DISAGREEMENTS CAN BE DEADLY

A couple takes witty revenge on their honeymooning exes in Judith Kelman's "Just Desserts." Gillian Roberts's "Heart Break" explores the dark side of staying together. In Sarah Lovett's "Buried Treasure," a hint-dropping stranger changes the life of an imperiled widow, while Edna Buchanan tells of how a man's nostalgia for the Florida of his youth threatens to cost him his family and his life in "Miami Heat."

"Satisfyingly twisted. . . . Although this anthology contains twenty original short stories, most of which are very good, it's worth the asking price just for Joyce Carol Oates's entry, 'Tusk.' There, a teenage boy, whose home life is tormented, brings a knife to school; as the day passes, his anger builds toward a terrible climax. . . . Laurie R. King's '*Paleta* Man,' the story of an ice cream vendor who walks the streets of a barrio neighborhood and knows the secrets of its inhabitants, was nominated for the Edgar, Anthony, and Marcavity awards. Jan Burke, meanwhile, evokes the spirit of Georgette Heyer's Regency novels in 'An Unsuspected Condition of the Heart,' her vibrant tale of murderous goings-on at a nineteenth-century stately home. . . . Bill Pronzini, an expert at concise but suspenseful stories, tells the riveting tale of a husband and wife who keep escalating their quarrels during a series of hot summer nights in 'Wishful Thinking.' On the lighter side, former trauma nurse Eileen Dreyer has some farcical 'Fun with Forensics.' "
                                                    Publishers Weekly

IRRECONCILABLE DIFFERENCES

LIA MATERA, Editor

AVON BOOKS
An Imprint of HarperCollins*Publishers*

This is a work of fiction. Names, characters, places, and incidents are products of the author's imagination or are used fictitiously and are not to be construed as real. Any resemblance to actual events, locales, organizations, or persons, living or dead, is entirely coincidental.

AVON BOOKS
An Imprint of HarperCollins*Publishers*
10 East 53rd Street
New York, New York 10022-5299

ISBN: 0-06-109733-0
www.avonbooks.com

First Avon Books paperback printing: April 2001
First HarperCollins hardcover printing: December 1999

Avon Trademark Reg. U.S. Pat. Off. and in Other Countries, Marca Registrada, Hecho en U.S.A.
HarperCollins® is a trademark of HarperCollins Publishers Inc.

Printed in the U.S.A.

10 9 8 7 6 5 4 3 2 1

CONTENTS

INTRODUCTION

The phrase *irreconcilable differences* has become, for over half the married couples in America, an unwelcome and painful fact of life. A catchall legal basis for modern divorce, the doctrine was designed to take the "fault" out of separation. But it has certainly not taken the sting—nor the crime—out of breaking up a household. No bland legal euphemism could ever disguise the cut-to-the-quick resentments, violent recriminations, and chilling betrayals of love gone wrong.

When I asked the writers in this anthology to use this phrase as a springboard for original short stories, I suppose I expected them to take a lawyer's view of the theme. But I was surprised and delighted to see how much more broadly they interpreted it. My years as a lawyer had, it seemed, limited the words for me, narrowing them to diminished potency. Appropriated by divorce statutes, *irreconcilable differences* had lost some of the vigor and complexity of its earlier, less specific usage.

Though not all differences can be reconciled, our legal system would have us believe, as hard as we are able, that every dispute can and must be resolved peaceably. Courts and arbitrators and special masters are, in theory, equipped to cut through differences, however irreconcilable. Several bodies of law exist for the sole purpose of standing between disputants.

But judging from crime statistics, a great many conflicts continue to cry out for vengeance, either in blood or money or tears. Satisfaction is supposed to be available through legal means. But too often, this comfortable assumption is undercut by the click of a trigger or the downstroke of a knife.

And unfortunately, these passions know no age minimum. You do not have to be "this tall" to climb aboard.

Joyce Carol Oates, winner of the National Book Award and author of numerous acclaimed novels, enters into the private hell of a teenage boy. In her story "Tusk," family conflicts become so overwhelming only a Gordian action can cut through the irreconcilable differences in a young man's heart. Amanda Cross, master storyteller and Columbia University professor emerita, also considers the teenage years and the fierce desire to be accepted by one's peers. In "The Perfect Revenge," the dissonance between a writer's portrayal of the past and its reality makes an editor balk. Jeffery Deaver, known for plot twists that leave readers gasping and writers envious, also looks backward. In "Eye to Eye," a young man returns to his hometown to find that the rowdy tormentors of his high-school years are now wearing badges. And John Lutz, whose thrillers set the standard for sensitivity and suspense, examines the painful differences teenagers are ill-equipped to reconcile. In "Stutter Step," it is urgent that a football-playing adolescent find his voice.

But while old wounds might burn deepest, nothing rankles more incessantly than domestic conflict. In "Miami Heat," Pulitzer Prize–winning journalist and best-selling novelist Edna Buchanan shows a city in turmoil and a household torn apart by a man's nostalgic refusal to accept the changes in his hometown. In "Wishful Thinking," multiple-award-winner Bill Pronzini shows us a small-town couple attempting to ride out a searing heat wave and a sizzling mutual hatred. And in "Up at the Riverside," the "mother of the American mystery novel," Marcia Muller, assesses the structural damage a partner's secret can do to a relationship, a hotel, and a community.

Sometimes a friend or a newcomer can provide needed relief. Edgar Award-winner Laurie R. King looks through the eyes of a bystander as a neighborhood ice cream vendor tries to chill out a hellish marriage in "*Paleta* Man." Best-selling mistress of psychological suspense Sarah Lovett describes a hint-dropping stranger's visit to an imperiled widow in "Buried Treasure." Jan Burke, acclaimed author of the Irene Kelly mysteries, also offers an outsider's view in "An Unsuspected Condition of the Heart," where the only way out of a bad situation is in a good Samaritan's carriage. And attorney Jeremiah Healy, creator of the award-winning John Francis Cuddy series, helps an ailing grandmother search for the kind of justice courts can't deliver in "Legacy."

But most of the time, divorced people must find their own personal ways of coping with the continuing conflicts of relationships gone bad. Not every Samaritan is a good one. And while courts may put marriages asunder, divide property, settle custody issues, and apportion assets, they can't quiet a seething heart. Most irreconcilable differences must be borne—or avenged—alone.

In "Fresh Paint," Julie Smith, Edgar Award-winning author of the Skip Langdon series, paints a perfect picture of a scorned artist's scheme to claim the recognition her lying ex-husband has stolen from her. In "Just Desserts," international best-selling suspense writer Judith Kelman offers a witty portrait of a couple's should-be delicious revenge on their honeymooning exes. Edgar Award-winner Margaret Maron also adds a twist of irony to second marriages in "Half of Something," when a timid man's hope of putting his first marriage behind him grows fainter after his remarriage. Anthony Award-winner Gillian Roberts explores the dark side of staying together in "Heart Break," where a wife's transgression is forgiven but not forgotten. And in

"All's Well That Ends," American Mystery Award-winner Joan Hess proves that revenge doesn't have to be swift or sweet to be worth it.

But divorced or not, married or not, anyone can be blindsided by irreconcilable differences. Sarah Shankman, author of four mainstream novels and seven acclaimed mysteries, spotlights one of life's most maddening conflicts. In "Love Thy Neighbor," a sleep-deprived woman tries everything to quiet a neighbor who just won't let up. Exploring a different kind of unneighborly conflict, Pete Hautman takes us into a local hangout in "Showdown at the Terminal Oasis." There, two regulars are still hashing out a thirty-year-old fight. In Eileen Dreyer's "Fun with Forensics," members of a fledgling forensics association try to handle—or perhaps dispatch—a new member bent on disgracing them. And in "If It Can't Be True," by Lia Matera, a brother and sister are still trying to cope with the long-ago derision of their neighbors.

With great pleasure, I bring you some of today's best writers as they push our universal hot buttons, exploding some of the emotional dynamite that constitutes irreconcilable differences. These contributors include winners of every major mystery award and numerous literary prizes, including the National Book Award and the Pulitzer Prize.

From a dark, moody study of the current consequences of past infidelities to a seriocomic dissection of modern devotion, from a near fatal misunderstanding in a rural prison to a *folie à deux* with a difference, these top crime and literary writers make their way across the excruciatingly intimate minefield upon which relationships, marital and familial and social, are built.

Joyce Carol Oates has written twenty-eight novels and numerous short stories, and is a winner of the National Book Award and the PEN/Malamud Award. She has also been a finalist for the Nobel Prize and the PEN/Faulkner Award. She is the Roger S. Berlind Distinguished Professor in the Humanities at Princeton University. In "Tusk," she takes us into the heart of a teenager determined literally to cut through the turmoil of his life.

TUSK

by Joyce Carol Oates

As the knife fitted into Tusk's hand, an idea fitted into his head.

Look at me! God damn here I am.

Exactly what he'd do, he'd make up when he got to the place it would be done in. Like a quick cut in a movie, you get to the place where something's going to happen. Or when he saw the person, or persons, it would be done to. Like jazz, what's it called, you make it up at the piano not toiling away for hours practicing scales and arpeggios and shitty Czerny exercises like he'd been made to do by his dad in the grim dead days before he was Tusk—*improvisation* it was called.

That's what Tusk was famous for, or would be famous for: *improvisation.* Forever afterward at East Park they'd be saying of Tusk, *That Tusk! Man, he's one cool dude!* And over in the high school they'd be saying it, too.

Exactly why they'd be saying this, shaking their heads in that way meaning *no shit,* blinking and staring at each other lost in wonderment, Tusk didn't yet know. But he would.

It was his dad's knife. Out of his dad's desk drawer. A souvenir from 'Nam. You had to wonder how many gooks the knife had killed, right? Tusk grinned contemplating such freakiness. *They did the DNA and it's more blood types than they can figure. Wei-ird!*

Probably it was going to happen at school, or after school. He was headed for school. His mom calling anxiously after him but he hadn't heard, on his way out fast like his new Nikes were carrying him. He'd been waking through the night charged with electricity like sex and it felt good. Liking how it was just an ordinary weekday, a Tuesday. Couldn't remember the calendar month—April? May? It was all a background blur. It was just the pretext for what came next. On the TV news, that was what they'd be saying. *Just an ordinary weekday, a Tuesday. At East Park Junior High in the small suburban community of Sheridan Heights. Thirteen-year-old Tusk Landrau is a ninth grader here.* Tusk hoped they wouldn't get into the honors-student shit, anything to do with old Roland. Anyway he wasn't going to plan much. He had faith the knife would guide him. When he'd been Roland junior for twelve fucking years he'd planned every fucking thing ahead of time. Laid out school clothes the night before, even socks. Socks! Homework had to be perfect. Brushing his teeth, never less than ten vigorous brushings to each part of the mouth. Until the gums bled. Going down a flight of stairs he was compelled to hit each stair at the identical spot. Setting up the chessboard to play with his friend Darian (when they'd been friends), he'd been compelled to set his pieces up from the back row forward as his dad had always done, always king and queen first. And his game planned as far as he could see it, until mist obscured his vision. Even wiping his tender ass with a prescribed length of toilet paper one two three four *five* rhythmic swipes. But no more! Now he was Tusk and Tusk moved in one direction only: fast-forward. He'd left every dork friend (like Darian) behind. His brain worked in quick leaps. Like *Terminator III*. Rapid fire and stop. Rapid fire and stop. Reload and *pop!* and stop. His brain was wired. His brain was fried. He didn't have to smoke dope or pop pills (though sometimes for the hell of it Tusk did) to get to that place. His head was quick starts and stops and reloads and pops and *bam! bam! bam!* and stop. Tusk was a new master of the video arcade. The older guys admired him. One cool dude! That strung-out look, dilated eyes. Certain of the girls thought him sexy-looking. Wild. Hours rushed by in this state. It was an OK state. If he stepped sideways out of it he'd feel like shit enveloped his entire soul so why? One direction only: fast-forward. *Bam! bam! bam!* and *blip!* on the screen. And the sweet explosion that follows.

Now you see Tusk, now you don't.

God damn here I AM.

Weird that a souvenir from 'Nam had been manufactured in Taiwan. Stainless steel with a seven-inch blade and an aluminum grip of some strange burnished metal or possibly mineral with a greenish glow. Tusk told kids his old man had fought in Vietnam but in fact his old man had been in intelligence probably just sitting on his ass until it was time to fly home again. He'd

bought the knife probably from some dumb fuck
who'd actually "seen action." Tusk tested the blade by
running it along his throat and wasn't sure it was as
sharp as it needed to be. You get your chance you don't
want to fuck up, right? There was a fancy knife sharp-
ener in the kitchen but better not. If his mom discovered him? A weekday morning? On his way to school?
Why, Roland, what's that in your hand? (Jesus, maybe
he'd stick *her!*)

So no way, Tusk's out of here.

Dad's knife shoved in his backpack with his homework.

If this was a movie they'd pick up next on Tusk pushing
into school like any other morning. A pack of round-
head kids, muffin-face kids, kids looking more grade
school than junior high. Tusk is the barracuda here. Not
tall but slouched, lean like a knife blade, fawn-colored
hair in flamey wings lifting from his face and that glis-
ten in his skin like he's got a fever. And shadowy hawk
eyes that are greeny glow-in-the-dark like the Assassin
in his new favorite video game XXX-RATED. He's
high but it's a natural high. He's a ticking time bomb
but there's no defusing. There are only a few cool
dudes in the junior high like Tusk and they're dressed
hiphop style in baggy T-shirts, baggy jeans and the
cuffs dragging the floor, but Tusk's mom won't allow
him to dress like a savage like some black ghetto gang-
ster she says so he's in just a regular T-shirt, regular but
hole-pocked jeans and his flashy new Nikes. No ear
studs, no nose ring. (Which the school dress code
doesn't allow anyway.) No punk streaked hair. That
isn't Tusk's style. Tusk isn't a goth or a freak, he's the
X in the equation.

But shit, when there's no camera you're invisible.

Tusk uses his elbows pushing some kids out of his way, you'd think the little jerk-offs would know to steer clear of him by now. Tusk says loudly, "It's a damn good thing there's no metal detectors in this school." And some girls giggle like this is a joke?

At his locker Tusk couldn't remember the fucking combination and so banged and kicked the fucking door. You can ask one of the nigger janitors but he'd done that just last week, and a few times before. So fuck that. Tusk was thinking almost he wishes there *were* metal detectors in the school like in some serious big-city school. He'd figure out some ingenious way to smuggle the blade in. That'd be the lead-in for the TV news that night: *Despite metal detectors at East Park Junior High, a ninth grader named Tusk Landrau succeeded in—* After that, his mind goes blank like in a slow soundless explosion.

Talking with some kids, and he's sighting Alyse Renke down the corridor, there she is and it comes to him in a flash *Stick Alyse. In her sweet cunt.* Alyse is Tusk's girl or had been or was gonna be, there's been a kind of understanding between them off and on all this year. Alyse is fifteen years old, she'd been held back a year and Tusk is thirteen, he'd been promoted a year (back in grade school) which his mom hadn't thought was a good idea but his dad pushed for. But Tusk is taller than Alyse and he knows he's sexy in her eyes because she'd all but told him once. Alyse is, for sure, *sex-y*. What guys in high school call a *cock-tease,* and she hangs out with them so they should know.

Fondling the knife through the nylon fabric of the backpack like it's Tusk's secret prick.

*Was a time he'd been Roland junior. Only twelve
months ago but can't remember old Roland except to
know the guy was a nork, a dorf, a nerd, a geek, a jerk-
off. That asshole Roland who busted his balls for his
old man getting high grades the old man examined like
something stuck to his shoe. Son, you know, and I know,
this isn't the best you can do.*

*Baptized himself Tusk. Where this name came from,
he didn't know. Only a few kids called him Tusk but one
day they all would. And his teachers too. (Alyse called
him Tusk now. Wrapped her pink tongue around
"Tusk" like it's his sweet cock she's sucking.)*

Staring at his skinny rib cage in the mirror still
steamed up from his shower (Roland had a habit of
hiding in the shower, water as hot as he could stand it,
running it for ten minutes or more believing himself
safe there, the door locked and you can't hear voices
in the shower unless they're voices in your head and
his mom wasn't so likely to knock on the bathroom
door if she heard the shower though of course she
would if he hid in there too long) contemptuous of his
puke-pale white-boy skin and the nipples that looked
like raspberries and skinny as he was a little potbelly
(visible if he stood sideways to the mirror and puffed
it out in disgust) and dangling from peach-fuzz red-
dish hair at his groin a skinned-looking little penis
maybe two inches long he'd try to hide from the other
guys changing for swim class which he hated. *Rol-lie!
Wow-ee! Let's see what Rollie's got!*

But all this was before Tusk. In that totally weird
space when he'd been Roland junior. And Roland senior had been what's called *alive*.

Buzzer sounds for homeroom. Everybody slams their
lockers and it's tramp off to homeroom. Tusk slouches
into his seat and lets the backpack fall gently. His usual
posture and deadpan style. Miss Zimbrig reading announcements. Tusk is nervous. Tusk is excited. Tusk is
sweating. Tusk is picking his nose. Needing to stoop to
touch the knife hidden inside the backpack. Taking a
chance maybe. He's twitchy, compulsive. If Zimbrig
calls out, *Roland, what d'you have there? Please bring
that backpack here.* Checking for drugs and the nosy
bitch is gonna get stuck like a pig in front of twenty-
seven bug-eyed ninth graders.

*Wow, you heard? Tusk Landrau whacked Zimbrig in
homeroom this morning, I mean totally wasted the bitch,
slitting her from throat to gizzard. His old man's combat
knife from 'Nam. Yeah, that Tusk is one bad dude!*

Except Zimbrig doesn't notice Tusk. Or, noticing,
wisely decides not to call him on the backpack. Zimbrig never knew Roland junior, through ninth grade it's
been Tusk and for sure she knows not to mess with *him*.
Not even to joke with him like she does with some of
the other cool dudes flashing skull tattoos on their biceps. (Tattoos are in violation of the East Park public
school's dress code. But these are just vegetable-dye
tattoos, not the real thing done with needles which is
the only kind of tattoo Tusk would wish for himself.
None of that chickenshit for *him!*) Could be, Tusk runs
into Zimbrig in the parking lot behind school, he'd get
the signal *Her! Stick her! She's the one.* But Tusk
doubts he can get it up for an old bag his mother's age.
(Though Tusk is vague about his mom's actual age.
Makes him squirm, he's fucking *embarrassed.* He'd

read in the obituary that Roland Landrau Sr., invest-ment attorney, had been forty-one when he'd bought the farm last year.) Tusk crouches down to check out the knife through the canvas fabric another time, man it's *there*.

PA announcements. Blahblahblah. Amazing to Tusk how shit-faced ordinary this day *is*. Not knowing he's squirming in his seat like he's got to go pee and picking his nose and there's Zimbrig casting him dirty looks, an old nervous habit of his, of Roland's, his mom scolded him in her anxious-hurt way for bad manners as she called it, and his dad slapped him for a dirty habit as he called it—*Dis-gusting, Roland! Stop that at once.* As if picking his nose till sometimes it bleeds was nerdy Roland's dirtiest habit. And there's Zimbrig definitely eyeing him through her black plastic glasses. Fuck, where's he gonna wipe the snot? The bitch glaring at him so he wipes it on his jeans at the knee where it sort of splotches in with the other greenish stains and crud.

Buzzer sounds. First period. Tusk wakes out of a dream and it's like XXX-RATED *bam pop* rapid fire and stop! and *pop!* and he's grinning like not knowing where the fuck he is. But on his feet, and the backpack heaved up and hugged to his chest and filing out of homeroom slouched and oily hair swinging in his face Tusk has to pass Miss Zimbrig's desk and the bitch smirks murmuring, "Here, Roland. Be my guest." Handing him a Kleenex out of the box on her desk. And kids looking on giggle. And Tusk winces, his face burns but he's been so fucking brainwashed to be polite to adults he actually mumbles, "Thanks, Miss Zimbrig."

And takes the Kleenex!

Bitch is gonna pay. Nobody laughs at Tusk. Nobody fucks with Tusk. The hour of reckoning is near!

Roland Landrau Sr. he can hardly remember. He hadn't known him all that well when the guy'd been his dad. Like the screen is zigzags and blurs and instead of rock music there's static. Like through a telescope he can see the three of them at the dining room table where the father had to discipline the son and took pleasure in the task, leaning forward on his elbows with an almost boyish eagerness so the tablecloth bunched and pulled toward him, and the father not noticing, quietly reprimanding little Roland (three years old? four?) for eating his food too quickly, or maybe too slowly pushing it around his plate, or for whispering to his mother instead of speaking to both his parents, or for chattering when he should have been silent because Daddy was trying to talk, or for sitting silent, his head bowed and sulky picking at his food when he should have been talking. Roland junior who never seemed to learn (dumb-ass kid! it's hard to feel sorry for such a shithead) that he must look Daddy in the eye and not shrink or cringe or burst into tears which really infuriated Daddy for implying that Daddy was "some kind of bully who'd pick on a small kid" and next thing you knew Roland junior was shrieking because he'd been slapped, or shaken by the shoulder like a beanbag, or what scared the most though it didn't hurt the most, his plump round face gripped in Daddy's big fingers so Daddy could lean within an inch to shout at him. (And where was Mom? Mom was at the table white-faced, worried, biting her lower lip until the lipstick was eaten off, Mom was such a pretty mommy and her hair so beautifully styled it was a puzzle why little Roland grew up not to trust her for there was a time when Mom would say these episodes at the dining room table didn't happen because they could not have happened explaining to Roland *Much of what you think has happened in a lifetime never did.*) And there was the time when Roland was six years old and no longer a baby and he'd run from the table when his dad began to discipline him and his dad had caught him on the stairs and yanked him back down and shook him till his teeth and his brains rattled in his head and Roland drew breath to scream but could not scream for the scream was trapped inside him like partly chewed food and his reddened face puffed up like a balloon to bursting and his eyes bulged in their sockets and he fainted and next thing he knew he was being wakened by someone he'd never seen before, in a place whitely glaring with light he'd never seen before, not wanting to breathe but forced to breathe, eyes rolled back in his head not wanting to focus normally but forced to focus normally and that was the occasion as his parents would afterward describe it in grave hushed voices of their son's first *asthma attack.*

This old shit, Tusk mostly can't remember. Like it did happen to another kid, some pathetic little nerd, now *gone.*

"Hiiiii Tusk."
   "Hi 'Lyse."
   "How's it goin'?"
Tusk shrugs eloquently. "You?"
Alyse Renke shrugs, too. In tight blue jeans and

purple cotton-knit Gap sweater displaying her pear-sized little breasts. Alyse wears six glinting ear studs on her left ear and her broom-colored hair has zebra streaks of black and her flirty eyes are outlined in black mascara deliberate as crayon and she's making a kissy-pouty mouth rolling her eyes at Tusk like it's a movie close-up. Saying in a growl, "Sort of OK. But kinda pissy, too, you really want to know."

Before Tusk can rack his brain for a clever reply Alyse moves on swinging her hot little ass so Tusk stares after her with *bad intentions* on his sweaty face like neon. At the door to her classroom Alyse will glance back at Tusk but Tusk has already shoved on, hugging his soiled backpack to his chest and blinking dazed into space.

Like, Alyse Renke *is* the one, maybe? And Tusk isn't gonna have any choice about it?

Next period, study hall in the school library, Tusk guesses he's calling attention to himself the way he's squatting for long minutes by the *World Book, Encyclopaedia Britannica* and other reference books nobody ever looks at unless there's an assignment. Tusk is making faces to himself paging through Human Biology and there comes Mrs. Kottler the librarian to say, "What are you looking for, Roland? Maybe I can help you." But Tusk won't meet her eye. Shrugs and mumbles what sounds like *Nah, I'm OK*.

At last he found what he was looking for: a cartoon drawing of a human being with bones, organs, arteries and nerves highlighted. The heart is lower in the chest than you'd think, Tusk sees. And there's bone protecting it, sort of. The neck? Those deep-blue blood vessels. *Carotid arteries supplying blood to the brain.*

Instinctively Tusk locates a hot pulsing artery in his own neck, below the jawline. The carotid artery is his best bet, probably. He'd only need to slash once, twice, maybe saw the blade back and forth. If his victim is Alyse Renke, she'll be easy to overpower, no taller than he is. If his victim is somebody bigger, like an adult, Tusk will be more challenged but *You want to bet Tusk can't do it?*

For all he needs is positioning and leverage. And the right timing. As in XXX-RATED. Strike by surprise! Rapid fire and stop and *pop pop pop! Game over.*

It was *pop! game over!* for Roland's dad. One minute he'd been talking on the phone and the next he was slumped sideways in his swivel chair behind his desk like a man surprised in an earthquake and paralyzed in the posture of that first second's terrible jolt. Had Mr. Landrau been arguing over the phone with a business associate?—had his son, Roland, twelve, upstairs in his room at his computer doing algebra homework heard his dad's voice lifting in pain and terror like a wounded animal? *Had the son heard his stricken father call to him for help?*

The business associate would afterward claim he'd assumed that Mr. Landrau had just hung up. Without saying goodbye. Not that Mr. Landrau was rude but he had ways of showing his impatience or moral indignation or disgust, and hanging up without saying goodbye or tossing the receiver down, off the hook, was one of them.

It was bad luck for Mr. Landrau that no one else (except his son) was home at the time of the emergency. For possibly he might have been saved. If an ambulance had been summoned, if he'd been rushed into neurosurgery, just maybe. This would be a subject for the grieving widow and the deceased man's relatives to ponder. But Mrs. Landrau was shopping at Lord & Taylor and the Puerto Rican woman who cleaned house so capably for the Landraus had gone home an hour before. And the door to Roland junior's room was shut. For since seventh grade the boy had begun to insist upon his right to privacy. So it was plausible *I didn't hear Dad. I didn't hear anything. I didn't!*

What popped in Mr. Landrau's brain was a weakened blood vessel. An *aneurysm.* An often undetectable and frequently fatal *abnormal dilatation of a blood vessel* in a brain. Roland Landrau Sr. would have ceased breathing by the time his wife returned home to discover him slumped in his swivel chair in his study, telephone receiver on the floor and his dead-white face so contorted as to be hardly recognizable. Mouth gaping open and eyes staring like a doll's eyes too round and shiny to be real.

Upstairs hunched over his computer keyboard Roland junior heard his mom begin to scream. A sound like tearing silk inside his skull he'll hear through his lifetime. He knows.

"Y'know who I'd like to whack someday? Fuckface Snyder."

"Wow, Tusk! Cool."

"This knife of my dad's I told you about, this thing like a dagger practically, already bloodstains on it, y'know?—from 'Nam?—that's what I'd use. Because a gun, even if I had a fucking gun, would make too much fucking noise, y'know?"

"Cool, Tusk! Rii-ight."

But these assholes don't take Tusk seriously, he can

tell. In the locker room fourth period. Tusk is slow and sullen changing his clothes, fucking resents fucking gym class. Today it's outdoor track and jumping he's lousy at, no more coordinated than when he'd been Roland junior shy and blinking at the guys yelling in a pack around him like hyenas. What Tusk hates is anything regimented like you're in the God damn fucking army or something. "Butch" Snyder clapping his ham-hands and puffing his cheeks and faggot eyes twinkling shouting like it's good news he's bringing them *All rii-ight, boys! Let's go, boys! Three times around the track to warm up, boys! C'mon, let's GET IT ON!* You'd think Tusk Landrau might be a runner, he's got that lean runner's frame, long slender arms and legs. But the poor kid gets breathless in five minutes, only the fat kids run slower, there's something wrong with his nasal passages or his sinuses, he's had asthma. Coach Snyder who's one of the popular teachers at East Park tries to sympathize. Tries to disguise his contempt for certain of these soft suburban kids. Spoiled rich men's sons he can tolerate if they're athletes who follow his instructions but the rest of them, sissies, punks and fuck-offs he's got no use for, like this "Tusk" pretending to be a cool dude grimacing and working his mouth like a schizo arguing with himself, and his baby-face oily with sweat like he's running a fever. "Roland, see me in my office, OK? Before you shower and change."

Tusk is scared. But laughing and telling the guys it's been a year since he's had a shower at school, what's Fuckface Snyder think, everybody's a faggot like himself?

In Coach's glass-brick cubicle office off the gym, with no window except opening onto the gym, Tusk grips the backpack on his knees. Christ, he *is* scared. Sweating and shivering and his teeth practically chattering. *He's going to stick Snyder. In the gut because Snyder's growing a gut and it serves the fucker right. Wild!* He's fumbling unzipping the pocket, slips his hand inside and there's the knife blade he touches first, it feels pretty sharp though maybe not razor-sharp, then he grips the handle, clutches it in his sweaty palm. But Coach breezes in and taps his shoulder, "OK, Roland, how's it going?" like Coach is Tusk's big brother or a different kind of a dad and before Tusk can handle it there's tears in his eyes, fucking tears spilling over and running like hot acid down his cheeks. Coach blushes pretending not to see this though for sure he's embarrassed as hell. Repeating, "How's it going?" in a kindly way that makes Tusk lose it even more so Tusk is on his feet wild-eyed stammering, "L-Leave me alone! You don't know anything about me! *Fuck you don't touch me, leave me alone!*" Tusk would yank out the knife from 'Nam, his right hand is actually shoved inside the pocket gripping the smooth handle (and this Coach will recall, speaking of the episode) but fuck it he's crying too hard, hasn't cried like this since he was a little kid, you forget how crying *hurts.* Coach is on his feet surprised saying, "Roland, hey wait—" but Tusk has already rushed out of the office hugging the backpack against his chest, can't see where the fuck he's going, choking for air, he'll hide out in a toilet stall in the lavatory off the storage room until the buzzer sounds for fifth period and the coast is clear and Coach figures he knows better than to follow a distraught adolescent.

What I'd do I thought was give the poor kid some slack, I could see he was upset but didn't think it was more than that, sometimes I don't involve anybody else at school to keep it off the kid's record. What I figured was, I'd give Mrs. Landrau a call at home that evening.

Yes. I knew the father was dead.

When the aneurysm went *pop!* there was Roland junior
upstairs in his room almost directly overhead. Yes he'd
heard his dad screaming. Not for him, or for help—just
screaming. Like a hurt, terrified animal. Yet, hunched at
his computer concentrating on his algebra homework
Roland junior who was a nervous twelve-year-old sort
of didn't hear. Or if he'd heard, he hadn't understood.
Dad had a TV in his study sometimes he'd switch it on
to watch news in the evening, so maybe that was it—
the strangulated scream. *Yes I heard. I heard something. Yes I knew it was Dad. Yes I knew something had
happened to him. Heart attack, I thought. Or somehow,
I don't know how, like in a movie or something—his
clothes were on fire. Always had a weird imagination, I
guess! Actually I'm kidding, I didn't hear anything
from downstairs. My room isn't over Dad's study really. Dad's study is at the corner of the house. I stayed
with the computer doing my homework. It was like I
was paralyzed I guess. From downstairs there was
nothing. No TV noises. I didn't hear anything until
Mom came home and started screaming.*

Then Roland junior ran into the bathroom connected
to his room and locked the door and switched on the fan
and even flushed the toilet pressing the sweaty palms of
his hands against his ears framing his head like a vise.

No! no! no! I didn't hear a fucking thing!

Red-eyed Tusk is skipping fifth-period math. Hanging
in the hall outside Alyse Renke's social studies class.
Framing his narrow paste-colored face in the door window so that Alyse can see him through her clotted eye-

lashes. He's excited, he knows that guys from gym class are talking and laughing about him. He knows exactly who they are. And there's Darian Fenner, his ex-friend now his enemy, who wasn't in that gym class but is a friend of a guy who was and in the corridor just now changing classes Tusk sighted Darian and this kid laughing together at Darian's locker and smiling in Tusk's direction. *There's baaad Tusk, sweated through his clothes unless some of that damp is he's peed his pants?* Just chance that Darian is in Alyse's class, Tusk doesn't want to be distracted by thoughts of Darian right now though his ex-friend has betrayed him and deserves to die—Tusk could drift into an open-eyed dream seeing this in slow motion—he'd corner Darian in the lavatory and saw the blade across Darian's throat until Darian's dorky head was severed from Darian's dorky-pudgy body and he'd position the head—eyes open—in the toilet so that's how they would discover Darian Fenner—*That Tusk! That cruel dude! You heard what he did to dorky Darian Fenner? Wi-ild!*

They wouldn't show the head on TV, though. Just photos of Darian when he'd been alive.

That's what happens, you mess with Tusk Landrau.

Tusk is hugging his backpack to his chest grinning and not-seeing Alyse Renke till she's practically in his face. Breathless and cutting her eyes at him saying she'd asked to be excused to use the rest room, how's about they get out of this dump?—"Just leave by the side door by the cafeteria, nobody's gonna notice."

He's heard his mom whining on the phone she didn't know what to do with him this past year, Roland isn't himself any longer and I don't know who he *is,* whining and sniffling and if he'd walk into a room with her she'd blink at him like she was scared of him and why the fuck did the pathetic bitch imagine she could "do" anything with him, like you'd "do" something with a dog or something, fuck it what's she think? "Like it's some choice of hers! Like, she'd better *learn*."

Alyse says, coughing as she smokes, waving smoke out of her face with her stubby fingers, maroon-polished talon nails, "Fuck *yes*. Same with my mom. And my dad, too, there's two of them constantly in my face. You ever thought about—y'know—" Alyse makes a slashing gesture across her throat with her forefinger, giggling, "—offing them?"

"Huh? *Who?*"

"Like, your mom and dad."

Tusk grins at Alyse sort of blank, dazed. Like he hasn't heard just right. "Uh, my dad's actually, like, dead. He's dead."

Alyse's pink-lipsticked mouth opens. Her mascara-ed eyes widen. She touches Tusk's bare forearm with her talon nails, and every hair stirs. "Jeez! I forgot."

"That's OK."

"Tusk, I'm sor*ry*. Jeez I knew that, I just forgot."

Tusk is embarrassed, shrugging. "Yeah, it's OK. It's cool."

"I mean—shit. I should *know*."

"Hell, it's no big deal, y'know? It was over a year ago it happened."

Tusk is surprised, and moved, that Alyse Renke is so apologetic and sincere-seeming, nudging close to him like she's his girl as they make their way along the edge of the school playing field and into a marshy wooded area sloping down to railroad tracks and a viaduct. This isn't the way Tusk walks home from school but he knows the terrain from bicycling, it's a no-man's-land except on the two-lane asphalt road East End but even on this road there isn't much traffic. In a movie, Tusk is

thinking, excited and nervous, there'd be a long shot of
the two of them walking here, sliding and stumbling
downhill through litter drifted like seaweed against the
stubby trees and bushes greening up, bursting with
tawny buds in the unexpectedly bright spring sunshine.
And the sky overhead is filmy patches of cloud and
hard blue sky like something painted. There'd be a way
the camera would zoom up to them to signal *something's gonna happen!* For every moment on the screen
is charged with electricity—and with meaning—not
like real life that's a fucking downer. Alyse is entertain-
ing Tusk in that bright sharp way of hers complaining
again of her parents, especially her mom "who if you
ask me is morbidly jealous of her own daughter for
Christ's sake" and of Mr. Thibadeau her social studies
teacher who's practically harassing her "grading me so
God damn low like I'm a moron or something," and
Tusk thinks he's never seen a girl close-up so sexy as
Alyse Renke with her pouty lower lip and slip-sliding
green eyes and a habit of sighing hard, drawing her
breath in deep so her hard little breasts stand out in her
plum-purple Gap sweater *and actually nudging against
him* like he's seen her do with older guys, high school
guys Alyse dates on the basis (as Tusk has heard) of
whether they have cars they can drive—and know how
to use condoms. In school, in the cafeteria where sometimes a gang of them hangs out, if other kids are around
Alyse is flirty and loud-laughing and sarcastic, and
Tusk isn't too good with trading wisecracks and gets
pissed off, and he never knows whether Alyse is putting him on like he never knows whether he's crazy
about her, crazy in love with her, or whether he actually
despises her, she's a cheap flirt and not too bright.
(There's been a rumor in their class since seventh grade
testing that a number of kids tested out with IQs below
100—and Alyse Renke is one of these. Roland Landrau

Jr. tested out at 139 which was a moderate disappointment to Roland senior who'd had reason to expect his only son would score higher, as he had at that age.)

Tusk murmurs, "Y'know—my old man?—I let him die, sort of."

Alyse maybe hears this or maybe doesn't, she's blinking and squinting nearsightedly across the highway. There's a 7-Eleven store not far away but they'll have to tramp through a marshy vacant lot and get their feet wet probably. But if they walk around the longer way, on pavement, that's twice as far, a bummer. "Yeah, what? That's cool. I mean—too bad," Alyse says vaguely. She's leading the way, must be they're going to tramp through the field. On this damply sunny day there are insects everywhere, droning and buzzing and fluttering, tiny flies, clouds of gnats, from out of puddles an eager trilling sound like castanets that's maybe—peepers? Alyse has said she's thirsty, dying for a diet Coke, she drinks maybe a dozen diet Cokes a day, smiling sidelong at Tusk who's staring at her with his fever-eyes saying it's how she keeps her weight down, lifting her sweater and tugging down her tight-fitting jeans just a bit so Tusk can see her warm smooth pale midriff and the glass-ruby stud glittering in her belly button, Alyse is vain about being thin but not *skinny,* not one of these *anorexics,* guys get turned off by that. Also, she's running out of cigarettes and he hasn't got any, has he?—and it's shitty, this state law, or maybe it's federal law—"You can't buy cigarettes if you're a fucking *minor.* Like that's supposed to stop you from *smoking,*" she says with withering sarcasm.

Seeing that little glass-ruby stud in Alyse Renke's belly button—oh, man. *Like, Tusk is turned on. Man, Tusk is TURNED ON.* It's got to be a signal, right? Alyse Renke has brought Tusk Landrau out here back of school because she wants to make out with him, right?

She's done it with lots of guys, Tusk has heard—Jakey Mandell, Derek Etchinson, Buddy Watts as long ago as seventh grade, and older guys in high school, must be she's giving Tusk Landrau the high sign she wants him to fuck her, right? It's his turn! It's his time! He's scared, and excited, hears himself saying sort of choked up, his voice a weird croak, "Uh, 'Lyse?—let's go over this way, OK? C'mon." Tusk is pointing toward the viaduct where there's a pedestrian tunnel beneath the railroad tracks, a rarely used tunnel strewn with debris and puddles glittering like glass, graffiti scrawled on the walls like shouts, and Alyse squints and wrinkles her nose, "Huh? Why? I want a Coke, I said." Her lipstick-pink lower lip is swollen, pouting. You can see she's a girl accustomed to getting her way, with no delay. There's a pimpled rash at her hairline where the black zebra stripes begin. Tusk says, choked, "Yeah. C'mon. OK?" Alyse shakes her head no, pettishly, but sees in Tusk's looming face, in his heated pasty skin and red-rimmed eyes, eyes like he's been crying, old-young eyes, *eyes like you'd never see in any boy his age I swear,* a promise of something interesting, something sexy, for a thirteen-year-old kid who'd been an honor-roll nerd only the year before, you have to grant Tusk Landrau is *cool.* So impulsively Alyse leans over and kisses Tusk—kisses him!—his first kiss from a girl, ever—on his parched lips light as a butterfly brushing against him and murmurs suggestively, "OK, maybe afterward. After the Coke and some chips, OK?" and nudges against him so the blank-staring boy gets her meaning, her left breast hard as a green pear against his electrified arm. Man, this is it. Tusk hears a roaring in his ears. Tusk is having trouble breathing. Fucking asthma! No, he's never had asthma, he's OK. He's always been OK. They tried to make a freak out of him but he's OK. He's got a hard-on like a knife. His hard-on *is* a knife. He'll drag this slut into the tunnel and fuck her till her brains fall out and he'll stick her with his dad's 'Nam knife like it was meant to do and the strength of this will carry him in his new Nikes flying a mile and a half to the five-bedroom green-shuttered white colonial on Pheasant Hill Lane where he'll stick his mom with the same instrument from 'Nam. It's time! It's his turn! *To put my mom out of her mercy, I mean misery, not like I hated her or anything, shit I loved her I guess—she was my mom, y'know?* Tusk will have to work out coherently what he's gonna tell the police and his lawyer, his statement for TV and the press, he's anxious he won't get a second chance, it will have to go down perfectly the first time. "Hey Tusk? You spaced out or what? Come *on!*"—flirty Alyse Renke giggling at him and he's staring at her seeing her pink lips move but can't hear what she's actually saying. *Alyse was my girl. I warned her from the first I would not share her with anybody! I would not be disrespected.* Tusk is hugging the nylon backpack against his chest wondering if this sounds OK. He thinks so. Maybe. Is it plausible? He is sort of crazy about Alyse, to tell the truth. He'd like to kiss her and kiss her in some dark place like the Cineplex. He'd like to hang out at her house like he's heard Jakey Mandell does, Saturdays. But Jesus, his hard-on is aching, his entire cock and balls, like a metal pipe or something inside his jockey shorts—how's he gonna *walk?* His old man was embarrassed telling him about sex, sexual experimentation as his old man called it, sexual reproduction of the species which is nature's imprint you might say upon the individual, but—how's he gonna *walk?* He'd take Alyse's stubby little hand to press against his bulging fly, give the slut a good feel and she'd shriek and giggle and snatch her hand away like it was burnt but she'd be impressed, too—wouldn't she?—except

Alyse is running across the field squealing and cursing
getting her feet wet, and Tusk hasn't any choice but to
trot after her, breathless and crouched over like he's got
a stomachache. "Hey, 'Lyse! Wait."

Fuck, he's getting his new Nikes wet.

In the tacky 7-Eleven they're the only customers. Alyse
knows the store and goes directly to the rear to get her
Coke. A staticky radio playing old-time rock from the
seventies and behind the counter staring unsmiling at
Tusk is this fattish gray-grizzle-bearded guy like a hippie going bald and what's left of his stringy hair is totally gray, he's wearing it in a ponytail tied with a piece
of yarn, a soiled Grateful Dead T-shirt straining against
his beer gut and bib overalls fitting him like sausage
casing and those steely eyes behind rimless bifocals are
fixed on Tusk immediately. *Fucker never gave me a
chance! What'd I ever do to* him? *Fucking Nazi like
I'm, what?—a nigger or something.* Alyse must know
the fat hippie, or anyway she's acting like she does,
chattering and flirting complaining why can't she buy a
pack of Virginia Slims at least?—"Who would ever
know, I mean it's just us in here, I mean—it's just common sense. Or you could give me the pack, y'know?
And I could, like, pay a little more for these chips?
Tusk, you got some change?" But the hippie pays Alyse no more mind than you'd pay a cloud of gnats, and
Tusk doesn't hear her either, nervously prowling the
aisles blinking at brightly packaged displays of Sunshine Cheez-Its, Doritos chips, Snak-Mix, Jif peanut
butter, Pringles Potato Crisps, Miracle micro popcorn,
Hungry Jack Bagel Bites and at knee level ten-pound
sacks of Purina Dog Chow and Kleen Kitty Litter. Tusk
is a shy boy actually, hunching his shoulders like he

wants to disappear, his chest practically caved in, that posture that so pissed off his old man he half expects to hear the old man's disgusted voice over the radio *Son!* Tusk is talking to himself which he never does in public only when he's alone, not audibly talking but his mouth is working, he's grimacing, puckered-up baby face that's close to crying. Heat prickling in his underarms like red ants. For Tusk seems to know before the hippie behind the counter speaks a single word to precipitate his doom *This is it! He's the one I been waiting for, the fucker.* "You, kid—yeah, you!—take your punk ass out of this store and keep on moving, you hear?" the hippie says in a sharp nasal voice pressing his gut against the counter, beefy muscled guy with wiry hairs bristling up through the Grateful Dead T-shirt and Tusk says stammering, "Say—what? I'm not doing nothing," and Alyse is protesting, "Tusk isn't doing a thing! Hey he isn't! Hey c'mon, mister," and the hippie ignores her saying to Tusk in a sneering voice, "Yeah? Like the other day you and your punk pals weren't doing anything except tearing open bags, right? Right on the shelves, right? Yanking pull-tops and leaving the fucking cans to drain on the shelves while I'm waiting on fucking customers, *right?*" Tusk is hurt, Tusk is shaking his head confused, saying, "Mister, I was never in this store before. I was *never.*" This is true!—Tusk's lower lip is trembling and his eyes are misting over but the hippie is furious and unforgiving stalking out from behind the counter waving his fatty-muscled arms, splotches of red in his face and his eyes steely-cold, "I said get out of my store, you little punk! You're a thief, you're a vandal and a thief and a punk and if I was your old man I'd blow out my brains, I want you out of this store right now before I break your skinny little—"

Suddenly then the hippie is gaping down at himself with this look of profound astonishment and wonder *where Tusk has shoved a seven-inch knife to the hilt in his guts.*

Following this, things happen swiftly.

And Tusk is watching, and Tusk is moving with it but it's like he's outside himself watching. Grinning dazed at his blood-splattered hands and jeans and he yanks the knife out of the fat man falling to his knees and stabs at him with it—"Fucker! You got no right! *I* got my rights! See how you like it now!" The hippie is on the floor screaming, trying to stop the blood from rushing out of his belly, Tusk is panting, triumphant, kicks himself free except he's splashed with God damn blood—his jeans, his new Nikes—shit!—he's excited, pissed—only just a little scared—runs behind the counter to the cash register reasoning *I will need money if I go underground* but the fucking cash register is shut up tight and there's no way to open it Tusk can figure, tearing at the drawer with his hands and breaking his fingernails leaving blood-smears on the metal he knows are fingerprints to incriminate him but what's he gonna do?—it's all happening so swiftly.

This buzzing in his ears like a trapped hornet, he can't figure where it's coming from. Old-time rock music at high decibels and somebody screaming? Then Tusk remembers with a tinge almost of nostalgia as if it had all happened long ago and they're flying away from each other like the universe is said to be broken into an infinity of isolated parts rushing away from one another at nearly the speed of light: the girl with the zebra-stripe hair. Alyse Renke. Alyse who's *his* girl. Her face wizened like a monkey's contorted in rage rather than horror *What the fuck are you doing Tusk! Just what the fuck are you doing you sorry asshole!* as in a frenzy he'd stabbed the fat hippie as many times as he could draw the knife blade out and sink it into the man's flesh like blue flames were licking over his brain until practically he was coming in his pants and panting he'd turned glassy-eyed toward the furious girl and seeing his face she backed off as the situation registered upon her—the knife, the gushing blood, the adult man thrashing and groaning at Tusk's feet. And now he doesn't know where she is. "'Lyse? Hey 'Lyse?" he hears himself yelling in a raw hurt voice, almost he's laughing, "—you hiding on me? *Hiding?*" But she isn't anywhere in sight. Isn't in the store. Just Tusk in the store, and the whimpering man. Just shelves of merchandise, rows of tins and paper packages and on the farther wall a flyspecked Coors clock showing 2:25 P.M. and it flashes through Tusk's mind that school's still in session, no wonder there's no kids hanging out at the 7-Eleven. The fat hippie, lying on his back, gasping and twitching his left leg in a pool of neon-glistening liquid like varnish is all that Tusk can see and then Tusk sees the girl outside, running toward the road and possibly she's screaming, Alyse has left him? Alyse Renke his girl running from *him?* when she'd been kissing him just a few minutes ago? and he'd done this for *her?* to show her how serious he is, how serious about *her?* Tusk runs to the door and calls plaintively, "'Lyse! Hey come back! Hey—" but Alyse doesn't hear, she's waving her arms running and stumbling in the road now and there's a station wagon approaching and it's going to stop, Tusk knows.

Where they find him only a few minutes later, it wasn't where he might've planned to be. Or at this abrupt time, either.

Back of the 7-Eleven, behind the smelly overflowing Dumpster. The slippery knife in his fingers as he's groping for the artery, what is it, carotid artery, in his throat. His fingers are clumsy, anxious. *I never heard him calling me. Never heard him scream. I didn't!* Hearing now a faint train whistle. A dog's forlorn persistent barking in the distance. A siren. A siren coming closer? He's got to hurry. Doesn't want to fuck up like he's fucked up just about everything else today but he's got to hurry. There's no going back because he could not live this day again nor any other day recalling what he'd learned in science class of how the sun is promised to continue shining for five billion more years before at last swelling and vaporizing the entire solar system but Tusk could not endure even one more day. Not one more! Drawing the knife across the artery he's located pulsing hot beneath his jawbone, a sharp burning sensation and at once he's bleeding but the cut isn't deep enough so he tries again, holding his right hand steady with his left and pressing with his remaining strength, on his knees swaying, gasping for air, choking on something hot and liquid. Shit, he's dropped the knife, can't see to pick it up, groping amid wet newspaper on the pavement, crinkly yellow Doritos wrapper, but there's the knife, the blood-glistening knife that's his only consolation, he picks it up and tightens his fist around it and tries again.

AMANDA CROSS *is the pseudonym of Carolyn Heilbrun, who is world-famous for her nonfiction works of feminist analysis and social history. As Amanda Cross, she is the author of twelve critically acclaimed, bestselling novels featuring Professor Kate Fansler. She is also a professor emerita at Columbia University, and was recently president of the Modern Language Association and vice president of the Author's Guild. In "The Perfect Revenge," an editor struggles to keep both her integrity and her job when she is forced to edit an old acquaintance's revisionist history.*

THE PERFECT REVENGE

by Amanda Cross

I am an editor by profession, rather long in the tooth these days when most "acquiring editors," as they call themselves, are not old enough to have got their wisdom teeth, let alone anything definable as wisdom. But I've been around, have connections and continue to work successfully as an editor of famous writers who still want guidance and expertise in something beyond marketing skills. True, my writers want to be marketed well and advertised widely and often, but until they have reached the marketing stage they still feel the need of someone who can read, advise, console, and encourage. So here I am, and here for some time I shall persevere.

There was, however, a time not long ago when it looked as though I might not remain, as though the practicalities of publishing these days had got beyond my ability to cope. It didn't turn out that way, but it

might have, and sometimes the closeness of my escape
haunts me. Still, I outmaneuvered the opposing forces,
so mostly what I feel is pride. Quiet pride.

As anyone who spares even a cursory glance at the
New York Times Book Review can tell you, memoirs are
in. I admit to having grown a trifle tired of so many detailed recollections, and even more fatigued with childhoods. I consider memories of childhood to be tedious,
clearly fictitious, and marred by a ubiquitous tendency
to blame one's parents, and particularly one's mother,
for everything difficult in the adult life. Credit for
achievements, of course, is due to one's grown-up self.
But remembered childhoods sell.

Children on paper are part of my job, and so I peruse
many memoirs and offer to publish the ones I think will
do best. Not, please note, those I like best. Personal
tastes are essential in a good editor, but must be grati-
fied with discretion. I am, I suppose, so successful at
my job because I maintain a neat balance between my
sensitivities and my publishing instincts. This even-
handedness is sustained, in part, by the young and eager neophytes I engage as my assistants. If they express
intense admiration for a manuscript, I try to look at it
from a juvenile vantage point; after all, the young buy
books, having few familial demands upon their purses.

It was, in fact, my newest and greenest assistant who
came upon Nancy Carmichael's memoir. She found it
touching and, within the realm of those examples she
had read in this (as even she realized) overworked
genre, unusual. Entitled "Four Generations of Plucky,
Family-loving Women," it covered a century of memories from great-grandmother, grandmother, mother,
daughter, daughter's daughter (also a mother, but,
thankfully, with progeny too young to put pen to paper).
Each of these women had had a marriage blessed with
felicity and devoid of anger; each had had children who

were the light of their lives, each had used her privileged
education to strengthen her family, to remain always
available to them and, in any time left over from domestic responsibilities, to volunteer on behalf of their com-
munities and their church.

To say that I almost barfed on reading the report of
my neophyte assistant would be true, but hardly sufficient. I found the writing an accumulation of simple
sentences designed to attract the most inattentive of
cursory readers. The cloyingness of the paragraphs,
themselves rarely more than two sentences long, left
me with the sensation of turning pages that had been
dipped in warm caramel. In short, I thought that if
each of these women had had the pen wrenched from
her hand, the task of editors would have been greatly
enhanced, and the world would have lost nothing.

But that was not all. As it happened, I had gone to
school with Nancy Carmichael, the mother in this
march of feminine virtue with two generations to either
side of her, that is, before her and after her. I remembered Nancy Carmichael well, although her name at
school had been Nancy Smith. Naturally, each of the
women in this line of devoted grandmothers had taken
her husband's name and therefore shared, however
much else, no surname with any of her precursors or
followers. A revolting history if ever I heard one. I had
turned to the end of the manuscript in the wild hope
that the youngest of the mothers might have been, as
they say today, single. No such luck.

Nancy Carmichael's account of her days at the elegant Episcopal academy we both attended would have
done credit to that school's brochure, except that the
brochure would have run into some opposition from
the state office committed to maintaining truth in ad-
vertising. Before my astonished eyes appeared decla-

rations of how we loved each other, worked together, encouraged the weak and modulated the strong; we were devoted to our studies and even to our vigorous athletics, divided as we were into two school-wide teams, the green and the yellow, teams that successfully encouraged loyalty, skill, and the rewards of ardent competition. All this beauteous experience was made luminous by school prayer and daily chapel attendance. Detailed Bible studies were undertaken at each grade level.

This last sentence is the only one with some faint aroma of truth adhering to it. True, the Bible was studied, or at any rate, those texts dwelt upon and memorized which emphasized racism, sexism, classism and anti-Semitism, although the last of these "isms" was the only one we had heard of by name in those long-ago days. As to the rest of the claims, they were, not to put too fine a point upon it, garbage. Never, in a long life of reading silly manuscripts, have I cast my eyes upon such hogwash. The truth? We were assigned within a hierarchy at school, from the most popular girls down to the least endowed—that is to say, the least pretty, flirty, rich, well-dressed. Far from devoted to our studies, we spent most of the time speculating about our teachers' sex lives, or lack thereof, sneering at their old-maid state, their clothes, and the way they spoke to us in class. I remember with particular poignancy our English teacher, who tried to invoke in us some appreciation of great poetry, and our chemistry teacher, who was quite literally driven to madness by the rudeness of the students. It was assumed that, since all of the teachers were unmarried, they were all sexless beings. Looking back, I suspect that some of them had secret love affairs, that several of them at least lived in satisfactory lesbian partnerships. Most of the teachers were kind to me because I clearly wanted to learn, because I was despised by the most arrogant of the girls, and because I honored them for their knowledge and their professional status.

The worst of it, of course, was that Nancy Carmichael portrayed herself, like her precursors and followers, as the kindest of individuals, while I remember her and her mother—these two generations, thank the Lord, were the extent of my acquaintance with her family—as the two snottiest, meanest, most self-satisfied and hypocritical of all those I have confronted over the long years since. I recall with particular pain how Nancy's well-dressed mother glared down at my mother's shabby shoes and then turned brusquely away. (Am I unique in remembering with affection and gratitude my gentle, hardworking mother, and in resenting still the arrogant disdain offered her?)

At last emerging from these unpleasant memories, I summoned my assistant, waved her to a seat, and demanded an account of what, exactly, she had found attractive about this offering. Leaving aside for the moment any reference to the veracity of the account or my knowledge of the author, I asked whether she considered the soggy writing, the self-congratulatory tone, or the pride of class and family the most persuasive feature. I realize that I am a blunt, downright person, often a shade intimidating to those who have not known me long, and I expected blushes, apologies, and a stammering explanation of her report on the manuscript.

Not at all. She thought this was exactly the sort of family about which everyone wanted to read, a family to be held up as an ideal. I stared at her for what must have been many seconds, and then asked if her family was like the one portrayed in the manuscript. Well, yes, in a way, except that she didn't care for her mother or grandmother, but thought that it was possible to live their lives in a better way, as suggested by this manuscript, and she for one intended before long to try.

"Then why are you working as an editorial assistant?" I asked, obviously the natural question under the circumstances. Her answer must have impressed her as equally self-evident: "I want to get some work experience before I settle down, and I've always enjoyed reading books."

I must pause here to say that I have never known another editorial assistant—and their number has been legion over the years; some of them are now senior editors of stature—who would have answered that way. Certainly, being young, they all assumed that they would have successful careers, happy marriages, and children; realistic expectations have never been a notable characteristic of the unfledged. But most of them had actually admired literature, as distinct from "books," and came to publishing from a sense that those they met there would share that admiration and the complex moral issues that great literature evokes. Complexity seemed to be a concept beyond the reach of this ingenue. When my phone rang with a call I had been awaiting, I waved her from the office; I was devoid of appropriate comment, a circumstance to which I was rarely exposed. I made a note, while conversing with my caller, to find out who had recommended this paragon.

But despite my attempts to dismiss that miserable manuscript and the memories it stimulated from my mind, I could think of little else. How well I remembered Nancy Carmichael in school, the leader of the "popular" girls. Not only was I not one of them for more reasons than I can now recall, I also was condemned for being Jewish. Nancy took delight in telling me that her English cousins prayed in their school for the conversion of the Jews. I think we few Jews were tolerated in that elegant academy because it seemed the right thing to do after World War II, and because the Jewish students were smart and got into the best colleges, even those with strict, if secret, quotas. In a school filled with the daughters of alumnae, brains were not always developed to the most desirable scholastic point. Or they might well have had adequate brains, but becoming celebrated in that school for interest in the curriculum was not the path chosen by the "best" girls.

By our last two years of Episcopalian education I had become something of a celebrity. I'd had a story published, and later a poem. I well remember that one of the girls' mothers had said she was certain the poem was stolen, that she had read it somewhere. Never shall I forget the powerful sense of innocence brought me by that accusation. I rejoiced to picture her poring over poetry anthologies looking for the poem contrived within my own head. As a result of my achievements, however, I became for the first time an object of interest to my classmates, and it must have occurred to Nancy that perhaps she had better enlarge her circle a bit. I was invited in.

How I would like to announce that I told them off, refused their inducements, steered clear of invitations. Alas, I welcomed the delicious sense of belonging. Thus, in the fullness of time, I was invited for a "sleepover" at Nancy's country house, actually a week's stay. Always a lonely child and certainly an observant one, I did not require extensive experience in the way of marriages to see what was the matter with Nancy's parents. In short, they could not speak without arguing, they could not argue without shouting and flinging insults, all of this, needless to say, totally subdued in the presence of company, adult visitors, the members of their social world. Perhaps they assumed I was deaf and impervious, as the English have been said to have assumed about their servants. My own parents, worried about money because of their extensive family obligations and regretting their Jewishness while refusing to deny it, were hardly the happy couple Nancy was to present her own family as being, but my parents liked and respected each other and, though I could not have used those words then, I understood that they perceived and comforted each other's pain. The intense disregard of Nancy's parents for one another's feelings was an unforgettable revelation to me.

No smallest allusion to any of this marred the giddy memoir of these four generations of conventional twerps. Turning the pages with a violence that, in the privacy of my office, escaped observation, I became even more incensed upon reading Nancy's paean to her wonderful marriage (to say nothing of her mother's similar marital gush) where she claimed that they never argued and almost never disagreed about anything. Nancy's explanation was that both she and her husband disliked confrontation (to which, in school, she was frighteningly addicted) and that she had set out to be a good wife to her financially proficient husband, who labored long hours on Wall Street. As it happened, I had, inadvertently I need hardly say, become a neighbor of Nancy and her husband when both he and I were at the start of our careers and Nancy was being the "model wife." So I knew at first hand that her account of her relationship with her husband was even closer to rubbish than her tales of school.

Not that I hold anything now against Nancy or her nasty parents. But her claims about her unruffled marriage do grate. Nancy had determined, I realized as soon as I got to know her husband even superficially, to marry someone who would not hurl accusations at her or expect her to hurl accusations at him: an understandable resolution. But what she very soon came to see was that her husband would never hurl anything at anyone; he understood money and noticed little else. He was agreeable, to be sure, but the sort of man who is agreeable to everyone; anyone in the world could have got along with him. But to arouse him to some sort of awareness, to raise his attention to even the lowest possible point, one had to shout, to scream, to threaten, to condemn. This Nancy did. After a while, I think, she understood that nothing would arouse him, that she was stuck with pleasantness and would have to find excitement elsewhere, if at all. In her memoir, she transmogrified his inattention and her endurance into happiness.

We moved apart after a few years, and I don't know where she found excitement, if she learned to do without it, or if, as sometimes happens, she took her frustrations out on her children. What was so unbearable about the blasted manuscript was that there wasn't a word of truth or complexity or trial by fire in it. The only "value" it honestly succeeded in promulgating was hypocrisy.

Eventually, I abandoned this farrago of lies and told my naive assistant to turn it down; it was not publishable, I said, and she ought to learn to recognize a publishable manuscript if she intended to remain, however temporarily, in the editorial trade. The writing was execrable, the substance simplistic, and the narrative line nonexistent. Four generations of women lying to themselves and about each other do not, I announced, a memoir make.

After a day or two, I began to see the funny side of the episode, and the irony of the manuscript's coming to me. My poor former classmate, so ardently right-wing, could hardly have known that her sorry memoir would end up in the hands of an editor who had seen through "family values" a long time since, and who further-more remembered the author all too well. I determined to let the new assistant go if she didn't sharpen up, and the whole incident had become but another annoying, unmemorable past occurrence when Leon, the head of the trade division, summoned me to lunch. This was curious, although not necessarily ominous. Leon wasn't given to lunches as a regular thing, and certainly not with anyone other than authors and agents; but I as-sumed there was some further shake-up in the hierar-chy of our publishing firm about which he thought I ought to know. Shake-ups, and indeed the sale of whole publishing companies, had become almost everyday occurrences in our profession.

Having ordered, we had hardly sipped our nonalco-holic beverage when he launched into what was evi-dently going to be a difficult subject.

"You're not going to like what I have to tell you," he said.

"Leon, if I'm out, just say so, and I'll go and slit my throat in the ladies' room as quietly as possible. No, don't worry," I added, putting my hand on his for reas-surance, "I'm ready to take up farming, I really am. Maybe I'll raise horses. Proceed."

Leon and I are old colleagues, he, like me, being one of the seniors still left on board, edging into fifty, maybe beyond. Leon is bisexual, as he puts it; I think he's gay, really, and since his marriage broke up he's had a male companion. He's childless, like me, and we both admit to finding children among the less appealing representatives of the human race.

"If it were a matter of firing you, I wouldn't bring it up at lunch," Leon said. "I'd arrive at your apartment with a bottle of vodka, a lime, a six-pack of tonic, an appropriate CD, and—"

"What would the appropriate CD be?" I interrupted.

"I have no idea; I would have to depend on inspiration at the time. But since it is not that time, let's get on with this, shall we?"

"By all means," I said. I lifted my fork to begin eating and gazed at him steadily, indicating my full attention.

"You know that manuscript you turned down a few weeks ago?"

"Which one?" I asked. This was quite honest. Like all publishers, we turn down many, many times more submissions than we publish.

"I thought you'd remember. Your assistant seemed to think you were unusually exercised about it and turned it down with considerable vigor."

"Oh, that one," I said. "Did she talk to you about it, the little snipe?"

"Yes, she did. And I sent her off with a bee in her bonnet."

"Go on."

"Someone representing one of the far-right foundations went to the head honcho. Having heard of the book's rejection, they offered a fancy sum to back the book's publication, disguised as a fellowship to the author to revise the manuscript under our direction, and agreed, furthermore, to purchase thirty thousand— have you got it? Thirty thousand—copies at retail price for their own distribution among the faithful."

"You're kidding. You have to be."

"My dear, parody, irony, Wildean oxymorons and

contradictions have become useless. Reality has out-
done rhetoric in these departments. I'm afraid it's all
quite, quite true."

"And the honcho is burning to accept."

"He did have the grace to consult me, as head of the
trade division. Consult, in this context, means inform
me of a done deal. I'm really sorry. But of course, I'll
put another editor on it. Unless you want to quit with
me, hand in hand, which would be one glorious momentary gesture, but the bloody book would still be
published and a sad profession would have lost two of
its few honest souls."

"I have to think," I said.

"Well, think away. But do remember, please, that I
was strictly forbidden to tell you about this, and that I
have done so must absolutely remain our secret, yours
and mine. The world, including everyone in the firm,
is not to know of this shoddy deal, of which I think
our honcho is more than a little ashamed. As far as
anyone else will ever know, we did not discuss this,
and you were shocked, shocked, when the news broke
that the book was being published."

"Believe me, secrecy is even more important to me.
Because, as I said, I have to think about this."

"Think away, but do remember that any adverse publicity for the book will simply make for more hype and
more sales."

"I do know that. But what worries me is—this lunch
is a bit unusual, I mean you and I having a business
lunch. I think we ought to decide what we will say, if
pressed, that we were discussing. I suggest something
really memorable."

"I've got it," Leon said, giggling. "Remember how
we used to joke, after a few drinks at one of our rather
raucous dinners, that we should put an egg of yours,
sperm of mine, into a petri dish, and get them to plant it

in a uterus-for-rent? The child would be a miracle of publishing know-how. I think we abandoned the idea because neither of us was prepared to bring it up."

"Excellent," I said. "That will really get their attention and divert them from any suspicions they might have harbored that we were discussing business."

"I'm damn sorry all the same," Leon said.

"I know. Eat up. After all, how often do you ask me to lunch? How often do we contemplate producing progeny? Anyway, I have to go off and cogitate."

"Should I worry?" I could see he *was* worried, about the book, and about what I might do.

"Let us take another vow of absolute secrecy," was all I said. I had a feeling, even as he agreed, that this request did nothing to calm his fears.

I admit that I started with simple violence. I know, I know, violence is never simple, and that thought was not slow in occurring to me. While it would have been satisfying, in the most basic, beastly way, to remove Nancy Carmichael and perhaps her whole family from the face of the earth, I had to abandon this idea even had I been capable of seriously considering it. Apart from all reasons obvious to anyone in favor of gun control, the publicity of such murders would simply send the book off to a flaming start.

My next brilliant idea was to write a book refuting everything she had said. But the same problem prevailed. Quite apart from the effort of writing the damn thing and getting it published, we would be providing the talk shows with a wonderful chance for debate and much-desired publicity.

Then I got even meaner. I well remembered when Nancy Carmichael, a charter member of Operation

Rescue, had had an abortion. The whole story of that episode would, indeed, make juicy publicity, but I abandoned it for three reasons, two of them practical. I had, as a matter of fact, a letter from Nancy thanking me for my financial help on that occasion, but I wasn't sure that, even if I could locate the document, it would actually contain what the law would consider evidence. Second, many anti-choice types had had abortions, so this would hardly be original news; hypocrisy is perhaps the salient feature of far-right religious groups. But the third and most compelling reason was simply that I didn't believe in this kind of personal betrayal. She had trusted me, knowing I was both trustworthy and, more to the point, a saver of money, and I loathed the idea of betraying such a confidence. After all, she had not personally attacked me in her so-called memoir, and I was a follower of the Henry James moral precept that actions be based on the morality of the doer and not on that of the proposed victim, however deserving of punishment.

I had heard that if one is having trouble solving a problem, it is best to stop thinking about it, to give one's attention to something else, and to let the subconscious muddle along on its own. Following this advice, I got down to work, bartering with agents, planning publishing schedules, encouraging authors, embroiling myself in the necessary and to me dynamic practice of my craft. At the end of the day, I went home still pondering how a much-valued author of mine might shorten his book without injuring it.

It was while I was dressing the next morning that the answer came to me, whole, complete, in all its lovely details.

We had had a letter from Nancy Carmichael, addressed to the head honcho and sent on to me from him, since I had agreed to continue with the editing of her manuscript. It seemed best, Leon and I agreed, not to call attention to myself in connection with this manuscript, not even by refusing to edit it; needless to add, I had no intention of editing it. The letter, oozing gratitude and eagerness for editorial advice, gave her address and telephone number in case we wished to reach her to discuss suggestions for revision. She lived in Greenwich, Connecticut.

Early Saturday morning, when I am famous for sleeping until well past noon and letting my answering machine cope with calls, I arose at dawn (no mean effort) and carefully removed the alarm setting from my clock. I intended to make certain that no one could possibly find a Columbo- or Poirot-type clue should I be suspected, unlikely as that was. I exited my building by the garage door, seen by no one, and rode the subway to Grand Central Station. From there I got a train to Greenwich. I took the fact that airplane travel was not, under the circumstances, possible as a heartening sign—after all, she might have lived at some distance, which would have been perhaps too much of a challenge: airplanes require identification, while railroad tickets can be bought for cash. I bought a round-trip ticket.

Once in Greenwich, I wandered around for a while, making my way toward the center of the town. Fortunately, post offices, as with so many former services, had stopped putting full zip codes on their postmarks. I dropped my letter into a postbox that announced, on a printed notice, a pickup at eight A.M. on Saturday morning. Since it was now well past that time, I hoped—though it did not really matter—that the letter would not be picked up, and therefore not postmarked, until Monday. I returned to the station, arriving, via train and subway, home; the entire trip had taken a matter of hours. I entered again by the garage door and plunged back into bed long before I would have awakened on an ordinary Saturday.

This was the easy part of the task. Composing the letter had been the hard part, but it was made easier by Nancy Carmichael's idiotic belief that everyone would be fascinated to learn even the smallest details of her conventional life. In her letter to the head honcho she had informed him that she had just learned to use a computer for working on her book, the original manuscript having been typed by a hired person. She had also bought a Canon Bubble Jet printer and was ready to get to work. I nastily hoped that the whole outfit would rot before she found a publishable use for it.

One lunch hour, I had dropped into a large computer store and murmured to a busy, fully occupied clerk that I just wanted to try his Bubble Jet printer; I had a disk, I said, it wouldn't take a minute. He waved toward a computer with a Bubble Jet printer attached. I inserted my disk, printed off my letter, and left the store before he got around to trying to sell me anything.

The letter, which I had written with great care and in careful imitation of Nancy's style, was addressed to a columnist I knew who worked on a daily paper. She was always in search of good copy, but was honorable enough to check her stories; she also shared my political anti-Gingrich views and so might like the news I was devising for her reception. The letter gushed happily about the arrangement made with my publishing firm, giving details (the ones I knew from Leon) and offering to discuss the matter with the columnist should she wish to call Nancy for confirmation: telephone number included.

I had, of course, to hope that Nancy was too naive in the ways of publishing firms to know for certain that this was *not* good publicity, and that the head honcho would, at the very least, wring her neck if he knew what she was doing. Scarcely daring to hope this would indeed work, but remembering Nancy Carmichael all too well, I posted my letter in Greenwich as described and waited for events. My only suspicious act during this whole endeavor was to buy the evening paper in which my columnist friend held forth, an uncharacteristic action but one I could not prevent myself from taking, whatever the risk.

If the letter was picked up on Monday, it might, if the post office did not make one of its frequent goofs, reach my columnist friend on Wednesday. She would immediately call to verify, and might print the item on Friday at the earliest. I continued praying, or what passes in agnostics for prayer, that Nancy would confirm the news in the letter she had not written; if the news was confirmed, what columnist would care who wrote the letter?

The wait was interminable, but . . .

The item appeared on Monday. I had correctly deciphered, from both memory and her writing, the sort of fool Nancy would be under the circumstances. I had had that advantage, and I made full use of it.

To say the head honcho was upset was to describe a tornado as a summer shower. Leon and I looked as horrified as our boss, innocently shocked by the news and more than slightly abashed by the revealed malfeasance. (The news of our possible in-vitro baby had swept happily through the office, despite our embarrassed denials that we intended any such thing.) The contract, which had not been signed—I had hoped to achieve this by acting quickly—was declared null and void, and Nancy Carmichael together with her manuscript disappeared into the sunset.

Leon and I never mentioned the matter again, even when we were alone. He never asked, I never told, as though we were gays in the military. Well, perhaps we were, in a manner of speaking.

As to the new assistant, she went, together with Nancy Carmichael's contract. I never knew if she had played any part in the right-wing financial arrangements, and I didn't ask. I was happy enough to see the last of her. Politics aside, I can't have an assistant editor who is devoid not only of experience but of taste as well. Four generations of family values indeed!

EYE TO EYE

by Jeffery Deaver

I'd help you if I could," the boy said. "But I can't."

"Can't, hm?" Boz asked, standing over him. Peering down at the top of the brown cowlick. "*Can't?* Or don't wanta?"

His partner, Ed, said, "Yup, he knows something."

"Don't doubt it," Boz added, hooking his thumb around his $79.99 police baton, imported and gleaming black.

"No, Boz. I don't. Really. Come on."

An engine-block-hot dusk. It was August in the Shenandoah Valley and the broad river rolling by outside the window of the Sheriff's Department interview room didn't do anything to take the edge off the temperature. Other towns, the heat had the locals cutting up and cutting loose. But Caldurn, Virginia, about ten miles from Luray—yeah, that's the one, home of *the* cave—was a small place, population 8,400. Heat this bad usually sent most of the bikers, trash and teens home to their bungalows and trailers where they stared, groggy from joints or Bud, at HBO or ESPN (satellite dishes being anticrime measures out here).

But tonight was different. The deputies had been yanked from their own stupors by the town's first armed robbery/shooting in four years. Sheriff Elm Tappin was grudgingly en route back from a fishing trip in North Carolina and FBI agents from D.C. were due later tonight as well.

Which wasn't going to stop these two from wrapping up the case themselves. They had a suspect in the lockup and, here in front of them, an eyewitness. Reluctant though he was.

Ed pulled his tan uniform shirt away from his chest and sat down across from Nate Spoda. They called him "boy," behind his back, but he wasn't a boy at all. He was in his mid-twenties and only three years younger than the deputies themselves. They'd been at Nathaniel Hawthorne High together for a year, Nate a freshman, the other two seniors. He was skinny as a post, had eyes darty and sunken as any serial killer's and was known throughout town for being as kooky now as he was in high school.

"Now, Nate," Ed said kindly, "we know you saw *something*."

"Come on," the boy said in a whiny voice, fingers drumming uneasily on his bony knee. "I didn't. Really."

Boz, the fat cop, the breathless cop, the sweaty cop, took over when his partner glanced at him. "Nate, that just don't jibe with what we know. You sit on your front porch and you spend hours and hours and hours not doing diddly. Just sitting there, watching the river." He paused, wiped his forehead. "Why d'you do that?" he asked curiously.

"I don't know."

Though everybody in town knew the answer. Which was that when Nate was in junior high his parents had drowned in a boating accident on the very river the boy would sit beside all day long while he read books and magazines (Francis at the post office said he subscribed to some "excruciatingly" odd mags, about which she couldn't say more, being a federal employee and all) and listened to some sick music, which he played too loud. After his parents' deaths an uncle had come to stay with the boy—a slimy old guy from West Virginia, no less (well, the whole town had an opinion on *that* living arrangement). He'd seen the boy through high school and when Nate hit eighteen off he went to college. Four years later Ed and Boz had served their stint in the service, becoming all they could be, and were back home. And who showed up that June, surprising them and the rest of the town? Yep, Nate. He booted his uncle back west and took to living by himself in that dark, spooky house overlooking the river, surviving, they guessed, on his folks' savings account (nobody in Caldurn ever amassed *anything* that lived up to the word *inheritance*).

The deputies hadn't liked Nate in high school. They hadn't liked the way he dressed or the way he walked or the way he didn't comb his hair (which was too damn long). They hadn't liked the way he talked to girls—never brushing up against them accidentally on purpose or joking about boobs or pussy, the way normal guys did, but just *talking*. Jesus, he'd been in *French* Club. He'd been in *Computer* Club. *Chess* Club, for Christ's sake. Of course he didn't go out for a single sport, and you could just think about all those times in calc when nobody could answer Mrs. Hardon's question and Nate—they'd advanced the faggot nerd bone-whacker a couple years—would cringe like a squirrel and sashay up to the board to write the answer, in his fem handwriting, getting chalk dust all over him. Well, *naturally* he got pounded in the parking lot after. *Naturally* they'd tie his Keds laces together and bolo the shoes over a power line. *Naturally* they'd pee on his gym suit before class. Who wouldn't?

Nope, hadn't liked him then. Didn't like him now. Sitting on his porch, reading books (probably porn) and listening to this eerie music (probably satanic, another deputy had suggested) . . . Well, sir, that was simply unnatural.

And speaking of natural: Every time a report of a sex crime came in, Boz and Ed thought of Nate. They'd never been able to pin anything on him, but he'd disappear for long periods of time and the deputies were pretty sure he'd vanish into the woods around Luray to peer through girls' bedroom windows. They knew Nate was a peeper; he had a telescope on his porch, next to the rocker he always sat in—his mother's chair (and, yep, the whole town had an opinion about what *that* living situation had been like too). Unnatural. It explained a lot.

So the Caldurn Sheriff's Department deputies—Ed and Boz at least—never missed a chance to do their part to, well, set Nate straight. Just like they'd done in high school. They'd see him buying groceries and they'd smile and, real sarcastic, say, "Need a hand, ma'am?" Meaning: Why don'tcha get married, homo?

Or he'd be bicycling up Rayburn Hill and they'd come up behind him in their cruiser and hit the siren and shout over the loudspeaker, "You're goin' too slow! You're a hazard!" Which'd once scared him clean into some blackberry bushes.

But he never took the hints. He just kept doing what he was doing, wearing a dark trench coat most of the

time, living his shameful life and walking out of Ed and
Boz's way when he ran into them on Main Street. Just
like in the halls of Hawthorne High.

Oh, it felt pretty good, Ed had to admit, having him
trapped in the interview room. Scared and twitchy and
damp in the summer heat.

"He had to've walked right by you," Boz continued
in his grumbling voice. "You must've seen him."

"Uhm. I didn't."

Him was Lester Botts, presently sitting unshaven
and stinking in the nearby lockup. The scruffy thirty-
five-year-old loser had been a sore spot to the Caldurn
Sheriff's Department for years. He'd never been convicted of anything, but the deputies knew he was behind a lot of the petty crimes around the county. He was
white trash, gave the nasty eyeball to the good girls in
town and wasn't even a lip-service Christian.

Lester was currently the number-one suspect in this
evening's robbery. He had no alibi for five to six P.M.—
the time of the heist. And though the driver and his partner hadn't seen his face, what with the ski mask, the
robber'd carried a nickel-plated Colt revolver—exactly
the type of gun that Lester had drunkenly brandished at
Irv's Roadside not long ago. And there'd been a report
last week that somebody with Lester's build had stolen
a half pound of Tovex from Amundson Construction.
Which was the same explosive used to blow the door off
the Armored Courier truck. At 6:30 tonight they'd
picked him up—he was sweating up a storm and acting
plenty guilty—hitching home along Route 334, even
though he had a perfectly good Chevy pickup at home,
which fired up the first time Ed turned the key, just to
test out if Lester's claim that it "wasn't runnin' " was
true. He'd also been carrying a long hunting knife and
fumbled the answer when they'd asked him why ("Well,
I just, you know, *am*").

The Sheriff's Department procedure manual had explained all about motive, means, and opportunity in investigating felonies. Boz and Ed had scoped all that out in this case. It was sweet and simple. No, there was no doubt in their minds that Lester had done the job. And because Nate's property was on a direct line from the heist to where they picked up Lester there was no doubt that Nate could place him near the scene of the crime.

Boz sighed. "Just tell us you saw him."

"But I didn't. That wouldn't be the truth."

Nerd then, nerd now. Christ . . .

"Look, Nate," Boz continued, as if speaking to a five-year-old. "Maybe you don't get how serious this is. Lester whacked the driver of that armored car over the head with a wrench while he was peeing in the men's room at the Texaco on Route Four. Then he went out to the truck, shot the driver's partner in the side—"

"Oh, no. Is he okay?"

"Nobody's okay, they get shot in the side," Boz spat out. "Lemme finish."

"Sorry."

"Then drives the truck to Morton Woods Road, blows the back door off. He loads the money into another car and takes off, heading west—directly toward your place. We pick him up on the *other* side of your property a hour ago. He had to go past your house to get to where we found him. What d'you think about that?"

"I think it . . . Well, it seems like it makes sense. But I didn't see him. I'm sorry."

Boz reflected for a minute. "Nate, look," he finally said, "we just don't see eye to eye here."

"Eye to eye?" Nate asked uncertainly.

"You're in a different world from us," the deputy continued, exasperated. "We know the kinda man Lester is. We live in that sewer every day."

"Sewer?"

"You're thinking you'll just clam up and everything'll be okay," Ed filled in. "But that's not how it'll work. We know Lester. We know what he's capable of."

"What's that?" Nate asked, trying to sound brave. But his hands were clenched, trembling, in his lap.

"Using his damn knife on you, what d'you think?" Boz shouted. "Jesus. You really *don't* get it, do you?"

They were doing the good and bad cop thing. The procedure manual had a whole section on it.

"Say you don't finger him now," Ed offered gently. "He gets off. How long you think it'll take for him to find you?"

"Find you and gut you," Boz snapped. "Why, it'll be no time at all. And I'm beginning not to care."

"Come on," Ed said to his partner. Then he looked at Nate's frightened face. "But if we get him for armed robbery and attempted murder, he'll go away for thirty years. You'll be safe."

"I want to do the right thing," Nate said. "But . . ." His voice trailed off.

"Boz, he wants to help. I know he does."

"I do," Nate said earnestly. And scrunched his eyes closed, thinking hard. "But I can't lie. I *can't*. My dad . . . You remember my dad. He taught me never to lie."

His dad was a nobody who couldn't swim worth shit. That's all they knew about his dad. Boz plucked his shirt away from his fat chest and examined the black patches of sweat under his arms. He walked in a slow circle around the boy, sighing.

Nate cringed faintly, as if he were afraid of losing his gym shoes again.

Finally, Ed said in an easy voice, "Nate, you know we've had our disputes."

"Well, you guys used to pick on me a lot in school."

"Hell, that? That was just joshing," Ed said. "We only did it with the kids we liked."

"Yeah?" Nate asked, eyes brightening with cautious hope.

"But sometimes," Ed continued, "I guess it got a little out of hand. You know how it is? You're fooling around, you get pumped up."

Neither of them thought this little salamander had *ever* been pumped up (for Christ's sake, a man does at least *one* sport).

"Look, Nate, will you let bygones be bygones?" Ed held out his hand. "I'll apologize for all of that stuff we done . . . and I promise it'll never happen again."

Nate stared at Ed's meaty hand.

Burning bushes, Ed thought, he's gonna cry. He glanced at Boz, who said, "I'll second that, Nate." The procedure manual said that after the subject has been worn down the bad cop comes around and starts to act like a good cop. "I'm sorry for what we done."

Ed said, "Come on, Nate. What d'you say? Let's put our differences behind us."

Nate's timid face looked from one deputy to the other. He took Ed's hand, shook it cautiously. Ed wanted to wipe it after they released the grip. But he just smiled and said, "Now, man to man, what can you tell us?"

"Okay. I did see someone. But I couldn't swear it was Lester."

Ed and Boz exchanged cool glances.

Nate continued fast, "Wait. Let me tell you what I saw."

Boz—who of the two of them had worse handwriting but better spelling—opened a notebook and began to write.

"I was sitting on my porch reading."

Playboy, probably.

"And listening to music."

"I love you, Satan. Take me, take me, take me . . . "

Ed kept an encouraging smile on his face. "Go ahead."

"Okay. I heard a car on Barlow Road. I remember it because Barlow Road isn't real close to me but the car was making a ton of noise so I figured it had a bad muffler or something."

"And then?"

"Okay . . ." Nate's voice cracked. "Then I saw somebody running through the grass, heading down to the river across from my place. And maybe he was carrying some big white bags."

Bingo!

Boz: "That's near the caves, right?"

Not as glamorous as Luray's but plenty big enough to hide a half million dollars. Ed glanced at him and nodded. "And he went into one of 'em?" he asked Nate.

"I guess. I didn't see exactly 'cause of that old black willow."

"You can't give us *any* description?" Boz asked, smiling but wishing oh so badly that he could be a bad cop again.

"I'm sorry, guys," Nate whined. "I'd help you if I could. All that grass, the tree. I just couldn't see."

Pussy faggot . . . but at least he'd pointed them in the right direction. They'd find some physical evidence that would lead to Lester.

"Okay, Nate," Ed said, "that's a big help. We're going to check out a few things. Think we better keep you here till we get back. For your own protection."

"I can't leave?" He was whining again, brushing at the cowlick. "I really wanta get home. I got a lot of stuff to do."

Involving *Playboy* and your right hand? Boz asked silently.

"Naw, better you stay here. We won't be long."

"Wait," Nate cried. "Can Lester get out?"

Boz looked at Ed. "Oh, hey, be practically impossible for him to get outa that lockup." Ed nodded.

"*Practically?*" the boy asked, twining his narrow fingers together.

"Naw, it's okay."

"Sure, it's okay."

"Wait—"

Outside, they walked to the squad car. Boz won the toss and got in the driver's seat.

"Oooo-eee," Ed said, "that boy's gonna sweat up a storm every time Lester rubs his butt on his chair."

"Good," said Boz, and sped out onto the road, flipping on the light bar and siren not because he needed to but because it was fun.

They were surprised.

They'd been talking in the car and decided that Nate had made up most of what he was telling them just so he could get home. But, no, as soon as they started down Barlow Road, they spotted fresh tire tracks, even in the failing evening light.

"Well, lookee at that."

They followed the trail into the grove of low hemlock and juniper and, weapons drawn, as the procedure manual dictated, they came up on either side of the low-riding Pontiac.

"Ain't been here long," Boz said, reaching through the grille and touching the radiator.

"Keys're inside. Fire it up, see if it's what the boy heard."

Boz cranked the engine and from the tailpipe came the sound of a small plane.

"Stupid for a getaway car," he shouted. "That Lester's got wood for brains."

"Back her out. Let's take a look."

Boz eased the old car into a clearing, where the light was better. He shut off the engine.

They didn't find any physical evidence in the front or back seat.

"Damn," Boz muttered, poking through the glove compartment.

"Well, well, well," Ed called. He was peering into the car.

He lifted out a large Armored Courier cash bag, plump and heavy. He opened it up and pulled out thick packets of hundred-dollar bills.

"Phew." Ed counted it. "I make it seventeen thousand bucks."

"Damn, my salary without overtime. Just sitting there. Lookit that."

"Where's the rest of it, I wonder."

"Which way's the river?"

"There. Over there."

On foot, they started through the grass and sedge and cattails that bordered the Shenandoah. They looked for footprints in the tall grass but couldn't find any. "We can look for 'em in the morning. Let's get to the caves, have a look-see there."

Ed and Boz walked down to the water's edge. They could clearly see Nate's house overlooking the bluff.

"Those caves right there. Must be the ones."

They continued along the riverbank to the spindly black willow Nate had mentioned.

This time Boz lost the toss and dropped to his hands and knees. Breathing heavily in the hot murky air, he disappeared into the largest of the caves.

Five minutes later Ed bent down and called, "You okay?"

And had to dodge another canvas bag as it came flying out of the mouth of the cave.

"Lordy, whatta we got here?"

Eighty thousand dollars, it turned out.

" 'S the only one in there," Boz said, climbing out, panting. "He must've planted the bags in different caves."

"Why?" Ed wondered. "We find one around here, we'd just keep searching till we found the rest."

"Wood for brains is why."

They poked through a few other caves, feeling hot and itchy-sweaty and sickened by the stink of a dead catfish, but didn't find any more money.

They looked down at the bag. Neither said a word. Ed glanced up at the sky through a notch in the Massanuttens, at the nearly full moon, glowing with brilliance and promise. Standing on either side of the bag, the two men rocked on their heels like nervous boys at a junior high dance. The shoal beneath their feet was smooth and black and soft, just like a thousand other banks along the Shenandoah, banks where these two had spent so many hours fishing and drinking beer and—in their daydreams—making love with roadhouse waitresses and cheerleaders like Emma Rae.

Ed said, "This's a lot of money."

"Yeah," Boz said, stretching a lot of syllables out of the word. "What're you saying, Edward?"

"I'm—"

"Don't beat around the bush."

"I'm thinking, there's only two people know about it, 'side from us."

Nate and Lester. Boz knew that. Keep going.

"So what would happen . . . I'm just thinking out loud here. What would happen if they got together—accidental, of course—in a room back at the station? If, say, Lester had his knife back."

"Accidental."

"Sure."

"Well, he'd gut Nate and leave him like that catfish over there."

" 'Course, that happened," Ed continued, "we'd have to shoot Lester, right?"

"Have to. Prisoner gets loose, has a weapon . . ."

"Be a sad thing to have happen."

"But necessary," Boz offered. Then: "That Nate, he's a true geek."

"Never liked him."

"Dangerous too. He's the sort'd go postal in a year or two. Climb up to the South Bank Baptist Church tower and let loose with an AR-15."

"Don't doubt it."

"Where's that knife of Lester's?"

"Evidence locker. But it could find its way back upstairs."

"We sure we want to do this?"

Ed opened the canvas bag. Looked inside. So did Boz. Stared for a time.

"Let's get a beer," Boz said.

"Okay, let's."

Even though alcohol on duty was clearly prohibited by the procedure manual.

An hour later they snuck in the back door of the station.

Boz went down to the evidence room and found Lester's knife. He padded back upstairs, made sure that Sheriff Tappin hadn't returned yet, and slipped into the main interview room. He left the knife on the table—under a folder, hidden but not too hidden—and slipped innocently outside.

Ed brought Lester Botts up to the door, hands cuffed in front of him, which was definitely contrary to procedure, and escorted him inside.

"I don't see why the hell you're holding me," the tendony man said. His thinning hair was greasy and stuck out in all directions. His clothes were muddy and hadn't been washed in months, it looked like.

"Sit down, shut up," Boz barked. "We're holding you 'cause Nate Spoda ID'd you as the one stashing Armored Courier bags down by the river tonight."

"That son of a bitch!" Lester roared, and started to rise.

Boz shoved him back in his seat. "Yep, ID'd you right down to that tattoo of yours, which is the ugliest-looking woman I have *ever* seen, by the way. Say, that your mother?"

"That Nate," Lester muttered, looking at the door, "he's meat. Oh, that boy's gonna pay."

"Enough of that talk," Ed said. Then: "We're going downstairs for five minutes, see the commonwealth's attorney. He's gonna wanta talk to you. So you just cool your heels in here and don't cause a ruckus."

They stepped outside and locked the door. Boz cocked his head and heard the shuffle of chains moving toward the table. He gave Ed a thumbs-up.

At the end of the corridor, thick with August heat and moisture, they found Nate Spoda by the vending machines, sitting at a broken Formica table, sipping Pepsi and eating a Twinkie.

"Come on down here, Nate, just got a few more questions."

"After you, sir," Ed said, gesturing with his hand.

Nate took another bite of Twinkie and preceded them down the hall toward the interview room. Ed whispered to Boz, "He'll scream. But we gotta give Lester time to finish it before we go in."

"Okay, sure. Hey, Ed?"

"What?"

"You know I never shot anybody before."

"It ain't *anybody*. It's Lester Botts. Anyway, we'll shoot together. At the same time. How's that? Make you feel better?"

"Okay."

"And if Nate's still alive, shoot him too, and we'll say it was—"

"Accidental."

"Right."

Outside the door, Nate turned to them, washed down the Twinkie with the soda. There was Twinkie cream on his chin. Disgusting.

"Oh, one thing—"

"Nate, this won't take long. We'll have you home in no time." Ed unlocked the door. "Go on inside. We'll be in in a minute."

"Sure. But there's something—"

"Just go on in."

Nate hesitated uncertainly. He started to open the door.

"Nate," a man's voice called.

Boz and Ed spun around to see three men walking up the hall. They were in suits. And if they aren't federal agents, Boz thought, I'm Elvis's ghost.

"Hi, Agent Bigelow," Nate said cheerfully.

He *knows* them? Ed's heart began to race. They interviewed him while we were gone? . . . Okay, think, goddamnit. What'd he tell 'em? Whatta we do?

But he couldn't think.

Wood for brains . . .

"Where you going?" The agent was a tall, somber man, balding, his short blond hair in a monk's fringe just above narrow ears.

"The deputies wanted to talk to me again."

Bigelow and the others flashed IDs—yep, FBI—and asked, "You're Deputy Bosworth Peller and you're Deputy Edward Rankin?"

"Yes sir," they offered.

Boz was thinking: Lord, failure to secure a prisoner is a suspendable offense.

Ed, thinking pretty much the same, turned to Nate and said, "Tell you what, Nate, let's us go back to the canteen. Get another soda?"

"Or Twinkie. Those're good, ain't they?"

"It's cooler in here," Nate said, and pushed inside.

"No!" Boz shouted.

"What's the matter, deputy?" one of the FBI agents asked.

"Well, nothing," Boz said quickly.

Both Boz and Ed found themselves staring at the door, behind which Nate was probably being stabbed to death at this moment. They forced their attention back to the federal law officers.

Wondering how they could salvage it. Well, sure . . . if Lester came out in a rush, all bloody, holding the knife, they could still nail him. The agents might even join in.

Damn, it was quiet in there. Maybe Lester had slit Nate's throat real sudden and was trying to get out through the window.

"Let's go inside," Bigelow suggested, nodding toward the door. "We should talk about the case."

"Well, I don't know if we want to do that."

"Why not?" another agent said. "Nate said it was cooler."

"After you," Bigelow said, and motioned to the two deputies.

Who looked at each other and ignored the curious glances the agents gave them when their hands went to their service revolvers as they stepped through the door.

Lester was sitting in a chair, legs crossed, cuffed hands in his lap. Sitting across the table from him was Nate Spoda, flipping through a battered copy of the

Sheriff's Department procedure manual. The knife was just where Boz'd left it.

Thank you, Lord in heaven . . .

Boz looked at Ed. Silence. Ed recovered first. "I suppose you're wondering why this suspect's here, Agent Bigelow. I guess there was a mix-up, don't you think, Boz? Wasn't the commonwealth's attorney supposed to be here?"

"That's what I'd say. Sure. A mix-up."

"What suspect?" Bigelow asked.

"Uhm, well, Lester here."

"You better charge me or release me pretty damn soon," the man barked.

Bigelow asked, "Who's *he?* What's he doing here?"

"Well, we arrested him for the robbery tonight," Boz said. His tone asked, Am I missing something?

"You did?" the agent said. "Why?"

"Uhm" was all that Boz could muster. Had they jeopardized the case with sloppy forensics?

A fourth FBI agent came into the room and handed a file to Bigelow. He read carefully, nodding. Then he looked up. "Okay. We've got probable cause."

Boz shivered with relief and turned a slick smile on Lester. "Thought you were off the hook, huh? Well—"

Bigelow nodded his shiny head and in a flash the other agents had relieved Boz and Ed of their weapons and belts, including the overpriced, made-in-Taiwan billy club Boz was so proud of.

"Officers, you have the right to remain silent. . . ."

The rest of the Miranda warning trickled from his somber lips, and when it was through, they were cuffed.

"What's this all about?" Boz shouted.

Bigelow tapped the folder he'd received. "We just had an evidence response team go through the getaway car. Both your fingerprints were all over it. And we found dozens of footprints that seem to be from police-issue shoes—like both of yours—leading down to the water near Mr. Spoda's house."

Mr. Spoda. Oh, gimme a break.

"I backed the car out to search it," Boz protested. "That's all."

"Without gloves? Without a crime scene unit?"

"Well, it was an open-and-shut case. . . ."

"We also happened to find a total of ninety-seven thousand dollars in the back of your personal car, Officer Rankin."

"We just didn't have a chance to log it in. What with all—"

"The excitement," Boz said. "You know."

Ed said, "Check out those bags. They'll have Lester's prints all over them."

"Actually," Bigelow said, as calm as a McDonald's clerk, "they don't. Only the two of yours. And there's a chrome-plated thirty-eight in your glove compartment. Tentative ballistics match the gun used in the robbery. Oh, and a ski mask too. Matches fibers found in the armored truck."

"Wait. It's a setup. You ain't got a case here. It's all circumstantial!"

"Afraid not. We have an eyewitness."

"Who?" Boz glanced toward the corridor.

"Nate, are these the men you saw walking by the river near your house just after the robbery this afternoon."

Nate looked from Boz to Ed. "Yes, sir. This's them."

"You liar!" Ed cried.

"And they were in uniform?"

"Just like now."

"What the hell is going on here?" Boz snapped.

Ed choked faintly, then turned a cold eye toward Nate. "You little—"

Bigelow said, "Gentlemen, we're transferring you to

the federal lockup in Arlington. You can call attorneys from there."

"He's lying," Boz shouted. "He told us he didn't see who was in the bushes."

Finally Bigelow cracked a smile. "Well, he's hardly going to tell *you* that you're the ones he saw, is he? Two bullies with guns and nightsticks standing over him? He was terrified enough telling *us* the truth."

"No, listen to me," Ed pleaded. "You don't understand. He's just out to get us because we picked on him in high school."

The agent beside Bigelow snickered. "Pathetic."

"Take 'em to the van."

The men disappeared. Bigelow ordered the cuffs off Lester Botts. "You can go now."

The scrawny man glanced contemptuously around the room and stalked outside.

"Can I go too?" Nate asked nervously.

"Sure can, young man." Bigelow shook his hand. "Bet it's been a long day."

Nate Spoda put on a CD. Hit the PLAY button.

Mostly, late at night, he listened to Debussy or Ravel. Something soothing. But tonight he was playing Rachmaninov. It was boisterous and rousing. As was Nate's mood.

He listened to classical music all day long, piped out onto the front porch through thousand-dollar JBL speakers. He played it louder than he should have, he guessed, but ever since he'd overheard Boz's smirking complaint about the "weird" music Nate listened to, he made sure to keep the volume up nice and high.

Sorry it ain't Garth. . . .

He walked through the house, shutting off lights,

though he left on the picture lights illuminating the Miró and the Jackson Pollack—his mood, again. He had to get to Paris soon. A dealer friend of his had acquired two small Picassos and had promised Nate first pick. He also missed Jeanette; he hadn't seen her in a month.

He wandered out onto his porch.

It was nearly midnight. He sat down in his mother's JFK rocker and gazed upward. This time of year the sky above the Shenandoah Valley was usually too hazy to see the stars clearly—the local joke was that Caldurn should've been named Caldron. But tonight, where the black of the trees became the black of the heavens, a brilliant dusting of stars spread in a dome over his head. He sat this way for some minutes, taking pleasure in the constellations and moon.

He heard the footsteps long before he saw the figure moving up the path.

"Hey," he called.

"Hey," Lester Botts called back. He climbed the stairs, panting, and dropped four heavy canvas bags on the gray-painted porch. He sat, as he always did, not in one of the chairs but on the deck itself, his back against a post.

"You left *ninety-seven* thousand?" Nate asked.

"Sorry," Lester said, cringing, ever deferential to his boss. "I counted wrong."

Nate laughed. "Probably was a good idea." He was thinking Boz and Ed would have fallen for the scam if they'd seeded as little as thirty or forty thousand in the cave and getaway car. You wave double a man's annual salary, tax free, in front of his face and nine times out of ten you've bought him. But a job this big, it was probably a good idea to have a little extra bait.

They'd still net nearly four hundred thousand.

"We've gotta sit on it for a while, even if it's cash?" Lester asked.

"Better be real careful with this one," Nate said. As a rule they never operated in Virginia. Usually they traveled to New York, California, or Florida for their heists. But when Nate learned from an associate in D.C. that the local Armored Courier branch was moving a cash shipment up to a new bank in Luray, he couldn't resist. Nate knew the guards would be lightweights and had probably never handled anything but check-cashing runs on paydays at the local plants. The money was appealing, of course. But what tipped the scale was that Nate figured that in order to make the scam work they needed two unwitting participants, preferably law enforcers. He didn't have any doubt whom to pick; adolescent grudges last as long as spurned lovers'.

"You *have* to shoot him?" Nate asked. Meaning the guard. One of his rules was no gunplay unless absolutely necessary.

"He was a kid. Looking like he was going to go for that Glock on his hip. I was careful, only tapped a rib 'r two."

Nate nodded, eyes on the sky. Hoping for a shooting star. Didn't see one.

"You feel sorry for them?" Lester asked after a moment.

"Who, the guards?"

"Naw, Ed and Boz."

Nate considered this for a moment. The music and the fragrant late-summer air and the rhythmic symphony of insects and frogs had turned Nate philosophical. "I'm thinking about something that Boz said. About how I didn't see eye to eye with him and Ed. He was talking about the heist, but what he was really talking about was my life and theirs—whether he knew it or not."

"Most likely didn't."

"But it makes sense," he reflected. "Sums things up

pretty well. The difference between us . . . I could've lived with it—if those boys'd just gone their own way, in school and afterwards. But they didn't. Nope. They made an issue out of it every chance they could. Too bad. But that was their choice."

"Well, good for us y'all *didn't* see eye to eye," said Lester, introspective himself. "Here's to differences."

"Here's to differences."

The men clinked beer cans together and drank.

Nate leaned forward and began to divvy up the cash into two equal piles.

JOHN LUTZ *is the author of numerous bestselling thrillers acclaimed for their gorgeous prose and almost unbearable scariness. Two of them,* Single White Female *and* The Ex, *have been made into motion pictures. He has won several awards, including the Edgar Allan Poe Award, and is a past president of Mystery Writers of America. In "Stutter Step," justice depends on a young athlete's ability to speak his mind.*

STUTTER STEP

by John Lutz

Eddie Hayes slowed almost to a stop after the football was snapped, then sprinted down the sidelines, whirled at the fifty-yard line, and there was the ball. Willard, the quarterback, had made a perfect pass, and all Eddie had to do was reach out and pluck the ball from the air as if he were picking fruit. He tucked the football beneath his arm as he spun back toward the opposing team's goal line and broke into a run.

The defensive end hadn't been entirely fooled, and Eddie glimpsed him in the corner of his vision, closing in fast for the tackle. That was when Eddie executed his favorite football maneuver, the stutter step. Maybe he liked it because he stuttered himself when he talked, and this was almost like making his halting speech physical in a way that could win football games and acceptance with his classmates. The stutter step was kind of like taking a quick stride and a half without speeding up, keeping your feet going faster than you were, so that on videotape it looked a little like a momentary fast-forward. Eddie was good at it. He broke stride just enough to throw off the defensive end's timing, changed direction, and felt arms slip around his right thigh, then slide down and away. He pulled free and was running full tilt again toward the goal line.

Footsteps sounded behind him and he knew the enemy linebacker hadn't been fooled, either, and had dropped back to cover the pass and was now after him. Eddie had soft hands and could catch whatever he could reach, but he knew he didn't have speed. He lowered his head and ran straight for the goal line twenty yards away, staying barely in bounds along the left sideline.

He made it to the ten-yard line before a freight train struck him from behind and he went down hard, remembering to tighten his grip so the football wouldn't squirt from his grasp on impact. His right shoulder and his face hit the ground first. As he slid, his metal face guard scooped up mud that stuck to it and for an instant obscured his vision as he turned his head to the left.

He was looking through the Norwood High bleachers, empty because they were so far from the fifty-yard line and because hardly anyone came to Norwood High's games anyway, and as his eyes focused he caught movement back in the field near the parking lot. He opened his eyes wider as the linebacker placed his weight on him to straighten up at the shrill sound of the official's whistle, and he was looking at the figure of a man bending over a girl on the ground. The man was holding something in his right hand, and the girl raised one long leg almost lazily high into the air, then let it drop. At the sound of the whistle the man froze for a moment, then looked around, stood up, and ran toward the rows of parked cars.

Eddie scrambled to his feet, grabbing the linebacker's jersey to stop him from jogging upfield for the next play.

"D-D-D-Did you s-s-ee—" was all he managed to get out as the enemy linebacker glared at him, knocked his hand away, and continued upfield.

Eddie tossed the ball to the official. "D-D-Did you—"

But the official was already following the linebacker. The clock was running.

Eddie stared toward the bleachers. The man was gone now but something was still on the ground, a patch of blue against the green grass. And maybe some red. Eddie couldn't look away.

The whistle trilled again.

"Eddie! Eddie!"

Coach Evans was waving to him, summoning him to the bench and the sidelines. Players from both schools were standing still, staring at him.

Eddie realized Norwood High was going to be penalized for having too many men on the field. His fault.

Detective Sergeant Jack Anderson watched the ambulance jounce slowly across the grass field toward the paved parking lot. The girl's body had been examined and removed from the taped-off crime scene. The medical examiner had needed only a cursory look at it to determine cause of death; the girl's throat had been slashed.

Anderson was a wrinkly suited man with a kindly round face and wildly curly brown hair that was too long at the nape of his neck. He'd been on the Norwood police force for sixteen years, had just turned forty, and had never investigated a murder. He looked at the blood on the grass, looked away, then walked several feet from the crime scene and spat an unpleasant coppery taste from his mouth. It came back immediately to lie along the edges of his tongue. The scent-taste of blood and the faint beginnings of decay. He sighed and began trudging toward the two-story brick high school on the other side of the deserted football field.

It was time to try making sense of the brutal chaos of a young girl's violent death, if there was sense to be made of it. Time to talk to people.

It soon became evident that no one had seen or heard anything unusual, which depressed Anderson. Already the word from his partner, Art Toomey, was that the girl's friends and family could think of no one who might harm her. Eleanor Jarvis, the victim, seemed to have led the life of a typical bright and attractive teenager. She had dates, good grades, good friends, and now she had death.

Anderson was about to leave the tiny counselor's office the school had lent him for his questioning when a stocky blond man wearing Levi's and a sweater walked in and introduced himself as Charley Evans, Norwood High's athletic director and football coach.

"I think one of my players saw something that might interest you," he said. And he told Anderson what Eddie Hayes claimed to have seen when he was tackled on the ten-yard line.

"Why wasn't I told this sooner?" Anderson asked.

"It took Eddie a while to tell me—I mean, to make himself understood. At first, during the game, nobody paid any attention to him."

Anderson was dumbfounded. "He said he saw a girl murdered and no one paid attention? Was the game *that* important?"

"It wasn't anything like that, Detective. Eddie's got a problem. He's a heckuva good kid, but . . ."

As Evans himself struggled for words, a tall, dark-haired boy with blue eyes and broad shoulders shyly entered the office.

"This is Eddie Hayes," Coach Evans said.

"G-G-G-Glad to m-m-meet you," Eddie said as he shook Anderson's hand. He kept his chin tucked in, so that he seemed to be looking up at Anderson even though he was the taller of the two.

Anderson understood now what Evans had been trying to say, and realized Eddie must have been standing or sitting just outside the open door, around the corner in the anteroom.

"Is what Coach Evans said the way you saw it?" he asked.

Eddie nodded.

"Could you identify the man if you saw him again?"

"I d-d-don't know for sh-sh—C-Can't be p-positive."

Anderson took a closer look at the boy. Handsome, an intelligent gleam in his blue eyes. Probably a junior or senior, already needing to shave maybe every third day. The stuttering problem must be rough on him in school. Out of school.

Anderson handed the boy one of his cards. "Get in touch with me if you remember anything else," he said.

"What I s-s-saw . . . is it impor-por-por-"

"Important," Coach Evans finished for Eddie.

Anderson smiled at Eddie. "I hope it will be."

As the boy was leaving, Anderson called his name and Eddie turned.

"Your team win the game, Eddie?"

Eddie smiled sadly and shook his head. "We l-l-lost."

A few seconds after the boy was gone, Evans stepped closer to Anderson and said softly, "I think you'll find Eddie's a winner no matter what the final score is."

"I kind of thought he might be," Anderson said. "It has to be hard for him, though."

"Harder than you know," Evans said, and left the office.

Two days later Detective Laura Bains stopped by Anderson's desk. She was a small blond woman who'd been on the force for five years and risen quickly to detective grade. She sat perched sideways on the edge of his desk and looked down at Anderson. "Whatya got on the Jarvis homicide?" she asked.

"Not much," Anderson said. "No apparent motive, no suspect, no weapon."

"What about DNA? Had the girl been sexually assaulted?"

"No sign of it, no semen. She wasn't a virgin, though."

Bains shrugged. "She was a sixteen-year-old girl. Even in Norwood a lot of them are sexually active. You talk to any boyfriends?"

"Two. One admitted relations with her. One was two hundred miles away at a family reunion, and the other was across town playing ice hockey. Scored a goal just about the time Eddie said he saw the murder."

Bains's eyes widened. "You've got a witness to the crime?"

"Sort of. One of the Norwood High football players. He's not sure he can identify the killer. And he has a speech problem that might make his testimony in court less effective."

Now Bains smiled. "You might not need it if you play your cards right. A patrolman in the second precinct told me a woman came in and almost reported her husband was molesting their daughter."

"Almost?"

"She couldn't quite bring herself to actually accuse

him. You know how it is with child molestation and incest. The mother doesn't want to believe it herself,
much less tell someone about it. But most of them do
tell someone eventually. It's the kind of thing that has
to get told."

Anderson had stood up without realizing it. "We
talking about Mrs. Jarvis?"

Bains smiled. "We sure are. I figured you might
want to speak with her."

But Anderson was already on his way to do exactly
that.

When he steered his unmarked police car onto York
Avenue fifteen minutes later and approached the
Jarvises' small clapboard house, he saw a police cruiser
parked in the driveway, its red and blue bar lights flashing against the afternoon glare.

He parked behind the cruiser and climbed out of his
car. The house's front door opened and a uniformed
cop stepped out. He was a big man with a barrel chest
and bulldog features. Anderson had seen him around
and knew his name was Hammond.

When Hammond approached, Anderson flashed his
badge though he knew it wasn't necessary. He was a little puzzled. "Detective Bains send you here?" he asked.

Hammond looked confused. "No, we got the call fifteen minutes ago through the dispatcher."

"Fifteen minutes?"

A siren off in the distance had gradually grown
louder. Now it was deafening as an ambulance turned
onto York Avenue. The siren growled to silence and the
bulky white and red vehicle parked in front of the
Jarvis house.

"What's going on here?" Anderson asked.

"Thought you knew," Hammond said. "Mr. Jarvis
said he called us soon as he found the body."

"Body?"

"Mrs. Jarvis. She fell down the basement steps. Steep steps, nasty fall."

"Are you sure she's—"

"If you saw the skull fracture and the angle of her neck, you'd know she was dead," Hammond said.

Anderson stood numb with impotent rage.

Hammond stared at the ground and shook his head. "Poor Mr. Jarvis, he's all broke up."

Anderson sat down across from District Attorney Norman McDill in McDill's gloomy, paneled office. The place smelled of dust and the libraries of Anderson's youth, with its tattered law volumes and court transcripts stacked and leaning in walnut bookcases. He liked the skinny, hatchet-faced D.A. because McDill was more interested in justice than in appearances or political traction. Anderson knew McDill wanted to nail Carl Jarvis, murderer of his own daughter and then his wife, as much as anyone.

"There's no way to bring charges against Jarvis for his wife's murder," McDill said. Anderson noticed gray in his curly black hair. McDill was beginning to show his age—like Anderson.

Anderson wasn't surprised about McDill's view of the wife's death. It was one of those simple homicides difficult to prove, perhaps even an impulsive act on the part of the killer. Was the victim pushed down the steep basement steps, or did she trip and fall? Since there were no witnesses, and little physical evidence, no one other than Jarvis would ever know.

"We don't need two convictions to send Jarvis to the execution chamber," Anderson pointed out. "We have a witness to the daughter's murder."

McDill sat back in his swivel chair and slowly shook

his head. "I've talked to Eddie Hayes. Because of his stuttering, he wouldn't make an effective witness. And Jarvis's attorney would carve him up on cross-examination, destroy him and our case. It would be a cruel thing to put that boy on the stand."

"Murder's a cruel thing."

"Eddie's testimony wouldn't change that. And it would be doing Jarvis a favor."

Anderson knew McDill was right. He couldn't get the two victims out of his mind, his dreams. But there was no point in compounding the tragedy by scarring a sensitive and vulnerable boy, creating a third victim. "What about getting Eddie's deposition as to what he saw?"

"Written testimony won't sway a jury in a murder trial. And Eddie Hayes would still have to endure cross-examination. Jarvis has the legal right to face his accuser in court, and his lawyer would make sure that he would. Don't think a defense attorney won't do everything to exploit Eddie's stuttering, to make him appear slow and unreliable, no matter how destructive it would be to Eddie. He's a good kid, a nice kid . . . it would be terrible for him." McDill sighed hopelessly. "Not to mention ineffectual as testimony. The sad fact is, all we've got is Mrs. Jarvis's conversation with a policewoman that did no more than leave the general impression her husband might be molesting their daughter. You read the report—it could be interpreted that Mrs. Jarvis might just as easily have come in to confess to leaving the scene of a traffic accident."

"Then lost her nerve and walked out?"

"It happens. The guilt suddenly seems a lighter load to bear when you're sitting in a police station."

Anderson stood up and paced angrily, then spun and faced McDill. "So we're gonna let Jarvis walk?"

"Yes. Unless you can come up with some other evidence."

"We both know he was molesting Eleanor, and she told him she was going to talk, so he killed her. But the mother'd been aware of the incest all along—they usually are even if they don't admit it to themselves or anyone else—and after Eleanor died she confronted Jarvis and he killed her too, to keep *her* from talking."

"Knowing isn't proving," McDill pointed out. He fired up a curve-stemmed pipe, like the one Sherlock Holmes smoked, and puffed and sucked on the stem to get the tobacco burning evenly. Years ago McDill smoked the pipe so he'd appear older; now it simply made him look wiser. His shrewd gray eyes squinted through the resultant haze at Anderson. "Maybe the victim confided to a girlfriend about the molestation."

"I followed that line," Anderson said. He didn't smoke, but he liked the pungent scent of McDill's tobacco. "None of Eleanor's friends remember her even hinting that her father was molesting her. But it's something a teenage girl wouldn't talk about even to her closest friend."

"What about her boyfriend?"

"He's a kid named Walter Sanders, honor student, basketball player. He says Eleanor was moody and acted funny around her father sometimes, but she never mentioned anything was wrong."

"Show me a teenage girl who isn't moody around her father sometimes," McDill said, holding his pipe out and gazing at it the way pipe smokers do, maybe thinking it was slowly killing him and wondering why he kept smoking the damned thing.

"I'm going to keep probing," Anderson said, moving to the door. "Jarvis isn't going to get away with this. Eddie Hayes is a bright kid. He'd make a good witness if he didn't stutter, and with his help we might be able to at least put Jarvis away."

"But he does stutter," McDill said. "And he's a

teenager. The witness stand in a murder trial is no place for him."

Anderson talked to Eddie's mother, a heavyset, fifty-ish woman who was as reluctant as McDill to put the boy on the stand. He talked some more to the dead girl's schoolmates, and to close friends of the late Mrs. Jarvis. No one could—or would—attest to the fact that Jarvis might have been molesting his daughter.

Then Anderson paid a visit to Irene Marasso, a slender blond girl Coach Evans had mentioned that Eddie favored but was too shy to approach. She was a sophomore with bright green eyes that tilted up slightly at the corners like a cat's. She would mature into a sensual and attractive woman, but now she had a demeanor almost as shy as Eddie's.

"Who told you I was Eddie Hayes's girlfriend?" she asked, in her family's living room with her mother and father seated side by side across from her on the sofa, monitoring the conversation.

"No one said exactly that," Anderson said. "Only that you were friends and he, er, liked you a lot."

"Eddie likes me that much?" She seemed surprised and pleased.

"You have a shared interest in books."

"Sure, we talk about good books. We both like to read. But we know each other, is all." She glanced at her mother and father. Protesting too vigorously, Anderson thought.

"Is he the kind of boy who'd stretch the truth to gain attention?"

"Eddie?" She looked astounded, her mouth open so wide Anderson noticed for the first time that she had metal braces on her lower teeth. "Attention's the last thing Eddie'd want. He's a very private person."

"And an honest one?"

"Nobody's more honest than Eddie!"

Anderson saw the mom and dad exchange looks of growing awareness. They, and he, knew what was happening here. Irene wasn't going to say anything that wasn't in defense of Eddie. Anderson chatted pleasantly with the three of them for a few minutes, then thanked them and left.

Eddie hadn't been home when Anderson had talked to his mother; she'd mentioned he'd gone for his regular appointment with his speech therapist. Anderson called Eddie's mother and got the therapist's name.

The Macklin Speech Clinic was in Carterville, fifty miles west of Norwood. Eddie made the drive every Thursday in the family car to attend therapy sessions.

The clinic was on the third floor of a small office and professional building. Anderson let himself in through the lettered oak door, found himself in a tiny waiting room, and pressed a buzzer to announce his presence. He'd phoned ahead, and Bonnie Macklin, Eddie's therapist, had agreed to talk with him between sessions. Judging by the directory in the lobby, the size of the office, and the lettering on the door, she worked without colleagues and *was* the Macklin Clinic.

Anderson sat in a red plastic chair and idly looked over clippings pinned to a nearby cluttered cork bulletin board. There were articles about stutterers who'd conquered their speech problem and achieved fame and fortune as actors or news anchors, a country-western singer who could sing without stuttering even though he still stuttered in interviews, historical figures like Charles Darwin and Isaac Newton and the Roman emperor Claudius, not to mention Moses. There were also items about how to deal with the isolation and psychological impact of stuttering, about how school-age children might cope with being teased in class and on the playground. Anderson thought about Eddie Hayes, what it took for him to survive in the sometimes cruel world of the teenager, what it took for him to come forward and report what he'd seen.

A door to an inner office opened and a skinny teenage boy emerged, glanced tentatively at Anderson, then went out the door to the hall.

"Detective Anderson?" said a woman's voice.

Anderson turned to see an attractive, dark-eyed woman in her thirties. Her direct gaze suggested a forthrightness and honesty. Her smile was friendly.

"I'm Bonnie Macklin," she said. "You wanted to talk to me about Eddie Hayes."

"About him possibly testifying in a murder trial," Anderson said.

"I gathered as much," Bonnie Macklin said, and invited him into what looked like a small conference room. At one end a cabinet was opened to reveal a computer setup. A chair sat before the computer, with some sort of equipment draped on its back, wires with earphones, and a strap with wires leading to it.

"That's CAFET," she said, noticing him staring at the computer. "Stands for 'computer aided fluency establishment training.' It teaches breath control in order to regulate the flow of air through the vocal folds."

"It cures stuttering?"

She smiled again, this time sadly. "Only sometimes. But almost always it helps to alleviate it or its symptoms."

She sat down at one of the wooden chairs arranged around the mahogany table. He sat opposite her.

"No one knows for sure exactly what causes stuttering," she explained. "One theory is that there are irreconcilable differences between the brain's left and right hemispheres, that they send conflicting speech signals.

It's been described as two sparrows chattering different messages simultaneously. For now, we have to settle for treating the result of those differences, the stuttering itself."

"I understand you treat Eddie Hayes."

"Yes, he's been coming here for sessions for the past four years."

"Is he one of those who can learn not to stutter?"

"It's possible but not likely. Too much time passed before he was given help. He can certainly improve his fluency, and he has. Someday he'll do just fine. He's a gritty kid. I like him. And if courage and determination were the whole story, he'd be my best subject. But the older a stutterer gets, the more the brain becomes hard-wired into stuttering, and a measure of concentration and breath control in speech will usually be necessary."

"How might a jury react to his testimony in court?" Anderson asked.

"Depends on the jury. They might pity him, or get impatient with his speech and tune him out, or underestimate his intelligence. All those alternatives would be a mistake. Eddie's past the point where he needs pity, and like most stutterers, he doesn't speak unless he has something to say that's worth hearing. And I've found that people who stutter are generally above average in intelligence. Eddie's IQ will probably be higher than anyone's on the jury."

"What about the effect testifying would have on Eddie?"

Bonnie Macklin's smile was back, warmer this time. "You ask as if you really care, Detective Anderson."

"I do care. Cops are misunderstood, just like stutterers."

"I think Eddie can handle it," she said. "He's got a wide streak of character in him. But it won't be easy for him. This trial will receive a lot of publicity and he'll be in the spotlight, expected to perform. That's a lot of pressure for any teenage kid, much less one with a speech problem."

"If he agrees to testify, will you help him?"

"I'll be there for him," she said without hesitation.

That should be enough, Anderson thought, assessing the woman again, not exactly in a coplike manner. For an instant he was sorry he didn't stutter.

McDill had himself been coached by Bonnie Macklin and handled his questioning of Eddie Hayes skillfully, pausing to let Eddie finish his sentences, staying firmly on the subject and asking questions that required only short answers. Seated beside Bonnie in the front row of the courtroom, Anderson decided Eddie had done very well. He thought, at the end of the second day of the trial, that the prosecution had presented a strong case against Jarvis.

Almost as soon as the defense had begun its presentation, Jarvis's attorney, a suave fashion-model type named Kniver, called Eddie to the stand.

"Mr. Hayes," he asked with a smile, "have you ever heard the expression 'Here's mud in your eye'?"

"I th-th-"

"Well, for those of you who haven't heard it, it's a toast among drinkers who sometimes don't see so straight. When you were tackled on the ten-yard line, Mr. Hayes, were you not hit from behind so hard that your metal face guard dug into the mud and obscured your vision?"

"It di-didn't ob-ob—I c-could—"

"Mr. Hayes?"

"Let the witness finish his answers," said the gray and venerable Judge Adam Proctor from the bench.

Kniver merely nodded, staying locked in on Eddie. "When an athlete strikes the ground with such force and suddenness, vision—even without a face guard and mud to obstruct it—can become jarred and indistinct, isn't that so?"

Eddie's lower lip trembled and he stared at Bonnie, who stirred beside Anderson.

Kniver sighed and waited. "Mr. Hayes? Eddie?"

"It—"

"And wasn't the scene you *think* you saw occurring—*if* it did occur—behind the bleachers, some distance from the football field itself?"

Eddie's gaze traveled to his mother, who was glaring at Kniver. Then Eddie looked at Irene Marasso, who sat three rows back, biting her upper lip and squirming in discomfort. Eddie looked quickly away from her and hung his head.

"Mr. Hayes?"

Eddie's mother stood up.

"I think we'll recess for twenty minutes," Judge Proctor said.

As court adjourned, Anderson glanced at Bonnie, who looked furious. On the other side of the room, McDill was seated next to Eddie with his arm slung across the boy's shoulder.

"Let's get out of here for a while," Anderson said to Bonnie.

"No, I think I'd better go to Eddie."

Anderson nodded, then stood up and walked from the courthouse into the brisk, bright autumn afternoon. The parking lot was bordered by large trees whose brown leaves still clung in the warming sun. It was eleven-thirty, and the early lunchers at the nearby high school were out, some of them driving past on Elm Avenue, which ran past the side of the brick and gray stone court building. One of the car's windows were open, and rapid drumbeats and the staccato rhythm of rap music wafted to Anderson where he stood with a foot propped on the concrete edge of a fountain that wasn't running. The world was moving faster all the time, he thought as the heavy bass and machine-gun lyrics of the music faded. How must it be if you couldn't voice your thoughts rapidly enough? Bonnie had said that in most conversations there was a time to express yourself, then it was gone. The speech-impaired couldn't avail themselves of the opportunity, and lost their chance sometimes forever. Grown men still mourned that they never expressed their love for their high-school sweethearts.

Anderson stood looking up at the cloudless sky for a few seconds, then smiled slightly and returned to the courtroom. He summoned Bonnie over from the group at the prosecution table so he could talk to her.

She was dubious at first, then finally gave in and went to talk to Eddie.

"Are you still so sure?" she asked Anderson, sitting down next to him as they waited for Judge Proctor to enter so the court could be called in to session.

"No," Anderson admitted. "If the jury reacts wrong, if they laugh, the kid is dead."

"Eddie's willing to risk it," she said. "And he won't die because he's laughed at by ignoramuses. He's better than that."

She spoke with barely contained rage at the thought of anyone laughing at Eddie. Anderson thought he might have to do something to contain her in court if things went wrong. He liked that about her.

When Kniver resumed his cross-examination of Eddie, there were a few nervous twitters and embarrassed coughs, but no one laughed. Judge Proctor, who had agreed to McDill's request, swept the room with a glare calculated to freeze laughter in the throat. Kniver didn't like it when Eddie sang his answers to questions, but he couldn't prevent it.

Each of the wily lawyer's questions was answered in a calm, clear manner, and in a tune whose melody no one could place but that sounded familiar. Jarvis, seated at the defense table, began to perspire.

"This is the first time I've ever conducted a cross-examination to music," Kniver said to the judge, standing with his hands on his hips.

"If there's an appeal," Judge Proctor said, "you might get your chance again." He waited for Kniver to resume his questioning. For Eddie to resume his answers in song.

The jury sat transfixed by this oddly hypnotic singsong interplay of word and wit. Gradually it became apparent that Eddie's honesty and credibility, and his intelligence, were more than a match for Kniver.

Kniver knew it. Jarvis knew it. The jury knew it.

The guilty verdict was a foregone conclusion.

When the trial was over, court had been adjourned, and the media were finally gone, Anderson walked with McDill and Bonnie across the gravel lot toward where their cars were parked beneath the trees bordering Elm Avenue. Eddie was with Irene Marasso, several hundred feet ahead of them, going in the direction of the high school. They were strolling close together but not touching, almost but not quite holding hands.

"We wouldn't have gotten a conviction if you hadn't remembered stutterers usually can sing fluently," McDill told Anderson, around the curved stem of the pipe clamped in his teeth.

"I read about it in an article on Bonnie's office bulletin board," Anderson said. "I figured if a stutterer could build a career as a country-western singer, Eddie might be able to get through an hour on the witness stand."

"I've heard of witnesses singing on the stand, but this is the first time I've actually heard it."

"He did it with Bonnie's support," Anderson pointed out.

"Eddie did it by himself," Bonnie said, glancing ahead. But Eddie and Irene were out of sight. "Knowing him as I do, I'm not surprised."

Anderson stopped walking, and the others stopped with him.

"What's the matter?" McDill asked.

Anderson stood still with his head cocked to the side and smiled.

"Listen," he said. "Do you hear singing?"

EDNA BUCHANAN was a Pulitzer Prize–winning reporter for the Miami Herald *before turning her attention to fiction. Her best-selling series starring crime reporter Britt Montero has been nominated for every major mystery award. In addition, she has written two nonfiction books about the reporter's life. In "Miami Heat," a man's nostalgia for the Florida of his youth threatens to cost him his family and his life.*

MIAMI HEAT

/

by Edna Buchanan

I want to live in the USA," Jennifer said, then raised the knife. She carved a thick slab of homemade meat loaf, placing it before him like an offering. A single tear trickled down her cheek. "I want my children to grow up to be Americans," she whimpered. "I miss home. . . ."

Charles drowned his mashed potatoes with mushroom gravy and sighed. Her reference to little Amanda and Chuckie as "my children," not "ours," was not a good sign.

"But honey, I was born here in Miami." He sighed again. "I promise, it won't always be this way."

"It will be, for our lifetime, and probably theirs." She glanced at the children, who sat up straight in their places, solemn eyes wide.

What scared him was that, in his heart of hearts, he had begun to fear she was right.

"How old is the man now?" he asked. "He can't live forever."

"Eight presidents thought the same thing. He's still in power, and where are they?" She pushed away her untouched plate. "If the CIA, the U.S. government and the Mafia couldn't get rid of him . . . He's not going anywhere."

Jennifer leaned across the table to dab at Chuckie's milk mustache with a napkin. Charles looked wistfully at the galaxy of golden freckles sprinkled across the decolletage of her scoop-necked shirt, forgot Fidel and remembered sex. How long had it been?

"The supermarkets here don't even carry grits, never heard of 'em," she said, pouting. "But they sure have got cassavas and malangas, whatever they are—looks like roots rejected from a potato farm. How would you even cook 'em?

"Nobody serves a decent cup of hot tea, the coffee is unspeakably vile, and the men make those disgusting kissy noises when I walk by—" Her voice broke.

"I'm lonesome all day," she mourned. "Our neighbors on both sides speak no English, and you know that even if they did . . ."

"I know, I know." He winced, preferring not to relive it, particularly at the dinner table. That thing with the goats had gotten them off to a bad start from day one.

The drums had convinced Jennifer a party was in progress next door. "Must be having a barbecue," she'd said, all aglow, insisting this was the perfect time for them all to troop out to the backyard fence and introduce themselves to their new neighbors. What they saw had freaked them all out, particularly tender-hearted little Amanda. How do you explain Santería rituals to your kids? You know you're in Miami, Charles thought ruefully, when your next-door neighbor knows more than three unusual uses for a goat.

Nothing had turned out the way he planned. Two things he knew: This was not the sweet Southern girl he'd married, or the town he'd grown up in. Would either ever again be what it once had been?

He had stolen Jennifer from his college roommate at Northwestern. She landed a job after graduation, he stayed to court her, and they remained in Chicago for the first six years of their marriage. But he had missed the big, brilliant blue skies, the Technicolor sunsets, the pink clouds at night, the silken sands stretching endlessly beneath star-studded skies, and the night music of the Everglades.

He wanted to share it all with his own kids and see them grow up the way he did. His south Florida childhood had been a paradise of year-round swimming, fishing, camping and boating, back in a time when people still thought of Tom and Huck when they saw a raft. He had explored the spoil islands of Biscayne Bay, the Miami River, the myriad canals and waterways, seen alligators, manatees, and dolphins. Boaters were now more likely to spot dismembered bodies or weighted corpses and risk being run down by go-fast boats with no running lights, operating at high speeds under cover of night.

Instead of wading birds, wild orchids, exotic butterflies and white-tailed deer in the Everglades, you had to stay alert for stray bullets fired by Cuban militiamen playing at war or poachers stalking the surviving alligators. And then there were the morbid tourists eager to snap shots of where the Valujet flight had plummeted in flames and was swallowed by the swamp without ever yielding a single corpse of the 110 souls aboard.

Charles hadn't realized how much Miami had changed, but it was still the place he loved, more for what it once was than what it was now.

He listened to Jennifer, still complaining, and sympathized. A journalist, she had worked for the *Chicago Sun-Times* until Amanda was born. Then she wrote advance obits, part time, interviewing well-known citizens for stories to be published *post mortem*. She was unable to find similar work in Miami, where journalists had to be bilingual. Charles found it easier. His late father's insurance business, which he had taken over, had a long-established clientele. He worked harder, and both of them liked her being a stay-at-home mom. He understood her disappointment at learning that even volunteer work went to the bilingual, but thought she overreacted when finding that the meetings of the PTA moms at Amanda's school were conducted in Spanish.

"Are you listening to me?" Jennifer demanded.

"Of course, sweetheart," he lied.

"Because I'm talking *d*-word here."

D-word? Dessert, he hoped. Her face told him otherwise. Divorce? His stomach flipped into a free fall. My God. Had it come to that? How could she think divorce while he was thinking sex? How long had it been? Weeks? No problem until that night on the beach and that long moonlit walk along the sand. The surf pounded, she laughed like the girl he remembered, that flirtatious look in her eye—when out of nowhere, shouts, panic, chaos. More than a dozen Cubans, splashing and spilling from a rickety sailboat, police officers, border patrol and INS agents descending with searchlights, demanding identification from Charles and Jennifer as though they, too, had survived a week navigating the Florida straits in a leaky boat.

The evening was ruined, but inspired his plans the following weekend. He rented a boat. They would picnic in the Keys, explore the islands of his childhood. Not his fault they were swamped by the speeding boats of the *democracia* movement, an entire flotilla of Macho Militants racing to thumb their noses at Fidel from the safety of international waters outside the twelve-mile limit. He and Jennifer were lucky that Brothers to the Rescue had spotted them and alerted the Coast Guard.

He was trying, she had to see that.

She sent Amanda and Chuckie into the Florida room to play, then returned to the table, voice hushed.

"I caught them at it again, Charles. That's why I've been so upset. This cannot go on."

Caught who? Was this something he was supposed to know? The neighbors? His mind raced.

"Caught them at what, Jen?"

"Playing that awful game."

"Game?"

"The kids, don't you listen?" She rolled her eyes, exasperated. "Do you ever pay attention to me? The *d* game!"

"Doctor?"

"Dope dealer!" She shuddered. "I hate even saying the words. Remember we found them playing it in the garage right after school started? Well, I caught them again this afternoon."

She saw the relief in his face.

"I'm serious. At this rate they'll be carrying weapons to school by third grade. This town is no place to raise children."

"I was raised here," he protested.

"You know it was different then."

"Not that much," he argued staunchly. "Are you sure that's what they were playing? How do you know?" he demanded.

"They took a box of Baggies from the pantry," she said, speaking succinctly. "Had leaves and stuff in some of them. Poured talcum powder in the others.

Had a wad of play money from the Monopoly set. Here. Look at this!" She took a fistful of small plastic bags from the cupboard.

The leaves and twigs looked remarkably like marijuana and the white powder a lot . . . What clever little creatures, he thought. "Where did they pick up this stuff?"

"In the backyard," she said distractedly, raking her fingers through her blond bangs. "The hedge—"

"No, I mean the whole idea."

"At school, from their friends, I guess. Amanda claims that all the kids play it. Good Lord, Charles, who are the parents?"

"Kids pick it up from TV," he said soothingly. "You'll find this everywhere. The networks—"

"Oh no! I can assure you, Charles, that across the rest of the country, kids are playing normal games. Hopscotch. Hide-and-seek . . ."

"Doctor," he offered.

"They are in need of counseling," she said solemnly, "and so are we. But most of all, we need to move back to the USA. Why not sell your dad's business?" she pleaded.

"Sell the business?" he yelped. "Throw away everything my father spent his entire life building? So you can live closer to your mother?" His voice rose. "She's the one putting these crazy ideas in your head, isn't she?" Her mother had never really liked him. Mother and daughter called each other daily. She was behind this, he thought furiously.

"I work too hard all day to come home and listen to this kind of talk!" He shook his finger.

"Don't you shake your finger at me, Charles. You know I'm right. Show a little respect for the mother of your children, and their grandmother, who is more th—"

"Respect is earned. You're just a little girl who

wants her mommy! Why don't you grow up? Try to be a woman and a wife for a change!" He stormed out the front door.

"Where are you going?" She followed him.

"None of your damn business!" He heard Chuckie begin to cry and Amanda call out, "Daddy!" He hesitated, then climbed into the Buick and slammed the door. Sometimes a man just has to take a stand. Angrily, he jammed the key into the ignition and sat clutching the wheel, trying to think.

Jennifer tapped on his window, startling him. The kids were watching from the front porch.

She'll have to apologize, he decided, and rolled down the window.

"Where are you going?" Even with her face flushed, eyes brimming, she still looked beautiful, he thought, wavering.

"I told you, none of your business."

"Then go, and take these with you!" She flung the kids' dope dealer Baggies into the car, rushed up the steps, herded the kids inside and slammed the door.

Now he had to go somewhere, like it or not. He floored it and screeched out of the driveway, burning rubber and narrowly missing a strolling neighbor.

The twilight sky was orange with mountains of lavender rain clouds towering to the west. He drove aimlessly as downtown lights began to appear, a sparkling skyline reflected in mirror-bright bay. Deco neon glowed hot pink and turquoise along the elevated Metro Rail tracks high above the streets, and a rosy glow across the bay warmed the sky over South Beach. How could you not love this place?

Yes! he thought. He was a man of the city and this was his city. How did the song go? He hummed it. Yes. A man of the streets. He began to feel better, remembered the schedule in the glove compartment, and fumbled for it at a stoplight. Sure enough, the Heat were playing basketball tonight at the Miami Arena. If he hurried, he could just make the tip-off.

The arena was built in Overtown, a dangerous inner-city neighborhood of barren, high-crime streets, in the hope that the fans who came would rejuvenate and re-vitalize the area. Another theory shot down. Die-hard fans swooped in for games, then fled to safer environs the moment they ended. The arena itself had become obsolete in less time than it took to build. Construction was already under way on a lavish new waterfront arena. But the Overtown facility was safe, as long as fans stayed on the main arteries and parked in the well-lit, security-patrolled lots.

He drove into the park-and-lock beside the arena, forked over $10, went to the box office, got a relatively good seat and thoroughly enjoyed the action.

Jennifer will hate missing this, he thought, wishing she was there as he munched a hot dog and drank a couple of beers. The game was great, the Heat dancers were smoking and an added bonus: both Madonna and Jack Nicholson at courtside, not together, each with an entourage.

The Heat were so far ahead that most fans left early, but Charles bought another beer and stayed until the end. Happy fans filtered out as a full moon burned a hole in the overcast night sky. No point fighting departing traffic. Headlights stabbed the night and horns blew around him as Charles sauntered to the parking lot, aware of a slight buzz from the beer. Just enough to feel mellow.

He unlocked the Buick and slid into the driver's seat content. Not until he turned to back out did he see the greenish glitter. Broken glass all over the back seat. The rear passenger window shattered. "Son of a . . ." Charles checked the glove box. His proof of insurance, tire warranty, owner's manual were all still in there. Missing was a roll of quarters and, of course, the Baggies and play money. He never should have left the kids' drug paraphernalia out in plain view. Charles got out and went to find the parking lot attendant. Maybe they had insurance, he thought hopefully.

The lot emptied fast and the man who had collected his money was gone. Charles nearly flagged down a passing patrol car, but what would he say, that his kids' fake marijuana and cocaine were stolen? Besides, he'd had a few beers. And no point making a report for insurance purposes, since the damage was less than his deductible. He sighed. With any luck, Jennifer would never know; he'd have the glass replaced in the morning. He returned to his car, alone in the empty lot, and drove toward Biscayne Boulevard.

But cops, emergency flashers and K-9 dogs with their handlers blocked his path. Red-faced officers, huffing and puffing as though they had been chasing a suspect, were directing traffic into a detour. He would have to turn west and circle the block to go back east. But the next street was a one-way. He turned at the block after that. He did not know that dark and barren street was a dead end. Vandals must have removed the sign. He wheeled into a hurried U-turn in a trash-strewn lot. Hard to believe it was so dark so close to downtown. Most streetlights here had been burned, broken, or shot out. Many were simply missing. It had been in the news. Urban loggers harvesting light poles, hauling them off to sell for scrap. Charles cursed and twisted the wheel, forced to make another right. Back where he started. He tried to turn east at the next corner but cops blocked that intersection, too. Disobeying an impatient wave, then an irate blast from a whistle, Charles drove up to the officer.

"*Siga! Siga! A la izquierda!*" The officer tried to wave him to the left.

"I just came from the game at the arena and I need to get to the boulevard. How do I—"

"*Muévase. Váyasa!* Move it, buddy, move it, or I move it for you. Go! Go! Go!"

The husky loud-mouthed cop accented his orders with a swift kick to the Buick's fender. "Go! Go! Go!"

What the hell was going on? Charles wondered, turning hastily down the unfamiliar street the cop indicated. He wondered if Jen was waiting up for him.

He groaned aloud when another cop waved him west at the next intersection. He needed to go *east*. He checked the dash. Damn it to hell! The needle on his gas gauge pointed to somewhere below empty. He had to stop somewhere, soon. Thank God he was out of Overtown, passing small houses and businesses.

An open Texaco station, at last. He drove under the welcoming lights and up to the gas pump. The place seemed deserted except for two men lounging on crates outside the small office surrounding the cashier's bulletproof cubicle. One was unshaven, built like a Clydesdale. He wore a red scarf tied around his head, and tattoos decorated his beefy biceps. The other, scrawny and mustachioed, sported a gold earring. Neither looked friendly. Charles decided to only pump ten dollars' worth and get out of there. The battered machine refused to accept his credit card, so he went inside. One of the men mumbled something in Spanish but Charles avoided their eyes and ignored them.

All he had was a twenty, so he dropped it in the metal tray. Something changed in the eyes of the obese middle-aged woman in the booth, an odd look. Charles followed her gaze.

Three bikers rolling up on Harleys. The two men outside sprang to their feet. Shouts, apparent insults, were exchanged.

"Who are they?" he asked the cashier.

"Ay, Dios mío!" she said.

The dialogue under the lights became more heated, the body language more threatening. The scrawny Hispanic suddenly came up with a twelve-gauge shotgun pulled from somewhere behind him.

"That thang ain't loaded!" a biker challenged.

"You think somebody should call the police?" Charles asked. The woman did not answer. She was gone, the booth empty. Then he saw the soles of her feet barely visible from beneath the counter where she had taken cover. Time to panic. No bulletproof glass in front of him. His only chance was to make it to the Buick, burn rubber and pray there was enough gas left to take him out of the line of fire. The hell with his twenty.

He stepped cautiously out into the warm, moist night and the rumble of rolling thunder. Ten more bikers riding into the station, between him and the Buick.

The argument grew uglier. A biker's hand flashed toward an ankle holster. Another yanked something dark out from beneath his leather vest. Charles did not wait to see what it was. He hurdled the fence bordering the station. The sloppy leap, unlike his high-school and college days, ended with a sharp pain coursing through his ankle. He slumped sidelong to the ground, breathing heavily, relieved that no one seemed to notice his flight.

He glanced about. This building looked like an old motel converted to apartments. Eager to create some distance between him and the station, he limped toward several cars parked outside. Just far enough so when it ended, he could easily make his way back to the Buick.

Behind him they were shouting.

"El es un muerto!"

"No dispare! No dispare!"

Charles wondered what they were saying, as a shotgun blast shattered the night. Then the *pop, pop, pop* of pistol shots.

Something buzzed past his ear like an angry insect and a chunk of stucco exploded off the building, just above his head.

He ducked, then pounded on the nearest door in panic. Inside, children yelped in fear and he heard someone skittering about. He thought of Amanda and Chuckie. "Open the door!" He tried it but it was locked. "Open the door!" he shouted, and rattled the knob.

Terrified, he peered over his shoulder, then heard a muffled crack and splintering wood in the door in front of him. The shot had been fired from inside the apartment where he sought refuge.

"*Váyase ahora mismo!* Go away!" a man shouted from inside.

Charles flung himself away from the door, then ran for his life. He crashed blindly through hibiscus bushes and cherry hedges, stumbling, throbbing ankle forgotten. Lights bloomed in the windows of small houses protected by burglar bars, dogs barked, outdoor lights flashed as he activated motion sensors, throwing eerie shadows across the yards, and voices shouted, "There he is! *Ayá está!*"

"*Ahí va!* There he goes!"

They meant him. He stumbled against a padlocked tool shed and stopped to catch his breath. Lights went on in the house. A knobby-kneed man clad only in rumpled boxer shorts appeared on the porch, a woman in a yellow nightgown and curlers screamed warnings behind him. As Charles stumbled toward them, to ask for help, he saw the man assume a shooter's stance and aim a large handgun at him.

"*Pare! Alto! No se mueva!*" The man clutched the weapon in both hands.

Charles scrambled around the tool shed, heart

pounding, gasping for breath. Did everybody in Miami have a gun? Panting and sweating, he slid along the side of the building until his shirt snagged on something sharp and tore. His Father's Day shirt. How would he explain to Jennifer and the kids? Would he ever see them again? Falling to his knees, he kept moving, creeping through clouds of mosquitoes as the rain clouds finally closed in and it began to drizzle. From behind him came shouts and pursuers pounding through the dark.

He found a small metal gate and fumbled for the latch. Thank God it was not padlocked. He scrambled through it. He thought the heavy breathing he heard was his own at first, then saw the luminous eyes. Moonlight glistened off the giant wet tongue. Pit bull!

"Ssshhhh," he whispered. "Good dog, nice doggy."

The animal cocked its giant head. A bone-chilling growl rumbled up out of its throat as Charles sprang forward like an Olympic runner breaking for the forty-yard dash. He grasped the chain link at the far side of the yard and with his last surge of strength vaulted over and crumpled to the ground, as the dog hurled himself at the fence.

Before his runaway heart allowed him to move, the dog was mercifully distracted by pursuers, racing to greet them at the gate Charles had left open.

The animal's owners were shouting, lights everywhere. If Charles could make his way through the yards to the next street, he could simply walk off, find a phone or a cab.

He trampled through wet flowerbeds along the north wall of a yellow rancher, collided with a life-size stone statue of the Blessed Virgin and then burst free onto the rain-slick street. Trying to catch his breath, he limped briskly to the corner to find a street sign and get his bearings.

He began to recognize the neighborhood from his high-school days, expecting an all-night drugstore with a soda fountain on the next block, but there was a *botanica* on that site instead, its windows dark. Where was he? He peered up at the street sign. General Maximo Gómez Avenue? He moved down the block to another sign. Humberto Quinones Way? Where was SW First Street? He was uncertain now which way it was back to his car. Should he try Pedro Luis Boitel Avenue?

He hated to leave the Buick all night. But he no longer cared if it was stolen, stripped or towed. All he wanted now was to go home, to sleep in his own bed. But first he had to get his bearings. Where the hell was he? His ankle throbbed with each step and his wet shoes squished, though the rain did seem to be letting up.

Calle Benito Juárez? Who the hell were these people? Whatever happened to SW Third Street? Where was he? He'd been wrong. He was no man of these streets. This was not his city. Jennifer was right, he thought, eyes wet with rain, or were they his own tears? They had to get out of here, take the kids and escape before it was too late.

Had tonight gone a bit differently, he might never have seen them again. His family filled his thoughts as he stood at the crosswalk waiting for several cars to pass. One slowed, the passenger's window glided down. Two men. Perhaps, he thought, they could give him directions, maybe even a lift back to the Texaco. He approached their car. "Hey guys, I'm kinda turned around here. Lost, actually. If you could give me . . ."

Leaving the engine running, the driver stepped out without a word. So did the passenger. Young men, relatively well dressed. Charles' stomach lurched when he saw the gun. The driver grabbed his arms. The passenger hit Charles with the gun, a solid blow above the right eye. He blacked out for a moment, his knees buckled and he felt himself being lowered to the pavement. This could not be happening, he told himself. Would his children remember him at all? Or worse, remember him slamming the door, ignoring their cries? Would their mother remarry? Charles thought of them as the two men expertly rifled his pockets. He did not resist as they stripped him of his wallet and his car keys. He felt one of them remove his wristwatch. His shoes! They were taking his shoes! He opened his mouth to object, but thought of the gun and swallowed the words. Head aching, blood dripping in his eyes, he heard the car drive off. In less than a minute they had taken his valuables, his pride and his dignity. He intended to lie there until police came and an ambulance.

But it rained harder. Nobody stopped. No one came. Eventually he sat up, then struggled to his feet. He felt dizzy, but took a few wobbly steps to try out his legs. They worked. He felt like he was going to be sick and wished he had not eaten that hot dog—was it only two hours ago? He padded along the wet pavement in his stocking feet. The soaked socks bunched up, so he sat down on the curb and peeled them off.

He plodded on, splashing through puddles, until finally, up ahead, he saw the welcome glow of an all-night convenience store. He groped his pockets; they were torn. Not even a quarter to call home. Surely the clerk would lend him one under the circumstances. He saw people loitering out front, smoking and talking loudly, as he approached. Why were they there at this hour? He glanced at his watch, then remembered it was gone. What could these strangers do to him? He had nothing left to take.

Then he saw that they wore hot pants and halter tops, with bare midriffs. A herd of hookers, four or five of them.

"Honeey! What happened to you?" A big girl, as tall

as he was, waxed sympathetic. She wore a thigh-high black skirt and shiny boots.

"A long story." He shook his head and reached for the door handle.

"You're bleeeeding! Here, baby, let me see that." He winced as she touched his head. "Baby, what happened?"

Her touch was gentle. He felt a little unsteady. "They got my car keys and my shoes," he said, noting the gold ring in her navel.

"Poor baby." Her name was Rose, she said, and, bracelets jangling, she assisted him through the door. He hobbled forward, leaning gratefully on her strong shoulder, envisioning them as wounded soldiers, survivors helping each other off the battlefield that was Miami.

The clerk glanced up from his *Playboy* magazine, then did a double take. "No! Nope. No way!" The small man held up both hands like a traffic cop. "Don't you bring him in here, Rose. No! No! No!" He stepped from behind the counter. "Look! Look! Look at that! He's bleeding all over the place! Outside. Outside."

"Orville! What's wrong wit' you? Can't you see this man is injured? Been robbed and carjacked," she scolded. "All beat up and left in the street."

"I only want to call my wife," Charles muttered.

"Out! Out! Look at that! He's all wet. Use the pay phone outside." He rushed them, making sweeping motions toward the door.

"Orville, you got no heart, no soul, you silly-ass piece of—"

"Would you lend me a quarter?" Charles asked, turning to the door.

"Sure thing, baby."

He dropped the coin in the phone outside while she dabbed at his head wound with a fistful of crumpled tissues from her little fringed purse. The number rang once, twice, as he closed his eyes, trying not to think about where those tissues had been.

Jennifer answered on the third ring.

"Jen, it's me. I need you to come pick me up. Bring the other set of keys to the Buick."

"Charles, where are you? It's nearly three A.M. Are you all right? What—"

"Don't ask questions, sweetheart. Just get here. Please hurry."

"Okay," she said uncertainly. "Give me the address. I'll have to bring the children along. I can't leave them alone."

The hookers provided the address and directions. "I'm on the way," Jennifer said.

He hung up, knowing that he would never be happier to see anyone.

Rose bought him a Styrofoam cup of hot coffee and insisted on applying first aid as Charles began to ponder her true gender. Her bare legs, though curvaceous, were extremely muscular. Her voice, though pleasant enough, was very deep. And could that be an Adam's apple?

The girls began to mutter and roll their eyes, reacting to an approaching Miami police patrol car. "Where was he when I needed him?" Charles murmured.

"Tell me about it," Rose said, hands on her hips.

"Ain't that the truth," the red-haired one said.

Charles took a deep breath and stood up straight to greet the officer who edged his cruiser to the curb.

"It's Swink," one of the girls said.

"Hi, Bernie," they chorused as the man in uniform stepped from his car.

"You." The officer pointed at Charles. "Could you step over here, please?"

A second man, a civilian, emerged from the far side of the patrol car. He looked oddly familiar.

"That's him," he said flatly. "That's the guy!" He

pointed to Charles with his finger this time, instead of a gun. "He was runnin' through my backyard, right after the chooting. He had chews on then."

"You have any ID?" the cop said.

"No," Charles said. "I was—"

"Whatcha doing? The hell's the matter wit' you?" Rose demanded loudly, up close in the cop's face. "Can't you see he's the victim here? Don't you have eyes? Are you crazy?" As the rest of the girls hooted, Charles's accuser climbed back into the patrol car and rolled up the window.

"How the hell you ever get outta the police academy?" Rose shrieked. "They musta been giving out badges in Cracker Jack boxes! You a reject from the Burger King?"

"You be quiet," the cop warned.

Orville opened the door. "Officer," he called, "none of this originated from the store. Would you kindly refrain from mentioning this address in your report?"

"You! You're another lousy jerk!" Rose screamed. "Get your ass back in there before I kick the hell outta . . ." She swung her booted foot at the clerk.

"Officer, did you see that?" he yelped. "She tried to assault me. We try to keep this element away, but . . ."

"Calm down," the cop was saying as Rose swung a powerful left hook at him and the rest of the girls began to curse and shout.

In a clear moment of revelation Charles saw how this would end. Jennifer and his children were going to arrive and find him handcuffed to a hooker.

Hopeless, he turned his back on the growing melee and wistfully scanned the street. Passing traffic moved slowly as drivers gawked. Like a mirage, a big Buick rolled into his line of vision. Charles blinked. The Buick was very much like his. Exactly like his, in fact. It *was* his.

"Hey," he yelled. "That's my car. They stole my car!"

The scuffle between Rose and the cop froze. "You sure?" the cop said.

"Absolutely." Charles realized that he was prancing barefoot in excitement.

"Don't move," the cop warned him, then blasted his whistle and waved the car over. The driver appeared startled, then pulled up to the curb.

With a dubious glance at Charles, the cop stepped toward the car and bent to peer in at the driver. "License and registration, please."

The driver smiled, nodded, then shot him.

The cop dropped, his gun half out of the holster. The girls screamed and scattered. Orville dove back inside, locked the store, and killed the lights. The gunman, who'd been half out of the car, slipped back behind the wheel. Charles stood stunned in the semidarkness, his fury rising.

The cop lay sprawled on the sidewalk, blood gushing from a neck wound. Charles pushed his hand aside, yanked the gun the rest of the way out of the holster and snatched up the cop's radio. "Officer down," he said, pushing the button. "Officer down! Mayday! Mayday!"

Forgetting his ankle, he sprinted barefoot after his Buick, hoping the cop's gun had no safety. He did not know how to release it. He had never fired a handgun before, he just jabbed it at his Buick and pulled the trigger. It was so loud when it fired that he nearly dropped it. But he pulled the trigger again and again. The heavy weapon bucked in his hand like a living creature and hurled balls of fire into the dark.

The Buick slowed.

"Gimme my goddamn car back!" Charles yelled. It would not go far, he thought, if the thief failed to gas up.

He must have fired at least six shots. The gun must

be out of bullets, he thought. But it kept firing. Had to be at least a dozen now.

The car jerked, then stalled. The door swung open. Charles ran toward it, then realized the driver did not bail out and run. He was leaning over the car leveling his own weapon. Gritting his teeth, Charles fired back, expecting each time to hear a click, to be out of ammo. But the gun kept firing.

The driver broke and ran, then cried out, stumbled and went down, clutching his ankle.

"Don't move!" Amazed, Charles padded purposefully up to the man, pointing the gun and trying to remember how they did this on *NYPD Blue*. He glared to show he meant business. "Freeze!"

The man hesitated, the fire fading from his eyes. He dropped his gun on the sidewalk. Charles kicked the weapon away, painfully injuring his bare toe. He hopped and winced as the man held his bleeding ankle with both hands and glared back.

Sirens converged.

"It kept shooting," Charles said stupidly as he handed the wounded officer's gun to a sergeant. "It never ran out of bullets."

"It's a Glock," the sergeant said. "Holds eighteen rounds."

"I kept shooting, but it never came up empty," Charles repeated.

The sergeant examined the weapon. "It's empty now," he said.

Chaos reigned at the convenience store. Reporters, TV news crews, and city officials descended—even the mayor. The man didn't look as swarthy in person as he did on TV, Charles thought.

When Jennifer finally found the address, the mayor himself rushed to greet her. She looked bewildered.

"I want to be the first to shake the hand of our home-town hero's wife," said the mayor. He kissed her cheek, then the kids, all bathed in the dazzling radiance of television lights.

Charles was being interviewed by reporters. The officer would survive, thanks to him, they said. The shooter, they said, had been featured three times on *America's Most Wanted,* was responsible for a cross-country crime spree and a major manhunt near the area earlier in the evening. He would have made good his getaway had it not been for Charles.

"What made you go after this guy, knowing he's dangerous, knowing he just shot a cop?" a reporter asked Charles, then shoved a microphone in his face.

Charles held Amanda's hand, his arm encircling Jennifer as she cuddled a sleepy-eyed Chuckie against her shoulder. "Sometimes," he said softly, "a man just has to take a stand."

Camera shutters clicked and whirred and cops congratulated him as he turned to his wife. "Didn't I tell you, honey? Isn't this a great city?"

BILL PRONZINI has published more than fifty novels, including three in collaboration with his wife, Marcia Muller, and twenty-five in his popular "Nameless Detective" series. He has received two Shamus Awards and a Lifetime Achievement Award from the Private Eye Writers of America. He has been nominated for six Edgar Awards and is the winner of France's Grand Prix de la Littérature Policière. In "Wishful Thinking," a husband and wife try to make it through the dog days of summer without killing each other.

WISHFUL THINKING

by Bill Pronzini

When I got home from work, a little after six as usual, Jerry Macklin was sitting slumped on his front porch. Head down, long arms hanging loose between his knees. Uh-oh, I thought. I put the car in the garage and walked back down the driveway and across the lawn strip onto the Macklins' property.

"Hi there, Jerry."

He looked up. "Oh, hello, Frank."

"Hot enough for you?"

"Hot," he said. "Yes, it's hot."

"Only June and already in the nineties every day. Looks like we're in for another blistering summer."

"I guess we are."

"How about coming over for a beer before supper?"

He waggled his head. He's long and loose, Jerry, with about twice as much neck as anybody else. When he shakes his big head, it's like watching a bulbous flower bob at the end of a stalk. As always these days, his expression was morose. He used to smile a lot, but not much since his accident. About a year ago he fell off a roof while on his job as a building inspector, damaged some nerves and vertebrae in his back, and was now on permanent disability.

"I killed Verna a little while ago," he said.

"Is that right?"

"She's in the kitchen. Dead on the kitchen floor."

"Uh-huh," I said.

"We had another big fight and I went and got my old service pistol out of the attic. She didn't even notice when I came back down with it, just started in ragging on me again. I shot her right after she called me a useless bum for about the thousandth time."

"Well," I said. Then I said, "A gun's a good way to do it, I guess."

"The best way," Jerry said. "All the other ways, they're too uncertain or too bloody. A pistol really is the best."

"Well, I ought to be getting on home."

"I wonder if I should call the police."

"I wouldn't do that if I were you, Jerry."

"No?"

"Wouldn't be a good idea."

"Hot day like this, maybe I—"

"Jerry!" Verna's voice, from inside the house. Loud and demanding, but with a whiny note underneath. "How many times do I have to ask you to come in here and help me with supper? The potatoes need peeling."

"Damn," Jerry said.

Sweat had begun to run on me; I mopped my face with my handkerchief. "If you feel like it," I said, "we can have that beer later on."

"Sure, okay."

"I'll be in the yard after supper. Come over anytime."

His head wobbled again, up and down this time. Then

he stood, wincing on account of his back, and shuffled into his house, and I walked back across and into mine. Mary Ellen was in the kitchen, cutting up something small and green by the sink. Cilantro, from the smell of it.

"I saw you through the window," she said. "What were you talking to Jerry about?"

"Three guesses."

"Oh, Lord. I suppose he killed Verna again."

"Yep."

"Where and how this time?"

"In the kitchen. With his service pistol."

"That man. Three times now, or is it four?"

"Four."

"Other people have nice normal neighbors. We have to have a crazy person living next door."

"Jerry's harmless, you know that. He was as normal as anybody before he fell off that roof."

"Harmless," Mary Ellen said. "Famous last words."

I went over and kissed her neck. Damp, but it still tasted pretty good. "What're you making there?"

"Ceviche."

"What's ceviche?"

"Cold fish soup. Mexican style."

"Sounds awful."

"It isn't. You've had it before."

"Did I like it?"

"You loved it."

"Sounds wonderful, then. I'm going to have a beer. You want one?"

"I don't think so." Pretty soon she said, "He really ought to see somebody."

"Who?"

"Jerry."

"See who? You mean a head doctor?"

"Yes. Before he really does do something to Verna."

"Come on, honey. Jerry can't even bring himself to

step on a bug. And Verna's enough to drive any man a little crazy. Either she's mired in one of her funks or on a rampage about something or other. And she's always telling him how worthless and lazy she thinks he is."

"She has a point," Mary Ellen said. "All he does all day is sit around drinking beer and staring at the tube."

"Well, with his back the way it is—"

"His back doesn't seem to bother him when he decides to work in his garden."

"Hey, I thought you liked Jerry."

"I do like Jerry. It's just that I can see Verna's side, the woman's side. He was no ball of fire before the accident, and he's never let her have children—"

"That's her story. He says he's sterile."

"Well, whatever. I still say she has some justification for being moody and short-tempered, especially in this heat."

"I suppose."

"Anyhow," Mary Ellen said, "her moods don't give Jerry the right to keep pretending he's killed her. And I don't care how harmless he seems to be, he could snap someday. People who have violent fantasies often do. Every day you read about something like that in the papers or see it on the TV news."

" 'Violent fantasies' is too strong a term in Jerry's case."

"What else would you call them?"

"He doesn't sit around all day thinking about killing Verna. I got that much out of him after he scared hell out of me the first time. They have a fight and he goes out on the porch and sulks and that's when he imagines her dead. And only once in a while. It's more like . . . wishful thinking."

"Even so, it's not healthy and it's potentially dangerous. I wonder if Verna knows."

"Probably not, or she'd be making his life even more

miserable. We can hear most of what she yells at him all the way over here as it is."

"Somebody ought to tell her."

"You're not thinking of doing it? You don't even like the woman." Which was true. Jerry and I were friendly enough, to the point of going fishing together a few times, but the four of us had never done couples things. Verna wasn't interested. Didn't seem to want much to do with Mary Ellen or me. Or anyone else, for that matter, except a couple of old woman friends.

"I might go over and talk to her," Mary Ellen said. "Express concern about Jerry's behavior, if nothing more."

"I think it'd be a mistake."

"Do you? Well, you're probably right."

"So you're going to do it anyway."

"Not necessarily. I'll have to think about it."

Mary Ellen went over to talk to Verna two days later. It was a Saturday and Jerry'd gone off somewhere in their car. I was on the front porch fixing a loose shutter when she left, and still there and still fixing when she came back less than ten minutes later.

"That was fast," I said.

"She didn't want to talk to me." Mary Ellen looked and sounded miffed. "She was barely even civil."

"Did you tell her about Jerry's wishful thinking?"

"No. I didn't have a chance."

"What did you say to her?"

"Hardly anything except that we were concerned about Jerry."

"We," I said. "As in me too."

"Yes, we. She shut me off right there. As much as told me to mind my own business."

"Well?" I said gently.

"Oh, all right, maybe we should. It's her life, after all. And it'll be as much her fault as Jerry's if he suddenly decides to make his wish come true."

Jerry killed Verna three more times in July. Kitchen again, their bedroom, the backyard. Tenderizing mallet, clock radio, manual strangulation—so I guess he'd decided a gun wasn't the best way after all. He seemed to grow more and more morose as the summer wore on, while Verna grew more and more sullen and contentious. The heat wave we were suffering through didn't help matters any. The temperatures were up around one hundred degrees half the days that month and everybody was bothered in one way or another.

Jerry came over one evening in early August while Mary Ellen and I were having fruit salad under the big elm in our yard. He had a six-pack under one arm and a look on his face that was half hunted, half depressed.

"Verna's on another rampage," he said. "I had to get out of there. Okay if I sit with you folks for a while?"

"Pull up a chair," I said. At least he wasn't going to tell us he'd killed her again.

Mary Ellen asked him if he'd like some fruit salad, and he said no, he guessed fruit and yogurt wouldn't mix with beer. He opened a can and drank half of it at a gulp. It wasn't his first of the day by any means.

"I don't know how much more of that woman I can take," he said.

"That bad, huh?"

"That bad. Morning, noon, and night—she never gives me a minute's peace any more."

Mary Ellen said, "Well, there's a simple solution, Jerry."

"Divorce? She won't give me one. Says she'll fight it if I file, take me for everything she can if it goes through."

"Some women hate the idea of living alone."

Jerry's head waggled on its neck-stalk. "It isn't that," he said. "Verna doesn't believe in divorce. Never has, never will. Till death do us part—that's what she believes in."

"So what're you going to do?" I asked him.

"Man, I just don't know. I'm at my wits' end." He drank the rest of his beer in broody silence. Then he unfolded, wincing, to his feet. "Think I'll go back home now. Have a look in the attic."

"The attic?"

"See if I can find my old service pistol. A gun really is the best way to do it, you know."

After he was gone Mary Ellen said, "I don't like this, Frank. He's getting crazier all the time."

"Oh, come on."

"He'll go through with it one of these days. You mark my words."

"If that's the way you feel," I said, "why don't you try talking to Verna again? Warn her."

"I would if I thought she'd listen. But I know she won't."

"What else is there to do, then?"

"You could try talking to Jerry. Try to convince him to see a doctor."

"It wouldn't do any good. He doesn't think he needs help, any more than Verna does."

"At least try. Please, Frank."

"All right, I'll try. Tomorrow night, after work."

When I came home the next sweltering evening, one of the Macklins was sitting slumped on the front porch. But it wasn't Jerry, it was Verna. Head down, hands hanging between her knees. It surprised me so much I nearly swerved the car off onto our lawn. Verna almost never sat out on their front porch, alone or otherwise. She preferred the glassed-in back porch because it was air-conditioned.

The day had been another hundred-plus scorcher, and I was tired and soggy and I wanted a shower and a beer in the worst way. But I'd promised Mary Ellen I'd talk to Jerry—and it puzzled me about Verna sitting on the porch that way. So I went straight over there from the garage.

Verna looked up when I said hello. Her round, plain face was red with prickly heat and her colorless hair hung limp and sweat-plastered to her skin. There was a funny look in her eyes and around her mouth, a look that made me feel uneasy.

"Frank," she said. "Lord, it's hot, isn't it?"

"And no relief in sight. Where's Jerry?"

"In the house."

"Busy? I'd like to talk to him."

"You can't."

"No? How come?"

"He's dead."

"What?"

"Dead," she said. "I killed him."

I wasn't hot anymore; it was as if I'd been doused with ice water. "Killed him? Jesus, Verna—"

"We had a fight and I went and got his service pistol and shot him in the back of the head while he was watching TV."

"When?" It was all I could think of to say.

"Little while ago."

"The police . . . have you called the police?"

"No."

"Then I'd better—"

The screen door popped open with a sudden creaking sound. I jerked my gaze that way, and Jerry was standing there big as life. "Hey, Frank," he said.

I gaped at him with my mouth hanging open.

"Look like you could use a cold one. You too, Verna."

Neither of us said anything.

Jerry said, "I'll get one for each of us," and the screen door banged shut.

I looked at Verna again. She was still sitting in the same posture, head down, staring at the steps with that funny look on her face.

"I know about him killing me all the time," she said. "Did you think I didn't know, didn't hear him saying it?"

There were no words in my head. I closed my mouth.

"I wanted to see how it felt to kill him the same way," Verna said. "And you know what? It felt good."

I backed down the steps, started to turn away. But I was still looking at her and I saw her head come up, I saw the odd little smile that changed the shape of her mouth.

"Good," she said, "but not good enough."

I went home. Mary Ellen was upstairs, taking a shower. When she came out I told her what had just happened.

"My God, Frank. The heat's made her as crazy as he is. They're two of a kind."

"No," I said, "they're not. They're not the same at all."

"What do you mean?"

I didn't tell her what I meant. I didn't have to, because just then in the hot, dead stillness we both heard the crack of the pistol shot from next door.

MARCIA MULLER, recipient of the Private Eye Writers of America Lifetime Achievement Award, has been called the mother of the American private eye novel. Her long-standing Sharon McCone series has won Shamus, Anthony, and American Mystery Awards, and has produced one of the best-known and most beloved characters in American fiction. In "Up at the Riverside," the author presents Sharon through the eyes of her office manager as they try to save a historic hotel from falling victim to its owners' lovers' quarrel.

UP AT THE RIVERSIDE

by Marcia Muller

Duck if you see a cop, Ted."

And so we were off on our mission: my boss, Sharon McCone; my partner, Neal Osborn; and me, Ted Smalley. She, the issuer of my orders, drove her venerable MG convertible. He sat slouched and rumpled beside her. I was perched on the backseat, if you could call it that, which you really can't because it's nothing more than a shelf for carrying one's groceries and such. And illegal for passengers, which is why I had to keep a keen eye out for the law.

I think our minor vehicular transgression made Shar feel free—far away from her everyday concerns about clients and caseloads at the investigative agency she owns. I knew our excursion was taking Neal's mind off the rising rent and declining profits of his used-book store. And even though I entertained an image of myself as a sack from Safeway, my thinning hair ruffling like the leaves of a protruding bunch of celery, I still felt like a kid cutting school. A kid who had freed himself from billing and correspondence, to say nothing of keeping five private investigators and the next-door law firm in number-two pencils and scratch pads.

Soon we were across the Golden Gate Bridge and speeding north on Highway 101. It was a summer Friday and traffic was heavy, but Shar made the MG zip from lane to lane and we outdistanced them all. Our mission was a pleasurable one: a stop along the Russian River to look at and perhaps purchase the jukebox of Neal's and my dreams, then a picnic on the beach at Jenner.

Our plans had been formulated that morning when Shar called us at the ungodly hour of six, all excited. "One of those jukeboxes you guys want is advertised in today's classified," she said. "Seeburg Trashcan, and you won't believe this: it's almost within your price range."

While I primed my brain into running order, Neal went to fetch our copy of the paper. "Phone number's in the 707 area code," he said into the downstairs extension. "Sonoma County."

"Nice up there," Shar said wistfully.

"Maybe Ted and I can take a drive on Sunday, check it out."

I issued a Neanderthal grunt of agreement. Till I have at least two cups of coffee, I'm not verbal.

"I've a feeling somebody'll snap it up before then," she said.

"Well, if you'll give Ted part of the day off, I can ask my assistant to mind the store."

"I . . . oh, hell, why don't the three of us take the whole day off? I'll pack a picnic. You know that sourdough loaf I make, with all the melted cheese and stuff?"

"Say no more."

Shar exited the freeway at River Road and we sped through vineyards toward the redwood forest. When we rolled into the town of Guerneville, its main street mirrored our holiday spirits. People roamed the sidewalks in shorts and T-shirts, many eating ice cream cones or by-the-slice pizza; a flea market in the parking lot of a supermarket was doing a brisk business; rainbow flags flapped in the breeze outside gay-owned businesses.

The town has been the hub of the resort area for generations; rustic cabins and summer homes line the riverbank and back up onto the hillsides. In the seventies it became a vacation-time mecca for gays, and the same wide-open atmosphere as in San Francisco's Castro district prevailed, but by the late eighties the AIDS epidemic, a sagging economy, and a succession of disastrous floods had taken away the magic. Now it appeared that Guerneville was bouncing back as an eclectic and bohemian community of hardy folk who are willing to yearly risk cresting floodwaters and mud slides. I, the grocery sack, smiled benevolently as we cruised along.

Outside of town the road wound high above the slow-moving river. At the hamlet of Monte Rio, we crossed the bridge and turned down a narrow lane made narrower by encroaching redwoods and vehicles pulled close to the walls of the mainly shabby houses. Neal began squinting at the numbers. "Dammit, why don't they make them bigger?" he muttered.

I refrained from reminding him that he was overdue for his annual checkup at the optometrist's.

Shar was the one who spotted the place: a large sagging three-story dirty-white clapboard structure with a parking area out front. The roof was missing a fair number of its shingles, the windows were hopelessly crusted with grime, and one column of the wide front porch leaned alarmingly. On the porch, to either side of the double front door, sat identical green wicker rockers, and in each sat a scowly looking man. Between them, extending from the door and down the steps, was a series of orange cones such as highway department crews use. A yellow plastic tape strung from cone to cone bore the words DANGER DO NOT CROSS DANGER DO NOT CROSS DANGER DO NOT CROSS . . .

In as reverent a tone as I'd ever heard him use, Neal said, "Good God, it's the old Riverside Hotel!"

While staring at it, Shar had overshot the parking area. As she drove along looking for a place to turn around she asked, "You know this place?"

"From years ago. Was built as a fancy resort in the twenties. People would come up from the city and spend their entire vacations here. Then in the seventies the original owner's family sold it to a guy named Tom Atwater, who turned it into a gay hotel. Great restaurant and bar, cottages with individual hot tubs scattered on the grounds leading down to the beach, anything-goes atmosphere."

"You stayed there?" I asked.

Neal heard the edge in my voice. He turned his head and smiled at me, laugh lines around his eyes crinkling. It amuses and flatters him that I'm jealous of his past. "I had dinner there. Twice."

Shar turned the MG in a driveway and we coasted back toward the hotel. The men were watching us. Both were probably in their mid-fifties, dressed in shorts and T-shirts, but otherwise—except for the scowls—they were total opposites. The one on our left was a scarecrow with a shock of long gray-blond hair;

the one on the right reminded me of Elmer Fudd, and
had just as bald a pate.

When we climbed out of the car—the grocery sack
needing a firm tug—Neal called, "I phoned earlier
about the jukebox."

The scarecrow jerked his thumb at Fudd and kept
scowling. Fudd arranged his face into more pleasant
lines and got up from the rocker.

"I'm Chris Fowler," he said. "You Neal and Ted?"

"I'm Neal, this is Ted, and that's Sharon."

"Come on in, I'll show you the box."

" 'Come on in, I'll show you the box,' " the scarecrow mimicked in a high nasal whine.

"Jesus!" Chris Fowler exclaimed. He led us through
his side of the double front door.

Inside was a reception area that must've been mag-
nificent before the oriental carpets faded and the
flocked wallpaper became water-stained and peeling.
In its center stood a mahogany desk backed by an old-
fashioned pigeonhole arrangement, and wide stairs on
either side led up to the second story. The yellow tape
continued from the door to the pigeonholes, neatly bi-
secting the room.

Shar stopped and stared at it, frowning. I tugged her
arm and shook my head. Sometimes the woman can be
so rude. Chris Fowler didn't notice, though, just turned
right into a dimly lighted barroom. "There's your jukebox," he said.

A thing of beauty, it was. Granted, a particular ac-
quired-taste kind of beauty: shaped like an enormous
trash can of fake blond wood, with two flaring red plastic side panels and a gaudy gilt grille studded with plastic gems. Tiny mirrored squares surrounded the grille,
and the whole thing was decked out with as much
chrome as a 1950s Cadillac. I went up to it and touched

the coin slot. Five plays for a quarter, two for a dime, one for a nickel. Those were the days.

Instantly I fell in love.

When I looked at Neal, his eyes were sparkling. "Can we play it?" he asked Chris.

"Sure." He took a nickel from his pocket and dropped it into the slot. Whirrs, clicks, and then mellow tones crooned, "Fly the ocean in a red biplane . . ."

Shar shook her head, rolled her eyes, and wandered off to inspect a pinball machine. She despairs of Neal's and my campy tendencies.

"So what d'you think?" Chris asked.

I said, "Good sound tone."

Neal said, "The price is kind of steep for us, though."

Chris said, "I'll throw in a box of extra seventy-eights."

Neal said, "I don't know. . . ."

And then Shar wandered back over. "What's with the tape?" she asked Chris. "And what's with the guy on the other side of it?"

Neal looked as if he wanted to strangle her. I stifled a moan. A model of subtlety, Shar, and right when we were trying to strike a deal.

Chris grimaced. "That's my partner of many years, Ira Sloan. We've agreed to disagree. The tape's my way of indicating my displeasure with him."

"Disagree over what?"

"This hotel. We jointly inherited it six months ago from Tom Atwater. Did either of you guys know him?"

I shook my head, but Neal nodded. He said, "I met him." Grinned at me and added, "Twice."

"Well," Chris said, "Tom was an old friend. In fact, he introduced Ira and me, nearly twenty years ago. When he left the place to us we said, 'What a great way to get out of the city, have our own business in an area that's experiencing a renaissance.' So we sold our city house, moved up here, called in the contractors, and got estimates of what it would take to go upscale and re-open. The building's run-down, but the construction's solid. All it needs outside is a new roof and paint job. The cottages were swept away in the floods, but eventually they can be rebuilt. Inside here, all it would take is redecorating, a new chimney and fireplace in the common room on the other side, and updated kitchen equipment. So then what does my partner decide to do?"

All three of us shook our heads, caught up in his breathless monologue.

"My loving partner decides we're to do nothing. Even though we've got more than enough money to fix the place up, he wants to leave it as is and live out our golden years here in Faulkneresque splendor while it falls down around us!"

Neal and I looked properly horrified, but Shar asked, "So why'd you put up the tape?" Maybe a single-minded focus is an asset in a private investigator, but it seems to me it plays hell with interpersonal relations.

Chris wanted to talk about the tape, however. "Ira and I divided the place, straight down the middle. He took the common room, utility room, and the area on the floors above it. I took the restaurant, kitchen, bar, and above. I prepare the meals and slip his under the tape on the reception desk. He washes our clothes and pushes mine over here to me. I'll tell you, it's quite a life!"

"And in the meantime, you're selling off the fixtures in your half?"

"Only the ones that won't fit the image I want to create here."

"How can you create it in half a hotel?"

"I can't, but I'm hoping Ira'll come around eventually. I wish I knew why he has this tic about keeping the place the way it is. If I did, I know I could talk him out of the notion."

Shar was looking thoughtful now. She walked around the jukebox, examining its lovely lines and gnawing at her lower lip. She peered through the glass at the turntable where the 78 of "You Belong to Me" now rested silently. She glanced through the archway at the yellow plastic tape.

"Chris," she said, "what would it be worth to you to find out what Ira's problem is?"

"A lot."

"A reduction of price on this jukebox to one my friends can afford?"

I couldn't believe it! Yes, she was offering out of the goodness of her heart, because she'd seen how badly Neal and I wanted the jukebox, and she knew the limits of our budget. But she was also doing it because she never can resist a chance to play detective.

Chris looked surprised, then grinned. "A big reduction, but I don't see how—"

She took one of her business cards from her purse and handed it to him. Said to me, "Come on, Watson. The game's afoot."

"Mr. Sloan?" Shar was standing at the tape on the porch. I was trying to hide behind her.

Ira Sloan's eyes flicked toward us, then straight ahead.

"Oh, Mr. Sloan!" Now she was waving, for heaven's sake, as if he wasn't sitting a mere five feet away!

His scowl deepened.

Shar stepped over the tape. "Mr. Sloan, d'you suppose you could give Ted and me a tour of your side of the hotel? We love old places like this, and we both think it's a shame your partner wants to spoil it."

He turned his head, looking skeptical but not as ferocious.

Shar reached back and yanked on my arm so hard that I almost tripped over the tape. "Ted's partner, Neal, is in there with Chris, talking upscale. I had to remove Ted before *they* end up with a tape down the middle of their apartment."

Ira Sloan ran his hand through his longish hair and stood up. He was very tall—at least six-four—and so skinny he seemed to have no ass at all. Had he always been so thin, or was it the result of too many cooling meals shoved across the reception desk?

He said, "The tape was *his* idea."

"So he told us."

"Thinks it's funny."

"It's not."

"I like people who appreciate old things. It'll be a pleasure to show you around."

The common room was full of big maple furniture with wide wooden arms and thick floral chintz-covered cushions, faded now. The chairs and sofas would've been fashionable in the thirties and forties, campy a few decades later. Now they just looked tired. Casement windows overlooked the lawn and the river, and on the far side of the room was a deep stone fireplace whose chimney showed chinks where the mortar had crumbled. Against the stones hung an oval stained-glass panel in muddy-looking colors. It reminded me of the stone in one of those mood rings that were popular in the seventies.

By the time we'd inspected the room, Shar and Ira Sloan were chattering up a storm. By the time we got upstairs to the guest rooms, they were old friends.

The guest rooms were furnished with waterbeds, another cultural icon of the sybaritic decade. Now their mattresses were shriveled like used condoms. The suites had Jacuzzi tubs, once brightly colored porcelain but now rust-stained and grimy, set before the windows. The balconies off the third-story rooms were narrow and cobwebby, and the fabric on their lounge chairs had been stripped away, probably by nesting birds.

Shar asked, "How long was the hotel in operation?"

"Tom closed it in eighty-three."

"Why?"

"Declining business. By then . . . well, a lot of things were over."

It made me so sad. The Riverside Hotel's brief time in the sun had been a wild, tumultuous, drug-hazed era—but also curiously innocent. A time of experimentation and newfound freedom. A time to adopt new lifestyles without fear of reprisal. But now the age of innocence was over; harsh reality had set in. Many of the men who had stayed here were dead, many others decaying like this structure.

Why would Ira Sloan *want* to keep intact this monument to the death of happiness?

Back downstairs Shar whispered to me, "Stay here. Talk with him." Then she was gone into the reception room and over the tape.

I turned, trying to think of something to say to Ira Sloan, but he'd vanished into some dark corner of the haunted place, possibly to commune with his favorite ghost. I sat down on one of the chairs amid a cloud of rising dust to see if he'd return. Against the chimney the stained-glass mood ring stone seemed to have darkened. My mood darkened with it. I wanted out of this place and into the sun.

In about ten minutes Ira Sloan still hadn't reappeared. I heard a rustling behind the reception desk. Shar—who else? She was removing a ledger from a drawer under the warning tape and spreading it open.

"Well, *that's* interesting," she muttered after a couple of minutes. "Very interesting."

A little while more and she shut the ledger and stuffed it into her tote bag. Smiled at me and said, "Let's go now. You look as though you can use some of my famous sourdough loaf and a walk by the sea."

When we were ensconced on the sand with our repast spread before us, I asked Shar, "What'd you take from the desk?"

"The guest register." She pulled it from her tote and handed it to me.

"You *stole* it?"

Her mouth twitched—a warning sign. "Borrowed it, with Chris's permission."

"Why?"

"Well, when I went back to talk with him some more, I asked how the two of them decided who got what. He said Ira insisted on his side of the hotel, and Chris was glad to divide it that way because he likes to cook."

Neal poured wine into plastic glasses and handed them around. "Bizarre arrangement, if you ask me."

Shar was cutting the sourdough loaf, in imminent danger of sawing off a finger as well. I took the knife from her and performed culinary surgery.

"Anyway," she went on, "then I asked Chris if Ira had insisted on getting anything else. He said only the guest register. But by then Chris'd gotten his back up, and he pointed out that the ledger was kept in a drawer of the desk that's bisected by the tape. So they agreed to leave it there and hold it in common. Ira wasn't happy with the arrangement."

I filled paper plates with slices of the loaf. Its delicious aroma was quickly dispelling my hotel-induced funk.

"And did the register tell you anything?" Neal asked.

"Only that somebody—I assume Ira—tore the pages out for the week of August thirteenth, 1978. Recently."

"How d'you know it was recent?"

"Fresh tears look different than old ones. The edges of these aren't browning." She flipped the book open to where the pages were missing.

"So now what?"

"I try to find out who was there and what happened that week. Maybe some well-known person who was still in the closet stayed there. Or somebody who was with a person he wasn't supposed to be."

I asked, "How're you going to find out if the pages're missing?"

She stabbed her finger at the first column on the ledger page, then at the last. "Date checked in, date checked out. Five individuals who checked in before the thirteenth checked out on the eighteenth. My job for this weekend is to try to locate and talk with them."

"Hey, Ted, come along with me!"

Shar was in the driver's seat of the agency van, parked on the floor of Pier 24½, where we have our offices. I was dragging tail down the iron stairway from the second level, intent on heading home after a perfectly outlandish Monday. I went over to the van and leaned in the open window. "What's happening?"

"With any luck, you and I are going to collect your

jukebox this evening and have it back at your place by the time Neal closes the store." Anachronism, Neal's used-book store, is open till nine on Mondays.

I jumped into the van, the day's horrors forgotten. "You find out what Ira Sloan's problem is?"

"Some of it. The rest is about to unfold."

I got my seat belt on just as she swerved into traffic on the waterfront boulevard outside the pier. Thanked God I was firmly strapped in, a grocery sack no longer.

The house was on a quiet street on the west side of Petaluma, a small city some forty minutes north of the Golden Gate. It used to be called the Egg Basket of the World, before the chicken boom went bust. From what I hear lately, it's turning into yuppie heaven.

As we got out of the van I looked up at the gray Victorian. It had a wide porch, high windows, and a fanlike pediment over the door that was painted in the colors of the rainbow. This, Shar had told me, was the home of Mark Curry, one of the men who had stayed at the Riverside during the second week of August 1978. Surprisingly, given the passage of time, she'd managed to locate three of the five who'd signed the register before the missing week, and to interview two so far.

"Ted," she said, "how long have gays been doing that rainbow thing?"

"You mean the flags and all? Funny—since 1978. The first rainbow flag was designed by a San Francisco artist, Gilbert Baker, as a sign of the gay community's solidarity. A version of it was flown in the next year's Pride Parade."

"I didn't realize it went back that far." She started up the walk, and I followed.

The man who answered the door was slender and

handsome, with a fine-boned face and a diamond stud in one nostril, and a full head of wavy gray hair that threatened to turn me green with envy. His wood-paneled parlor made me envious too: full of Chippendale furniture, with a gilt harp in the front window. Mark Curry seated us there, offered coffee, and went to fetch it.

Shar saw the way I was looking at the room. "It's not you," she said. "In a room like this that jukebox would look—"

"Like a wart on the face of an angel. But in our place—"

"It'll still look like a trash can."

Mark Curry came back with a silver coffee service, and got down to business while he poured. "After you phoned, Ms. McCone, I got in touch with Chris Fowler. He's an old friend, from the time we worked as volunteers at an AIDS hospice. He vouched for you, so I dug out my journal for 1978 and refreshed my memory about August's stay at the Riverside."

"You arrived there August eleventh?"

"Yes."

"Alone?"

"No, with my then partner, Dave Howell. He's been dead . . . do you believe nearly sixteen years now?"

"I'm sorry."

"Thanks. Sometimes it seems like yesterday."

"Were you and Mr. Howell staying in a cottage or the main building?"

"Main building, third floor, river side. Over the bar."

"D'you recall who else was there?"

"Well, the place was always full in the summertime, and a lot of the men I didn't know. And even more people came in over the weekend. There was to be a canoeing regatta on Wednesday the sixteenth, with a big barbecue on the beach that evening, and they were gearing up for it."

I said, "*Canoeing* regatta?"

Mark Curry winked at me. "A bunch of guys, stoned and silly, banging into each other and capsizing and having a great time of it."

"Sounds like fun."

Shar said, "So who *do* you remember?"

"Well, Tom Atwater, of course. His lover, Bobby Gardena, showed up on Tuesday. Bobby had a house in the city, divided his time between there and the river. Ira Sloan, one of Tom's best friends, and the guy who inherited that white elephant along with Chris. He was alone, had just broken off a relationship, and seemed pretty unhappy, but a few months later Tom introduced him to Chris, and they've been together ever since. Then there was Sandy Janssen. Darryl Williams. And of course there was . . ."

Shar dutifully noted the names, but I sensed she'd lost interest in them. No well-known figure who customarily hid in the closet, no scandalous mispairing. When Mark Curry ran out of people, she said, "Tell me about the week of the thirteenth. Did anything out of the ordinary happen?"

Mark Curry laughed. "Out of the ordinary was *de rigueur* at the Riverside."

"More out of the ordinary than usual."

Her serious—and curiously intense—tone sobered him. He stared into his coffee cup, recapturing his memories. When he spoke, his voice was subdued.

"The night of the regatta, you know? Everybody was on the beach, carrying on till all hours. A little before two, Dave and I decided we wanted to have a couple of quiet drinks alone, so we slipped away from the party. I remember walking up the slope from the beach and across the lawn to the hotel. Everything was so quiet. I suppose it was just the contrast to the commotion on the beach, but it gave me the shivers.

Dave, too. And when we went inside, it was still quiet, but . . ."

"But what, Mr. Curry?"

"There was a . . . an undercurrent. A sense of whispers and footfalls, but you couldn't really identify whose or where they were. Like something was going on, but not really. You know how that can be?"

Shar's face was thoughtful. She's had a lot of unusual experiences in her life, and I was sure she *did* know how that could be.

Mark Curry added, "Dave and I went into the bar and sat down. Nobody came. We were about to make our own drinks—you could do that, so long as you signed a chit—when Ira Sloan stepped out of the kitchen and told us the bar was closed."

"But this *was* after legal closing time."

He shook his head. "The bar at the Riverside *never* closed. It was immune to the dictates of the state lawmakers—some of whom were its frequent patrons."

"I see. Did Ira give you any explanation?"

"No. He asked if we wanted to buy a bottle, so we did, and took it up to our room and consumed it on our balcony. And all night the noisy party on the beach went on. But the quiet in the hotel was louder than any cacophony I've ever experienced."

When we got back to the van, Shar took out her phone and made a call. "Hi, Mick," she said. "Anything?"

Mick Savage, her nephew, computer specialist, and fastest skip tracer in the West.

"I see. . . . Uh-huh . . . Right . . . No evidence about a gas leak on Friday the eighteenth? . . . Yes, I thought as much. . . . No, nothing else. And thanks."

She broke the connection, stuffed the phone back

into her bag, and looked at me. Her expression was profoundly sad.

"You've got yourself a jukebox," she said.

"Before I go into this," Shar said to Chris Fowler, "there's something I ought to say."

The three of us were seated at a table in the bar at the Riverside. The dim lighting made Chris look curiously young and hopeful.

"Secrets," Shar went on, "are not necessarily harmful, so long as they remain secrets. But once you put them into words, they can't be taken back. Ever."

Chris nodded. "I understand what you're trying to tell me, but I need to know."

"All right, then. I spoke with three men who were present at the hotel on Wednesday, August sixteenth, 1978. Each gave me bits and pieces of a story, that led me to suspect what happened. A check I had run on a fourth man pretty much confirmed my suspicions.

"On August sixteenth of that year, a canoeing regatta was held at this hotel—a big yearly event. The cottages and rooms were all full, but we're only concerned with a few people: Tom Atwater and his lover, Bobby Gardena. Ira. And my witnesses: Mark Curry, Darryl Williams, and Sandy Janssen.

"All three witnesses came up here the Friday before the regatta. Ira arrived on Sunday, Bobby Gardena on Tuesday. It soon became apparent to everybody that Tom and Bobby weren't getting on. Bobby was baiting Tom. They quarreled frequently and publicly. Bobby confided to Sandy Janssen that he'd told Tom he'd quit his job and put his San Francisco house up for sale, with the intention of moving to New Orleans. Tom accused him of being involved with somebody else, and

Bobby wouldn't confirm or deny it. He taunted Tom with the possibility.

"After the regatta there was a barbecue on the beach. Everybody was there except for Tom, Bobby, and Ira. Bobby had told Darryl Williams he planned to pack and head back to the city that night. Ira was described by Mark Curry as alone and unhappy."

I heard a noise in the reception area and looked that way. A thin scarecrow's shape stood deep in shadow on the other side of the desk. Ira Sloan. I started to say something, then thought, No. Shar and Chris are discussing him. He has a right to hear, doesn't he?

"Something unusual happened that night," Shar continued. "Mark Curry noticed it when he returned to the hotel around two. Sandy Janssen described a strange atmosphere that kept him from sleeping well. Darryl Williams talked about hearing whispers in the corridors. The next morning Tom told everybody that Bobby had left early for the city, but Darryl claims he saw Bobby's car in the lot when he looked out his window around nine. An hour later it was gone. None of my three witnesses ever heard from or saw Bobby again. The skip trace I had run on him turned up nothing. The final closing on the sale of his city house was handled by Tom, who had his power of attorney."

Chris Fowler started to say something, but Shar held up her hand. "And here's the most telling point: On Thursday night, all the guests received notice that they had to vacate the premises on Friday morning, due to a potentially dangerous gas leak that needed to be worked on. A leak that PG and E has no record of. The only men who remained behind were Tom and Ira."

Chris sat very still, breathing shallowly. I looked at the reception area. The scarecrow figure in the shadows hadn't moved.

"I think you can draw your own conclusions," Shar added. She spoke gently and sadly—not the usual trumpeting and crowing that I hear from her when she solves a case.

Slowly Chris said, "God, I can't believe Tom killed Bobby! He was a gentle man. I never saw him raise his hand to anybody."

"It may have been self-defense," Shar said. "Darryl Williams told me one of his friends had an earlier relationship with Bobby, an abusive one. Bobby always threw the first punches."

"So an argument, a moment of violence . . ."

"Is all it takes."

"Naturally he would've turned to Ira to help him cover up. They were best friends, had been since grade school. But that doesn't make Ira a murderer."

"No, it doesn't."

"Anyway, you can't prove it."

"Not without Bobby's remains—which are probably somewhere in this hotel."

Chris glanced around, shivering slightly. "And as long as they're here, Ira and I will be at a stalemate, estranged for the rest of our lives. That's how long he'll guard them."

I was still staring at Ira Sloan's dark figure, but now I looked beyond it, into the common room. The stained-glass oval hanging on the fireplace chimney, that I'd fancifully thought of as the stone in a mood ring, gleamed in the rays from a nearby floor lamp: pink, red, orange, yellow, green, blue, indigo. The seven colors of the rainbow.

I said, "I know where Bobby's buried."

"When I saw this stained glass yesterday," I said, "I couldn't tell the colors, on account of it being hung where no light could pass through. A strange place, and that should've told Shar or me something right then. Tonight, with the lamp on, I see that it's actually the seven colors of the rainbow."

We—Shar, Chris, and I—were standing in front of the fireplace. I could feel Ira Sloan's presence in the shadows behind us.

"It's the only rainbow symbol in the hotel," I went on, "and it was probably commissioned by Tom Atwater sometime in 1978."

"Why then?" Shar asked.

"Remember I told you that the first rainbow flag was designed in seventy-eight? And that a version of it was flown in the seventy-nine Pride Parade?"

She nodded.

"The seventy-eight flag was seven colors, like this panel. Respectively, they symbolized sexuality, life, healing, sun, nature, art, harmony, and spirit. But the flag that was flown at the parade only had six colors. They dropped indigo so there would be exactly three stripes on either side of the street. That's the one that's become popular and is recognized by the International Congress of Flag Makers."

Chris said, "So Tom and Ira put Bobby's body someplace temporary the night of the murder—maybe the walk-in freezer—and after Tom closed the hotel, they walled him in behind the fireplace. But Tom was a sentimental guy, and he loved Bobby. He'd've wanted some monument."

Behind us there was a whisper of noise, such as I imagined had filled this hotel the night of August 16, 1978. Shar heard it—I could tell from the way she cocked her head—but Chris didn't.

Bitterly he said, "It couldn't've been self-defense. If

it was, Tom or Ira would've called the county sheriff."

"It wasn't self-defense," Ira's voice said. "It was an accident. I was there. I saw it."

Slowly we turned toward the reception area. Ira Sloan had come out of the shadows and was backed up against the warning tape, his face twisted with the despair of one who expects not to be believed.

"Bobby was leaving to go back to the city," he added. "He was taunting Tom about how he'd be seeing his new lover. They were at the top of the stairs. Tom called Bobby an ugly name, and Bobby went to hit him. Tom ducked, Bobby lost his balance. He fell, rolled over and over, and hit his head on the base of the reception desk." He motioned at the sharp corner near the stairway on his side of the hotel.

Shar asked, "Why didn't you call the sheriff?"

"Tom had been outspoken about gay rights. Outspoken and abrasive. He had enemies on the county board of supervisors and in the sheriff's department. They'd have seen to it that he was charged with murder. Tom was afraid, so I did what any friend would do."

Chris said, "For God's sake, Ira, why didn't you tell me this when we inherited the hotel?"

"I wanted to preserve Tom's memory. And I was afraid what you might think of me. What you might do about it."

His partner was silent for a moment. Then he said, "I should've let you keep your secret."

"Maybe not," Shar told him. "Secrets that tear two people apart are destructive and potentially dangerous."

"But—"

"The fact is, Chris, that secrets come in all varieties. What you do about them, too. You can expose them, and then everybody gets hurt. You can make a tacit agreement to keep them, and by the time they come out, nobody cares, but keeping them's still exacted its toll on you. Or you can share them with a select group of trusted people and agree to do something about them."

"What're you trying to tell me?"

"The group of people in this room is a small and closemouthed one. We all know Ira can keep his own counsel. Bobby Gardena's been in his tomb a long time, but I doubt he's rested easily. Perhaps it would release him if you moved his remains to a more suitable place on the property and created a better monument to him."

Chris nodded.

I said, "A better monument, like a garden in the colors of the rainbow."

Chris nodded. A faint ray of hope touched Ira's tortured features.

I added, "Of course, a fitting monument to both Bobby and Tom would be if you renovated this hotel like you planned and reopened it to the living."

Chris nodded again. Then he went to Ira, grasped the warning tape, and tore it free from where it was anchored to the pigeonholes.

I rode in the back of the van on our way home to the city, making sure the Seeburg Trashcan didn't slip its moorings. Both Shar and I were quiet as we maneuvered it up my building's elevator and into the apartment.

Later, after Neal promised to become the fifth party to a closely held secret, I told him the story of August 16, 1978. He was quiet, too.

But still later, when we'd jockeyed the Trashcan into position in our living room and plugged it in, the nostalgic tunes of happier times played long into the night, heralding happy times to come.

Laurie R. King is the author of an Edgar Award–winning series featuring San Francisco homicide detective Kate Martinelli. She is also the creator of the critically acclaimed, bestselling Mary Russell series featuring the brilliant young wife of Sherlock Holmes. In "Paleta Man," an ice cream vendor's tragic past makes him more than merely empathetic toward an abused young wife.

PALETA MAN

by Laurie R. King

*E*llos me llaman «*paleta* man».

They call me "*paleta* man," and I must remember now to use the English language of this country.

Paleta is ice cream, so I suppose in English you would call me the ice cream man. But in the town where I now live, the ice cream man drives an old white truck whose sides are covered with pictures of his products and signs saying WATCH FOR CHILDREN, and he plays a song on the scratchy loudspeaker of his truck, the same notes playing over and over so loud they can be heard for a mile, a noise that drives all the adults crazy until they come out of their houses and shake their fists and throw rocks and beer cans at his truck.

I do not drive a white truck with loud music. Trucks cost much money, even the old ones, and I am a poor man.

Pero yo soy contento; I am content being a *paleta*

man. I own a small cart with three wheels and a handle to push it by, with thick insulated sides and a pair of harmonious bells that hang from the crossbar of the handle. The children listen for me, and when I turn the corner of their street and play my pair of bells, they run out with their coins in their hands to stand looking at the front of my cart where I have a line of pictures that show what the cart contains. The children make their decisions, and then they point or they tell me what they want and I reach in to pull out their *paletas* and close the top quickly to keep the cold in, and I take their money, give them their change if they have any coming, and I wish them a good day. They are polite children, most of them, as the children of poor people tend to be, and they thank me and they take the wrappers from their *paletas*, and I walk on, leaving them to their young pleasures of sweet ice. Here, now, I am a *paleta* man. I sell small measures of happiness in a way that allows me to be out in the open air, and gives me gentle exercise, and keeps me in contact with friendly children. Why would I not be content?

True, it is not much of a job for a man. Certainly it is a job beneath a man who has been to university, who was the headmaster of a village school, in the peaceful days before the soldiers came.

In a better time, another age, I would still be living in that village, writing mathematical problems on the chalkboard and telling the children about history and government and the rules of grammar. I would still have a wife and two sons to greet me when I came home in the afternoon and to sit around the table in the dinner hour and around the fire in the evenings, the boys and their father doing homework while the mother bends over her embroidery and mending. But the war began, and our village was very near to where the revolt first boiled up out of discontent and hunger and

envy and the two ways of life that can never be reconciled, and before we thought to worry, there were
rebels in the village, and then soldiers, and between the
rope sandals of the one and the leather boots of the
other, my quiet village was trampled to death.

I was away when the village died, off on a training
course for my school, when suddenly the room I was
sitting in began to buzz with rumor, and I left the semi-
nar and hitchhiked in trucks and on motor scooters and
ran in my city shoes until I reached my village to find
smoke and uniformed men and people with television
cameras and the tents of the Red Cross, filled with my
groaning friends and neighbors.

My younger son looked like he was sleeping, lying
peacefully against the big tree in our front garden
while men armed with guns and cameras trotted past
in the road outside the hedges and somewhere nearby
a woman shrieked and shrieked. Lying sleeping
against the tree where some soldier had caught him up
and thrown him, breaking his head against the hard
trunk.

My older son looked like he was dead. A bayonet or
a machete had entered him four or five times, but he
was still alive when I found him in the Red Cross tent.
He had been found in the door of my schoolroom, and
taken to the doctors, but he never woke, never heard my
voice again before he died. It still comes to me, all
these years later, how very strange it was, that one boy
with such terrible wounds could live longer than another boy whose head showed so little damage.

My wife died too. I will say no more about her
death, because when I do she haunts my dreams, and I
am ready to forget. I cannot forget, of course, any more
than my schoolteacher's hands can forget the feeling of
killing two of the men responsible for the death of my
village, once I had caught up with them. Blood is so

very hot; it shocks the skin when it spills, and the hands never forget the sensation.

But now I am no longer a schoolmaster, no longer a father taking his revenge. I am a *paleta* man, content to walk up and down the streets of my route in the footsteps of all the men who once would have gone here, the milkmen and delivery boys, the knife sharpeners and brush sellers and itinerant window washers. Now there is only me and the boy who delivers the paper from his bicycle in the afternoons, and the postman, who is friendly but who wears an official uniform and has no time to listen to problems or to help. Everyone else drives here in a car or a truck, and is kept alone by the metal skin of his vehicle.

Except for me. For perhaps ten months of the year I am here nearly every day, up and down my route, through the neighborhood that lies between the busy shops of the main street and the open fields and big concrete buildings where the town's deliveries arrive and are shipped away, the buildings where men come to buy pipe and gravel and women in polished cars drive to the wholesale bakery and take away to their large homes many strange and delightful foods like fresh tortillas and spicy empanadas and brightly colored Mexican pastries.

I call it my neighborhood, my *barrio,* because I work there, but I do not actually live there. I live a few miles away in a small rusty trailer grown over by a single, enormous rosebush with flowers of palest yellow, very like the rosebush my young wife planted at our front door in my village in the hills. Near the trailer I have built an arbor to hold the vines of melon and grape and chayote squash, which makes a cool shady area I can enjoy on the rare hot days I do not go to town. The trailer and arbor are surrounded by my garden of nopal cactus and tomatillo plants and marigolds, of chiles and summer squashes and other vegetables, all of it set in a square of ground fenced off from a big field that is planted with strawberries or lettuce or cabbages in different years. It is a long, dusty walk along the busy highway pushing my *paleta* cart, but it is my home, and although I have no family and few friends come to visit me, I enjoy my garden and my chickens. In the winter, when people do not buy as much ice cream, I dig in the garden and repair the arbor and read the books that I borrow from the library, and in the summer evenings when I have finished selling *paletas* I sit under the arbor or in the doorway of my trailer surrounded by the smell of roses and watch the cars fly past.

Most of the people who live in the neighborhood where I work would not stay there if they had another choice. Trains rumble too close to the houses, the big delivery trucks sit for hours with their engines running and make the air smell, and wandering dogs are hit and killed by speeding teenagers in their crazy bright cars. Or they are hit and not killed, and that is worse.

It was just such a thing that got me started on the other side of my work as a *paleta* man, a dog that was struck and half crushed and lay in the street, suffering loudly but refusing to die.

I was two streets away when I heard the shriek of the tires and the loud gulping howl of the dog, and I knew at once what it was. The noise did not stop. All the time I walked with my cart down one street and up the next, ringing my bells loudly, the dog continued to howl. When I finally turned the corner past the sweet-smelling *panaderia* and I saw the faces of the mothers and the children where they stood in a knot around the crushed dog, I knew that it would be up to me to stop the noise that had twenty small children clutching their ears, tears pouring down their twisted faces into their mouths.

I knew the dog, of course. Any man who walks the streets must know which dogs have to be watched and which are trustworthy, and this old bitch was a sweet-tempered, toothless old animal with dry yellow fur. Her boy loved her, and sometimes bought an extra ice cream just for her.

She was lying where the speeding car had tumbled her, and I knew she was howling from terror, not from pain—that spinal cord could no longer be carrying any messages from any part of her behind the shoulders. But she could not get to her feet to run away, and her nose must have told her of her injuries even if her other senses did not.

When a living body is violated and the skin breached, what spills out is too real for the eyes to accept it. Blood is too red, the organs too alive; the mind turns away. However, when a person has done as many things in a long life as I have, the eye is given distance. My eyes saw mostly the horror of the children, whose mothers should have hurried them indoors and turned up the televisions in their houses loud enough to dominate all other sounds.

I opened the top of my *paleta* cart and took out two ice cream bars, and I went over to the dog. I squatted down in front of her, where she could see me, and put out my hand—carefully, because a mortally wounded animal is an unpredictable thing.

She knew me, her eyes told me that, and though she kept howling mightily, she watched me, too. I held up one of the ice creams and began to unwrap it, and when it was free of its paper I took it by its stick and laid it along her rigid, howling tongue. It took a minute for the sensation to travel to her brain, but then the terrible noise faltered, and went by fits and starts, until finally she gave a last yip and her mouth closed greedily on the cold, creamy bar.

She slobbered and chewed and gummed the stick dry, and when she remembered and began to yip again I unwrapped the other one and placed it in her mouth with my right hand while I stroked her head with my left, talking to her in a quiet voice. I let her finish the ice cream bar, and then I bent over her so the children would not see what I was doing and I gently put both hands on her neck and with a clean jerk I put her beyond the reach of her misery.

One of the mothers brought an ancient rag of a curtain, which we draped across the old dog's back end, leaving only her peaceful, ugly face with the ice cream still on the muzzle. I encouraged the children to pat the face of their peaceful old friend, and sold them some ice creams, and we all went back to our work. Eventually the city came and removed the dog's body, and that was the end of it.

But it was also the beginning.

The incident with the dog occurred when I had only been in the town for three years, and it was my second season behind the *paleta* cart, but after that day I was everyone's *tío,* their helpful uncle. The women refused to let their children buy from the noisy truck when it ventured into my territory, just drove him off with their stares and their closed purses. They found small jobs, and paid me for them when they could, and when I would permit it. I carried groceries back from the market on top of my sturdy little cart, with pregnant women leading small children by my side; with my cart too I transported chairs, mattresses, and baby beds from one house to another in the neighborhood. I even did those small jobs in a house that women have never been taught and landlords put off—repairing a spitting light switch, putting a strong new lock on a door after an angry boyfriend has broken down the old one, opening a window sealed shut by the paint of years.

Then there were the tasks for which I would not take money, the wandering children, the small boy who had locked himself inside a bathroom, the old woman nobody had seen all day, lying in her bed in sheets wet with urine, taken away in an ambulance and placed in a home that people mentioned in lowered voices. For these tasks I could not, as a man, accept payment. I asked only that they bought my *paletas*, even if they were sometimes a little soft and the selection was limited, and turn their backs on the man in the white truck.

I see that I have gone on and on with my story, and yet only now is the story of Señora Robinson beginning. But I do not apologize, because without knowing about the cart and the crushed dog and the little jobs old Tío Jaime the *paleta* man was sometimes called on to perform, my involvement in one woman's problems would surely seem insane, ungodly as well as illegal, and even the stuff of an old man's imagination.

But now you know that I am Tío, the *paleta* man, and I am a friend to the neighborhood.

Because I walk through my *barrio* and do not steer a noisy truck down its streets, I get to know the people very well, even those who do not have children. I know when the husband of one house has a job, because his children buy real ice creams instead of the cheap frozen water pops. I hear when the teenage son of one family gets arrested, and when a girl gets in trouble, and which of the children leave school to go to work in the shops and fields and which families will struggle to give their sons and daughters the full four years of high school they will need to get a real job and move beyond the neighborhood. These things and more I know, because I have eyes and I have ears and I am on the streets for people to talk to.

So I knew that the husband of Señora Robinson beat her up regularly, on the first and third Fridays of every month. He would receive his pay, he would cash it at the cashing service next door to the bar on Main Street, he would go into the bar, and some hours later he would go home drunk and hit her. The next day she would not come out of her house. Two or three days later, she would emerge to buy from me one of the ice cream cups I sell to be eaten with a small flat wooden spoon, as a little reward, I think, for surviving another round with her husband's fists, and as a tiny gesture of revenge, that his money should be spent on her luxury.

On those days I did not want to accept her money. I did, because I thought that if I refused to take it, she would not come out to buy this taste of sweetness for herself. I also decided that in this matter, this woman's small pride might be more important than my own.

She was a nice woman, was Señora Robinson, pretty in that pale way some Anglos have when their hair is too dark to be called blond and too light to be brown. She was a tiny woman, smaller even than my wife, whose head used to rest beneath my chin when I wrapped my arms around her and held her close. Señora Robinson's house was the cleanest place in a neighborhood of clean houses—which could not have been easy, since it stood at the end of the busy road with its back on a field, from both of which the dust rose in clouds at every wind. She had a nice garden, too, vegetables and flowers, and when she bought her little cup of chocolate ice cream and peeled off the top to eat it slowly, sometimes we would stand and pass a few words about her garden. Two or three times I brought her cuttings or seeds from my own garden, so that next to her front door there grew a small rose of palest yellow. I looked at it every time I went past her gate, greeting it as a friend.

Señora Robinson had no real neighbors. On one side of her house lay the yards of a plumbing supply business, on the other rose up the high, blank wall of a warehouse. Across the street was a printer's, and behind her back fence stretched the fields. It was a busy place during the day, but everything shut down in the evenings, so that after dusk the street was deserted, and people rarely went there. She had no neighbors, although everyone in the neighborhood knew who she was, and if there was no true feeling for her, there was some sympathy.

One day, three days after the first Friday in the month of May, I sold her a cup of chocolate ice cream. She had trouble holding the flat wooden spoon because one of her fingers was in a splint. I said nothing and went about my business, but a short time later I stood with my elbow on the fence of another woman who lived not far from the Robinson house, making conversation.

Señora Lopez was a retired cannery worker whose children had grown and whose fingers itched for grandchildren to care for. She had spent most of her life organizing people, from her husband to the union, and I knew well that nothing would give her greater pleasure than organizing Señora Robinson. I leaned against the fence watching three children revel in the sugary pleasures of their *paletas*.

"Do you know Señora Robinson?" I asked her. "In the house near the plumbing supply?"

"Sure. She's very stuck-up."

Actually, what she said was that Señora Robinson acted like she had a stick up a part of her body. I said, "It's not the stick up there that troubles her, it's the fist she gets in her face."

"She's not the only one in this neighborhood," said Señora Lopez. She sounded as if she was throwing the problem away, but in truth I knew that she was one of those that women in trouble turned to, and she could be as fierce as a tiger in how she helped them. We often act in ways that conceal our true feelings, especially when those feelings are strong.

"That is true," I said, trying to sound like I was apologizing for all the wrongdoing by all the men who ever lived. "But she is also very young, little more than a child, and without friends and family. It is too bad she cannot find some way of reaching out for friendship. Maybe she could take a cooking class down at the adult school, if her husband would let her. She was asking me the other day about how to make *chiles rellenos*. What do I know? Ah well, I must be going. My ice creams will melt in this sun."

As I left, I let my eyes rest on the row of young, healthy chile plants she had along the side of her house. *Chiles rellenos,* indeed.

That is how Señora Robinson made friends in her neighborhood, and how she learned that Tío the *paleta* man was a helpful sort of fellow, and finally how there were services in the community to help women like her, and things you could divorce a man for that didn't involve calling the police. Señora Lopez told me one day that Señora Robinson had asked her what was meant by "irreconcilable differences." Señora Lopez had to explain the phrase to me as well, but when I understood it, I agreed that it was good that in this country a divorce could be had for such a simple reason.

Over the next few weeks I thought she was going to make it. It seemed to me as if the yellow rose nodded at me in approval when one third Friday of the month went past and on the Saturday morning she was at work in her garden. Señora Lopez brought other women to see the small, pale Anglo woman. The smell of chiles and cumin sometimes overcame the dust smell of the plumbing supply yard next door, and Señora Robinson began to blossom like a neglected plant given water and sun. I told myself what a clever fellow I was, to set such a thing in motion. Why, why do we never learn?

In truth, though, it should have ended happily. In my village it might have, because the women were strong and in and out of each other's lives all the time, and had brothers and uncles to help them. In this country it is not always that way. It is especially not that way for the poor.

Perhaps if I had not interfered, if I had not arranged for Señora Lopez to take Señora Robinson under her wing, then nothing worse would have happened other than Señora Robinson's black eyes and careful walk. I did mean well, but I saw only one week later that I was wrong, and I saw where it would end.

The following Wednesday Señor Robinson lost his job, and that evening his wife came very near to losing her life. If one of Señora Lopez's friends had not been bringing a paper bag full of tomatillos to Señora Robinson, and heard what was happening inside the house, and run to call the police, the husband might have murdered her. Instead, he was jailed for two days until Señora Robinson came home from the hospital with plaster on her arm, and when she would not press charges, he moved back home.

Two months later it happened again.

Six weeks after that, again.

I was no longer content in that neighborhood. The inability of the police to stop a man from beating his wife to death preyed on my mind and gave me nightmares when I saw my own wife's end come on her. A thick layer of invisible smoke seemed to lie over the whole area, and the *paleta* cart became heavier and heavier to push toward it as the cool mornings of autumn came along.

Señora Lopez did not give up. She checked on her Anglo friend every day. She brought her food, took her to visit other women, made her get involved in some committee that was working to force the city to install stop signs and traffic bumps. She took her to the doctor to have the plaster removed from her arm, and to the clinic to have the stitches taken out, and to the emergency room to have her ribs x-rayed, and all the while she talked to Señora Robinson about her options. She could divorce him, she could get a job, she could hide in the women's shelter, she could get something called a restraining order. Señora Robinson listened to all the advice, and nodded, and did nothing. She stopped coming out of her house to buy a cup of ice cream from me, her house stopped smelling like cumin, and when I caught glimpses of her, she seemed to me even smaller, stooped over and thin as a broomstick.

When Señora Lopez explained to me about the restraining order, I only looked at her. Señor Robinson was a very big man. Until losing his job for showing up at work drunk, he had made his living moving heavy objects from trucks to warehouses and back again, and his shoulders were massive. I could not imagine a piece of paper restraining those shoulders. Señora Lopez saw the doubt in my eyes and shrugged. He did not want his wife to leave him; no one in the neighborhood wanted her to stay. The differences in the two points of view were as far apart as those of the government and the rebels in my village. And as likely to lead to bloodshed.

That shrug of Señora Lopez's stayed with me all that day and into the night. I sat long in the doorway of my trailer, the last roses drooping off the vine above my head, and I looked off into the soft darkness, and heard the cars and trucks go by. If a woman wants to kill herself, the shrug said, what can we do?

I did not think that Señora Robinson wished to kill herself. I thought that she was trying to become so small that her husband would not see her, to make herself so without presence as a person that she would be invisible to his eyes. In that way, she would be safe. A restraining order, her spine said to me, would only make him more angry. A flight to a shelter, her bent head whispered, would only rouse his possessive fury.

I thought she was right. That night beneath the dying roses, I decided that she was right to be afraid, that the police were helpless to do anything permanent and the court system of Señora Lopez would be unable to move fast enough to stand in Señor Robinson's way. It was, in truth, a task for a single man.

I could not do it without her permission, though. I decided that the next day, if I saw her, I would ask Señora Robinson if she wished to be free of her husband. I would consider it my service to the peace of the neighborhood.

I dreamed of my wife that night, standing with both our sons in the door of our small house in the village. She said nothing, but I thought she was pleased with me. In my dream, the rose around the door was in full bloom. It smelled like my wife's hair when we lay in each other's arms.

I had made my decision, to perform this service to the neighborhood, and for pretty, childlike Señora Robinson, and for the shades of my family. I did not have a lot of time, though, because soon the rains would begin and a *paleta* man sells nothing in the rain.

During my hours of walking the route and ringing my two harmonious bells, I thought carefully about how I would do this thing. I did not wish to spend the rest of my days in prison, nor did I wish to have Señora Robinson accused. The man had to disappear.

In a hardware store I bought a strong pulley, a package of sturdy rope, and a metal object in the shape of an *S* to hold the pulley. Rough burlap sacks are almost unknown in this country, but I found some strong cotton sacks used to make sandbags when the river floods, and took those.

Everything else I already had: rubber gloves I used when mixing chemicals to spray in the garden, a box of heavy garbage bags I found by the side of the road one year, a shovel, and of course my knife.

In the sunny mornings I dug along the back fence of the property and planted cuttings of the pale yellow rose. Late in the evenings I removed the roses and dug the holes deeper, filled the cotton bags with the soil, and then put them back into the hole before planting the roses again. One wet day I constructed a tripod to hold the pulley. And I waited.

I very nearly waited too long. A day or two later, the sun came back out, the children were again interested in cold treats, and the *paleta* man loaded his cart with ice creams on sticks and frozen juice bars and a few cups with chocolate ice cream that you eat with flat wooden spoons.

Señora Robinson had been taken to the hospital again. This time she would be in for days, even a week. Her husband had been arrested, and was out on bail.

I stood looking at the child who told me this news, my mind whirling, until the gentle touch of a hand on mine brought me back to the street.

"Are you okay, Tío?"

"Yes of course, Tomás. Oh—I'm sorry. Here is your juice bar. No, I was only wondering if I remembered to turn off the heat under my coffeepot. I think I did. How is your mama? Good, good. And what do you want today, Esmerelda?"

I am an old man on the outside, but still there are times when the young heart beats as strongly within me as ever it did, when the blood rises up in disgust or rage or sometimes even lust. It leaves me shaken and empty when it passes, feeling as old as I look, but this time I would not allow it to pass until I had used it. I would hold it close and nurture it, and I would be a young man again, for a time.

The sun went behind clouds in the afternoon, and by dinnertime a light rain was falling, which was good. I left my *paleta* cart hidden behind one of those large metal refuse bins they call Dumpsters, and I walked home in the dark by a back way, where people would only see a man in a dark raincoat, not the *paleta* man without his cart.

In my trailer, I turned on lights, cooked a dinner and forced myself to eat it, cleaned up and watched the television, and turned off the lights at ten o'clock, only a little earlier than the houses nearby were used to seeing. I then changed into my oldest clothes, put my knife and my rubber gloves in my pockets, resumed my cold, wet raincoat, and walked back to town.

I had thought I would try to kill Señora Robinson's husband in the bathtub, to make cleaning up easier, but I changed my mind when I saw how the rain was coming down ever harder. There would be no reason to dirty his wife's house with my boots and his blood.

I knocked on his door at a quarter after eleven. I had to pound, over the sound of the rain and to wake him from his drunkenness in front of the television. He came to the door, blinking and holding on to the jamb, and I had to tell him twice how sorry I was that I drove into the side of his truck.

He roared when he understood me, roared like a bear and shoved me aside so that I nearly fell. I followed him down the steps, and then I stepped off the pathway and stood in the middle of the patch of lawn, waiting for him. He finished looking for the damage on his precious truck and staggered back toward me, soaked and furious, shouting and waving his fists.

There had been no one to hear when this man hit his

wife and made her cry out; the thing that protected him before would be his undoing now. I waited until he was standing in front of me, preparing to do to my face what he did to his wife's, and then I drew my knife from my pocket and I killed him.

The two soldiers I hunted down all those years ago had taught me much about killing. After the first, I learned that it is mostly when the knife comes out that blood is shed, and especially when it is removed before death. Señora Robinson's husband was dead before he fell to the lawn. I left the knife where it was while I turned off the house lights, closed the front door, and went to fetch my *paleta* cart from behind the Dumpster.

The cart is not large, and I am no longer a strong man, so I knew that I would have to transport him in two pieces. It was not pleasant, but that is what I did, placing his remains in the rain-slick garbage bags and running the garden hose for a long time in the place where I had worked. It took the entire package of bags, most of the night, and more energy than I thought I possessed, but I got all of him to my home before dawn. I left him in my garden shed along with the clothes I had worn, then scrubbed myself in all the hot water the trailer's small tank held, and finally fell into bed.

The next day the rain was less, but no one would expect the *paleta* man to be out. That too was a good thing, because the young strength of disgust and rage had left me by then, and I felt old and weak and more than a little sickened by what I had done. I lay in bed all that day. When darkness fell I rose and forced myself to eat, and then I set up my tripod and pulley, carefully took up the roses I had planted in the holes along the back fence and dug down into the soil beneath. The heavy sandbags filled with soil came up easily with the help of the tripod and pulley, and the first hole was quickly emptied. And filled again. Then the second one, with Señor Robinson's upper half.

They were both very deep holes. I dug them along the back fence line because I did not care to have the grapes and the melon vines that I eat from sinking their roots into that man, and to put him closer to the trailer would have given me bad dreams of his torso clawing its way across the ground to my steps. The back fence was much better.

The next day was clear and warm. I pulled a sheet of plastic from the pile of prunings I had been keeping dry, and I burned them, along with a few pieces of trash from the garden shed like soiled rubber gloves and some old clothing.

Then the *paleta* man loaded up his cart and went back to his neighborhood, to sell his *paletas* to the children who lived there.

All of that happened nearly two years ago. The police questioned many people about the strange disappearance of an unpopular man, but they made no arrests; after all, Señora Robinson was in the hospital when her husband went away. And who did she know who might have done away with her husband so efficiently? Her only friend was Señora Lopez, and troublemaker though that woman might be, the thought of Señora Lopez as part of a murder plot was impossible. No, Señora Robinson had no one who might have removed her husband for her; the man must have been involved in some bad affair, crossed some dangerous man while drunk. It was a mystery.

The other day I had two visitors, who drove into my yard about half an hour before sunset, when the shadows stretched long and the summer heat was beginning to cool from the air.

Señora Lopez had never said anything to me about the strange disappearance of Señora Robinson's husband. She did not say anything the other evening, either, when she and Señora Robinson, who was in truth a handsome woman, stood in my dusty yard admiring the garden. Señora Lopez studied the heavy leaves of the grapes on the arbor, the heavily loaded tomato and pepper bushes, and the great jungle the yellow rose has become over the front of the trailer.

The two ladies had spent the day making tamales, which is a dish a cook embarks on when she wants to share her kitchen with the world. They brought me a large plateful. I thanked them both, and we talked for a few minutes. They politely refused my offer of a cold drink, and then they left.

Just a friendly visit.

But before she got into her car, Señora Lopez looked long and hard at the glory of my back fence, where half a dozen cuttings now cover a hundred feet. She looked at it, and she looked at me, and she had a very small smile on her face as she drove away.

The pale yellow roses are, in truth, very beautiful.

Y soy contento.

And I am content.

SARAH LOVETT *is the author of three complex, bestselling psychological thrillers drawing on her experiences as a researcher at the New Mexico State Penitentiary. She has also written twenty-five nonfiction travel and science books, and has been a theater director and playwright. In "Buried Treasure," a late-night visitor helps a recent widow through the lingering perils of a bad marriage and a brutal murder.*

BURIED TREASURE

by Sarah Lovett

Dr. Magic was one of the ugliest men Candy Tosh had ever seen. He filled her doorstep like a toad, bloated, warty, bug-eyed. She liked him immediately.

"I'm here to talk about your husband's death," he said.

"Murder," she said, opening wide the door to the tract house.

"Murder," he agreed, reaching toward the lapel of his gray jacket. "I drove out from Los Angeles. I'm a psychiatrist. Sometimes I moonlight for the FBI." His hand—now clutching credentials—reminded Candy of a yellow kitchen glove, inflated. Cortisone, she thought. She'd worked as a receptionist in an oncologist's office for two years. She imagined she might end up with a career in a hospice someday.

"I believe you." She turned, inviting him to follow her inside. "Coffee's on. I take mine black."

"Same for me, then." Dr. Magic settled slowly. He was a man who explored a space by first examining its outer boundaries, in this case pitifully flimsy living room walls sprayed with some synthetic finish that resembled gray bread dough. Two pictures broke up the cheap monotony: one paint-by-numbers of a Joshua tree and one photograph of Candy Tosh and her eight-year-old mentally retarded son, Leon. They were both smiling like Cheshire cats.

"Harry didn't take that picture." Candy was referring to her husband, now deceased, blown to smithereens by a very competent pipe bomb.

"Who did?"

"My sister. You work late," Candy said, offering a mug of steaming coffee. She glanced at a clock on a small table, and the room was suddenly filled with a loud, ominous ticking. Selective awareness. Ten-forty-eight.

"I do. I'm a night owl. Hope I'm not keeping anybody up?"

Candy raised her coffee mug like the Liberty torch, her other arm extended in *ta-da* pose. "Nobody here but us No-Doz chickens." She took a sip of coffee, made a sad face, then shrugged. "Leon's staying with friends down the block. Poor baby. Until things die down . . ."

With that, both Candy and Dr. Magic peered out the prefab living room window as if Leon might appear on the dying patch of lawn outside at any minute. Leon failed to appear, but the full moon illuminated the asphalt cul de sac, the strand of ticky-tacky houses clustered like a pendant, the bald landscape beyond where stakes and drooping plastic tape delineated future cul de sacs, future pendants made of plywood, stucco, and asphalt.

Villas de Las Playas. Beach Village. At the temporary boundary between LA's suburban badlands and the Mojave Desert. Where there was no beach and no village. Just arid sprawl.

Watching that, Dr. Magic felt two things: a sharp sick pain in his gut and an urgency that Candy and Leon escape their grim fate. He sat, cueing her to take a seat, any seat, so they could get down to business.

"Detectives came by earlier," Candy said. "They didn't mention you."

"They probably didn't know about me." Dr. Magic's mouth flattened into a straight line. His pupils were dark hard beads. "Death in a circumstance like your husband's involves multiple law enforcement agencies—"

"And they don't talk to each other, I know." Candy sighed. "I just want to know when Leon and I can leave. Before he died, Harry cleaned out the bank accounts, pawned our wedding rings, even raided the cookie jar—but how could he do that *after* he died?" Her voice broke, she coughed, her face crumpled, then brightened. "So I wish you were the sweepstakes guy or the life insurance guy instead of a . . ."

"Psychiatrist?"

"Right." Something in his voice had tapped her solar plexus. She assessed him again, with great care, and raw instinct made her muscles contract. Her question was hesitant: "So . . . why are you here?"

"To tell you who killed your husband."

"I know who killed my husband. Harry Tosh. He murdered himself." It was a minor outburst—although major for Candy—and Dr. Magic, who wanted to hear bitterness, waited hopefully for her to continue. She didn't. For a while, the clock's heartbeat filled the silence.

Then he said, "One of my hobbies is profiling."

She nodded, understanding. "You study crimes and figure out who did it."

"Not quite. But I look at methods, infer motives, come up with personality traits, a hypothetical personality consistent with what I see. It's not Sherlock Holmes."

"I've watched *Profiler.*"

"Close enough." Dr. Magic considered Candy's tired face. Pretty, pert, and smart underneath the layers of fatigue and the beginnings of fear. Early thirties. From hardscrabble stock, expecting hardship as if the world never delivered anything else to people like them. Usually it didn't.

She said, "So Harry blew up, his body shriveled in the desert, his car a total write-off—and you can tell me who did it? Why should I care?"

"Bear with me."

"Sure," Candy said, her native courtesy rising in the moment. "Can I get you more coffee?" Her eyes widened when she realized he hadn't touched the first cup. "Oh."

"I'm fine, thanks. Really." Dr. Magic stood, moving stiffly from the sofa, where he left Harry's wife with a silent command to remain seated. "Your husband's killer was a professional. The bomb was well-made, the fuse was sophisticated, the timing device worked where and when it was supposed to work. The killer studied your husband's habits, knew them, knew you, knew Leon—with an intimacy that would frighten you. I'm quite certain the killer knew you better than your husband did."

Candy looked alarmed (she had the odd sensation that her heart was a musical instrument hitting every other note) but merely gripped her coffee mug. "Go on."

"It's most likely your husband and his killer never stood face-to-face. Personal proximity would defeat the purpose of a bomb, which is always distance to some degree. And his business associates would hire someone they had used before. Someone who prefers distance kills to close kills."

"The drug dealers, you mean," Candy said. "I guess they rate as business associates."

"Because of the money involved—"

"One-point-eight million."

"—I also believe the men who ordered your husband's death intended it as a warning to other parties." Here, Dr. Magic's speech slowed, perhaps in an effort to diffuse the negative content of his words. "Possibly a partner."

Automatically Candy nodded, turning thoughts around in her mind, reaching a bad conclusion. "*Me?* They think *I* know where the money is?" She shuddered. "Oh, my God . . . that's why the cops were so weird."

"Possibly." Dr. Magic's eyes had narrowed to provide the tunnel vision of a predator.

"Oh, but I *don't,*" Candy moaned.

"I believe you."

"Thank you," Candy whispered. In her eyes, Dr. Magic now appeared in harsh light, a bulb switched from dim all the way to full. Her voice was feathery and soft and shaky when she said, "Tell me more about my husband's killer."

"The bomb. Well-made, as I said. Its craftsmanship is consistent with other bombs used in similar murder-for-hire cases. The end caps are distinctive, the timing device is simple and efficient." Dr. Magic kept his back to his audience of one. "But there is one inconsistency: He made a mistake."

"A mistake?"

"He almost botched the job. The fuse was faulty." Dr. Magic's voice wavered. "Your husband would be alive today—"

"My husband slapped my son," Candy said sharply.

"He hit me. He was mean and he was stingy. So don't tell me about *woulds* and *mights*."

Dr. Magic nodded. "The killer is infirm. He's losing patience or interest in his work—which, in his case, means he's losing interest in life. He doesn't care anymore."

"He's dying," Candy stated, her voice stopping at a dead end.

"He must be," Dr. Magic murmured. "Or he would have come for you by now."

I understand was implicit in Candy's long silence. Still seated on the couch from Sears, she smoothed her small hands over her floral pedal pushers. Her fingers toyed with a thread. She'd grown up on a dusty line between Texas and Oklahoma. She'd seen crops fail, droughts win, and twisters blow—she'd seen double rainbows fill black skies. She'd known families who rotted from the inside out—and families who took in stray kids even when they couldn't feed their own. The world was filled with extremes of good and bad. Always had been, always would be.

She set her shoulders and gained a quarter inch of height. "You're close, but no cigar," she said, feeling satisfaction at the look of surprise on the doctor's face. "The man who murdered my husband . . . he's *not* losing interest in life." She shook her head. "I've seen lots of people who believe they're going to die."

"So has he. His business is death."

Candy nodded. "But he hasn't stopped caring. He needs something, doesn't he?" She hunched her body forward, excitement fueling her words. "He's seen dozens of people die unprepared. He killed them! As the years passed, he began to dream about his victims—what happened after they died, if there was a final judgment, how the scores were settled. He's not a young man anymore. He needs—" Her voice failed.

With eyes that were calm and fearless, she looked directly at Dr. Magic.

She asked, "Where do we go from here?"

Dr. Magic studied the young woman's face. He saw intelligence, pragmatism, fatalism, and an admirable lack of self-pity. Candy Tosh reminded him of the daughter he had somewhere . . . about the same age. Marnee Ann. Another planet, another life that had never ever belonged to him.

"Be patient." Dr. Magic pushed away the persistent little bull terrier of his own self-pity; he ignored his sadness and—more difficult—the clawing pain in his abdomen. "In spite of his flaws, your husband possessed above-average intelligence but little imagination. He was just smart enough to believe he deserved more than he got. He had envy issues. If we approach him from an Adlerian stance—among personality theorists, Adler is the most intelligent on envy—we find a little man with dreams of tropical beaches and women in sarongs." Dr. Magic's voice withheld judgment, overflowed with a weary patience. "He had you at home, and he dreamed of Dorothy Lamour. Foolish, foolish man."

Candy said nothing, but when her short thick eyelashes brushed her cheek, tears glistened. She was nodding, unconsciously agreeing with everything spoken.

Now Dr. Magic continued briskly, as if nearing the end of an unpleasant assignment: "Harry Tosh was obsessive-compulsive, a neat freak, who needed routine and ritual to appease his otherwise constant level of anxiety. He liked to squirrel things away at the office. He had compartments, niches, everything in its place— from rubber bands to petty cash."

"He even folded his dirty laundry . . ."

"When he died, there was garden soil in the trunk of his car."

". . . before he gave it to me to wash." Candy looked

up, abruptly alert. "What?" She smudged her fingers across her cheeks in a gesture common to children.

"Three shoe boxes filled with potting soil. In the trunk of the car."

"Harry really liked petunias," Candy whispered. For most of a minute she stayed propped on the couch, her floral knees digging trenches in the cheap foam cushions.

With effort, Dr. Magic moved his bloated body across the room until he stood inches from Harry Tosh's wife. "Petunias are nice," he said without emphasis. His suffering hands were still capable of quick and nimble movement.

Candy found words lodged in her throat. "The killer . . . cancer of the pancreas, colon cancer, maybe prostate cancer—any of them could kill a man. Rob him of his zest for life. Sometimes they're curable, even when they've progressed. Sometimes a man can steal back a year or two." She blinked, and soft air escaped her mouth. "But I don't think he's after money—"

To quiet her, Dr. Magic shook his head. Moonlight streamed through the window and washed Candy's face with soft color. Roses had returned to her cheeks. Her lips were delicate poppies. There were petunias in the garden.

Leon answered the door, thrusting a grin at the lanky detective who occupied the front porch. The detective couldn't resist returning a smile. He wasn't a penurious man, just a man preoccupied by the worries of the world.

"My mom's washing her hands," Leon crooned.

"I'm Detective Hansen, and you're Leon. I've been here before."

"I remember." Leon was small for his age. His eyes naturally came to rest on the detective's tan leather belt. "You gave my mom the hiccups."

Detective Hansen took this to mean he'd made Mrs. Tosh nervous. He felt a little bad about that. She seemed like a nice lady who'd been stuck with a creep for a husband. *So what else's new in the world?*

"She played in the garden," Leon said, swinging his arms in wide circles. "Mud pies are sweet, mud pies are good!"

For the first time the detective noticed the boy had a crushed petunia nestled in his red curls. He repressed the urge to tousle the kid's carrot top. Nice kid, too. Deserved better. "Can you tell your mother Detective Hansen is here to see her?"

"Come on in." Leon laughed as he dashed away, leaving the door wide. Nothing to hide in this world.

Detective Hansen stepped over the doorstop, stepped back, leaned inside. "Hello? Mrs. Tosh?" He jumped when he heard her light voice behind him.

"I didn't know you'd be back so soon." Candy Tosh stood on the lawn, sun bouncing off her red hair, hands planted on her small hips. Her sundress was yellow with purple flowers. Her sandaled toes were pink. She looked five years younger than she'd looked the day before. "Do you have news?"

"Are you going somewhere?"

"Just to visit my sister in LA." Her eyes brightened with defiance. "Unless that's against the law."

Detective Hansen watched her, saying, "We have your sister's address if we need you. Mrs. Tosh . . ."

She walked past him, through the door, and said, "Come on inside. It's hot."

He followed, stopping reluctantly in the small entry. He kept his voice low. "We know who killed your husband."

Candy said, "It's okay, Leon's out back." She moved into the living room. Sat on the couch. Listened to the clock. *Tick, tick.* Clasped her hands together. "The drug guys killed Harry."

"But they hired a man. A pro. He's got six or seven aliases. George Matheson. Match. Mapp." Hansen coughed. "He's also known as the Doctor."

"I see." Her voice was pancake flat.

"I don't want to scare you—no, I *want* to scare you, Mrs. Tosh. We have reason to believe he might come looking for you."

"Because the money's still missing."

"You have anything to add about that?"

She gazed up at the detective, her eyes wide and guileless. A tremor ran through her. "I wish I could tell you some clue. Anything." Her voice dropped. "I don't want to die. I don't want Leon hurt."

Hansen stood, nodding. "We'll do our best to see that doesn't happen. In the meantime, it's good you're going to stay with your sister. We'll notify the guys over there—they can check up on you." He reached into his pocket, fingers dipping into crisp cotton fabric; they came back with a small photograph.

Curious, Candy Tosh gazed down on the image of a killer.

Looking much, much healthier than he'd looked last night. The cortisone, Candy thought. And the cancer. The combination didn't do much for the man.

She asked only one question. "How many people has he killed besides Harry?"

Detective Hansen shrugged. "Too many. He was a sniper in Vietnam. He's been in the business ever since." The detective touched Candy's hair gently, pulling something from between red strands. "He's a very dangerous man. I'd hate to think of him here, in your living room, your house."

Candy looked straight back at the detective. She saw the concern in his eyes, she saw the wilted petunia in his fingers. She shook her head. "If he'd been in my living room, you and I wouldn't be talking. I'd be dead and buried."

JAN BURKE is the author of six suspense novels featuring reporter Irene Kelly. The series has been nominated for Anthony, Agatha, and Macavity Awards. In addition, she is the winner of the Ellery Queen Mystery Magazine *Readers Award* and the Macavity Award for best short story. Her essay about mystery short stories appears in Deadly Women, Volume 2. In "An Unsuspected Condition of the Heart," she changes venues and time periods to prove that in any era, it may not be safe to trust a gentleman.

AN UNSUSPECTED CONDITION OF THE HEART

by Jan Burke

Now and again you may call me a rattlepate and tell me I don't know what's o'clock, Charles, but even you will account me a man who can handle the ribbons. And a dashed good thing it is that I am able to drive to an inch—or I'd have bowled your cousin Harry over right there in the middle of the road. I daresay running him over is no less than he deserved, for he'd over-turned as beautiful a phaeton as I'd ever seen, which was a thing as nearly as bad as wearing that floral waistcoat of his in public—upon my oath, Charles, even the horses took exception to it.

"Oh, thank heaven," he cried, even before I'd settled the grays, "it's dear old Rossiter!"

Two days earlier, the fellow had all but given me the cut direct at Lady Fanshawe's rout, and here he was, addressing me as if I were an angel come down the road just to save him.

"Dallingham!" I replied. "What on earth has happened? I trust you've taken no hurt?"

"Nothing that signifies," he said, dabbing at a little cut above his left brow. "But I am in the devil's own hurry and here this phaeton has lost a wheel and broken an axle!"

"Let me take you up, then," I said. "Will your groom be able to manage those bays?"

"Yes, yes," he said, already climbing up next to me. "I'd just instructed him to take them back to that inn we passed—five miles back or so—and to see about repairs. May I trouble you to take me there? I must see if they've something I can hire—"

"Nonsense, Dallingham, can't imagine they'd have so much as a horsecart to hire. I'm on my way to Ollington—to see my aunt Lavinia. I'll take you along as far as that, and if you need—"

"Ollington! Why, I'm to dine at Bingsley Hall this evening, and—"

"Bingsley Hall?" I said. "Well, that is on my way. No trouble at all."

"My thanks, Rossiter!"

The grays were restive, and I put them to. A moment later, he said, "Perhaps you can save me from disgrace."

I doubted there was any possibility of such a thing, but I said, "Oh?" (Just like that, you know—"Oh?" I believe I raised a brow, but I can't swear to it.)

"Have you met Lord and Lady Bingsley?" he asked.

"Never had the pleasure. They do not go about much in society. I believe my aunt has some acquaintance with them."

"Damned recluses, the pair of them."

"I beg your pardon? Did you not just say you were invited to dine there?"

He smiled. "Oh no, I'm to stay there a fortnight!"

"A fortnight! With the Bingsleys!"

"Well, yes, as it turns out, we're related!"

"You are related to Miss Bannister's aunt and uncle?"

He laughed. "Wish me happy, Rossiter! I'm newly married!"

"Married!" I could not hide my shock.

"Yes, as of yesterday. And in future you must refer to Miss Bannister as Lady Dallingham. We were married by special license. She's gone on to Bingsley to—er, prepare my welcome."

Charles, I own I was left speechless. The grays took advantage of my lack of concentration, and a rather difficult moment passed before both my horses and my composure were back in hand.

"Well, then," I said, rather bravely, really, "I do wish you happy. Miss—er, Lady Dallingham is a lovely young woman."

"Oh, I suppose the chit's well enough," he said, "but there can be no doubt that her fortune's mighty handsome."

As you can imagine, this blunt speech left me appalled. Of course, all the world knew that Dallingham was hanging out for an heiress, and that he had followed in his father's footsteps—meaning that his gaming had finally destroyed whatever portion of the family fortune the old man had not already lost at faro and dicing.

I know you'll not take offense at my putting it so baldly, Charles—after all, neither your cousin Dallingham nor his father could be ranked among your favorites, and your father was estranged from his late brother for many years. I recall that Dallingham applied to your esteemed parent for assistance with his debts on more than one occasion, and that your father—quite rightly—showed him the door.

Of course, even as I took him up that night, I knew that Dallingham was not without friends. He could make himself charming when need be. I will own that Dallingham's handsome face made him agreeable to the ladies, but most matchmaking mamas steered their chicks clear of him, knowing he hadn't a feather to fly with, and that his reputation as a rake was not unearned.

I fear Miss Bannister was easy prey to such a man. She was an orphan. Her guardian was a half-brother who gave little thought to her; he gave her over to the care of her aunt and uncle, Lord and Lady Bingsley—Lord Bingsley also serving as the trustee of the large fortune that will come to her a few years hence.

But the Bingsleys, as I have said, do not go about much, and have not been seen in Town for some years. When Miss Bannister was old enough to make her come-out, therefore, her half-brother arranged that she would spend the season with her godmother, a most foolish woman, who could by no means be accounted a suitable chaperone.

I soon had it from Dallingham that her half-brother—undoubtedly misled by Dallingham's charm—had granted his consent to this hasty wedding.

"You think it unseemly, high stickler that you are!" Dallingham accused me now.

"I? A high stickler?" I said. "Oh no. One only wonders, what brought about a need for such haste?"

"Tradesmen and others," he replied, quite honestly.

"Forgive me if I speak of matters which do not closely concern me, Dallingham," I said, "but you find me all curiosity. Miss Bannister's godmother has bandied it about that Miss Bannister does not come into her fortune upon marriage. She must reach the age of twenty."

"Ah, and you wonder that I could wait so long? The expectation, my dear. The tradesmen foresee a day in the not-so-distant future when I shall be a very wealthy man. They are willing to forestall pressing me until that day. In fact, they are quite willing to extend my credit."

We turned to idle chitchat for a time, during which he let fall that the lovely phaeton he had so recently overturned was yours—I am so sorry, Charles!

I changed horses at Merriton, and we were well on our way again when he said, "Sorry to have cut you out where the Bannister was concerned, old boy. But I daresay my need was the more pressing. From all I hear, Rossiter, you're as rich as Golden Ball."

"No such thing," I said coolly.

He chuckled. "No need to cut up stiff with me," he said. "You've had your eye on her, haven't you?"

"My dear Dallingham," I said, "she is your wife. It would be most improper in me to respond to such a comment."

In truth, Charles, she had come to my notice. However, unlike most women—who are drawn to me by my fortune and rank—she had no need of either. This being the case, I was sure I held no attraction to Miss Bannister. While I don't suppose a *great* many children have been frightened by my visage, or told by their nursemaids that I shall come to steal them if they don't mind their manners, I've not Dallingham's handsome face.

I did not blame the ladies of the *ton* for being taken in by him, for I too readily remembered one beauty who flattered me into believing that all mirrors lie, and 'twas a heady experience. That was long after I'd had my town bronze, so what chance does a chit fresh from the schoolroom have against the influence of a handsome face?

By the time we arrived at Bingsley Hall, my spirits were quite low. These were by no means lifted when Dallingham, at the moment we passed the gatekeeper's lodge, announced with a covetous eye, "She's to inherit all this, too, you know! Bingsley dotes on her."

I had every intention of leaving at the first possible moment, but Lord Bingsley would not hear of it. For my part, I could not help but like the old fellow and his lady, who proffered every kindness imaginable—the upshot of this being my acquiescence to the Bingsleys' insistence that I stay the night. My relative was not expecting me at any certain date, and so I agreed to break my journey with them.

"Good man! For we've something of a celebration this night, haven't we?" Lord Bingsley said, clapping Dallingham on the back.

Dallingham, who had apparently already met Lord Bingsley, seemed relieved not to be met by an outraged relative when introduced to his wife's aunt. Lady Bingsley, if not quite as effusive as her husband, was nonetheless all that a hostess should be.

For her part, the former Miss Bannister seemed, as always, becomingly shy in the company of gentlemen and, to my own relief, was not at all demonstrative with her new spouse.

In fact, dear Charles, the two of them seldom looked at one another. Dallingham was eyeing the thick carpets, the beautiful vases and charming chandelier with the air of a man who is calculating the price each might fetch at auction. One would have thought him a solicitor's clerk, practicing the art of taking inventory of the Bingsleys' estate. He made little effort to hide his happy contemplation of taking possession of their goods upon their demise. He divided his time between this and the depletion of Lord Bingsley's cellars.

Watching him, I found myself seething, until I felt a gentle hand on my sleeve. "My dear Lord Rossiter," the new Lady Dallingham said softly, "how glad I am that you have come."

She moved away rather quickly, and spoke to her aunt, all the while blushing.

I did not suppose for a moment that Dallingham, a man whose name has been linked with two actresses and any number of fair Cyprians, thought her very lovely. She tended to plumpness a little. Her face was not that of a classic beauty, and no one would mistake her for a diamond of the first water. But there are other gems than diamonds, my dear Charles, and I found much in her that was admirable and becoming.

I wanted to ask if something was troubling her, if there was any way in which I might be of service, but I had no opportunity for private speech with her that evening—which was, I tell you plainly, easily one of the strangest nights of my life.

We were beset by real difficulties at table that evening. Dallingham wasn't paying the least attention to me or his wife; he was admiring the silver and china, repeatedly congratulating Lord Bingsley on his fine cellars, making gratifying comments to Lady Bingsley on the excellence of the soup *à la reine,* and remarking on the beauty of the epergne at the center of the table (it depicted tigers chasing one another round about—not to my taste, as frankly, I don't like to dine with figures of things that would just as soon dine on me).

But just as the second course—a haunch of venison, saddle of lamb, boiled capon, and spring chicken—was served, Lady Bingsley said in a ringing voice, "Pistols at dawn!"

Dallingham and I exchanged looks of some consternation, even as Lord Bingsley calmly replied, "You'll never do me in that way, my dear."

"I know a good deal about pistols," her ladyship replied. "Don't I, Amelia?"

"Yes, Aunt," the former Miss Bannister replied.

"Yes, yes," said his lordship, "but for all that you

know about them, you are an execrable shot." He continued to apply himself to the venison, even as her ladyship appeared to apply herself to the problem of shooting him. Dallingham, so far from being dismayed, seemed on the verge of losing any semblance of gravity still left to him, while his new wife calmly continued to take small bites of the lamb.

Within a few moments, his lordship looked up from his plate and said, "Arrow through the heart. While you sleep."

"I must say—" I began weakly.

"Nonsense!" said her ladyship firmly.

"It is not nonsense!" protested my host. "I'm a demmed sight better with the bow and arrow than you are with pistols. I'll creep into your room through that old priest's hole."

"Now, there you're out!" said her ladyship. "The priest's hole is in Lord Dallingham's room—the exit, in any case."

At this, Dallingham, who had been drinking steadily from the moment of our arrival, was overcome with mirth.

"I find nothing amusing—" I tried again.

"By Jupiter!" his lordship said. "You're right! Hmm. In that case, it shall have to be something more subtle. Perhaps when you go riding—"

"Please!" I said. "Your lordship, your ladyship . . . I beg pardon . . . not my place, really . . . but I can't possibly face the next course if there is to be nothing but this talk of murder!"

There was a moment of profound silence before his lordship said, "Not face the next course? Rubbish! There's to be lark pudding!"

And so the exchange of murder plots continued. I would have made good on my threat to excuse myself from the table, lark pudding or no, had not the former

Miss Bannister looked at me so beseechingly, I forgot all else.

By the time the ladies retired to the drawing room and Lord Bingsley offered his excellent port, though, I had heard our hosts exchange no fewer than twenty threats of foul play, and had decided to leave this odd household by first light, beseeching looks or no. Miss Bannister had married a bounder, but it was his place to take her away from such humbuggery, not mine.

But Dallingham was extremely well to live by then, as the saying goes—or at least, in too much of a drunken stupor to converse. Other than expending the effort required to continue to drink, he seemed to be using whatever powers of concentration remained to him to prevent himself from falling face first into the table linen he so admired.

Sitting there over port, blowing a cloud with his lordship, I sought an excuse for an early departure. But as if reading my mind, his lordship said, "Must forgive us, Rossiter. Her ladyship and I are not much in company, as you must know. You are outraged, as any good man would be." He paused and, looking at Dallingham, said in a low voice, "Unlike yon jackanapes! Were I twenty years younger, I'd darken his daylights! But here . . . well, we keep the ladies waiting. I only mean to ask you—nay, beg you, and I'm not a man who often begs!—to see your way clear to remain with us another day or two."

"My dear Lord Bingsley—" I began, but in what was becoming a habit in him, he interrupted.

"For Amelia's sake!" he whispered, then added, in a normal speaking voice, "You'll grow used to our havey-cavey ways, I'm sure."

I bowed to a man who—as I was to learn—was a masterful persuader.

Two stout footmen carried the jug-bitten Lord

Dallingham to his chambers that night. That his wife
slept apart from him did not surprise me in the least—I
only hoped that she had locked the door against him.

He did not appear at breakfast, when Lord Bingsley
asked if I would be so good as to accompany his niece,
who wished to ride her mare about the estate. "Going
to miss Bingsley Hall, she tells me. By God, Bingsley
Hall shall miss her!"

"Perhaps Lord Dallingham would like to join us," I
suggested.

"Daresay he would," Lord Bingsley said, "if he
hadn't eaten Hull cheese! My valet informs me he shot
the cat! Too blind to find the basin like a decent fellow, damn him. Wonder if he'll be so fond of that carpet now!"

"I—I believe I shall find Miss—Lady Dallingham,"
I said, feeling a bit queasy myself.

He offered to accompany me to the stables. We delayed some moments on the steps to exchange pleas-
antries with Lady Bingsley, who was to call upon an
ailing tenant that morning. His lordship, determining
that there was some slight chill in the air, begged her to
wait while her maid should fetch a shawl, and once this
item was retrieved, he solicitously placed it about his
lady's shoulders. He handed her up into the carriage,
and her little dog as well, and then a large hamper of
food for the tenant's family, and, after receiving assur-
ances from the coachman that he would not drive too
fast over the country lanes, stood watching the carriage
as it pulled away.

At the stables, he saw to it that I was very hand-
somely mounted on a fine gelding. I assisted his
niece—who wore a delightful blue velvet riding
habit—with her mare, and in the company of a groom
who stayed some distance behind us, we rode out.

Lord Bingsley's lands were in good heart, and if I

had been Dallingham, no doubt I would have been estimating their yields. But my mind was wholly taken up with the thought that I had forever lost the opportunity to ask the woman beside me to become Lady Rossiter.

"How do you fare this morning, Lady Dallingham?" I asked, trying to accept that fact.

"Oh, please do not address me by that hateful name!"

"Hateful? But—"

"May I count you my friend, sir?"

"Most certainly! If there is any service I may render—"

"I am afraid, Lord Rossiter, that I have been duped."

"By me?" I asked, aghast.

"Oh no, Lord Rossiter! Never by you!"

"I don't understand, Lady . . . er, beg pardon, but I don't know quite how one should address—"

"Amelia," she said. "I should like it above all things if you would call me Amelia."

"Very well, Amelia, and you shall please call me Christopher—no, dash it! Call me Kit."

"Do your friends call you Kit?"

"Yes."

"Well, then, *Kit*," she said—and by the saints and angels, Charles, she could have asked for the world from that moment on. She didn't.

"I am so sorry that a man of your sensibilities was forced to . . . to accustom himself to the odd behavior of my aunt and uncle," she said. "They mean well, but—"

"Mean well! Talking of poison and setting traps with old armor or contriving to make a fellow walk beneath loose roof tiles!"

"Oh, Kit, no! They are trying to get me to show a little—I believe Uncle calls it 'rumgumption.'"

"I beg pardon?" I said, all at sea.

"Oh, I know I shouldn't use cant—"

"No, no, I don't mind it—the cant, I mean—but what the blazes have you to do with their plans to do one another a mischief?"

"One another? Oh no, Kit—"

"Discussing—over the syllabub, mind you—how they're going to put a period to the other's existence!"

"But that is not what they are about, Kit! I am sure . . . that is, I begin to wonder . . . well, the thing of it is, perhaps I should murder Harry!"

"What!"

"Oh, yes. It's the only way out of this tangle I'm in."

"My dear Amelia! Surely—"

"You see," she said, exhibiting an inherited tendency to stop a fellow from saying what he ought to say, "Peter—he's my half-brother, you know—Peter told me that Harry had some—some rather displeasing information about my dear aunt, and that Harry would make it public if I didn't marry him straightaway. Only now I find out that my aunt doesn't care a fig about any of it, that it was some old scandal from long ago, and Uncle Bingsley called me a goosecap, and said that Peter and Harry had arranged it all between them, because according to my parents' will, a certain sum of money came to Peter on my marriage, which is why he wanted me to have a London season in the first place, which I wouldn't have cared for at all, because really it's quite exhausting and gives one the headache, except that it afforded me the chance to—to meet a few admirable persons, although he—they—seemed to take little interest in me, for which they can hardly be blamed, and so—and so I married Harry."

I was much struck by this speech, once I had sorted it out, and said, "The dastards! When I think what Dallingham and your half-brother have conspired to do! Why—why, I shall thrash the two of them! This is positively gothic!"

"Oh no, Kit, do not! I have made a great mistake, and I've been a sad featherbrain, as my uncle says—"

"But surely the marriage can be set aside!"

She turned very red.

"Beg pardon!" I murmured, a little crimson myself. "Don't know what possessed me to—"

"No, no! It is just—I was so very foolish! But to have a man with Lord Dallingham's looks and address tell me that only his desperate love for me drove him to such measures to bring me to the altar—well, I realize now that he was merely ensuring that our marriage could not be annulled. As for my giving into such nonsense—it is all vanity, I'm afraid. My head was turned. 'Perhaps he cares for me after all!' I thought. So silly of me. My aunt says it comes of reading too many novels. But she's mistaken, of course. It is because I am a plain woman, and—"

"Never say so again!" I protested.

She was silent for a time, then said, "You are kind. Perhaps you cannot know what it is like to be flattered in that way—"

"Oh yes, I can," I said.

"You? Oh, it isn't possible."

I laughed. "My dear, I have learned it was not only possible but probable, as it must be for every unmarried person of fortune."

She made no reply.

After a moment, I asked, "How came you to bring him here?"

"My uncle had come to Town, because Peter had sent word to him that he was owed money—on the event of my being wed. I had thought Uncle would be in a rage, but he was all that was civil, and merely told

Dallingham that perhaps he should like to come to Bingsley Hall for a fortnight, and saying that one day all his own wealth and property would come to me, so Harry may as well become acquainted with the place."

"And Dallingham couldn't wait."

"No." She sighed. "But I won't cry craven—I shall contrive to live with Lord Dallingham. I only wanted you to know—well, I was so surprised to see you with him, and so grateful. It has done my nerves a deal of good to know you are at hand, although undoubtedly you've found this visit quite dreadful!"

That evening, Charles, as we sat down to dine, I found my attitude toward murderous speech had undergone a sea change. I listened to my lord's and ladyship's schemes with rapt attention. And when Lady Bingsley was so good as to teach me the names and properties of certain plants in the nearby woods, I was an apt pupil.

Now, none of this has any bearing, of course, on the sudden death of Lord Dallingham. He died, as was ascertained by the magistrate, of an apoplexy brought on by an unsuspected condition of the heart. He had been drinking steadily throughout his visit to Bingsley Hall—Dallingham, not the magistrate, I mean—and an empty bottle of very fine port was found near his bed. This life of dissipation, the magistrate believes, led to the gentleman's untimely demise.

Like other gentlemen of the law in centuries before him, the magistrate did not observe the exit to the priest's hole. It is a very small hiding place indeed—as I discovered by viewing it from the entrance, which was in my own chambers.

Amelia puts off her black gloves in another week, when you may expect an announcement of our betrothal in the *Times*.

One other thing I must mention, though, Charles.

More than once—rattlepate that I am—it has occurred to me that now that the late Lord Dallingham has passed on to his reward without an heir, you are in line for the title. It has also occurred to me that you had never before allowed the late Harry the use of so much as one of your tenants' wheelbarrows, let alone your own new phaeton. I say, old friend—thank goodness you weren't in it when that wheel came loose!

However, should you ever feel the urge to loan another phaeton to someone, Amelia's half-brother may be glad to make use of your generosity.

How very good to be able to confide in you, my dear, dear Charles!

Your most Obedient & etc.—

Kit

JEREMIAH HEALY, *author of thirteen mystery and suspense novels, is best-known for his Shamus Award–winning series featuring Boston private eye John Francis Cuddy. He is also a lawyer and legal scholar who taught for eighteen years at the New England School of Law. He is a past president of the Private Eye Writers of America and the current North American vice president of the International Association of Crime Writers. In "Legacy," John Cuddy helps an ailing grandmother provide for children left destitute by their parents' divorce.*

LEGACY

A John Francis Cuddy Story

by Jeremiah Healy

It was a cold day in Boston, one of those with a crust of refrozen snow on the ground and still early enough in December that you couldn't even begin to think of the temporary reprieve Christmas might grant to the situation. Walking down Boylston Street with the Common on my left, I turned into Steve Rothenberg's building, taking the elevator—working for once—to his floor. The door to the office suite he shared with a rotating cast of other attorneys still had the vertical xylophone of names on different wood plaques next to the jamb, Rothenberg's appearing by patina to be oldest.

Which wasn't necessarily a status symbol.

Inside the door was a waiting area, the receptionist-cum-secretary sitting behind her desk and in front of a computer monitor. She had orange, spiky hair over a pair of small earphones, her shoulders rocking to something other than dictated correspondence.

When her head turned toward me, probably by accident, I said, "John Cuddy for—"

"Hey, Steve," she yelled, "that investigator's here."

A South Boston accent, the neighborhood where I grew up.

Just seconds later, Rothenberg's head came around a corner, almost like a clip from the Marx Brothers. "John, come on in."

As we entered his office, he waved me to one of the client chairs in front of a scarred and cluttered desk.

Sitting down, I said, "Your treasure with the orange hair. What's her name again?"

"I can never remember either."

Rothenberg lowered himself into the swivel chair backed by a drafty window. He was wearing his suit jacket for a change, the tie snugged up to his collar, probably more a function of the weather than any sense of decorum. The departing hair and fuller beard, both salt-and-pepper, even gave an illusion of frost to his features.

"So," I said, "you called my answering service?"

"I've got an interesting matter, John. A first-timer for me."

Rothenberg had been a criminal defense lawyer for most of his career, which is how I'd met him while doing a favor for a Boston police lieutenant. But lately Steve had been dabbling in other areas of legal endeavor.

He called it "diversification."

I looked at him. "Not a divorce case?"

"No."

"I don't do divorce, Steve."

"I know that, John."

"Okay, shoot," I said, leaning back in the chair.

Rothenberg did the same in his, swinging a little on the swivel point. "This woman named Dalia Looney came back north about five months ago with her two kids, a boy and a girl."

"That's D-A-H-L-I-A, as in the flower?"

"As in the flower, but she's Lithuanian, and they drop the *H*."

"Where does the 'Looney' come from?"

"She took her husband's name when they got married. He moved back up here, too. Works construction with his father over in Charlestown."

Another neighborhood of Boston. "And where's Mrs. Looney?"

"Your old stomping grounds."

"Southie?"

"Just off West Broadway. Dalia and the kids are living in her mother's house."

Husband with father, wife with mother. "Steve?"

"Yeah?"

"This is sounding suspiciously like a divorce case."

A smug smile and a shake of the head. "Already happened."

"What did?"

"The divorce. After the wedding, they lived up here for a while, him working with his dad. Then there was some kind of fight between Senior and Junior over how to run the construction business, right around the time the newlyweds' son was born. So Junior packs his family off to somewhere around Atlanta, for the building boom down there. Then to Florida for a while, and even Alabama before they end up in a little town with 'ville' at the end of it. Husband and wife get divorced, southern style, citing irreconcilable differences."

"Then why do you need a private investigator?"

Rothenberg came forward in his chair, hands spreading on top of his desk. "The court down there ordered Junior to pay child support, and he did. For a while. When the money stopped coming, though, Dalia had a tough time trying to get an enforcement order, and I guess she never really liked that part of the country. So she moved with their kids—the daughter was born during the Florida period—back up here."

"And now Mrs. Looney wants a Massachusetts court to order her husband to pony up."

"All eight months of arrearage, and a continuing obligation to—"

"Steve, this is a divorce case."

"Uh-unh." Rothenberg put a little passion into his voice. "All the real divorce work's been done for us."

Us.

"I'm a little hazy on the details, John, since this is my first time registering an out-of-state judgment. But based on what I've read about it, I just file a complaint with the Probate and Family Court up here, attaching certified copies of the official papers from down there."

"And what do I have to do, Steve?"

The passion in his voice was replaced by a twinkle in his eye. "A simple asset search."

"The husband's squirreling money?"

"Has to be. They were doing fine down south, financially speaking, anyway. Then once Junior's a bachelor again, he decides to stop paying child support and heads home to happier hunting grounds."

"Steve, the husband's such a good wage earner, how come he's working with the father he had a fight with?"

"Cover."

"Cover?"

"My client's positive her ex brought a pot of gold north with him and is working with his father just as cover for the money he's hiding."

"Sounds like you need an accountant more than an investigator."

"That might be too late. Once I file my complaint with the court, I can force formal discovery. But meanwhile they'd be on notice that Mrs. Looney is coming after them, and might just bury the stuff deeper."

"Steve, there are computer outfits that can search for assets on-line a lot faster than I can on foot."

"And we might use one. But I'd like your take on things first, because I trust your judgment."

Compliments are something private investigators rarely receive. I glanced down at my left wrist, the watch an old Timex with real hands on a face of twelve numbers.

Rothenberg said, "You have another appointment?"

"No. It's just that I'm paid for the hours I put in, Steve, and so far, I don't quite see where my fee's coming from on this."

"John." A note of disappointment in the voice now. "These are needy people. A single mother with two small children."

"Living with Grandma, Steve. I don't have that luxury."

"Meaning?"

"Meaning I pay my own rent, apartment and office, my own—"

"John, I smell money here."

"The husband's 'pot of gold.' "

"Yes."

"Which is where my fee would come from, if at all."

Steve Rothenberg sighed deeply. "Tell you what. I'll pay you out of my own pocket for the time it'll take to drive to Southie and meet these people. If you still decide against working the case, no hard feelings."

I thought about Rothenberg making things easier for me when I did that favor for Robert Murphy of the Homicide Unit. It also had been a while since I'd visited my wife, Beth.

Sleeping in her hillside in Southie, overlooking the harbor.

Rothenberg said, "John?"

"You have an address for the grandmother?"

It was a three-decker on a block of them within walking distance of the Lithuanian Club, where the fathers of some kids I went to grammar school with would hang out on their days off. The house itself had stonework around the front door and aluminum siding replacing the original wood, but some of the paint skin on the siding was peeling, and the front stoop's cement steps were crumbling, as though the owner hadn't stopped the damage when she could have.

Leaving my car at the curb, I walked up a solid part of the stoop. Three buzzers over the mailbox, but only the top and bottom ones showed slots for names, and only the bottom one actually had printing on it. VALECKAS.

When I pressed the button, I heard a bumblebee sound inside the house. I was on the verge of pressing it again when the door opened on what I at first thought must be an unusually strong spring.

Until I got a look at the person doing the opening.

She was maybe five-two, skinny rather than slim, with short, curly hair shading from blond to gray. I'd have pegged her age at mid-sixties, but the sunken eyes, hollow cheeks, and sagging flesh told me I couldn't rely on a first impression, because I'd seen all three aspects before.

In Beth, when she'd had her cancer.

I said, "Mrs. Valeckas?"

"It is pronounce Vah-*las*-kuss."

"My name's John Cuddy."

The eyes might be sunken, but they glowed now. "You are from my Dalia's lawyer?"

"Yes."

"You come in, out of the cold."

She had trouble with pulling the door wider, so I pushed a little to help.

"Thank you," said Valeckas.

The foyer had a staircase leading up to what would be a second and then a third landing, some sepia photos on the walls of people with a healthier version of my greeter's features standing around farm equipment.

"The land of my father, outside Vilnius. We have thirty hectares of potatoes, with orchards of cherries around our house. And a big cross of wood, tall as tree, to protect us."

"It looks like a pretty place."

"Then yes, before the Soviets." Valeckas walked toward the first floor door on the left. "My *dukra* waits in the parlor."

"Your . . . ?"

"In Lithuania, *dukra* mean daughter. After you talk to her, you come see me in my kitchen, yes."

Valeckas didn't phrase that last as a request, and I took it as an order. "I will."

After going through the door—opening onto a dining room—she pointed left but walked to the right. I followed her finger to a bay-windowed parlor that would have been filled with sun in the summer but at four-thirty on that wintry day lay shadowy, the only light a floor lamp. The rug and furniture were threadbare, an old and heavy walking stick like a squared-off shillelagh mounted over the couch.

Where three people were sitting.

One was a woman around thirty, with curly blond hair not yet graying and a full-cheeked face like Mrs. Valeckas must have had at her age. A little stolid from childbearing, Dalia Looney looked up at me and held the stare as I crossed the small room to her. She was flanked by a boy around seven and a girl maybe four. Both had looked up, too, when I came into view, then both looked down at the floor, as synchronized in their movements as an army drill team.

I didn't think the kids should have been there. "Mrs. Looney?"

"Yes." She took my hand, a brief, clammy shake. "This is Michael and Veronica."

A slight twinge of the South mixing with the Southie in her voice. The two bookends looked up again and down again, the girl rubbing one arm with the other hand, the boy coughing in a way my own mother would have called the croup.

I said, "Maybe it'd be best if we talked alone."

Looney nodded, then glanced left and right. "Michael, Veronica, y'all go into the kitchen with Gram, okay?"

Each looked at her, looked at me, and stood up. They were still small enough to walk abreast through the doorway. From a few rooms away, I heard Valeckas say, "My *anukas* and my *anuke*. We have currant cookies and milk, yes."

Then the sound of the boy coughing again before a swinging door creaked to a stop, closing him off.

As I took an armchair across from Looney, she said, "My mother's always baking cookies. Currants—both the black kind and the red—are just real popular over there."

"In Lithuania."

"Uh-huh."

A test. "Steve Rothenberg asked you to have the children with you for me, right?"

Looney hesitated, then nodded, almost enthusiastically. "He said you told him you might not want my case, but that Michael and Veronica ought to convince you."

"I just don't like to waste anybody's time, Mrs. Looney."

"Could you . . . would it be all right if you called me Dalia?"

"Did Steve tell you to do that, too?"

Looney looked hurt, and I regretted my words—and the edge in my voice—as soon as they'd hit the air.

She said, "Nobody told me nothing. I keep the Looney name for the kids' sake, but I just don't much like to hear it tied to me anymore."

"I'm sorry, Dalia." Give her a chance to convince. "Steve said you thought your husband—"

"Ex-husband."

"—ex-husband was hiding assets?"

Another enthusiastic nod. "When we were down south, he was doing just real well, every place we lived. The judge even said so, when he ordered Johnnie to pay the support."

First time I'd heard his given name. "Can you spell that for me?"

She did.

I said, "So, this judge ordered child support?"

"Uh-huh. And insurance, too. Medical for me and the kids, and a life policy on him, so we'd be okay in case anything happened. Then, after the divorce and all, Johnnie moved again—back to Florida—and I tried just real hard to make a go of it, but I couldn't once he stopped sending the checks. Mom kept up the insurance, account of the companies had to let us know that he wasn't paying them anymore, either. And that's when I came back home."

"To Southie."

The enthusiastic nod.

"You didn't pursue your husband in Florida?"

"No way. Never liked living there, and without the

support, I couldn't afford to, anyways." Another hesitation. "Besides, there was his gun, too."

Swell. "Which gun is that, Dalia?"

"Johnnie—back when we still lived up here—bought this revolver. He had a permit and all, so it was legal. Said we needed one in the house on account of the Castle Law."

Massachusetts has a home-defense statute, allowing someone to use deadly force if they fear an intruder means them severe bodily harm. "And he kept the revolver when you moved?"

"Wherever we moved. Down there, the states don't seem to care so much about people having guns."

"You think your husband would use his?"

"Johnnie was always kind of a hothead." Looney blushed. "That was what attracted me to him in the first place, back when we were in school here. But he's also a drinker, and I don't know what all Johnnie would do if he got it into his head that I was coming after him with a lawyer."

Or a private investigator. "Dalia, how do you think your ex-husband is hiding his money?"

"I don't know that, either." A weak smile. "I guess if I did, I wouldn't need Steve or you, huh?" Even the weak smile disappeared. "But Jake's been in the business a long time, and it was him doing funny things with the books that started them fighting in the first place."

"Jake being Johnnie's dad?"

"Uh-huh. Looney Construction, over in Charlestown." A shiver. "And if Johnnie can scare you, Jake's a lot worse."

This just got better and better. "Has either of them ever threatened you?"

"No. Fact is, Johnnie and Jake haven't even been by to see Michael and Veronica. Can you imagine that? A father and grandfather, and they don't care about their own kin?"

"If they feel like that, what do you think I can do?"

Dalia Looney shrugged, not just with the shoulders, but her whole body. And then the tears began running down each side of her nose. "Help us, maybe?"

"Mrs. Valeckas—"

"My name is Izabel, with the *z*. And this is not milk."

An amber bottle shaped somewhere between a pint and a quart stood in front of her on the kitchen table of stamped tin painted white. Sitting with her hands out of sight in her lap, Izabel Valeckas had sent her grandchildren back to their mother as soon as I'd come through the swinging door from the dining room. There were two more doors off the kitchen, in Southie probably a pantry and a half bath.

"Sit, sit. We have some *suktinis*."

"Sook-teen-as?"

Valeckas brought her right hand up and to the bottle, pouring a dram of liquid a little paler than amber into each of two jelly glasses. "It mean a dance like the polka, where the man and the woman spin around and around. You spin like that, too, you have very much *suktinis*."

I tasted it. Fiery, but with flavors of honey and . . . clove? "Excellent."

Valeckas said, "In English, the drink is call 'mead.' As old like beer from my country."

And "only" fifty percent alcohol, according to the label on the bottle.

I set down my glass. "Mrs. Val—"

"Izabel. I just tell you, remember?"

"I remember."

"And you. There is a business card I can see?"

I took one out, put it on the tin in front of her. She used the pinkie of her right, drinking hand to drag it closer to her.

"John . . . Francis . . . Cuddy." Valeckas looked up. "I thought at my front door you have the same name as my Dalia's husband. But since he leave her, I do not like that name no more, so I call you Mr. Detective."

"Izabel, why did you want to see me?"

She tossed her *suktinis* off in one gulp, returning the glass to the table and her right hand with my card in it to her lap. "You take my *dukra*'s case, yes."

"I don't know."

"Why not?"

"What Dalia—or her lawyer—wants done is very difficult with no information."

"How much of the information you need? You see she have two babies and no man to work for her family."

"Izabel, I can't just walk up to Dalia's ex-husband and say, 'Where are you hiding your money?' "

A smile of triumph. "So, you too think he hide it."

I shook my head. "If he's any good at all, he can bury his assets so deep nobody could find them."

"Bury." Valeckas dipped her head, the wattles under her chin shaking. "Soon my *dukra* must bury me."

When I didn't respond to that, Valeckas looked back up, the eyes aglow as they had been at the front door. "You know much about the cancer, Mr. Detective?"

"Some."

A change fluttered over her eyes. "I think more than some. But you do not have to know much to see I have it. And bad. The last doctor say I have six months, and then I am with my husband again. In the parlor, his walking stick I keep over the couch still. My Kazimieras is name for the patron saint of Lithuania. Dead five years now, my husband, but there is not one day, one hour, when I do not think of him."

"Izabel, I know how that can be."

Her turn not to respond.

I said, "But as far as helping your daughter is—"

"Legacy."

I stopped for a moment. "Legacy?"

"The lawyer word, for what we leave to our children. In Lithuania, there is no tax on the land, so my father could leave our farm to us, if the Soviets do not come. That is why he bring us to America, to give us the chance. I marry my Kazimieras here, and we work hard, buy this house. Then God bless us with Dalia, and now Michael and Veronica, too."

I looked around the kitchen. "Your daughter and her children will get this place, then."

"No." A weary shake of the head. "No, I pay the insurance when her Johnnie stop, but not the insurance for me."

"What about Medicare, or—"

A tight smile now. "How old you think I am?"

"I hadn't thought about it, Izabel."

"Do not play stupid with me, Mr. Detective. You think about it outside, when I open the front door and you see the cancer in my face." She waited a moment. "I am only fifty-three years, and I cannot get the Medicare."

When I didn't respond again, Valeckas said, "So I call the bank, and the nice man there give to me a reverse mortgage. You know what is this?"

I wished I didn't. "The bank sends you money each month in exchange for owning the house when you die."

"Just so. The doctors find the cancer two years ago. I think the reverse mortgage is a good idea, because my *dukra* has a husband who can take care of her, of my *anukas,* Michael, and my *anuke,* Veronica. My Dalia is a *gulbe*—a swan, Mr. Detective—but that Johnnie treat her like a crow. And then he divorce them. So now I have no legacy to leave except the walking stick of my Kazimieras, this bottle of *suktinis,* and the bill for my funeral."

"Izabel—"

"I have met my Dalia's lawyer. Steven Rothenberg is a good man, but he cannot upstand to that Johnnie like could my Kazimieras or my father." The eyes softened. "In Lithuania, my father a great hunter. We have the heads—the horns—of deer and elk and moose on the walls of our house, what he takes with his gun." The eyes hardened again. "You carry a gun, Mr. Detective?"

"Occasionally."

Now the eyes glowed angrily. "When my *dukra* comes home with her children, I help them to put away their clothes and things. Some are in boxes, and in one, I find these."

Valeckas brought her left hand in a fist up from her lap and over the table before turning her wrist palm down. When she opened her fingers, five cartridges fell to the tabletop, making a jarring, rattling sound on the stamped tin.

Valeckas said, "What kind of man would leave bullets from his gun where his children could find them?"

I had no answer for that one.

She leaned over the table and toward me, her breath foul but laced with the honey-and-clove flavor of the mead. "The lawyer man cannot upstand to Johnnie or his father. But you can, and you must, yes. For my Dalia, my Michael, my Veronica."

Valeckas then squeezed her eyes shut, and I could see a spasm wrack her body nearly off the chair.

When her eyes opened again, Izabel Valeckas said, "And for me."

My feet made a crunching noise on the icy path, the folks who maintain the cemetery doing a little better job of mowing the grass in summer than shoveling the snow in winter. When I got to her row, the wind began coming up from the water, stinging my face even before I laid the roses longways to where she was.

The stone still read ELIZABETH MARY DEVLIN CUDDY, although the lettering seemed more worn than the last time.

When was the last time?

John, it's too cold for you to be here.

"It's never too cold, Beth."

A pause. *Why do I feel it's not just the weather that's bothering you?*

"Maybe because I just met your match today."

Another pause. Then, *Someone you're interested in?*

"Interested . . . ? Oh, no. I meant your match in knowing how to handle a certain Irishman."

Tell me.

I went through it, from Steve's office to the grandmother's kitchen.

You told this Valeckas woman you'd help, didn't you?

"Worse than that. I promised her."

But what are you going to do?

The wind really began howling now, the stinging sensation superseded by a nearly ripping one, as though I were strapped into one of those astronaut accelerators that simulate Mach 5 or—

John, you still with me?

"Still here, Beth."

Well?

"How am I going to help the family?"

That's what I mean.

"Actually, Izabel Valeckas gave me the idea herself."

She did?

"Sort of," I said, deciding to leave the details till the following morning.

Just over the bridge from the old Boston Garden—now replaced by the Fleet Center—lies Charlestown. The people who live there call it simply "the Town" and themselves "Townies." The neighborhood was best known recently as the home of the poor white family in the late J. Anthony Lukas's book *Common Ground,* his version of Boston's school desegregation/busing crisis during the seventies.

But Charlestown is a mixed bag today. It provides a berth for the USS *Constitution*—"Old Ironsides"—at a wharf on the water. It supports the Bunker Hill Monument—"Don't shoot till you can see the whites of their eyes"—on the mound of the same name. In between, you have everything from tough housing projects bordering auto yards to spanking new condo complexes bordering the harbor.

And, on one of the main commercial drags, the headquarters of Looney Construction, Inc.

Sitting in my Prelude near a mom-and-pop convenience store, I went over what could loosely be called a strategy. Izabel Valeckas really had been the inspiration for it, by triggering my statement about not being able to just ask Johnnie Looney where he'd hid his money. Standing over Beth's grave the night before, doing exactly that seemed my best bet for getting the informal assessment Steve Rothenberg wanted.

When my watch read 9:00 A.M., I got out of the car and walked a half block to the freestanding brick building that once might have been a small branch of the lo-

cal savings and loan. There was a postage stamp of a
parking lot on the side holding one passenger car and
two blue pickup trucks with room for maybe a couple
more. Going in the front doors of the building, I nearly
collided with a stumpy guy about my age in charcoal
jeans, an army field jacket, and powder-blue hard hat
with SPENCE stenciled across the crown.

"Help you with something?" he said, a black hand
going up to mop a line of sweat on the broad forehead
despite the temperature outside hovering in the teens.

"I'm looking for Johnnie Looney."

"I ain't him."

"Mr. . . . Spence?"

The eyes rolled northward, as though trying to read
the stencil from the inside. "That's me, I guess."

"You know where I can find Johnnie?"

Spence took a half step backward, sizing me up.
"You the law?"

"In a manner of speaking."

A nod. Not a happy one, just an acknowledgment to
himself that, unfortunately, he'd gauged me right.
"Johnnie ain't here."

"When's he due back?"

"Can't say, man."

"I'll settle for Jake, then."

Spence spent a moment gauging something else,
then said, "First door on the right."

As Spence left the building, I moved into the hallway. The door to my right stood open, a man looming
over a drawing board as he clipped a blueprint to the
corners of it. His complexion was ruddy enough from
the weather—or the booze—you'd have called it
blotched. He wore a maize chamois shirt, sleeves rolled
above burly forearms. On top of his head was a toupee
so thick and so badly matched to the fringe of carrot

hair around his ears that it made me embarrassed to think we swam in the same gene pool.

"Jake Looney?"

He looked up. "Happens every time."

"What does?"

Looney gestured toward an empty desk on his left near the door. "Send the girl for some decent coffee, and I get interrupted by a guy's gonna make trouble for me."

"What makes you think I'm trouble?"

"You're wearing a suit, bucko, and I don't recognize your face. Maybe you're a new inspector from the city, maybe you're somebody's lawyer, maybe you're just a guy thinks he can sell me something without even needing samples to show."

"None of the above, though you were warm with the middle one."

Looney regarded me a minute. "Lawyer?"

I took out my identification holder. "Working for one. John Cuddy."

He glanced at the laminated copy of my license. "What's this about? I haven't had a guy injured on the job for going on a year."

"It's about your son."

"Johnnie?"

"And his obligations."

Looney squinted at me now, the toupee inching down bizarrely, as though extending his hairline by manifest destiny. "What obligations?"

"To his wife and children."

"Oh, that's just what I need." Looney made a face like he'd bitten into a sour lemon. "Tell you what, bucko, let me save both of us a lot of time. Sit in the girl's chair, and I'll give you the straight skinny."

I moved over to the empty desk as Looney went behind a bigger one against what might have been the bank's drive-up window. He said, "First off, Johnnie shouldn't never have married that broad. Don't work, you mix the bloodlines like they did."

"It's okay to hire them, but don't let them date your sister."

Looney squinted at me again, the toupee reaching toward his eyebrows again. "You making fun of me, Cuddy?"

"Yes."

A gruff laugh. "You ran into my house nigger on your way in, right?"

"I'd rather you didn't use that word."

"Or else what, you'll kick my ass?"

"Into next week."

Looney squinted a third time, but this time the toupee stayed put. "You and me are headed for troubles, bucko."

"Almost certainly. Which would waste our time instead of saving it the way you were hoping a minute ago."

The eyes opened halfway, and he blew out a breath. "Okay. I got to hire the blacks—and the Chinese, for that matter, they decide to turn in their chef's hat for a hard one. Otherwise, I got the state and the feds all over me. But that doesn't mean I trust them any more than I trust the Lithuanians, like that shrew of a grandmother over in Southie."

I got a slight impression of "He doth protest too much" from Looney's tone, but I shelved it. "You know Mrs. Valeckas, then?"

"From the wedding, where we didn't exactly hit it off, you might say. Turned up her nose at us like we were some kind of peasants and she was the fucking lord of the manor. Or lady, whatever. Well, her daughter—who meets Johnnie on account of busing, by-the-by—"

"Busing?"

"Yeah. When old Judge Garrity decided the neighborhood schools didn't work right. My son was going to the Eddie—the Edwards Middle School—only it was getting bad, and Charlestown High worse. So I dug deep and sent him to Catholic school, which is what the Lithuanian shrew decided to do with 'her Dalia,' too. Wasn't for Garrity and those goddamned buses, none of this ever happens."

"None of what?"

"The daughter wouldn't ever have met Johnnie, much less be able to do her best to get knocked up by him. And—surprise, surprise—along come two little yard apes."

"Your grandchildren."

"You'd think so, wouldn't you? Only their momma and her momma poisoned them against my side of the family from the word go, made them move down to the land of cotton and Negro spirituals."

"I understood the move south had more to do with Johnnie and you having a falling-out."

"See, that's just what I mean about the poisoning stuff."

"A falling-out over financials."

"Financials, huh? Well, let me set you straight, Cuddy. Johnnie and me had our differences, but it was more the father-son competition thing. Two years out of school, and the boy could see exactly how the old man was 'mismanaging' the company. The same general contractor that rebuilt half of Chelsea for the Jews after that fire. And half of the Town here, once the new lady executives found out they could walk to the State Street skyscrapers and even walk home without getting yanked into an alley for twelve angry inches of black salami. So I told Johnnie, 'Look, you want to run things, start your own company.' And—give the devil his due—he goes down to Georgia and does just that."

"And did well, from what I've heard."

"And that word *did* is the important—no, what the fuck do they call it? Yeah, yeah, the operative word. Johnnie did fine for a couple of years during the boom when any bozo with a hammer in his hand and nails in his mouth could make a fortune. Then the boom goes bust, and he's gotta move on. And on. Well, pretty soon the lovely blond bride becomes a fucking palomino horse, and the boy realizes he's made more than a few mistakes I warned him against. So Johnnie comes back north with his tail between his legs, realizing he can learn from his old man while he earns enough to live on."

"But not enough for his family to live on, too."

"Christ on a crutch, Cuddy, you know how the courts work. The judge looks at a couple of financials and listens to a couple of lawyers looking to feast off the fucking corpse of the marriage, and before you know it, the poor husband's supposed to be supporting his wife and kids in the fucking Taj Mahal."

"What happened to all the money your son made down there?"

"What happened to it is Johnnie likes to drink. They tell you that over in South Lithuania?"

"Yes."

Looney seemed a little surprised. "They also tell you he hit a kid with his car when he was over the limit, both booze and speed?"

Jesus. "No."

"I didn't think so. Way my lawyer here tells me, Johnnie would have been better off, he killed the kid. No 'established earning power yet' or some fucking mumbo jumbo. Anyway, the kid's never gonna walk again, and Johnnie's insurance wasn't enough to cover the verdict. So that means everything he worked for is up in smoke. My son's gotta move back north, come on bended fucking knee to the old man."

"I assume he's got all the paperwork on this."

A shifty look. "Paperwork?"

"On the accident case."

"Beats me, I think the lawyers sealed it or something, so nobody can get at who agreed to pay what."

Convenient. "You realize your son hasn't even been to visit his children since they've been back?"

Looney stood bolt upright from his chair, fists on the desktop in front of him. "You realize that fucking shrew won't let him in her house?"

"What?"

"Grandma Vel-las-kus or however you pronounce it. She told Johnnie he don't pay the support, he don't get to see his kids. She's even called here, asking me— *me*—to send her money I don't have."

I closed my eyes, reminded of why I didn't do divorce cases. "Mr. Looney, there's talk your son has a gun."

"A gun? He did, it'd be pawned by now. I'm telling you, Cuddy, Johnnie doesn't have a pot of gold. Fuck, he doesn't have so much as a pot to piss in. The poor kid drives a ten-year-old pickup and eats day-old bread. He lost his watch and can't even afford to buy a new one, tell him what time to be at work."

"Meaning he's late this morning?"

"Meaning you and I are finished talking. I hope I saved us both some time, but you want to settle this another way, there's lots of empty alleys in the Town."

"I'm already looking forward to it."

Going out the front door of the building, I saw Spence standing by one blue pickup truck as another bounced hard into the side lot, jerking to a halt across two of the precious spaces. The man who came out the driver's side stumbled a little on the running board. When

Spence called him over, I got a pretty good look at the face. Replace the rug with natural hair, and you had Jake Looney at age thirty or so.

Which would make the man walking unsteadily toward Spence son Johnnie.

I decided to join them.

Spence was speaking low and quickly, based on how fast his lips were moving. Looney shook his head constantly, using his palms to push away at the other, older man.

Kind of awkwardly missing him, truth to tell.

As I drew within earshot, Spence pointed toward me, and Looney turned. His eyes were bleary, and the first words out of his mouth rolled a cloud of whiskey fumes into my face.

"The fuck you want?"

"Johnnie Looney?"

"I'm the one doing the asking here."

"Johnnie," said Spence, "be cool, man."

"Fuck you, Harry. I'm gonna settle this here and now."

Spence glanced from his face to mine and back again. "I don't think that'd be too good an idea, Johnnie."

Apparently Looney didn't like the tenor of Spence's advice, because he threw a roundhouse left at me. The punch took about an hour arriving, so I just sidestepped it. Junior's second effort was a straight right, with enough weight behind it to do some damage. But even at twice the hand speed Looney was showing, his son Michael could have blocked it. I just parried the punch with my own left palm, letting Junior follow through. Then, swiping my right foot at his right ankle, I unbalanced Looney enough to send him facedown toward the macadam.

He landed so heavily you could hear the air leave his lungs in a whumping rush.

Spence watched me—probably making sure I wasn't going to follow up my advantage—then knelt down next to Junior, grabbing him by the belt and lifting up and down slowly and smoothly. "Johnnie, you got to breathe, man. In deep and out, or you'll plain pass out."

It took a minute, but Looney finally managed to gain his feet in a four-count movement, thanks to some levitation help from Spence. After two steps, though, Junior shrugged off the other man's hand, choosing instead to stagger toward and eventually through the doors of his father's brick building.

Harry Spence watched the boss's son until he disappeared inside, then turned to me. "Talk with you a minute?"

"Johnnie, he got himself a significant drinking problem."

We were standing next to the poorly parked pickup, the words LOONEY CONSTRUCTION, INC. on the dinged and faded driver's door, some jokester having scratched out the *e* in the name.

Which actually captured Junior rather well, I thought.

Spence waited for me to say something. When I didn't, he lowered his own voice. "I'm in the program myself, so I seen a lot of Johnnies, up close and personal."

"How long you been sober?"

"Two years, eight months, twenty-nine days."

"What's the longest Junior's been on the wagon?"

I thought Spence might take offense at my nickname, but he just said, "Need a stopwatch with a good second hand, man."

"He usually get physical like that?"

"Not usually. But I been where he's at, so I can identify with the boy. You hear what I'm saying?"

"I think so."

"Back in my drinking time, I chased away a pretty fine wife, too. She up and took off with our three kids. I never did find out where to."

"Your point?"

Spence rubbed his chin. "Maybe you could see your way to cutting Johnnie a little slack here, account of he so fucked up right now."

"Not my call."

"Maybe you can, like, persuade the one whose call it be."

"Maybe, if I was convinced Junior was really dead broke."

Spence grinned, a little theatrically. "Man, what's past dead in the broke department? Johnnie, he don't got his own pot to pee in. He driving this old truck, eating—"

"—yesterday's bread."

Spence dropped the grin, his voice growing a burr. "Maybe you oughta forget about persuading anybody about this thing, man. Maybe you just oughta butt out, like Johnnie told me to do over there."

"Unfortunately, I'm not very good at doing what other people tell me to."

"Might want to learn." Harry Spence sized me up the way he had when we met at the building entrance. "Be seeing you."

My turn to watch somebody walk toward the front doors of Looney Construction, Inc.

"Claire, John Cuddy calling."

"Hey, Cuddy," came her voice from the other end of

the line. "What time next month do you need whatever it is you want?"

"Claire, your computer can't be that backed up with traces."

"No, it's not. But I am, and you may not believe this, Cuddy, since you don't know shit from Shinola when it comes to the Ethernet, but the computer can't work unless I enter stuff into it."

"I thought it was called the Internet."

"Only by the uninitiated."

"Claire?"

"What?"

"This is a case for a single mother with two little kids."

"She should have thought of that before letting the guy duke—"

"Her ex-husband's a boozer, quasi-violent, who hasn't paid child support for eight months now."

"Cuddy, you got to stop. My heart's already bleed—"

"And the woman's own mother, who took the family in, is dying of cancer herself."

A silence at the other end. "You wouldn't shit me about this, Cuddy."

"No."

"I mean, this isn't something you cribbed off *Queen for a Day* or—"

"My hand to God, Claire."

Another silence. "Your wife died of cancer, right?"

"Right," I said, as evenly as possible.

"My dad, too. Shitty way to go."

"It is that."

"Almost makes you nostalgic for the good old days, when people just dropped dead from heart attacks."

"Claire?"

"Now what?"

"I'm in kind of a time bind here."

A third silence, followed by a sigh like the air leaving Junior's lungs on the parking lot's macadam. "All right. What've you got?"

"Asset check. Start with Looney, John Jr."

"This the deadbeat dad?"

"Yes."

"Any AKAs?"

"Try Johnnie, double *n* and *ie* at the end."

"Should run it with double *n* and *y,* too."

"Claire, I trust your expertise like no other's."

"Asshole," came over the line, but behind it the sound of computer keys clacking.

"I'm not coming up with much, Cuddy . . . car registration on a—Christ, some ten-year-old clunker of a truck . . . rent checks to a realty trust in Charlestown . . . balance in the account ranges between low three figures and overdrawn."

Silence, except for the clacking of keys.

"Claire?"

"I'm trying, Cuddy, but I think we're in blood-from-a-stone territory."

"How about John senior, AKA Jake?"

"The deadbeat dad's own father?"

"Right. And Looney Construction, Inc., over in the Town as well."

"Wait one . . . I'm doing the corp first, on the— Christ. Great group of people you're giving me."

"What've you got?"

"Looney Construction's up to its limit in bonding capacity. Unless they finish a project and get the surety company to let them off the hook, John the elder won't be starting a new one before the millennium."

"Anything unusual in the corporate holdings?"

"Holdings? Let me check the secretary of . . . yeah. Yeah, here we go. Security interest filings on a backhoe, a few small trucks—Christ, John the elder seems

to do all his buying on credit, Cuddy. Even some gaso-
line generators are on the float."

"Not much owned outright, then?"

"His hard hat, maybe a screwdriver or two. And
worse on the guy personally."

"How do you mean?"

"I've got a back door into the Commonwealth's cor-
rections records. Seems your construction exec did
two stretches in a secure hotel with three squares a
day."

"Charges?"

"One fraud, one assault with a deadly."

Dalia Looney wasn't kidding about Senior being
scarier than Junior. "What about assets, Claire?"

"Showing a four-year-old car, checking balance between a thousand and two. Nothing like a gold mine or
paid-off saltbox on the Cape."

I thought about it. And about Harry Spence's protec-
tive attitude toward the boss's son despite the father's
overtly racist attitude toward the employee.

"Hey, Cuddy, you still drawing oxygen there?"

"Try Spence, Harry, or variations."

"Wait one more." Clacking, sighing, more clacking.
Then, "Whoa, would our man be African-American?"

"He would."

"Win the lottery, maybe?"

"Not that he mentioned."

"Well, Spence, Harold, has deposited twenty to
thirty large each month since August."

Bingo. Maybe. "Any indication of the source?"

"That'd be in the paper records, not the electronic.
And you'd need a court order for it, not that you
shouldn't for what I've already—"

"Claire, print out what you've got anyway. And if
you find anything else, call my answering service, leave
a message."

"On the printout, you finally join the twentieth century with a fax, or should I messenger it over?"

"Use the bicycle folks."

"Cuddy?"

"Yes, Claire?"

"What kind of gun you carry, a flintlock?"

"Steven Rothenberg speaking."

"Steve, about that receptionist . . ."

"You have something for me on Looney?"

"I mean, she's chewing gum when she answers your phone, the Muzak starts as soon as she picks up, and I don't think *Twisted Sister's Greatest Hits* is exactly the image you want to—"

"John, please. It's been a long morning already. Tell me if you've got something."

I told him.

Rothenberg said, "I knew I smelled money."

"Only we don't know where Harry Spence got it from."

"Has to be the Looneys."

"Agreed. The father painted the man as just affirmative-action window dressing, but Spence's loyalty to both of them seemed to run deeper than the bands of mere employment. However, there's still the problem of which Looney's money he received."

A pause before, "I'll file the enforcement action tomorrow, maybe seek an *ex parte* attachment of—"

"Steve?"

"Yes?"

"You need me for anything else?"

"Just that printout of the asset search."

"It's being messengered over to me, and I'll hand-carry it to you."

"John, thank you. From both me and my client."

I dropped the printout at Rothenberg's within half an hour of receiving it. Returning to my own office, I sat down thinking that, all in all, it'd been a pretty good day.

At least until 4:47 P.M.

I lifted my receiver on its third ring. "John Cuddy."

"Mr. Detective," the voice hushed. "You know who is this?"

"Mrs. Valec—Izabel?"

"Just so."

"What's the—"

"There is outside my house a car up the street."

"A car?"

"A little blue truck. What do you call them?"

"Pickups. Is anyone inside it?"

"I think yes. Then, when I look again, I think no."

"Izabel, where are Dalia and the children?"

"They are out, but they come back soon."

"Call nine-one-one, then get out of there, too."

"No," she said, still in the hushed voice, then louder. "No, he does not scare me from my own house."

"Izabel—"

"Please, you promise me you help us. Come, come quick."

"First call—"

"And please, bring your gun, yes."

With the crosstown traffic, it took me half an hour to reach the head of Valeckas's block in Southie. Leaving the Prelude, I could feel the butt of my Smith & Wesson Chief's Special ease off the right kidney area enough to save me massaging back there. The swirling winter wind whipped across my cheeks and nose as I closed the door and did a quick survey of the street. About half the parking spaces were filled, one by a blue pickup.

If there was lettering on the truck's door, I couldn't see it from where I was standing, even with the high stoop light from a nearby house shining on it.

Slowly, I moved down the sidewalk opposite the pickup. Drawing even with it, I caught the Looney Construction lettering, the *e* still scratched off.

Junior's truck.

Two minutes later I was knocking softly at the rear door of the Valeckas house, and ten seconds after that, Izabel opened it for me.

"Come in, quick, quick."

I slipped through the door. Valeckas was wearing an apron over heavy pants and a sweater, her husband's walking stick leaning against the wall. When she reached for the stick, Valeckas held it in two hands like a club rather than one hand like a cane.

"I think I hear something back here before you knock, so I take the walking stick of my Kazimieras off the wall."

"What did you hear, Izabel?"

"The sound of glass, like somebody break it."

"Dalia and the kids?"

"Still gone."

I nodded, then put my fingers to my lips. She nodded back.

Easing the Chief's Special from its holster, I held it tight to my right shoulder, muzzle toward the ceiling. I checked the stairway to the cellar first, hoping not to get my feet shot out from under me as I descended the steps. Oil burner and tank. Hot-water heater. Boxes that might have contained her family's things as they moved back north.

I checked behind everything Junior could have used as a hiding space. Zero.

Back upstairs, Valeckas was standing by the doorway like a sentry in a castle, the walking stick at port arms.

I leaned into her ear. "Rear room now."

She nodded again.

The room faced the small backyard and wasn't much more than a closet with a window. All the panes seemed intact, though, and nobody there, either.

Valeckas came even with me.

I said, "Rest of this floor first, then upstairs."

A third nod.

There were three more doors off the kitchen. One was the swinging door to her dining room, the second probably the pantry, the third her half bath. The latter two were both closed, and each was at right angles to the other on different, short walls forming a corner.

Meaning no way to open both at once while covering each.

I pointed to the door on my right, and Valeckas moved against it. As I opened the one in front of me, a light came on overhead, surprising me and a pair of cockroaches, intent on some breakfast cereal.

A worse surprise was the sound of the other door opening, Valeckas yelping in pain.

But by the time I turned, the stars were already rising across the back of my head, and I felt my left wrist turn awfully funny as I landed heavily on it.

"He wakes."

I didn't recognize the voice, though I had the feeling

my eyes had vaguely registered her face. I concentrated on keeping both lids open at once, then focused on the woman standing next to my bed.

She was all in white, a name tag on her left breast pocket under some pens and little medical tools. I couldn't read the tag from where I was lying, and I couldn't even think about getting up.

She said, "I thought it might be a concussion, so we held you overnight. The wrist is just sprained."

I let my eyes loll over and down, seeing a soft cast on my left forearm all the way to the hand. "Peachy."

The woman reached into the name tag pocket. "However, I'm afraid your watch wasn't so lucky."

As she laid it gently on my night table, I could see the crystal cover was broken.

"Oh, and you have a visitor. If you're up to seeing him."

"Let me guess," I said. "He draws his salary from the city and he's smiling."

"Chuckling, I'd call it, but still not a bad prediction. Maybe you should play the lottery this week."

"I've the feeling I already have."

"Okay, Cuddy, how many fingers am I holding up?"

Just the middle one. "Not funny, Lieutenant."

He laughed a little anyway, pulling over a visitor's chair. Robert Murphy, appointed to Homicide in the long ago when a city councilor mistook surname for race, was around six feet tall and carried twenty more pounds of rumpled flesh than either his wife or the department's doctors preferred. His tie was knotted neatly, the fashionable pattern one of those I can't keep track of. A collar stay held the points of his shirt in formation, a small pad and gold pen contrasting against the black hands holding them.

Murphy's eyes closed to little slits in a Buddha-like face. "Lucky for you that Grandma was riding shotgun."

"I don't remember anything after hearing the bathroom door open."

"How's about you fill me in on what happened before that?"

I went through it for him, from the time I first spoke with Steve Rothenberg in his office two days earlier.

Murphy said, "Must be close to record time for you, Cuddy. Most folks don't decide to kill you till after a week or so."

"What went down after I did?"

"There's only one version of that, but I'll give it to you anyway. Mrs. . . . just a second . . . yeah, Vel-*las*-kus. Mrs. Valeckas says that as you opened that pantry door, this Johnnie Looney banged through the half-bath one, knocking her over. She assumes he hit you because when she looked up, Looney was standing over you, then started yelling at her for where his kids were."

"First time he'd showed any interest in them for a while, financially or personally."

"Be that as it may, Looney rampages through the first floor, then Grandma hears him climbing the stairs. She told me she wasn't too worried then, account of she knew her family wasn't home yet. So Mrs. Valeckas moves over to you, see if you're okay. She sees you're still breathing, then notices the butt of your gun sticking out from under your right arm."

I thought, Looney didn't take it?

Murphy flipped a page in his pad. "Anyway, Mrs. Valeckas figures she'd better put the gun in her apron, which she does. And that's when ex-son-in-law comes stomping down the stairs and back into the kitchen, still demanding to know where his kids are. Grandma said she could smell liquor on his breath."

"You confirm that?"

Murphy looked at me, then flipped another page. "Yeah. One of my team talked to a Spence, Harold, who works at the father's construction company."

"We've met."

"Which?"

"Both Spence and Looney senior."

"Anyway, Spence says Looney junior gets a telephone call. Apparently your Johnnie's half in the bag already, but he tells Spence there's some emergency and takes off for parts unknown."

"Southie."

Murphy nodded. "Another guy on my team talked to a bartender two blocks over from the Valeckas house. Says Looney came in, stayed about an hour while tossing down four whiskeys, straight up. Man must've had an aversion to ice and water, I guess. Oh yeah, and he kept asking the bartender what time it was."

"What time?"

"Yeah. Seems our construction worker didn't wear a watch."

I thought back to what his father had said about his son's losing the watch and not being able to afford a new one.

Murphy went back a page. "So where . . . right, right. Looney's in Grandma's kitchen with booze on his breath, telling her she doesn't come up with where the kids are, he's gonna put bullets in you till she does."

"And Valeckas stonewalls him."

"Tough little lady. Well, Looney turns and aims at you—one of your legs, she thought, but wasn't too sure, since she was more concerned with getting your piece out of her apron. Grandma yells at him to stop, and he swings around, his gun no more than two feet from her in that kitchen. Looney shoots once, and Mrs. Valeckas empties your Chief's Special into him. By the way, the techies recovered only four rounds at the scene."

"That's all I load, keep the chamber under the hammer empty."

"Old-fashioned, with the new half-cock safety."

Back to the point. "Lieutenant, all Looney's wounds were through and through?"

"That range? You bet. Left most of his vitals sliding down Grandma's walls in the corner there."

"And how is she?"

"Looney's slug took her just below the rib cage. Mrs. Valeckas is in a room down the hall and around the corner, though she's not in much better shape than him."

"Looney made it?"

"Dead at the scene, dead in the ambulance, dead on arrival." Murphy closed his pad. "In fact, you and Grandma were real lucky about the timing yourselves."

"I don't get you."

"By six, enough of the traffic's gone so your ride to the hospital got here in less than ten minutes, door to door."

"Six o'clock."

"Yeah. Of course, the Castle Law applies no matter what time of day, though I've always thought that once it's dark out, the homeowner should get even more benefit of the doubt." The lieutenant rose from his chair. "You got anything else to add?"

"Let me sleep on it," I said, but as soon as Robert Murphy left my room, I reached over to the nightstand.

Shit.

I closed my eyes, maybe for an hour. Or at least until I was pretty sure I'd worked things out as best I could on my own. Then I creaked out of bed and into the shirt and pants somebody had hung in my closet.

She was only seven rooms away from mine.

I looked through the little diamond window in her door. I could see Izabel Valeckas lying in bed, apparently zonked. Her daughter perched on a chair by the side of it, holding her mother's left hand in both of hers.

I didn't bother to knock.

Dalia Looney spun around, nearly dislodging the braid of tubes running into the older woman's arms and up her nose.

I said, "Sorry if I scared you."

Looney took a breath, the sound almost as ragged as her mother's was raspy. "I thought . . . I thought it was Jake, coming to take revenge on us."

"You ask for a policeman outside the door?"

"Yes, but that Lieutenant Murphy said he couldn't spare one for you and one for her, so he's just got an officer down in the lobby with a photo of Jake." Looney paused. "I guess they had some mug shots of him?"

"I guess they might have." I inclined my head toward Valeckas. "How's your mom doing?"

"She's trying, trying so hard, but I . . . I . . ." The tears started coming, more rapidly and harshly than in the parlor of the Valeckas house two days before.

I said, "We need to talk, Dalia."

She cupped her hands, using the heels to dam some of the tears. "About what?"

"I think maybe we talk first, yes."

Both of us looked toward the bed.

Izabel Valeckas, eyes now open, said, "Dalia, you will not sleep, go to get some coffee, so at least you stay awake better."

"Mama, I—"

"Go, my *dukra*. Mr. Detective and me are fine to-gether."

When Looney glanced in my direction, I said, "It might be best."

Once her daughter had closed the door behind her, Valeckas pointed shakily toward the empty chair. "Come, sit with me."

I went over, using my right hand to lower myself into the chair.

"That crazy man," she said, "he break your arm, too?"

"My wrist got sprained when I fell."

What passed for a nod from the pillowed head. "He try to shoot you, and me, too."

"And you shot him, to save both of us."

"Just so."

"No, Izabel."

The eyes blinked, her features contorting under the facial tubes. "What you say?"

"You set Johnnie Looney up to be killed."

The eyes closed. "Mr. Detective, you are crazy man, too."

"I think I've got most of it worked out, but feel free to correct me if I botch something. Your daughter comes back to live with you, because her husband has divorced her and isn't paying child support anymore for their children. Problem is, Johnnie's a drinker, which probably doesn't help him hold a steady job, and definitely doesn't help him when he hits a child down south while under the influence and speeding to boot. Whatever money Johnnie did accumulate went toward satisfying the accident verdict."

"He lie about that."

I thought back to my first talk with Valeckas in her kitchen. "So, you did know Johnnie had the accident."

A small, grudging smile. "You take advantage of me, a poor woman, shot in her own—"

"Fortunately, though, you'd kept up the premiums on insurance, especially health policies for Dalia and the kids, if not yourself. Oh, and that over-the-rainbow possibility of Johnnie dying young."

"What is 'over-the-rainbow'?"

"Watch *The Wizard of Oz* next time it's on TV. Only problem is, while Johnnie Looney's back up here and therefore within reach, he isn't coming around to see his children, and you're a little too sick to go hunting for him in a manner that'd let you get away with killing him."

"I am too sick for listening to you."

"So you need to set a trap. You convince your daughter to go to a softhearted lawyer, who in turn brings in a softheaded private eye. Nobody tells either of us about Johnnie's accident trouble down south. But you know from your daughter that Looney senior hasn't always been on the up-and-up regarding his bookkeeping. So you maneuver me to go stir things up over in Charlestown, riling them while diverting me from your real plan."

"I got no plan."

"You didn't just find those bullets when you helped your daughter unpack. Drunks often misplace things, like watches, for example. Well, Johnnie left the bullets and the gun together—probably forgetting where—and you found both."

"Why do I want his gun?"

"Because the police might not believe someone your size, weakened from cancer, could wrest a weapon away from a man who worked construction. A much better version would be Johnnie having his gun, and you having mine."

A deep sigh, and the grudging smile was back. "Very good, Mr. Detective. Very good."

"I know how you got me to come to your house last night. How did you lure Johnnie to your block and send him to sit in that bar?"

The smile stayed put. "Johnnie like to drink, and the bar have liquor."

"But getting him to Southie in the first place?"

"My Dalia is in the bathroom, making ready to take Michael to doctor for his cough. I call to Johnnie at his father's business. Michael is coughing bad then, and I say on the phone, 'Your son is very sick, you can hear him, yes.' And Johnnie say Dalia should take him to doctor. And I say she cannot, he must come because I am scare for my *anukas*. And Johnnie finally say he will come."

"And when he did arrive?"

"Dalia and Michael and Veronica, they are all at doctor. I tell Johnnie, 'Go off to bar, come back in one hour.' I see him at his truck—to get money, maybe— then walk for the bar."

"Which is when you called me."

"Just so." A different smile now, that one of triumph Valeckas first showed me at her kitchen table. "I put the fear in my voice, I hear same in you. Then I get the walking stick of my Kazimieras and wait for you to come."

"In order to lead me around the kitchen. Then you faked the bathroom door hitting you and rapped me with the stick."

"I would use the gun, but I think maybe I cannot hit you hard enough with my one arm only."

"And when Johnnie came back from the bar, you let him in."

"I tell him everyone is in kitchen. When we get there, he see you, he bend down. I yell at him, Johnnie turn around, and I shoot him as many time as you have bullets in your gun. When he is down on the floor, too, I kneel on my legs beside him, and I put the gun I find in my *dukra*'s pack box in his hand. I hold my arm away from my body, and I point the front of the gun at my side. I push on Johnnie's finger to shoot me once." The smile of triumph again. "It does not hurt so much as I think before. Then I call the police for ambulance to take us to here."

"You thought of everything, Izabel."

"Just so."

"Maybe not quite."

Valeckas dropped the smile. "What you mean now?"

"When Johnnie hit me, he 'forgot' to take my gun?"

"He is drinker, and drunk men not think so good."

A gambit. "When Johnnie got the phone call from you, he told one of his co-workers you'd called him."

"It is like I say. Johnnie is drunk man. He lie to worker, or worker lie to you." The smile came back. "Or maybe even you lie to me, Mr. Detective, yes."

"This is no lie, Izabel. The police can trace through the phone company that a call was made to Looney Construction from your phone at that exact time."

"So? I call to the boss father, ask him for money to feed his grandchildren. I do this several time before already. But yesterday, I get his crazy-man son, who come after me in my own house."

"Speaking of time, you called my office at four-forty-seven."

"If the phone company will say that, too."

I took out my ruined watch, dangling it by the strap in front of her eyes. "This broke when I hit the floor in your kitchen, after you hit me. The hands are frozen at five-twenty-three."

Valeckas blinked at the watch face.

I said, "It shows I was down and out over half an hour

before you called the police about Johnnie supposedly hitting me, then threatening to kill the two of us."

"I already tell police Johnnie threaten to kill only you. This I remember. And your watch?" She managed to sniff derisively, even with the tube up her nose. "It is cheap and old. Maybe it stop before six o'clock yesterday for many reasons."

I stood up. "You think you have all the answers, Izabel, and you might be good enough to pull it off. But I'm going to try and stop you."

"The police?"

"Yes."

"They talk to my doctor, they do not bother."

I stared at her.

"My doctor, he say to me that the bullet through my side go too close to the liver, already weak from my cancer. I would not live to see the trial you want for me."

"Then I'll turn to the insurance company that wrote the policy on Johnnie's life."

A troubled look now. "So they do not pay my Dalia the money?"

"That's right."

"For what purpose, Mr. Detective? Johnnie is dead, I will be dead, too. Together we leave a legacy to my *dukra* and her children, the money to have a real chance at life in this country."

"Because you killed your former son-in-law."

The glow rekindled in her eyes. "You promise to help us. In my kitchen, the first time you come two days ago. You call to insurance company with these little things you say, maybe you look very bad to the other detectives."

I stared down at her. Valeckas might not know chapter and verse, but she was as wise as anybody I'd ever dealt with.

Or been up against.

I rose and turned to leave the room.

"So, Mr. Detective, you come to my funeral, yes."

I yanked on the door handle. "Don't wait for me."

Izabel Valeckas said, "I know these are your words before they come out your mouth."

Without looking back, I could picture the smile of triumph on the grandmother's lips.

JULIE SMITH *has been nominated for numerous awards and won the Edgar Allan Poe Award for her richly textured Police Detective Skip Langdon series, set in New Orleans. Her earlier Paul Anderson series deservedly retains its cult followings. In "Fresh Paint," a divorced artist finds an exceptional way to paint her lying ex-husband into the tightest possible corner.*

FRESH PAINT

/

by Julie Smith

Officer, would you like some coffee? I made some for the ladies and gentlemen of the press, but they too excited to have any—gettin' they pictures and all. Wonder who call the po-lice on me? Maybe it wasn't them atall. Coulda been Tomika, 'cross the way—she always did have a thing for Cleon.

Now, don't you worry 'bout Cleon; he be all right. Come on, let me get you some coffee, then we talk about it. What? You gon' let him loose now? Oh, you want me to. Uh-uh. You take the key—*I'm* not lettin' 'im loose. He can stay handcuffed to that bed the rest of his miserable life as far as I'm concerned. He a piece of art himself now. Got videos, got photographs; only thing I regret is you ain't gon' give me time to paint him.

Oh, yeah, *'course* I already painted him. I mean, next I want to paint the bed, with him lyin' in it painted up like he is. That'd make a right good picture, don't ya think? Where's that art critic? Mr. Turkelson? Hey, Mr. Turkelson—what you think of that one? Look authentic to ya? You gon' take back what ya said in court?

'Scuse me, Officer, I got a laughing fit comin' on. Every time I look at that picture, I get a fit of the giggles. Would somebody give me a handkerchief, please? 'Scuse me, I just can't seem to stop.

All right.

All right, Officer. I know it must be hard on you, bein' the odd one out like this. But you don't need to get so upset about it. Say, you one o' those new out-o'-town recruits they gettin'? 'Cause otherwise you mighta heard of Cleon and Orietta Banks. We famous. And *he* rich.

In fact—oh, me, I got another laughin' fit comin' on—in fact, if you went lookin' in your po-lice computer, you'd see Cleon famous in there, too. Oh, yeah. Car theft, strong-arm robbery, armed robbery, assault, bank robbery—least some of those. Possession of this, sale of that, burglary, shopliftin'—I know he did 'em all, just not sure which ones they got him for.

What's that? Has he done time? Ohhh, yeah. Forgive me for laughin' again, Officer. Oh, yeah, Cleon's done time. Cleon's done time big time. See, tha's part of his gig. He a outlaw. If he wasn't a outlaw, he be just another dude can't draw worth a damn, but he a *outlaw*. Young girls put up with that stuff.

Can't say they like it; won't say that. But Cleon and me had a baby together twenty-five years ago—I wasn't but seventeen at the time. Cleon, he was twenty-two if I remember right. I thought I was queen of the Magnolia Project. Had myself such a good-lookin' man, already grown-up and out of high school. He was doin' good, too. Had a job and everything. Worked at a warehouse. He tol' me, "Ori, the folks at this place are so dumb I wouldn't lower myself to work with 'em if I didn't know what was gon' happen—they gon' make me a supervisor soon. I'm gon' do real good and I'm always gon' be there for Shawana." Shawana—that's our daughter. And you know what? He didn't lie. I mean, he didn't *quite* lie. He always been there for Shawana. Whenever he out of jail.

Well, in a kind of a way he has.

I b'lieve he was right, though—he probably *was* smarter than the folks at that warehouse. Ain't nothin' dumb about Cleon—he just like a cat. Know how to get somebody to take care of him, no matter how bad he scratch up the furniture. He probably wasn't lyin' about his future, either—probably *woulda* been a supervisor, brains had anything to do with it. But Cleon—just like he know how to get around people (specially me)—he know how to mess up. Did in those days, anyway. Can't afford to no more—he got two convictions; can't get another one. Mmm mmm, no sir. He ain' gon' go back to Angola for the rest of his life—had to figure out somethin' else.

How 'bout a doughnut to go with that coffee, Officer? Cleon all right. He gon' sleep at least another half hour, maybe forty-five minutes. I *know* the man. I got some nice muffins here—won't you have one?

What's that? Oh, yeah, the warehouse. Well, he worked at some place sell TVs and things—Circuit City, Campo, some kind of thing like that. I don't know if they didn't have guards or what. And I *really* don't know how he think he could get away with it; all I know is the rest of the way Cleon think. He think what's yours is his, you understand me? So Cleon just take home whatever look good to him—run a little re-sale business, right out of his house.

What's that, Officer? Maybe I did say he was a little bit smart—mostly I said he *say* he smart. Well, you right. He got caught. 'Course he got caught.

Got caught, got convicted, went to jail.

He get out of jail, he start doin' drugs. Smokin' 'em, snortin' 'em, sellin' 'em, everything. All of a sudden, Cleon the drug *king*. Well, maybe he do drugs before, but never like this. I wouldn't have nothin' to do with him. Oh, and by this time, I got another child with him. Baby boy name Kwayne.

What you mean, why was I still seein' him? I wasn't, then. Got pregnant just about the time he got caught. Had the baby while he was in jail, and wouldn't let him nowhere 'round me once he start doin' all them drugs. My mama didn't drop me from no turnip truck.

Matter of fact, I wouldn't even let him see his own baby boy. But Cleon, he a good father. No, Officer, really. He love his babies. And he hate to see us so poor. I'm sorry to say I was on welfare at the time, and you know how welfare is. Can't hardly get off it, 'cause it's so hard to get a job that pays enough to cover ya child care. And can't make much money and keep ya benefits. So all I had at the time were little cleanin' jobs— two or three little half-day things. We havin' a hard time, Shawana and me and Kwayne.

So you know what Cleon do? I give him credit for this, give him all the credit in the world. He clean up for a while there. He get off drugs—go to some neighborhood detox place—but he always say, "Ori, I ain't no addict, just don't have the addictive personality, I can do drugs if I want, I just don't want to right now. Want to get my family back."

My family! he say. We weren't no family, Officer— at the best of times, Cleon, he come 'round once, twice a week. Tha's the kind of family it was. But this time he impress me. He clean up, he get a job, and we get married.

We had a real nice time there for a while. Cleon, he a good father. Even go to church on Sunday. Work hard, come home at night—everything copacetic. Had some job in a hospital, didn't really mean much, but it was all right. It was just fine till he got fired.

What's that? No, it wasn't for stealing drugs. Officially, he was just laid off, but you know what it really was? Somebody's kid needed that job. Political thing, you know what I mean? Well, everything still mighta been all right if he'd a just gone out and got another job. Which he could have. No, he didn't really have no skills, but there lots of jobs for people who show up on time—that's all you gotta do, just show up. 'Stead, he let those fool friends of his talk him into robbin' a bank.

He say he gon' *get* a job, he just need the money to tide us over. Well, in a way it make sense—we didn't have enough money to last till he got a paycheck. Still, the landlord probably wasn't gon' throw us out just 'cause we two weeks late on the rent. 'Course it would-n'ta been the first time, and he'd threatened and every-thing. But my mama woulda taken us in, maybe. Just no need to go rob a bank. No need in the world.

'Scuse me, Officer? Yeah. Sure did. Got convicted again. Went to Angola again. Two-time loser, tha's what you call that, ain't it, Officer?

'Cept this time Cleon come out a winner.

He learn a skill in prison. Well, really he kind of teach it to himself. But he had help; I'm not sayin' he didn't have help. He had a inmate friend called Blind Joey who show him a whole new way to be. Now Blind Joey couldn't see his hand in front of his face, but he could paint. I gotta stop and laugh a little here. Least, there was this New Orleans gallery thought he was the Michelangelo of the penal system. He'd paint these little stick figure scenes, folks out in the fields, or maybe standin' around on the porch of a sto'—you ever see that kind of picture? Yeah, you right—everybody has.

Well, Blind Joey's was more innerestin' than most because he couldn't see his paints, so you never knew what color anything was gon' be, and also, he couldn't see what he already painted, so things got jumbled up a little. Yeah, go ahead and laugh. Dahveed—he the gallery owner—I'm sure he prob'ly laugh all the way to the bank. But I gotta give it to him—those ol' jumbled-up, funny-colored pictures come out pretty good. They got they own style, you know what I mean? Blind Joey ain't paintin' no more, though—somebody stab him seven, eight years ago—jealous, I guess.

'Course Dahveed love that—couldn't be better for business. He handle what they call outsider artists. You unnerstand what that is? It's kind of self-explanatory, ain't it? Well, for outsiders, you can't hardly beat outlaws, officer. Yeah, I see you makin' that face. You think you feelin' sick now, I'm 'bout to *really* turn your stomach. You know some of the most famous murderers behind bars is artists now? Anybody can do it. Or mos' anybody. And it pays so good it's almost like robbin' a bank. I guess tha's one of the main things attracted Cleon—that and the fact he couldn't afford no more mess-ups.

While he and Blind Joey both at Angola, he ax Blind Joey some things, like what kind of paint to use and how to mix it up—few little things like that. And then he just dig in and paint.

What, Officer? I hear ya. I *know* how bad that make ya feel, out tryin' to make a livin', and this outlaw get somethin' for nothin' just 'cause he *is* a outlaw. No, it ain't right. I agree with you on that one.

It might not'a been right, but all the same I was overjoyed. I was the man's *wife*, after all. It wasn't dangerous and it was legal. Only thing was, it wasn't exactly lucrative. Somebody like Blind Joey, now, he made pots o' money. But Cleon—well, frankly, Cleon wasn't all that good. He a little too—I know this gon' sound funny, considerin' we talkin' 'bout a bank robber here, but Cleon just a little too timid. No, I'm tellin' you the truth—what it was, he didn't have the confidence of his own convictions. Or maybe he just didn't have no convictions; wouldn't be surprised. To my mind, he draw everything too little—kinda constipated-lookin', scared to get up there and be what it is. Then he be stuck with a great big sky, and he fill it in with flyin' crosses, kind of like polka dots. I ax him once why he put 'em there and he say he don't know what *else* to put there, and people like Jesus, so he thought he'd try him some crosses. Can you credit that, Officer? That was the best answer he could come up with.

No, them crosses didn't have wings. They was more like floatin' than flyin', maybe, just kind of hangin' there in the part of the canvas that wasn't filled in.

Well, I tell him that and he say, "You think you can do better, bitch?" Just like that. Tha's the way my husband talk to me.

I jus' want to make peace in the family, so I say, "You know what I think's real good? I like that little dancin' man there."

The picture we was lookin' at was a man playin' a piano and some people dancin', only they mostly look like they got flagpoles up they butts. 'Scuse me, Officer, but how would *you* say it? There was this one man, though, look like he was havin' fun. So I say to Cleon, "Why don't you do just this one man? Make him real big and don't have nothin' much else in the picture."

And Cleon say, "Shut up, Ori, you don't know what you talkin' about."

So I show him. I go ahead and I paint it. I paint it

kinda like he paint it and kinda different. I make the man dance crazier; crazier and wilder with his hair flyin' all around. And Cleon, he don't say nothin'. But then, next day, I get me another idea; I want to put a moon over the dancin' man's head. But I can't find the picture.

I ax him where my picture is and he say he don't know. But then I notice all of a sudden he doin' what I said. He tryin' to make all his people bigger, tryin' to fill up the canvas with 'em, really make 'em stick out. But somehow—now there ain't nothin' wrong with this, it's just the way Cleon paint—somehow they don't look right. It just ain't Cleon style, tha's all. His style be makin' a whole lot of little figures, look like they 'mos lost on the canvas.

Now, I go to church reg'lar and I can certainly open up my heart when I know I been wrong. So I say, "Cleon, I'm real sorry for what I said. You was right all along. I shouldn'ta messed with what you tryin' to do. You tol' me I didn't know what I was talkin' about and it was true."

He say, "No, Ori. No, I think you got somethin' there. I just got to get the hang of it, tha's all. How 'bout you do me another one, maybe another couple, so I can study 'em."

Now in all these years of marriage, I could probably count on the fingers of one hand the number of times Cleon concede me a point. I shoulda realize somethin' was fishy. But you know what? I really did enjoy paintin' that picture—it was somethin' I just kind of knew I could do and sure enough I could. So when Cleon say make him a couple more, I look forward to it. I wait till the chirren off at school and I turn on WWOZ and I sit down to paint and I think, "Now what am I gon' paint?" Well, they playin' a Billie Holiday song on the radio and I think, "Yeah! I'm gon' paint

Billie Holiday. I'm gon' make her real beautiful, more than she really was, because she deserves it, an' then I'm gon' put a gardenia in her hair."

So I make me a midnight blue background, 'cause Billie the blues queen, and then I paint me a great big *beautiful* picture of her. She wearin' a kind of wine-color dress, with red tones in her skin, and she got a gardenia that's not really white, but maybe kinda yellow and kind of gold in certain places. Beautiful. Just beautiful.

The whole picture about two feet wide, maybe three feet tall—different shape from what Cleon paint. See, he like horizontal shapes—that way he can get in all them little bitty figures, and he don't have that much sky to fill in with flyin' crosses.

Well, Billie never look so good. She got everything but an audience. So, know what I did? I put in that little dancin' man—same one I made big that I kinda lost track of.

By this time, I was feelin' so pleased with myself I start to get ideas. I think, what about if I paint African-American musicians? (I was still listenin' to WWOZ.) So I thought maybe some old-timey ones—like Robert Johnson, with that ol' derby hat—and then I could do livin', breathin' ones, nothin' says I couldn't. What about if I just got out a old CD cover with a picture of Aaron Neville on it and paint Aaron himself? Hey, how 'bout Fats Domino? Ernie K-Doe? These gentlemen not gettin' any younger. Could do with some recognition, maybe. Then I really get grandiose. I think, what if I paint Fats Domino from a photograph and then maybe photograph the paintin' and send it to him? Maybe he buy it. See what happen to me, Officer? One mornin' paintin' one picture and already I got big ideas.

Fantasies, really. I didn't really b'lieve none of that—I was just havin' fun. Well, I did paint Robert

Johnson and I see he need something, just like Billie. So I give him the dancin' man for a audience as well, and about then Cleon come home. I say, "What you think?" And he say, "Tha's pretty interestin', Ori. Kinda childlike, doesn't show much technique, but I b'lieve I'm gon' think on it some."

Next day, the chirren be off to school, Cleon out somewhere chewin' the fat with his friends, and I go in the garage, which Cleon use for a studio in those days. I go out there, but I don't see my pictures.

Humph, I think; that's pretty strange. But I don't really care, because I want to do Fats. So I do him, and this time I put a bit more care into it, take my time a little—yesterday I was in a big hurry because Cleon ax me to do a couple. I realize now I was afraid I wouldn't get 'em done. So I do Fats real careful—just a *beautiful* picture of Fats, but he don't look right without the Dancin' Man, so I put him in the corner. And then Cleon come home and he so happy I think he even more loaded than usual. "Orietta! Honey, we done struck gold," he say, and he come up behind me, put his arms around me and near about make me mess up my beautiful picture.

But I couldn't get mad if we struck gold, so I turn around, happy as a new bride, and I say, "What is it, Cleon, honey? You have a good day at the track?"

And he say, "Lot better than that, Miz Banks. Our ship has come sailin' right into the harbor. You know that first picture you did? The Dancin' Man? Dahveed sold it for a thousand dollars! So I took him the other two pictures and he say he can get even more for 'em—maybe twice as much, he say."

Well, I'm just starin' at him, my mouth open, my eyes big as saucers, and he say, "Orietta, we really on to somethin' here. That new paintin' style of ours gon' take me a long way. Yessir! Dahveed say I'm gon' be rich and famous—say I've just made a artistic breakthrough."

Yeah, Officer, you notice that, too? I never was *that* good at grammar, but I know the first person singular when I hear it. So naturally I say what has to be said and Cleon get mad. He say, "Woman, don't ruin this for us! I'm the one got the name; not you. Dahveed can't say Orietta Banks paint those pictures—whoever heard of Orietta Banks? Also, you a woman. You see the problem there? You just name me a famous woman artist. Was Michelangelo a woman? Leonardo da Vinci? Go ahead. Name one."

I shoulda name Clementine Hunter, but he sneak up on me. All I can say is, "Famous? You gon' be famous, Cleon?"

"And rich," he say.

Well, yeah, Officer, I do see what happen to my pronoun, but he had me. He tell me Dahveed don't handle no women artists, he'd laugh me right out of there if I come in and say I done those pictures. So I just shut up about it.

And you know what? Everything Cleon predicted come to pass. Cleon got famous and we got rich. Well, yeah—you mentioned you never heard of us. Well, Officer, with all due respect, are there that many artists you can name? You know 'bout a man put a little blue dog in all his pictures? No? Well, he even more famous than Cleon—come to think of it, probably got the dog idea from us, 'cause after that I put the dancin' man in every picture I ever paint. For luck.

And oooeeee—did we have it. Everybody buy those pictures. What's that? Yep, white folks did. And black folks! Officer, I can tell you in all modesty that there is hardly any African-American celebrity who doesn't have a Cleon Banks—and there's part of the problem right there.

I'll get to that part in a minute, but right now I want you to understand the point I'm tryin' to make with you. Maybe you aren't real up on the art world, but if you went to Cleon's house in Eastover, you'd see how successful he is. I mean, you wouldn't think so from this place of mine, but now maybe you gettin' some inkling what this whole show's about.

What's that—you got a cousin in Eastover? Mighty fine neighborhood, ain't it? And I know what you thinkin'—you thinkin' once we started makin' it, my life musta been real sweet. Uh-huh. I knew you was thinkin' that.

Well, it mighta been; it coulda been. And up to a point it really was. Only problem was Cleon. The man drinks, Officer, honey.

Oh. Oh, I see. I'm sorry, Officer, I meant no disrespect. I just thought, since you a woman, too, you might understand a man who gets a snootful and then get too big for his britches. Well, now, come to think of it, I take that back. Cleon too big for his britches the minute he wake up to the minute he go to bed—or more likely, pass out drunk. The minute Cleon get a one-man show and start gettin' reviewed by the *Times-Picayune,* he decide he a celebrity and he like that *fine.* He go out every night with his no-account friends and he argue about art and politics and he get interviewed by magazines, and all of a sudden he look around and notice he got so many women after him, ain' no way he can get aroun' to 'em all.

Tha's Cleon. Me, I stay home and paint. Now, seems like he got the better part of the bargain, but mostly I like my life and Cleon don't like his. Because he know he livin' a lie. So the more I work and enjoy my work, the more he got to put me down.

Meanwhile, he gettin' so famous, all kind of celebrities start wantin' him to paint they portraits. He make the appointments, go out to lunch and dinner with 'em,

take me along to "take notes" while he do his "prelimi-
nary sketches," while really I be the one makin' the
sketches.

You'd think that'd be humiliatin' enough, but he got
to bring women around. He start doin' that and I get
mad just like I'm s'posed to and finally he start havin' a
thing with Sondra Bartell. Yes ma'am, *that* Sondra
Bartell. Maybe the best vocalist this country has ever
produced since Billie Holiday herself. I'll tell you, I
was mighty thrilled to do that job. Then, Cleon break
my heart. Tha's right—he had women before, and lots
of 'em. But he didn't have no hot love affair right in
front of my eyes with maybe the number one person I
admire in this world.

He really want to make me feel bad about it, so he
tell her he gon' need several sketchin' sessions and he
make me go with him, watch her come love on him just
like I wasn't there. Come put her arms aroun' his neck
and look at his little first-grade drawings, pretend like
she think they good; then he kiss her, nuzzle her neck,
and me just sittin' there.

Did she know I was his wife? Why, yes, Officer, she
did, and she just didn't care. Well, you right, Officer. I
shouldn'ta put up with it. I shoulda just walk on out of
there.

And the first time it happen we had a big old scene
afterward, end with Cleon sayin' how much he love
me, I'm the only woman he really want, and then gettin' all romantic—tryin' to, anyway. But he get too
drunk and fall asleep before he get around to anything.
Ha! Jus' like always.

Second time it happen, I do walk out. Walk right
over to my lawyer's office and say I want to file for divorce. I don't need this shit—we got community property laws in this state; with only half what I made

paintin' pictures over the years I figure I can be a wealthy woman. Don't *need* no Cleon Banks, right, Officer? Wrong.

What I didn't know is Cleon went and "invested" the money. Invested in what, I don't know. Wine, women and song, maybe.

No, I oughta be fair. Gave some to his brother for his plumbin' business—brother's doin' fine now, thank you. Then some other friend start up a restaurant—you know how many restaurants succeed and how many fail? Tha's right—and this one in the "fail" category. Anyway, buncha things like that. So we got no bank account.

Well, still no problem. What we do have is a whole basement full o' pictures ain't been sold yet—probably half a million dollars down there; maybe more. But meanwhile, I moved out to this little place, and Cleon got control of the basement.

Tha's right, Officer. Put your head on the table and cover your ears. 'Cause you *know* what's comin' next. Suddenly, those pictures can't be found.

What's that? Well, *'course* I testify that I'm the one paint the pictures. And Cleon, he testify that I already lie about the pictures in the basement, I'm crazy and always have been, I'm the one who drink, and I'm the one havin' affairs. You name it, he say it.

So my lawyer say he gon' prove I'm the real artist; we gon' have a paintin' contest right there in court. I'm gon' paint a dancin' man picture and Cleon gon' paint one and then we gon' get a art critic to express his opinion right in front of the judge.

Well, the judge won't go for it. Cleon lawyer call it a frivolous claim and the judge go for that instead. No, the judge wasn't white. Funny question for you to ask—you white as rice yourself. I b'lieve if the judge *had* been white, I'd'a had a better chance. This man *like* Cleon. They two of a kind; got the two biggest dicks in town. That judge didn't have *no* use for me; none atall. Cleon his main man.

So we divide up all the property in sight which, at this point, consists of nothin' but the house. And the house, because of certain business deals Cleon didn't bother to tell me about, turns out to have a third mortgage on it.

That leave me with about enough money to pay my lawyer, and Cleon with half a million dollars in paintings which he can now claim he producin' right along. Maybe he's even gon' say he cuttin' down his production so they go up in value. But then he's *s'posed* to give me spousal support, so maybe he's gon' sell 'em privately—not even go through Dahveed. That probably double the value of 'em, and there wouldn't be no record of the sales. So he wouldn't owe me anything. Oh, yeah, I wouldn't put nothin' past Cleon.

Meanwhile, I got no income.

So, here's what I do. I say to Cleon, look, you need me for one last thing and I need money real bad, so you come on over and let's talk about it. I tell him I might do that portrait of Sondra Bartell if he'll let me have the money for it.

Well, I know I got him—'cause he need the portrait to keep her interested. But of course he gon' try to argue down the price, say he should get half. So he pass by, and he standin' on the porch, lookin' real scared. And I say, oh, come on in and have a drink. Well, that's a invitation Cleon never *could* resist.

So I give him a drink and Cleon say, "Baby, we sho' did have some good times, didn't we?"

Officer? Officer, you okay? You need a damp cloth or anything? I'm used to it, see—I live with the man twenty-five years. I know what he's like.

So I say, "Yes, Lord, we sure did." And I start to reminisce with him. Meanwhile, he have another drink, then another. Pretty soon he start gettin' flirtatious.

You say somethin', Officer? Well, *yeah,* he got a lot of nerve. But I jus' told you—he think his dick so big you can't hardly get in the room with him. So I flirt back and pretty soon he start kissin' on me. I say, "Cleon, honey, I ain't had none of that in a *long* time. How 'bout we get in bed and talk some more?" So we do, and he say, "This is a mighty fine new brass bed you got." And sure enough it is—the kind with brass bars at the top and more at the bottom.

And I say, "I was thinkin' of you when I bought it."

And then I say, "Why don' you let me rub ya back, baby?" So he turn over and I get started and pretty soon, I hear snorin'.

Yeah, you right, Officer. Just like I knew I was goin' to.

Well, you figured out the rest already, ain't you? I already got just the right bed so I could handcuff his hands to the headboard and his feet to the footboard. So I go ahead and do it.

And then I paint Sondra Bartell right on his butt. I put her face right in the one place he couldn't put it himself. Uh-oh, I think I'm gon' have another laughin' fit.

Woo. 'Scuse me, Officer. Sure did feel good. Didn't it? I notice you crackin' a smile your own self.

Well, anyway, once I get my paintin' done, I call up a few friends in the press I happen to know from my divorce trial and they record that picture once and for all for God and everybody.

I bet now I'm back in the paintin' business, what do you think? Oh, yeah, sure—I am if I manage to beat the rap on this.

Why, no, he didn't wake up all the time I was paintin'. Not even while the reporters was here.

Yeah, he sleep pretty sound most of the time. What's that? *'Course* I didn't put nothin' in his drink.

Oh, wait a minute—wait a minute, now. I jus' remember somethin'. Come to think of it, he say he got a little cold, and I did see him take a couple of pills. Not sure what they was, Officer, but I know you gon' find the rest of 'em in his pants pocket.

You smilin' again, Officer? I didn't know you had it in ya. Yeah, I did wash those glasses. I'm a pretty tidy person—tha's one reason I was such a good wife.

Unfortunate thing, though—one of 'em broke on me. Had to throw away the pieces.

Well, looka there—here come the medics. I guess they'll prob'ly want to pump his stomach. He be all right, though. Like I say—I'm a pretty tidy person.

Well, now, thanks, Officer. Good luck with your career, too. Why, sure. I'd be glad to paint you sometime. You can be my second client.

JUDITH KELMAN's suspense novels have topped best-seller lists all around the world. She is a member of the renowned Adams Roundtable and has contributed stories to their anthologies, among others. In "Just Desserts," a love affair between the ex-spouses of a honeymooning couple needs only a garnish of revenge to turn out perfectly.

JUST DESSERTS

by Judith Kelman

Mort Garbis could not recall a more satisfying evening. The house special sirloin with béarnaise had filled the chronic void in his belly, and his brain was buzzing nicely from the 1987 Opus One. The crab cake appetizer and the *crème brulée* dessert had proven a perfect foil for the meat, as were the sides of shoestring potatoes and sautéed mushrooms. The wine had proven well worth the two-hundred-plus-dollar splurge, especially given that his lovely companion had been so quick to sign the check to her room. Mort bore no antiquated reservations about women paying their way. Quite the contrary.

His thin lips retracted in a besotted grin. Alma Rudolph had far exceeded his most optimistic expectations. Her wide brown eyes and robust laugh were most engaging. The jade silk dress and matching shoes complemented her figure, so the broad hips seemed magically slimmer and her feet, which were rather oversized for someone of her short stature, appeared a far more rational size. In this low light, one barely noticed how an excess of plastic surgery had stretched her skin so taut that she bore an expression of perpetual unpleasant surprise.

Actually, Mort found her attractive in a number of ways. Alma appreciated him as he had not been appreciated in years. She responded to his favorite jokes and listened raptly when he explained the season's invigorating prospects for his favorite hockey, baseball, basketball, football, rugby, and women's five-two-and-under luge teams. She valued his interest in fashion and fairly squealed with pleasure when he confessed that shopping for clothing was among his favorite pastimes.

Alma considered herself a contemporary hunter-gatherer as well. What could be more bracing than foraging in the wilds of the mall, armed with a keen eye and a quiver full of high-credit-line plastic? Like Mort, in addition to shopping for clothes, Alma also enjoyed buying accessories and luxury goods and household items and unspecified other goods as the spirit and sale circulars moved her.

The uncanny similarities between them did not end there. They enjoyed the identical TV shows. Like Mort, Alma would never miss the Monday night comedy lineup on CBS or Tuesdays on Fox or NBC Thursdays. Like him, she knew everything there was to know about every member of the cast, past and current, since the historic inception of *Beverly Hills 90210,* which they both recognized to be a work of complex and far-ranging cultural significance.

"Certain to be a classic," Alma pronounced.

"Of *Dynasty* proportions."

"The Young and the Restless, perhaps."

"I'm afraid that's going too far, Alma," Mort said sternly.

"I suppose you're right. *Y and R* is in a class by itself."

Mort peered fondly into Alma's wide brown eyes. As a result of her earlier crying jag, they resembled a poignant Keene painting, rimmed with smudged mascara.

When he told her as much, she delighted him further by admitting that Keene was her favorite artist also. In a burst of giddy intimacy she confessed that often when she was moved to tears at home, she indulged in a soothing snack of baby food.

"Let me guess," Mort said with a rakish hitch of his brow. "Gerber's peaches and Beechnut squash?"

"How did you know?" Alma said.

"I've never told this to anyone, but I like them too," he whispered. "I keep mine stashed in the back of my closet."

"Unbelievable. Me too."

Mort sighed. This was the best he'd felt in the two years since the divorce, better by far than he'd felt in the three years, four months, two weeks, three days and six hours since Geena told him she wanted out of their twenty-year marriage. He would never forget that day, that moment, the shock of it so profound that Mort felt as if he had been kicked in the chest by a kangaroo.

For twenty years he had devoted himself to that woman. He had adored her completely, complimented her constantly, and attended unstintingly to her needs. In twenty years he had never once strayed or betrayed her in any way. He had been with no other woman since they wed, except, of course, for bachelor parties, business trips and guy getaways, which, as everyone knew, did not count. He had done everything in his power to promote Geena's career and further her ambitions.

Alma had done the same for her wretched ex-husband, Gary, who had abandoned her in a similar crushing way. She had been the perfect wife, steadfast and true. She had labored constantly both at home and at work. While Gary was off chasing his silly millions, she had done something with true social significance, building her gift basket business from a dream to a flourishing reality.

It had started with her proudest invention, the welcome baby Baskinette. She had expanded to include the bridal shower special, containing sufficient soaps, deodorants and perfumes to guarantee that the recipient's body would smell uninhabited. She also offered a hostess basket, with stationery and sachets, and her famous bereavement baskets, featuring comforting snacks and sleep and digestion aids. Business was now so good, she employed up to four teenagers after school weekdays and two almost full time during the busy Christmas vacation.

Mort stared across the restaurant terrace at the sea. Jewels of moonlight gleamed on the undulating surface. Lace-capped waves lapped the shoreline. Little Bliss Island perched at the dark horizon like a malignant mole.

The waiter brought the half bottle of rare vintage port Mort had also placed on Alma's tab. He raised his glass. "To tomorrow and Little Bliss."

"To *no* bliss for certain deserving someones," Alma said. "It's about time everyone got precisely what was coming to him."

"And her," Mort added with a rakish clink of her glass.

"Definitely her," agreed Alma.

Dawn brought dense, hazy sunshine and a strident flare of heat. Mort stumbled out of bed near six A.M. His tongue felt like the prickly side of Velcro, and his head thumped as if Oprah Winfrey was doing step aerobics on his skull. He felt a trifle better after two Bufferin and an Alka-Seltzer. Remembering the day's plan brought a further measure of fizzy relief.

Tossing open the shades, he spotted the ark of their salvation bobbing at the dock. She was officially named *The Getaway,* but Mort and Alma had dubbed the boat *The Get Even,* for the noble mission she was destined to perform.

Finding the craft had proved a knotty problem. Mort had taken it for granted that boats for hire would be plentiful in the area. On arrival, he had been appalled to learn that local insurance laws forbade boat rentals. They could have engaged someone to ferry them back and forth to Little Bliss, but that would have burdened them with a potential witness.

Given the potential risk of legal consequences, they had taken every precaution to ensure that no one would know of their plan. They had masked their ticket purchases through a complex series of bookings and cancellations. They were registered under false names at the hotel. Their purchases had been made with cash and traveler's checks to avoid any telltale paper trail. Those few people in their lives who might be prone to care had been offered cover stories. Mort had told everyone he would be holed up working on a memoir, whose working title was "Shopping Is My Bag." Alma had only to say that she would be indisposed for a couple of weeks and her friends presumed she was scheduled for one of her regular cosmetic surgeries.

In a rare show of resourcefulness Mort had inveigled a wizened local fisherman to sell them a craft, the oldest fishing boat in his small fleet. No doubt the old man could be persuaded to buy the boat back when they returned. Otherwise, he was confident that someone else would take *The Getaway* off their hands, quite possibly at a profit. Mort had assured Alma that this would prove to be the soundest ten-thousand-dollar investment she had ever made.

Right after breakfast, they would set off for Little Bliss. The trip to the remote deserted island would take about an hour and a half. Preparations there would require four or five hours. With any luck, they would be safely back at the hotel in ample time to enjoy another sumptuous dinner tonight.

Mort strolled into the lobby at the stroke of seven, as they had agreed. Promptness was a virtue he embraced. Ditto loyalty and fidelity. A deal was a deal, as far as Mort was concerned. And his contract with Geena had read "till death do us part." But that had not stopped her from breaking her vows and their bond. Without hesitation, she had left him for worse, not to mention for poorer. The ache of his lost Visas and MasterCards lay in his heart like cold stone. No more titanium Visa, no credit line with Optima, no house charge at Barneys or Saks. The last time he stopped by to browse at Brooks Brothers, Sergio, his regular salesman, had been positively frosty.

How could Geena reduce him to this? The woman had no scruples, no compassion, not a scrap of moral decency. Despite her lying protestations to the contrary, Mort knew that she had left him for that snake, Gary. She would never have broken up their idyllic home had Gary not slithered into their lives, infecting Geena with his venomous deceits.

Mort could barely believe his ears last year when Geena sat in the courtroom and claimed, under oath no less, that she had sued for divorce because of extreme mental cruelty. With a straight face, that du-

plicitous harlot had claimed that Mort was an overbearing, irrationally jealous bully and a severe shopa-
holic who had sapped her hard-earned funds and
imperiled her credit rating. She'd asserted that Mort
had undermined her career and subjected her to
countless public humiliations. In particular she re-
counted the opening night of her private showing at
the Sheridan Gallery on Fifty-seventh Street. Instead
of thanking Mort for spiriting her out of harm's way
when that sleazy creep from SoHo started oozing all
over her, she claimed that Mort had cost her an important contact with one of the country's foremost
collectors of modern art. Geena had honestly believed that creature with the ratty hair and the earring
when he claimed that he planned to purchase several
of her works and offer them for permanent loan to the
Museum of Modern Art. Obviously, the woman was a
babe in the woods. How right Mort had been to protect her over the years from her own misguided instincts.

Mort's cheeks burned with anger. He would protect
that wretched ingrate no longer. Quite the contrary,
this very day he would see that she got just what she
deserved.

The clock beneath the hotel's signature stuffed pink
pelican read 7:15. Where on earth was Alma? Mort dialed her beachside *casita* from the house phone, but after seven rings, there was no answer. He worried that
she had overslept. Worse, perhaps she was ill. Or
maybe some predatory islander had stolen into her tiny
shack in the middle of the night. Mort had suggested
that taking one of the isolated cabins was reckless and
foolhardy.

He believed in security, even though Geena had always made fun of his prudent precautions. Despite
her, Mort remained convinced that everything was

better off insured in every possible way. No matter that Geena chided him for checking and rechecking the row of locks on their house before they went to sleep and for always setting the burglar alarm, including the interior traps, even during the day. He wished Geena were here now to see how wrong she'd been. Poor Alma. One foolish lapse of judgment, and the dear woman lay bleeding and unconscious, quite possibly dead.

"Come quickly. You must help me," Mort urged the gum-cracking clerk behind the desk.

"I move"—*crack*—"I get canned." *Crack.* "You got problems, handle them yourself." *Crack crack.*

Mort raced to the *casita,* heart thumping, and shoved his considerable heft against Alma's faux bamboo door. The flimsy panel gave almost at once, and Mort sprawled on the mock Mexican tile floor.

Alma swiveled from her perch at the vanity table. Her bulging eyes bugged further and her hand flew to her mouth like a flame-bound moth. "What the hell are you doing, Mort? You scared me half to death!"

"I thought you'd been attacked. I thought you'd been raped and slashed with a machete and left for dead."

She stared into the magnified mirror and scowled. "You made me ruin the liner. Now, I'll have to take off everything, right down to the foundation, and start again."

"I'm sorry. I didn't mean it."

"Whether you meant it or not, I'll need to cleanse again, tone, exfoliate, almond scrub, mint mask, sun protect. Now get out of here and let me finish getting ready."

Mort took an appraising look at her ensemble: beige linen walking shorts, a delicate silk floral shirt and a matching clutch and sandals. "Perhaps you didn't hear me, Alma. This is going to be hard, dirty work."

"I'm the girl, Mort."

"Yes, but as I explained, I have a bad back. Very fragile. The doctor doesn't want me to do heavy lifting or anything like that."

"You play tennis and golf."

"Recreational strain is allowed."

She waved him off. "We'll discuss it on the way over. Now, go."

Mort paced the lobby, striding in the rhythm of the clerk's cracking gum. The clock read 7:30. 7:45. If they delayed their departure much longer, they might not be back in time for happy hour. The bitter loss of those free Coco Locos stung Mort's throat.

At least he didn't have to deal with Geena's carping that he drank too much. He was sick to death of explaining that he was a social drinker in a highly social world. He should have been the one to charge extreme mental cruelty. Geena was the overbearing, unsympathetic one. He still reeled remembering how she'd explained his professional career. "He calls himself an *entrepreneur,* Your Honor, which I gather must be French for 'between jobs.'"

At long last, Alma appeared. She had traded her earlier outfit for a flowing pastel sundress and a straw hat bound with a gossamer chiffon scarf. She teetered across the indoor-outdoor carpeting on four-inch heels thin as bug feelers. The spikes made her size eleven feet look almost petite. Very attractive, Mort thought, though hardly practical.

Then, this was a day for triumph, not practicality. This day would be dedicated to sweet justice and even sweeter revenge.

In an ebullient mood, Mort offered Alma his arm and squired her to the boat. He helped her aboard, though the action caused a vexing twinge in his lower back. Alma claimed to diet constantly and work out every day, but she had the kind of hourglass figure that could measure time in months.

Mort had always eaten what he pleased and exercised when the spirit moved him. Fortunately, unlike Alma, he was blessed with an excellent metabolism. Geena used to carp that he'd gained an unhealthy amount of weight over the years, but in fact, his body had merely chosen to replace countless fat cells with muscle, which weighs twice as much.

"There you go, Cap'n. Take the helm," said Mort.

Alma flushed. "To tell the honest truth, Mort, I've never exactly driven a boat."

He sputtered. "But you said you were a seasoned boatswoman. Ahoy and avast, you said. Anchors aweigh." He flashed back to Geena's claim that Alma was a pathological liar.

"Lighten up!" she snapped. "Don't make a goddamned federal case!"

Something in her tone made Mort want to roll on his back with his paws up. He held up his hands instead. "Okay, okay. I'm sure I can figure it out."

"Do that, Mort. Don't be a total wimpy jerk."

"Yes, Alma. Whatever you say, my dear."

"I say, this tub reeks of fish and looks about as sound as a three-dollar bill. How could you possibly buy this hunk of junk?"

Technically, he had not. Alma had signed the traveler's checks, not Mort. But it seemed wisest not to quibble.

"It's the best I could do, Alma. And it's only for today."

She pinched her sculpted nostrils. "Some educated consumer you are."

The smile dried on Mort's face like salt spray as he started the engine and maneuvered the boat from the dock. Piloting the craft was simple enough, and soon they were slicing through the currents at a bracing clip.

Mort lost himself in the mesmerizing rhythms of the ride and the delectable prospects that lay across the sea.

A bloodcurdling shriek wrenched him from his reverie. He protected his head and peered up, expecting to see a swooping seagull. But the screech had come from Alma.

"Slow down, Mort! What are you trying to do, you crazy idiot? Kill us?"

"I'm just anxious to get there."

"How about I toss you overboard and you hitch a ride with Jaws? How about I stick a torpedo up your butt and launch you? How about—"

He killed the throttle, slowing the boat to a limp.

They chugged to the dock at Little Bliss two hours behind schedule. Novice that he was, it took Mort four tries to maneuver the craft close enough to reach the dock with the stern line. At last he helped Alma onto the rickety planking.

"Tie her up to that whatchamacallit," he said.

"Okay, Mort. But if I break a nail, you'd damned well better have silk wrap, glue and skills."

"Tie her up gently," he said.

Wispy clouds veiled the sun, and the air was filled with drenching humidity. Dragging in the heat, they off-loaded their provisions from the boat, or rather Mort transferred their bundles to the shore while Alma stood by, tapping her oversized foot and complaining. "You forgot the Evian, Mort. How am I supposed to enjoy my chicken sandwich with no Evian?"

"Maybe there's some here. We'll deal with that when it's time for lunch. Don't worry."

"And look at this sunscreen. It's only fifteen. Don't you understand that anything under thirty causes premature photoaging of the skin? What are you thinking, Mort? Are you thinking at all?"

"Relax, Alma. Let's focus on getting the place ready for the happy couple, shall we?"

The curl of her frown reversed itself in a mischievous little smirk. "You're absolutely right, Mort. Things must be perfect for them. Let the games begin."

Over the dunes, they found the island's sole cottage, a freeform pool, a hot tub, a tennis court, a library, and all the amenities any newlywed couple could hope to have. Little Bliss was the ultimate romantic retreat, offering complete luxury and absolute privacy. The tiny island was available for rental on a weekly basis from mid-December through the end of May, after which it was closed through the shoulder, off, no-see-um, and hurricane seasons. This was the final week of the island's operation for this year. Geena and Gary had planned their wedding for this day in order to be able to honeymoon at this idyllic remove.

Alma and Mort strode around the cottage. The larders had been crammed with gourmet meals that had only to be warmed and devoured. There was a decadent abundance of tropical fruits, rich pastries, French cheeses, Belgian chocolates, sorbets and ice creams, tins of pastries and cookies and the finest Beluga caviar. The bar brimmed with a staggering variety of libations, including vintage wines and plenty of top-of-the-line bubbly.

The king-sized bed in the master suite boasted creamy sheets and inviting mounds of plump down pillows. Orchid petals in the shape of Cupid wielding a bow and arrow had been scattered artfully over the lace coverlet.

"Is that enough to turn your stomach, or what?" Alma groused.

"I could definitely use a Zantac," Mort agreed. "Maybe two."

A bilious swell rose in his throat as he pictured Geena and Gary in that bed. He could not dismiss a nagging image of Gary burying his beak in Geena's creamy cleavage. He was haunted by phantom sounds of Geena in the throes of passion: *"Yes, Gary! Yes!"*

"Let's start here." His voice was a locked cell, menacing and constricted. He scooped up the flower petals and tossed them in the toilet, which by fortunate bonus stuffed the fragile plumbing. When Mort flushed, fetid water slopped up from the bowl and rushed in a smelly mess over the hand-painted tile. Mort skittered out in delight and closed the bathroom door behind him.

Alma was shredding the satin linens with a steak knife. Her blade slashed the mattress ticking and the pillow covers, and soon swirling feathers and clumps of foam filled the air. Her taut features warped with rage. "Take that, Gary. That's what you deserve for discarding a perfectly wonderful wife after twenty-three years. And you, Geena, you shameless slut. May your hair fall out. May your teeth rot. May your breasts hang like hot water bottles. May everything you put in your mouth turn to cellulite."

"Amen," declared Mort. "And may the dog pee on your best paintings. And you, Gary, you sexual Svengali. May you lose all those millions you made in investment banking. May your Jaguar give you nothing but headaches. May you suffer from impotence and flatulence and piles."

Alma clapped her pudgy hands in delight. "And may the two of you come to hate and detest and loathe each other and suffer terminal irreconcilable differences and wind up in a nasty miserable divorce that goes on for decades."

"Amen."

Alma looked at Mort fondly. "I'm so glad I had the

good common sense to call you after that whore you were married to stole my Gary."

"No gladder than I am, Alma. You were the perfect person to talk to after that evil pimp you were with stole my Geena."

She sighed. "Having you to share concerns and information with has been such a comfort to me, Mort. Truly."

"Yes, Alma. And to me."

Her guffaw pierced Mort's eardrum like a knitting needle. "Let's get back to it, Mortie boy. I can hardly wait to get this dump in perfect shape."

They embarked on an orgy of destruction. First, they threw all the provisions in the pool, where the exquisite food blended into a sodden, revolting mess. At Mort's suggestion, they reserved three ounces of caviar and a bottle of Dom Perignon. "So we can toast the happy couple before we leave," he said with a devilish hitch of his brow.

"Great idea."

Alma tore pages from the classics and best-sellers in the library, while Mort chopped holes in the pristine clay surface of the tennis court. They collected all the extra sheets, towels and paper goods, including the toilet paper, and buried the lot at sea.

They stuffed the hot tub with palm fronds and other debris until the motor coughed and died. Alma bashed the ceiling fan like a piñata, while Mort poked holes in the roof thatch and window screens, inviting in the tropical rains that struck almost daily at sundown and the nocturnal swarms of ravenous mosquitoes. Finally, Mort found the island's electrical generator and poured water into the air intake until it stopped cold.

When he reported this to Alma, she chortled with delight. "That's priceless, Mort. Imagine the Garden of

Eden without light or air-conditioning. Imagine paradise without hair dryers or microwaves. That's what I call preposterous."

"Indeed."

Alma, having discovered a six-pack of Evian, set a bottle aside for lunch and used the others to soak the emergency radiophone until it buzzed with a lethal short circuit. While Mort poked additional holes in the roof, she teetered to the shore and tossed all the matches and candles and emergency flares into the sea.

Once the staff boat dropped Geena and Gary at the dock, they would be stranded on this hellhole for a week until the launch returned to fetch them. They would have no food, no comforts, and no means of signaling their distress. Their sole remaining amusement would be to observe themselves and each other in the harsh light of day and realize what wretched, revolting souls they were.

Glancing at his watch, Mort was startled to find that it was nearly three P.M. So absorbed had they been in their enterprise, they had not paused to rest or eat. Now, sapped by the crushing heat and their exertions, he gathered their picnic provisions and sank in the shade of a coconut palm.

Alma staggered beside him and planted herself with a thud. "God, I'm pooped. I want you to know, Mort, I don't normally do any manual labor."

"Neither do I. But this is a special occasion."

"Very special. I must say, we did real, real good."

"Eloquently put." Mort popped the cork on the Dom Perignon.

Alma guffawed, a grating blast of sound that gave Mort palpitations. "What was that?" he demanded.

"I was just picturing Geena and Gary sucking up chlorinated mush from the pool, busting coconuts to keep alive, trying to boil the salt out of seawater. Does my little heart good."

Mort had to chuckle himself. "Not to mention lying on the wrecked, soaked mattress swatting mosquitoes all night. Scratching themselves and getting mildewed. How romantic."

"No lights, no air-conditioning. No toilet and no toilet paper. I give them twenty-four hours before they're at each other's throats."

"I give them twelve, maximum. Geena always accused me of being a spoiled brat. Well, let's see how she does living off the fat of the land, roughing it. We'll see who's the big brave adventurer."

"Not Gary, that's for sure. He always made a big deal about my demanding too much help. But it's not like he didn't benefit from having Helga clean and Marta do the laundry and Manuel for the garden and Celeste come in twice a week to give me a massage. I mean, I'd hardly say a trainer and a facialist and a therapist and a driver are excessive, especially given that we had the means."

"You're absolutely right," said Mort. Visions of all those lovely services danced in his head. Alma really did look fetching in chiffon.

"Let's see how that creature likes doing without his creature comforts," she huffed. "I wish I could be here to see it."

"I'd give anything," Mort agreed.

"Let's see how Gary feels about having to live in reduced circumstances."

"He's not going to like it. Not one little bit."

"Good for him," Alma intoned. "It's exactly what he deserves. When I think about that judge demanding that I get nothing but the house and the condo and somehow live on a mere twenty thousand a month alimony, I could absolutely scream!"

Scream she did, so sharp and shrill, Mort's blood congealed like instant Jell-O. But the thought of twenty thousand dollars a month in play dough set his arteries humming again. He had a sudden urge to wrench off Alma's size-eleven spikes and suck her toes.

Mort restrained himself. Tonight, back at the hotel, would be soon enough to begin courting this irresistible wench. He offered her a chicken sandwich and poured her a glass of champagne. "To us," he said.

"Indeed. And to everyone getting just what he—"

"Or she."

"—deserves."

They ate with prodigious appetite. Alma devoured two chicken sandwiches and Mort ate his hero followed by a ham and cheese on rye; they dispatched a pound of German potato salad and a pound of macaroni salad and six large sour pickles. For dessert, they had brownies and chocolate chip cookies and passion fruit and chocolate mints. Still hungry, they ate all three ounces of beluga caviar, scooping the succulent roe directly into their mouths.

"Too bad no toast points," Alma lamented as she gobbled.

"Too bad no capers," said Mort.

"Too bad no chopped hard-boiled egg."

"I hate those," Mort admitted.

"That's amazing. So do I."

Their eyes fused in a sizzling electric circuit as they drank the remains of the Dom Perignon. Alma drained her glass and drew a breath and belched.

"Are there any potato chips?" she asked.

Mort stared into the empty bag, and his face fell. "Sad to say, no. Nothing at all. Let's head back, get cleaned up, and have a nice hearty dinner. Shall we?"

"Absolutely. My treat."

"If you insist."

Mort struggled to his feet and raised Alma like a cement block on a derrick. A swell of affection gave him the extra leverage he required. Unsteady on her bug-feeler heels, she stumbled. Mort caught her and, for a heady instant, their bodies melded. Mort felt the swell of Alma's breast implants, the firm thrust of her tucked tummy, the press of her liposuctioned thighs.

His corpuscles sprang to attention. After years of fruitless searching and wrong turns, he had found the perfect woman. Alma was precisely the one to fill the gaping hole Geena had torn in his heart.

As if on cue at a climactic moment in *90210,* the sky went dark. Lightning flared and the ground shook with a menacing growl of thunder. The first plump raindrops slapped the arid ground, raising a steamy haze.

Mort viewed the gathering storm with alarm. "Oh my. It looks like a hurricane, or maybe a tornado brewing. What if there's a tidal wave? What if the island floods? What if our boat is dashed at sea? We could drown. We could capsize. There are poisonous jellyfish in these waters. Piranha. Sharks. Plus, I'm dreadfully allergic to plankton."

"Can I ask you a teeny favor, Mort?" Alma said sweetly. "Would you *shut the hell up!*"

That shocked Mort free of anxiety's grip. A drape of calm descended upon him. "Of course. You're right. We'll be fine. I'm sure this will blow over in a couple of minutes. Why don't we wait in the cottage?"

"Because the roof is Swiss cheese, remember? Plus there's sewage on the floor and it stinks."

"Right, of course. What do you suggest?"

Alma picked up a fallen palm frond and fashioned it into a makeshift rain bonnet. "Let's head for the boat and get off this rock. Place gives me the creeps."

They raced across the dunes, buffeted by driving rain, gusting winds, and her ceaseless shrill complaints.

"Damn it, Mort. My dress is getting ruined. My hair is frizzing. And my five-hundred-dollar Manolo Blahniks are soaked!"

"Okay, Alma. I hear you. You can dry off in the hold."

"With the fish guts and herring cooties? Not on a bet. This is your fault, Mort Garbis. Every damned bit of it."

"How is it my fault? I didn't make the storm."

"Don't try to worm out of it. That's so typically Gary. Excuses, excuses. It makes me sick!"

"Be reasonable, Alma. No one's responsible for the weather."

"Don't give me that. If you weren't so busy stuffing your face and spending money like it's going out of style and boozing all the time, we wouldn't be in a fix like this."

Mort's stomach churned. He couldn't wait to get back to the hotel and away from the pointed spear of Alma's accusations. They were almost at the dock.

He ran harder, eager to be under way. Then, approaching the rickety plank, a startling sight stopped him cold.

"Where's the boat?"

Alma planted her hands on her hips. The palm frond lay like a huge dead bug on her head. "Don't be cute, Mort. I may have pretended to like your stupid jokes, but this does not amuse me one little bit."

"This is no joke. The boat's gone."

"How could that be? I looped the rope around three times."

"You *looped* it? I told you to tie her up."

"Gently, you said, Mort Garbis. Don't try to blame this on me, you porky drunken parasite."

"Look who's talking," Mort muttered.

"What did you say?"

"Nothing, Alma. Not a word. Look. Let's try to stay calm and figure this thing out."

She frowned in thought. "Hah! Got it!" Alma dipped into her clutch and pulled out her cell phone. She dialed the hotel and listened, her scowl playing tug-of-war with her overstretched skin. "I can't get through."

"Try calling the operator."

She did. Still nothing. Alma spotted the tiny mobile phone in Mort's shirt pocket. "My Nokia's digital, and the service seems to be spotty around here. Try calling on your StarTac."

Mort pulled out the flip phone and held it to his ear. "No luck," he said. "I guess there's no service here."

Alma wrenched the phone from him and listened to the recorded announcement.

"Helps to pay the bill," she snapped.

"That happens to be a sore subject, Alma. Let's try to find some shelter and keep calling, shall we?"

They slogged back over the dunes and huddled in the driest corner of the smelly cottage. Alma kept dialing, but she could not raise a clear connection. "Must be the storm."

"It has to blow over soon. Maybe you should save the battery."

"Don't give me any of your damned overbearing, controlling advice, Mort." She played the phone like a slot machine, stabbing the REDIAL button again and again until true tragedy struck.

Alma's scream caused Mort's ears to curl like cheap linoleum. "My God," he said. "What happened? What's wrong? Are you hurt?"

"Hideously, horribly, terribly. I broke a nail. Look. It's really, really bad."

Squinting hard, he managed to spot the tiny chip at the peak of her left index finger. "It's nothing."

"Don't give me that, you tubby boozehound bum."

"Who are you calling a tubby boozehound bum, you lying lardass shrew?"

That took Alma's mind off her troubles. She flew into a rage that made the ferocious storm outside seem a light summer zephyr by comparison. She assailed Mort's manhood and his earning capacity, his looks and personality, his physique and his emotional health and his shopping ability. "You can't tell your Armanis from a hill of Geoffrey Beenes."

Mort clutched his heart. "Now that really hurts, Alma. Ouch."

Slowly, her temper cooled. "All right, dung breath. I'm going to try the mainland again. It had better connect, if you know what's good for you."

Mort didn't bother protesting her illogic. He eyed the leaky roof and offered up a silent prayer.

"Yes!" Alma raised her flabby arm in triumph. "Hello. Listen. This is Alma Blake. I'm stuck over here on—"

She fell silent.

"What?" asked Mort.

"Ssh."

Her expression darkened like the sky before a storm.

"What is it, Alma? What?"

"Don't tell me that," she screeched. "I do not want to hear that. Just get somebody over to Little Bliss to pick us up—*right now!*"

There was a series of frantic beeps. Alma eyed the phone with fury, then hurled it across the cottage. Mort scrambled to rescue the instrument from a large fetid puddle.

"Don't bother, Mr. Deadbeat. It's out of battery."

Panic looped around Mort's neck. "Well, then thank goodness help is on the way."

"Help is not on the way, poophead. All I got was a damned recording. The storm has done major damage.

There are small- and large-craft warnings. Cruise ships have been turned back. The airport's shut down. Power is out, phone lines down, normal services are not expected to be restored for weeks."

"That can't be," Mort sputtered. "We can't be stuck here."

"Tell me about it. I'm not exactly enjoying the so-called pleasure of your company."

"There's no air-conditioning, not even a ceiling fan. And no lights."

Alma sniffed. "That's not the half of it. Look what you've done to this place. It's a disgusting, uninhabitable mess."

"No food, no bar, no stores," Mort lamented. "We'll starve to death and then we'll die of dehydration and then we'll get mosquito bites and yellow fever and sunstroke and perish all over again."

Alma screeched, "Would you shut your trap and let me think, Mort? My Lord."

"I'm hungry," he whimpered. "I want my Geena. I want a drink."

"Ssh." Her spike-heeled shoes made slurping sounds as she paced the cottage. "All right. Here's the situation. We're stuck here for now, but we're bound to think of something. Right?"

"I don't know. I'm not very good at problem solving."

Alma rolled her bulging eyes. "Naturally, neither am I. How would they handle a thing like this on *90210,* do you suppose?"

"Prettily," offered Mort. "Perkily, sexily. With a tan."

Alma sighed. "I'm hungry too." She started poking in the closets, checking cabinets. "There must be something left to eat in this dump. Come on, Mort. Help me look."

They rummaged through every corner of the damp, dismal place. Finally, in desperation, they strode through the rain to the pool. There, floating amid the swirling slop, were several tins of pastries and cookies.

Mort stirred the revolting currents with his hands until one of the tins bobbled into his grasp. He pried the top off. The wafers were slightly damp but edible.

Mort and Alma filled their mouths and chomped greedily.

"You'd better think of something, Mort. And meanwhile, you'd better get busy fixing up this dump and cleaning. I want the toilet working and the generator humming and the roof patched and all that yucky phooey off the floor—"

"But we'll be out of here in no time. I'm sure of it."

"And I want decent food. Fresh fruits, veggies, lean meat and fish. If I eat just desserts, I'm bound to gain."

"Someone is sure to come along and rescue us. Matter of time."

"Don't give me that, Mort. I want you to clean out the pool and fix the screens and figure out how to improvise some beauty aids and fitness equipment. Do you understand we could be here for *six months?* My Lord, I'll miss my touch-up with Christophe. I'll miss my laser peel. I won't know whether Lucy marries Sven and becomes her own mother-in-law on *Y and R.*"

Mort groaned. "This can't be happening. The Yanks are headed for the playoffs and the U.S. has a terrific shot at the Davis Cup. And there's a fabulous sale next week at Saks. Forty percent off on Canali and Joseph Abboud. Some intermediate reductions have been taken. I can't miss that."

"I'm not interested in your stupid problems, Mort. This is entirely your fault, and I'm not going to let you forget it. You will pay for this. Every second of every minute of every hour of every day we're stuck here, you will pay. And when we get home, I'm going to sue your lazy, useless butt for every last red cent you have."

"Please, Alma. Stop hollering. I'm getting a terrible headache."

"I'll give you a headache, you useless, worthless, obese lump of lard. I'll make your head ache so bad you'll wish you'd never been born."

Mort retrieved several more pastry and cookie tins from the pool. Numbed by Alma's relentless berating, he slogged back to the cabin. Weary to the bone, he sprawled on the soaked, ruined bed.

"Don't just lie there, you lazy lump. Get to work!"

Someone would come to rescue them, he thought. Someone had to come. He could not go on like this for another day, much less six months. He would drown Alma, then himself. Or maybe he'd go first.

"Get up and *do* something, dick brain. Build me a hair dryer. Blend me some natural cosmetics. Give me a shiatsu massage!"

To think he'd been duped enough to believe they were kindred spirits. Who could blame Gary for leaving that wretched, impossible, spoiled, selfish witch? Mort saw now that Alma had gotten just what she deserved.

Everyone did, he supposed. Eventually.

MARGARET MARON'S fine mystery series featuring Judge Deborah Knott has won numerous prizes including Edgar, Anthony, Agatha, and Macavity Awards. Her earlier mysteries remain coveted collectibles. She is a past president of Sisters in Crime and the American Crime Writers League. In "Half of Something," a man struggles to live down an ill-fated marriage long enough to make a fresh start with a new wife.

HALF OF SOMETHING

by Margaret Maron

Adam Gallardin willed himself not to look nervous or uneasy in any way.

He had thought to be out of here by noon, yet it was almost ten after, almost as if that serious young man across the desk from him was trying to draw things out.

If he chose not to approve this loan, fine. There were other banks, other towns, although this history-laden little village on the southern coast of North Carolina was everything Adam had dreamed of when he married Marjorie back in *un*historic, landlocked Nebraska— charming streets that dead-ended at the water, friendly people with small-town values, antique stores filled with beautiful pieces to satisfy an aesthetic longing that had never been satisfied, white clapboard houses that had solidly withstood coastal hurricanes and warm salt breezes for a hundred years.

The house he hoped to buy wasn't as big as the

house of his dreams, but then his personal fortune wasn't as big as he'd planned either.

Half of something's better than all of nothing, he reminded himself. In the end, that's probably what swayed the jury back in Nebraska.

"If Adam Gallardin had cold-bloodedly murdered his wife for her money," his defense attorney had thundered, "would he have immediately offered her daughter half of the estate when Marjorie Gallardin had willed him everything she possessed? No, ladies and gentlemen of the jury. The Gallardin marriage was brief but happy, a marriage built on love and mutual trust. Mrs. Gallardin's fall was indeed the tragedy the D.A. has pictured, but it wasn't murder. You must not, you *cannot* convict this bereaved husband of killing the most precious person in his life."

Of course, it had also helped that Marjorie's daughter came across as a greedy, spoiled young woman when she took the witness stand. Ten minutes of Sally's nasal whine and the jury felt they knew exactly why she'd been disinherited.

"Another ten minutes," his attorney had whispered jubilantly, "and they'd have been ready to indict *her* for your wife's death."

The jury had acquitted him, but their friends—Marjorie's friends, as it turned out—were less charitable. By the time the trial was over, nearly three years had passed since her death, three years of virtual solitude.

The attorney had taken a quarter of the estate for saving his hide. Because Sally's shrill accusations had fueled his arrest in the first place, Adam felt completely justified in deducting that quarter from the half he'd originally offered her.

Even so, it left him with much less than he'd hoped. The bulk of Marjorie's investments had been in real estate and that market hadn't yet reached its fullest potential. "This area's growing," his financial adviser told him last month when Adam spoke of liquidating so he could leave Nebraska for good. "Another year, two at the most, and you can name your price. Right now, though—"

Which was why he was sitting here in South Cove's only bank to hear if he was going to be approved for a mortgage instead of purchasing the house outright. He stole another look at his watch and wondered why the delay. There was no reason for Marjorie's death or the trial to show up in his credit history, but the way computers linked in everything today, maybe this poker-faced loan officer was searching for a polite way to tell him that not only was his loan refused but the good citizens of South Cove would appreciate it if he'd get the hell out of their town.

On the other side of the desk, Chad Easling looked at his own watch, glanced through the glass door of his office, then closed the folder he'd been reading.

"I see you're a widower, Mr. Gallardin."

Here it comes, Adam thought.

"So sad," Easling said sympathetically. "Was it her heart?"

"N-No." Adam's throat was so dry he could hardly speak. "A-An accident."

"Too bad," Easling said as an attractive blonde in a turquoise sundress suddenly appeared beyond the glass door. "Still a young woman, no doubt."

Young? thought Adam as Easling held up a wait-one-minute finger to the woman at the door. Marjorie had been eight years older than he—almost fifty when she fell downstairs and broke her neck. That must mean that the bank's credit search had limited itself to only those facts with dollar signs attached.

The blonde made an impatient face and pushed open the door. Her flowing turquoise skirt swirled around slender ankles and shapely legs. As she stood there only a few feet away, Adam caught the scent of a subtle and expensive perfume.

"You said twelve sharp, Chad, and it's already ten after." Her words rebuked but her voice was music.

"Sorry, love. We're almost finished. This is Mr. Gallardin, Ruth Anne. He's going to be your neighbor, right across the street from you. I've just approved his mortgage on the Broughton house."

"Really?" asked Adam, hope rising in his heart.

"Oh, yes," said Easling with a smile that was suddenly boyish and friendly. "I'm a good judge of character, Mr. Gallardin, and I knew from the first day you applied that you'd have an excellent credit rating."

The woman looked at Adam Gallardin with interest. "The Broughton house? Oh, I'm so pleased. It's been neglected for ages. I've been dying for someone to love it."

"My big sister's an interior designer," said Easling proudly.

"Big" was clearly an affectionate phrase left over from their childhood, for she barely came up to Easling's shoulder.

"Amateur only," she demurred.

"You own that house with the elaborate widow's walk, Miss Easling?" asked Adam, impressed. The historical plaque by the front door of that three-story white house dated it at 1822, forty-five years before Nebraska even became a state.

"It's Mrs.," Easling corrected. "Mrs. Haywood."

"Don't be stuffy, Chad," she scolded, and turned back to Adam. "If we're to be neighbors, you must call me Ruth Anne."

"And I'm Adam," he said, taking the small hand she offered him.

"Why don't you join us for lunch and we can finish up the paperwork after," Chad Easling said, and his sister immediately chimed in, "Oh, yes, please do!"

They ate in a restaurant overlooking the water and Adam felt as if he'd finally come home: the ocean, soft southern voices all around him, Ruth Anne Haywood's intelligent interest in antiques, her brother's easy charm.

By the time their bowls of she-crab soup arrived, he decided that Ruth Anne was older than her girlish slenderness had led him to believe. Faint laugh lines around her clear blue eyes and reference to a major world event "just before I started to school" confirmed his impression that she was no more than a year or two younger than his own forty-five years. By the end of lunch, he knew that she was at least ten years older than her brother, that she was twice widowed, childless, and lived alone in that antebellum jewel directly across from the house he'd soon take possession of.

"You'll have to show Adam what you've done with your place," said Easling. "Maybe give him some pointers. My big sister's a demon on historical accuracy," he told Adam. "Let her pry off a little chip of plaster from your walls and she'll not only tell you what color they were first painted, she'll take you down to the paint store and match it with the right shade."

Ruth Anne shook her head with a rueful smile. "Chad exaggerates, but it *is* exciting to help a house come back to its original beauty." She looked at him anxiously. "You *do* plan to restore, don't you? Not just remodel?"

"Absolutely," said Adam. "Maybe you could advise me. If that's not too big an imposition?"

"Deal," she said. "I love helping people spend money."

Her blue eyes sparkled like noon sunshine on the water as they shook in mock solemnity over the remains of lunch. Adam almost hated to let her hand go.

"Well, this is all fine and good for you people of leisure," said Chad, "but some of us still have to work for a living. If you want to come back to the office with me, Adam, we'll sign the papers and I'll give you the keys."

He reached for the check, but Adam beat him to it.

A hour later, Adam pulled up to the curb in front of the home that would be his as soon as the real estate agent could arrange the closing. When he stepped onto the porch with the keys jingling in his hand, he found Ruth Anne sitting on a lovely old wicker swing wide enough to hold three people.

"I didn't know I had a swing," he said, delighted to be seeing her again so soon.

She laughed. "You didn't. I had my handyman hang it. A housewarming gift."

He invited her to tour the interior with him and discovered that Chad hadn't been exaggerating Ruth Anne's expertise. She knew the history of the house—who built it, which owner had boarded up the fireplaces, and where he might find antique mantels to replace the ones ripped out twenty years ago. She even promised him the phone numbers of craftsmen who could restore the plaster ceilings and put the house's pocket doors back into working order.

The sun was still high in the sky when they returned to the porch. Hoping to prolong the moment, Adam walked over to the swing. "Is it really strong enough to hold two people?"

"Absolutely," Ruth Anne said. "See how tightly the wicker is woven?"

She sat down on the swing and smoothed her skirt aside to make room for him. Huge live oaks shaded the porch and they could look down to the end of their street and straight out into the cove, where small boats passed in the bright distance.

The chain creaked restfully as they swung back and forth. Adam took a deep breath and savored the smell of salty air overlaid with the bouquet of Ruth Anne's perfume. "All we need right now is a big glass of lemonade," he said happily.

Her laughter came like ice cubes tinkling in a tall crystal goblet. "I should have brought some over. I made a fresh pitcher this morning."

"Really? I would have thought you were more the champagne or sangria type."

"Because of my house?" She dismissed that mansion with an airy wave. "Oh, honey, it came down through my last husband's family. You should have seen the house Chad and I grew up in, a sharecropper's shack over on the Neuse River. Our dad died when Chad was three and Mama worked herself into an early grave shucking oysters at the fish house to feed and clothe us and keep us in school."

Her unpretentious candor swept him away and in the weeks that followed, he felt himself falling helplessly, hopelessly in love.

Like the house, Ruth Anne wasn't the vision he'd kept in his head during that last tedious year of Marjorie's life. She was older and less curvaceous than he'd fantasized, but their interests meshed as if they'd known each other forever. Adam discovered he'd rather spend a day with her, treasure hunting through dusty old barns and back-road flea markets, than chatting up the nubile young cuties who hung around the marina. What was nubility compared to Ruth Anne's lovely smile and delicious sense of humor?

Adam even approved of the work ethic she'd inherited from her mother. She was so competent in everything she undertook, whether it was repairing a spinning wheel or coping with the balky carburetor on her outboard motor when it conked out on them the day she took Adam fishing. She volunteered for several charities, she freelanced as a design consultant, and she'd taken responsibility for her younger brother after their mother passed away.

She could have spoiled Chad, given him a big allowance and maybe turned him into a wastrel and idler. Instead, she persuaded her first husband to help him through college and then encouraged her second husband to start him on a fast track at the bank so that he could earn his own way.

Adam soon realized that Chad was basically lazy and relied more on charm than hard work. To his credit, although he grumbled about punching time clocks, Chad seemed equally devoted to Ruth Anne, and he appeared genuinely pleased as the relationship deepened between Adam and his sister.

"You're good for her," Chad told him. "She's been lonely too long."

Ruth Anne seldom spoke of her first two husbands except in passing, but various South Cove gossips were less reticent.

It seemed that Harry, a cardiologist, had died in a freak accident and left an estate of anywhere from a half million to a million five, depending upon who told the tale.

"A bad wire in the motor of his cabin cruiser sparked

an explosion," said his barber. "Ruth Anne was mighty lucky that she changed her mind at the last minute 'bout going out with him that day."

"Blew him halfway to Elizabeth City," said the mailman.

Michael, who'd owned a controlling interest in the bank where Chad Easling still worked, had died of carbon monoxide poisoning.

"Mr. Michael, now, he was a huge Duke fan," said Adam's cheerful young cleaning woman, a woman who would rather dish the dirt than clean it. "That night, an ice storm knocked out the power in the first quarter of the big Duke–Carolina game, so Mr. Michael went out to the garage to listen to it on the car radio while Mr. Chad bunked down in the guest room and Miss Ruth Anne went to bed. In the middle of the night, she woke up and went looking for him—motor was still running. They figured he musta got chilly and turned on the engine so he could run the heater and then fell asleep."

"Finding him like that near 'bout killed *her*," said his next-door neighbor.

"Left her a lot to live for, though," said the neighbor's more pragmatic husband. "All his bank stock, that big house, and a mighty tidy portfolio."

Six months later, with Chad's blessing, Adam proposed to Ruth Anne in an antique store in Wilmington.

"Oh, Adam, honey, I can't marry you," she'd whispered.

"But I love you. I thought you loved me back."

She sank down upon a red velvet love seat, and her blue eyes were miserable. "I do love you, oh, I *do*! But I loved Harry and Michael, too. My heart's been broken twice, Adam, and I'm too cowardly to go through that again."

Adam knelt down beside the antique love seat and took Ruth Anne's small hand in his.

"Third time lucky," he promised.

The ceremony was private—bride and groom pledged their eternal troth before the minister of a small coastal church, with only Chad and Chad's latest tall, leggy girlfriend as witness.

"And best man," Adam insisted. "If our loan session hadn't run over into your lunch date that first day, Ruth Anne and I might never have realized how much we have in common."

"Let me not to the marriage of true minds admit impediments," Chad quoted, lifting his champagne glass in toast.

After the honeymoon, Adam moved into Ruth Anne's spacious home, and for the first two months, the newlyweds seemed to float on a golden haze of connubial bliss. Half of something had become more of everything he'd dreamed of back in Nebraska.

Then the accidents began.

Somehow, the chemicals they used to clean pieces of folk art got muddled and Adam was nearly asphyxiated.

"He could have died!" Ruth Anne told Chad, who scolded them both for their carelessness.

The Tiffany lamp in their bathroom suddenly developed a short that could have electrocuted one of them if they'd touched it while standing barefooted on wet tiles. As it was, their cleaning woman got a nasty jolt.

Before renting out his own house, Adam had brought over some of the antiques Ruth Anne had helped him buy. He had hung his 1810 Sheraton tabernacle mirror over the dainty Victorian desk where she sat every morning after breakfast to return phone calls and plan her day.

A week after their near miss with the Tiffany lamp, the mirror's wire hanger somehow worked its way loose and five feet of silvered glass and gilded mahogany came crashing down on the desk, splintering the desk and shattering into a thousand sharp daggers of glass, daggers that could have ripped Ruth Anne to bloody shreds if she hadn't gone out into the kitchen to pour herself another cup of coffee two minutes earlier.

"I could have sworn those screws were too long to pop out like that," Adam said when Chad came over and saw the damage.

"Were you here when it happened?" Chad asked.

"No, I was up on the widow's walk with the telescope, watching a freighter that just pulled out from Morehead—and that reminds me, dearest. One of the railings feels a little wobbly. If you go up, do be careful," Adam said with seeming solicitation.

"*I* think you both ought to stay off and call your handyman right now," Chad said firmly. "No more accidents, Ruth Ann, okay?"

She patted his arm reassuringly. "No more accidents."

The next afternoon, when Chad stopped by on his way back to the bank after lunch, Ruth Anne told him that the handyman had put everything shipshape that morning. "Want to see?"

"Sure," he said, and tossed his briefcase toward the nearest chair before following her upstairs.

The briefcase teetered on the edge, then flipped over onto the floor.

By then Chad was halfway up the stairs.

"I'll get it," said Adam. "And I'll bring us up some lemonade. Unless you'd like something stronger, Chad?"

From the landing above, Chad said, "Better not. I have to get back to work."

As Adam lifted the briefcase, the top fell open and a couple of faxes slid out. Horrified, he realized they were copies of Nebraska newspapers. The top headline read WOMAN ACCUSES STEPFATHER OF MURDER.

He quickly riffled through the other sheets till he came to the smaller story headlined JURY ACQUITS IN GALLARDIN TRIAL.

The chemical fumes, the electrical short, the smashed mirror—they must have triggered Chad's suspicions about Marjorie's accidental death.

Before their wedding, he'd told Ruth Anne about Marjorie—the same version he'd told the jury—and Ruth Anne had wept for him, attributing to him the grief she'd twice endured. Of course, *she* hadn't been accused of murder, and he hadn't thought she needed to hear about that small difference in their circumstances. He'd been too afraid of her reaction. And now Chad was probably up there giving her all the gory details. Would she feel betrayed? These last few months had been the happiest in his life. Money was wonderful, but in his heart of hearts, he knew that he could live content in a rented room if Ruth Anne was there beside him. How could he bear to see her sweet look of love turn to horror?

He didn't realize how long he'd been standing there until he glanced up and saw a white-faced Chad looking down at him. Too late to pretend, he crammed the papers back inside the briefcase and held it out to Chad.

"Did you tell her?"

Chad shook his head grimly.

"Chad, I swear to you—"

"Don't bother saying it, Adam. I honestly don't care whether your first wife's death was purely accidental or not, but if Ruth Anne so much as sprains her ankle from here on out, these papers are going straight to the district attorney. You won't find North Carolina juries as understanding as Nebraska's." He looked Adam straight in the eye and said softly, "Cherish her, okay?"

"I will," Adam promised, almost weeping with gratitude. "I do."

His brother-in-law snapped the briefcase closed, straightened his tie, and headed for the front door.

"Well, back to the salt mines," he said with a semblance of his old cheerfulness. "Ruth Anne stayed up to watch a huge sailing yacht put in at the marina. She thought you'd want to see it, too."

Emotionally drained, yet with a lighter heart than he'd have thought possible five minutes ago, Adam stepped out onto the widow's walk balancing a tray with a pitcher of lemonade and two glasses. It took a moment for everything to register.

The newly mended railing had pulled away from the post and Ruth Anne was nowhere to be seen.

The tray fell from his nerveless fingers. Pitcher and glasses spun away as he rushed over to the gap.

Three stories down, one of the glasses hit the stone patio beside Ruth Anne's crumpled body and smashed into diamond-sized bits that caught the sunlight and mocked him with their bright sparkle.

"No!" Adam whimpered, knowing in that instant that his whole life was now as thoroughly smashed as that glass. No one would believe this was an accident. It would all come out about Marjorie's death, and they'd say he married Ruth Anne for her money, too, and then killed for it. Another trial, another public pillorying, and for what?

Even if they didn't send him to the gas chamber, what did it matter? They would certainly give him life in prison, and what good was life without Ruth Anne?

"No!" he moaned again, and stepped up onto the coping. He gazed out over the water with tear-blurred eyes and in that instant between launching himself into oblivion and oblivion itself, it suddenly pierced his numb brain that those faxes had been dated the day before his first meeting with Ruth Anne.

And there were no huge yachts anywhere in the cove.

GILLIAN ROBERTS *is the pseudonym of mainstream novelist Judith Greber, author of four bestselling novels including* Silent Partner *and* Mendocino. *As Gillian Roberts, she is the creator of the popular Anthony Award–winning series featuring witty Philadelphia schoolteacher Amanda Pepper. Her acclaimed* Emma Howe *and* Billie August *private eye series lends a character to "Heart Break," as Emma tries to counsel an old friend with a heartrending problem.*

HEART BREAK

/

by Gillian Roberts

Emma," Vivian Carter said, "I was thinking . . ." She lapsed off into dreamy silence, but through the years, Emma had come to expect these pauses. Vivian's thoughts meandered through private byways. Eventually, and at her own pace, she'd get back to whatever was on her mind.

Emma Howe was in no hurry. She was enjoying both her beer and the quiet. She'd tolerated Vivian's unfinished sentences for over two dozen years, amazing herself, because she wasn't excessively tolerant of anything, she'd been informed more than once, and Vivian's brain too often seemed covered with bubble wrap.

But this was a day for savoring Vivian-provided time lags, for remembering the point of living in California. After the endless battering of an El Niño winter, the air was scrubbed to a high polish as its light ricocheted off the bay onto every clearly etched object. She sat in the warm midst of the equivalent of an ice storm, only here, light coated each leaf and blade, light made the colors seem from a child's crayon box, and it extended across the bay to where San Francisco glittered, each building edged and highlighted with light.

On the north side of the bay, Emma sat at a table in an outdoor restaurant backed up to a hillside filled with long-stemmed matilija poppies. They looked blatantly false with their oversized white crinkled petals and bright yellow centers.

Emma felt a knotted portion of her innards relax. Vivian's invitation had come at just the right time. That morning, George, generally the most agreeable of men, had pushed her as close to a declaration of war as an unmarried, uncohabiting middle-aged woman felt willing to endure before calling it quits.

It had been ridiculous. All she'd done was be annoyed—with good cause—at her daughter, the oldest infant in the universe. "She's a whiner, nothing more and nothing less," she'd said. "Won't make up her mind or take responsibility and do something. It lets her get away with murder."

And blam, like that, George was on her case, accusing her, the most realistic of women, of seeing everything in black and white. "No grays!" he'd said, like an angry teacher flunking her for bad behavior. "You refuse to admit there's even such a color!"

That was nothing short of ridiculous. Emma was a private investigator. Her entire profession dealt with grays and the need to clarify and see through them. She knew gray. She just didn't like it. Didn't approve of it. Avoided it at all costs. Gray was dirt and fog and weariness. Gray was to get rid of.

Who could say what had set George off? Maybe he had hormonal problems. Male menopause or something as yet undiscovered.

Besides, when you got down to it, there *were* such things as right and wrong, and whining vacillation was on the column in Emma's ledger headed "wrong." Why should Emma change her views? They made sense. They organized the world, provided guidance.

And even if she spent her days plodding around on behalf of lawyers attempting to bend the law in their client's direction, that still was on the side of right. That was the law. Emma was against what was *wrong,* and she'd be damned before she'd apologize for keeping a clear head.

She tilted her face toward the sun like a creature just released from hibernation, pushing away the memory of George's disapproval.

"You aren't the deity, Emma Howe." He'd said it softly, but the words made her want to order him out of her house. "You aren't God and you don't *know* everything and everybody the way you sometimes think you do. Bend a little. Give a little more. You want every problem solved, every mystery answered. Some things just don't have ready answers."

She never claimed omniscience, but dammit, Emma was a good judge of people. Had to be to survive. The only seriously wrong call she'd made was with her late and unlamented husband, Harry, but she'd been young and in lust back then. And Harry, incessantly providing proof of how bad her judgment had been, had taught her to be more discerning about people. So what the hell was George talking about?

George was a good man. He must have gotten out of her bed on the wrong side. Luckily, the phone had rung at precisely the necessary moment, and Vivian's invitation saved the rest of the day from degenerating into gray. Into wrongness.

Instead, it was Technicolor. Life was good, indeed.

Good to have a Saturday to herself, out of the office, away from insurance cheats (bad) and missing teenagers (all pains in the butt were bad by definition) and sullen, reluctant witnesses (bad, period).

Don't try to tell her there were no absolutes. Maybe for paramecia there weren't, but humans with functioning brains knew right from wrong.

"I like that those are native plants," Vivian said, gazing toward the stand of matilija poppies. "I like that nobody invented or imported them. They planted themselves. They're real, and as intended. I love it that something that extravagant just pops out of the earth on its own. And that they look fake, like the crepe paper flowers we used to make to decorate the gym for dances."

And that was part of why Emma accepted Vivian's soft-sided mind. No other woman she knew would follow "I've been thinking" with a metaphysical appreciation of native flora. She nodded her understanding. (She *did* know people, no matter what George said. You could. You had to, in fact. That didn't mean you thought you were God.) "Those poppies are so overstated, they're horticultural Tchaikovsky," Emma said with a smile.

Vivian looked startled, momentarily confused, then smiled. "Oh, my God, I'd forgotten that." She nodded and sipped wine before speaking again. "I must have sounded like such an idiot. All that blather about life as a grand symphony. Oh, what I wanted out of poor old life!"

They'd been so young, embarking on marriage, speculating about how it would be, planning—now there was a laughable thought—the rest of their lives. Emma's own marriage had ended at the Tawdry-R-Us motel off the freeway, her husband's heart overwhelmed on yet another of its side trips into adultery. "Dead of a half-night stand" was the epitaph for Harry and their future.

But Vivian's unrealistic, impossible marriage that seemed so removed from the real world that it was doomed, endured. The picture was fresh and vivid in Emma's mind. Vivian, dressed all in black so the world would know she was a genuine artist, declaiming for a life that was "pure Tchaikovsky—oversized, passionate, nothing ordinary or bland. Ever."

Her words had been emblazoned in Emma's memory because—she said—she couldn't believe her ears, couldn't believe her friend was that hopelessly immature. The girl was marrying a medical student whose every drudgy nanosecond was devoted to his studies, his rounds, his patients, his future, and, in truth, to stunned self-wonderment. He was a good man, a dedicated man, but his first love was himself. Yet Vivian, whose two jobs would support them, saw them in a perpetual wild waltz, when everyone with normal vision knew she was going to barely see him at all for years. And when she did, they'd both be too tired to even dream about romantic excesses and their conversation was guaranteed to be about medical procedures.

But that wasn't the only reason Emma had remembered Vivian's words. They were etched on her brain cells because she'd secretly envied anyone who could think in those terms, whose imagination was large enough, unself-conscious enough to consider such an idea, whose cellular material wasn't made of one hundred percent washable, durable, unbreakable fabric.

"But look," Emma said. "Here we are in what is laughingly called middle age, although that assumes we'll live to be one hundred and ten—and you and Gene are still going strong, whatever the background music has become. You weren't a fool at all."

Vivian held her wineglass below her nose, as if sampling its bouquet. Her eyes were half lowered, her expression unreadable. "You're more or less the law," she finally said.

"Come again?" What road had led Vivian from poppy admiration through Tchaikovsky to Emma's relationship to the law? "Cops are the law," Emma said. "The law's the law, so lawyers are the law. But I'm . . . auxiliary law, at best. What made you say that?"

"I need to know." Vivian sighed as she ran her finger around the rim of the wineglass.

Normally, at such a juncture, Emma made it clear that she didn't have all day. But as it happened, she did. And she was with Vivian, whose clock was set to a different measure than the seconds and minutes the rest of the universe used.

"If I tell you something," Vivian said, "something terrible, do you have to report it? Or do you have to keep it a secret like lawyers and priests do?"

"A confession?" Emma asked, smiling. Vivian, unsmiling, nodded.

If Vivian Carter confessed to anything more serious than sampling unpaid-for grapes at the supermarket, Emma would go home and tell George he was absolutely right. That she didn't know squat about anybody.

Vivian was the gentlest of women. Not that she didn't deal with her portion of the real world. In fact, she nurtured it. She was an art therapist at a center for emotionally disturbed children, and was outstanding at quietly finding a way into a child's locked-up world. A year ago, Emma and George had gone to an event honoring Vivian. They'd sat with her husband, Gene, who never had acquired that haunted Tchaikovsky patina. Not in attitude and surely not in appearance. He looked wholesome and sturdy, scrubbed clean and trustworthy.

He looked the way a cardiologist should look, like someone you'd trust with your heart. His faith in himself had been justified by time as he won awards and an international reputation. But that night, he'd stared with open adoration at his wife as she was praised from the podium. He seemed completely contented to bask in his wife's reflected glory. They'd all grown up and learned new, less troublesome music. Nobody wanted Tchaikovsky making life-and-death decisions about them. You wanted somebody like Gene.

Vivian treated her husband like a beloved artifact, cushioning him in a home decorated in the same soft and glowing colors she painted onto her canvases. She raised three fine children without seeming to raise her voice. She was generous to a fault, and slow to anger.

All of which would have long ago put Vivian over the top of airy-fairiness and off Emma's list of acquaintances were all the sweetness and light not tempered by dollops of earthiness, good humor, intense honesty, surprising pragmatism, and talent. Vivian's paintings fascinated Emma, because they made it obvious that the woman, who lived only a few miles from Emma, inhabited an alternative universe with its own sky, earth, and bay.

None of which could account for the troubled dark in Vivian's amber eyes, a shadow that wasn't part of her usual hesitations and conversational wanderings. Emma stifled her urge to smile. "How terrible?" she asked.

"You didn't answer. Would you have to tell? Could you keep this confidential?"

"You're worrying me," Emma said. "What are we talking about here?" What would the queen of pastel see as "terrible"?

Cruelty, Emma thought. Any variety. A prank turned sour. Elder abuse. She probably suspected somebody—

a relative, a frail and elderly neighbor—was being neglected, or more actively abused. It would be like Vivian to notice—and like her to agonize over what to do.
That was fine. At least she asked for advice, and Emma
loved giving it. Loved being She Who Knows and
Never Dithers.

"We're talking about murder," Vivian said.

Emma pulled back in her chair as if to avoid the suddenly hard-edged light. "I'm a PI," she said quietly.
"I'm not allowed to be involved with an open homicide. It's only on TV that PIs meddle in police investi-
gations. I'd lose my license, even if I had a taste for that
sort of thing."

"You wouldn't be meddling into anything," she said
softly. "There is no investigation."

"If you have information about a murder that the police don't know about, you have to tell them, Viv."

"I can't."

"Then tell me and I'll tell them."

"They won't know what you're talking about." Vivian was almost inaudible.

"But you said—"

"It is murder," Vivian said more emphatically. "A
kind of murder."

Emma relaxed. Not exactly murder, but a kind of
murder. Of the spirit? The will? She'd been right in her
initial assessment. This was Vivian and her "murder"
wasn't the kind the law minds. Emma listened with tolerant amusement, waiting for what trivial mini-drama
Vivian would present.

"Can I tell you? And then you can tell me what to do.
You're always so sure of yourself, Emma. I get mired
down, but you always—I so admire that about you."

Emma was delighted to have someone acknowledge
what wasn't a fault, no matter what George thought,
but a talent. Vivian seemed about to speak, but waitper-

son Jenny, who so introduced herself as she materialized at the table, needed to take their orders. Truth was, no matter what George had said, real life wasn't gray. There were two options in this life, the right and the wrong. Imagine the Ten Commandments according to George: "Maybe thou should . . ." "Sometimes thou shalt . . ." The world was bad enough off with absolutes, but muddle things more with ifs and perhaps . . .

Furthermore, even Vivian, who might appear a ditz, knew what to do. People always did. They just wanted people like Emma around to insist they follow that right impulse. Emma was a professional prod, that was all.

Waitperson Jenny—Emma wanted to know why she had to know the name of someone she'd have a five-minute relationship with—chirped the list of specials, exotic foodstuffs that hadn't existed when Emma was young. Emma ordered a cheeseburger, rare, and got a savage pleasure out of the waitress's barely controlled disapproval. Vivian ordered a concoction of various forms of plant life. And another glass of wine.

"Begin," Emma said the moment Jenny bounced off.

"If I only knew where . . . ," Vivian said.

"At the beginning. Then go all the way through to the end." Fat chance having that be true with Vivian, but it never hurt to hope. All the same, Emma felt mild apprehension. Why wouldn't Vivian know where to begin?

"The beginning . . . maybe it was the Tchaikovsky life, maybe that was it. I had such high hopes. Correction. They were more than hopes. They were convictions. A credo. Gene was so . . . electric. More alive than other men. I can be a little, um, less than directed. He seemed so *passionate* compared to me. I thought we were a cosmic combination."

This "murder" was about her marriage?

"So did Gene. He wanted that bigger and better life just as much as I did. He wanted to feel things to his toes, to never live dully. We were alike in that."

He had an affair, Emma assumed. Or is having one. Their marriage was being murdered. Kind of. But first, the story of how wonderful it once was. Even women hiring her to spy on their wandering mates began with the story of how it once had been. Even they, buying her services in a cut-and-dried transaction, had to offer up the sad trajectory of their love, to explain why they weren't run of the mill, but tragic figures worthy of attention. Over the years, over how many tables and desks, lunches, dinners, and drinks had she listened to women recite this litany? And sometimes she'd been the one telling the tale.

"Gene got a lot of the adventure he wanted through his work. Through the instruments he's devised, the awards. In the world he chose, he's made it. The Eighteen-Twelve triumphal music is playing all the time in his background." She smiled, half proudly, half wistfully.

"But real life wasn't what I'd imagined, Emma. For a long time, with the work—mine and his during medical school and residency, and then the children—we were too busy to be Tchaikovsky. We were too busy treading water. I stopped painting, stopped all the art. Couldn't set up, couldn't afford sitters, couldn't find the time or even clear my mind long enough to see anything beyond the day itself. And then one day, I woke up and realized I was everything I hadn't wanted. I was ordinary as mud."

Emma's mind had wandered back to the days Vivian was remembering. Kids today—her own daughter, Caroline—had no idea what a different world it had been back then. Women like Vivian, sick for personal expression, were told they were maladjusted. Didn't like being female. "Hardly ordinary," Emma said. "Everybody's marriage was crumbling in those days. Everybody's except yours. And you must remember that you were painting, at least a little, and definitely well, because I remember an exhibit where you won first prize."

After half a dozen years and two children with Harry Howe, his inability to hold a job plus his talent for gambling away whatever he'd managed to earn, Emma had realized her life was not going to follow her carefully designed plan. The only jobs she could find for the longest time were poorly paid, menial, foot-wearying work that never advanced her life, just sustained it. She hadn't been to college, had no special skills. Just debts. So the winter of that painting award Emma watched Vivian's life flower with her growing family, their new economic stability, her art, his medicine. Emma watched Vivian, the dizzy one, manage to have it all. And she tried not to envy, not to let the chilling grasp of jealousy ruin the relationship.

"That painting," Vivian murmured. "I didn't say it then, felt as if I was cheating, but that was an old painting. I'd done it years before the show. So don't, Emma," she said softly, brushing imaginary crumbs off the table. "Don't try to console or reassure me. That's your view of my life. I'm trying to tell you how it actually was. I wasn't unhappy—but I wasn't happy, either." She looked up and stopped speaking as Jenny put Emma's hamburger down as if it were contaminated, then beamed at Vivian as she reverently placed the sprouty offering in front of her.

"I was ashamed of myself, too," Vivian said as soon as Jenny turned her back. "Here I was with everything I could want, and more, and I felt half dead. Numb inside. So I went for help."

Of course she would. Nobody opted to just plain get

over it. Grow up. That had been part of the heated discussion with George this morning. Caroline had been contaminated growing up in Marin, where there was a therapist on every street corner and an ordinance against experiencing even a moment's pain. You lived at the end of the rainbow and you'd better enjoy it. Caroline had spent half her life and most of her money on cure-alls ever since, and nothing at all was cured.

George considered her opinion narrow-minded. They were going to have to, as they said in these parts, work on that. But for now, she kept her mouth shut. Vivian had gone for help. Emma would now undoubtedly endure secondhand revelations and insights and know that the help hadn't worked. You could see its failure in Vivian's desperately unhappy expression.

"I fell in love with my therapist," Vivian said. "I know how that sounds. I know it's a cliché, and I knew it then. But I also knew, almost immediately, he was the perfect person in the world for me."

Emma waited.

"We had an affair."

Damn whoever it was. That was a terrible thing—but not the way Vivian probably meant. To take advantage of a client's vulnerability was disgusting, and she was glad of the chance to tell Vivian so. No need to debate this one. Take the bastard to court. Rip up his license. "Okay, Vivian, you asked me what to do, and I'll tell you. Take him to—"

"We didn't have the affair while I was his patient. I stopped therapy—he suggested it. Months went by before . . ." She looked up. "Nothing was rushed into. I was married and so was he. But eventually . . . it lasted a year and a half. Well, there you have it."

No. She didn't. That was the terrible thing? The so-called murder? "When was this?"

"Fifteen years ago."

For God's sake, it had taken Vivian long enough to decide this was a big moral issue. "You don't need my opinion about that. Besides, it's over."

Vivian shook her head and lifted her wineglass again, drinking from it almost as if it were water. Emma ate hamburger. It seemed the wrong choice of food while listening to a tale of passion, somehow tactless, but all the same, she thoroughly savored it during the pauses Vivian's stuttering memory provided.

"It ended because it was wrong," Vivian finally said. "Too hurtful. I was ready to leave my marriage, but he wouldn't do the same. There were good reasons. His wife wasn't well, and . . . in any case, it became too emotionally painful to continue. And I hated lying. Hated it. I decided to make my marriage work instead, to find my own way, get on with it. Gene and I saw a counselor together and talked things through, and . . ."

"He knew, then?"

She nodded. "I wanted the air clear between us. He was shocked, he was miserable, he was angry, he was depressed. He was all the things I guess people are. He was almost—pretty much—that passionate, crazy, over-the-edge man I'd thought I wanted. But I'd grown up, you see. It was awful. Most of all, he hated that I couldn't lie and say I'd never loved the other man. He wanted that to be the truth, but it wasn't. And he wanted me to hate the other man now that it was over, but I didn't. Why would I? He was loveable. He hadn't done anything to change that perception. I knew I'd love him till I died, although of course I didn't say that to Gene. But I didn't say the words he was aching to hear, either. I didn't lie. It was bad enough that I'd cheated and lied for a year and a half. Gene's such a . . . *rational* man, a problem solver, a healer. But then, he talked about revenge, getting back—useless, meaningless, insane things like that. Completely unlike himself. Which is when, and why, I realized I wanted him to be completely like himself. I wanted that calm intensity and steadiness. And I'd ruined it, I thought. Smashed it. Except eventually the rage and depressions passed, and the past began to feel like a disease we'd both recovered from. Life's been good ever since." She exhaled, as if after long exertion, and poked at her grassy salad. She looked at Emma directly. "Honestly. Very good." She looked down at her fork and grew silent again.

In the distance, a waterfall of fog spilled over the spires of the city, then seemed to stop and hover, waiting, as was Emma, for the point of the story. Happily ever after wasn't the end of her story and wasn't the story itself. Emma finished her hamburger, ate each and every french fry, drained her beer, ordered another and still she waited. And finally, Vivian looked at her, her amber eyes awash with moisture.

"He—I didn't see him all those years except three times when we found ourselves at the same event. We never spoke. Gene never mentioned it. But someone who didn't know my connection to him mentioned she'd been to a funeral. His wife's, it turned out. She said how bad the widower looked, that he was retiring sooner than expected for reasons of health.

"The last time I saw him, Gene wasn't with me, so I said hello, had a little more time to see him. I tried to hide my shock, he looked so crumply and gray—his skin, I mean. Not healthy. He was older than I was, but not old enough to look that way. He said his health had been poor, but he was hopeful of a change for the better.

"I didn't ask why. I should have, because then maybe ... I didn't put together the gray skin, how weak he looked, how slowly he walked up the one step in front of him. Maybe if I'd known ... But Emma, I didn't suspect a thing. Why would I have? It was fifteen years ago!"

Emma wished she'd ordered coffee instead of beer. It wasn't warm anymore. She wished she were inside anything. Protected in some way she suddenly felt she was not.

"He was on the heart-transplant list. I didn't know. If I had only asked, if I'd known . . ."

She was off again, lost somewhere. Emma was getting used to this rhythm, and she waited.

"Three days ago," Vivian said in a flat voice, "Gene came home from the office in a great mood. Buoyant and beaming like something great had happened, and when I asked, he said, 'Vivian, it's over at last.'"

"Of course, I had no idea what he was talking about. I thought about his projects, about anything on earth he'd been waiting for—grants, awards, equipment.

"He said, 'Your love affair is what's over. Finally. It took fifteen years, but he's out of your life. And mine. Out of his, too. He's dead. Why the hell would I let him qualify for a new heart after he broke mine? Go ahead, cry for him. Feel whatever you like. Love him. It no longer bothers me a bit. I hear he was a really nice guy.' And he smiled."

Emma shivered.

"If I'd known . . . I would have lied, Emma. I would have said I didn't, I never loved him. But I didn't know and Gene did. And he killed him," Vivian said. "On purpose. Isn't that murder?"

Intentionally killing someone. Yes, of course. Except. She could see Gene's clean healer's hands, could imagine him explaining the complex protocol for deciding who gets transplanted organs and who doesn't. Vivian said he'd been older than she herself was. That would put him near sixty. Borderline age, Emma assumed. In a rarified world, with a procedure as complicated as a heart transplant, Gene would produce scientific, compassionate, heartfelt, rational and irrefutable arguments. Gene was a physician. The expert in his field. He'd know things nobody else on the jury, in the courtroom, possibly could.

Murder—or speculation. Hysteria. Much too petty an act for the good Dr. Carter, whose entire career had been dedicated to saving lives.

And what would be gained? Gene's undeniable lifesaving talents would be rendered useless. Vivian's lover could never return. The situation would never repeat itself.

"I've moved out," Vivian said softly. "It's obvious that those fifteen years were a farce, that just below the calm, there was boiling lava. Fifteen years waiting for revenge; fifteen years of hate—it all came out in that greeting. In less than a minute. I can't live with him anymore, knowing that."

That fury, that murderous rage, that twisted passion. Straight out of a nineteenth-century opera. Be careful what you wish for. . . .

"What do I do now?" Vivian asked. "What's the right thing to do?"

Nothing would be made better if she went to the authorities. There was nothing they could do. And nothing would be made worse by silence. Nothing had been real for fifteen years. You can't lose what never was.

Emma was glad George wasn't here to witness the dismantling of her carefully calibrated systems. The clear-edged blacks and whites she'd flipped in front of him this morning had muddled into each other to form a noncolor. A veil she couldn't see through. "I don't know," she said softly. "I don't know that there's an answer."

"But Emma, you always—I thought you'd—"

"I thought so, too." Emma felt exposed as her absolutes fell away. "But I was wrong." She thought about hearts, their secrets and unknowable mysteries.

In the distance, a foghorn moaned. Emma turned. Fog had swallowed the city until all definition was gone, turned into a fuzzed and featureless wilderness of gray.

ALL'S WELL THAT ENDS

by Joan Hess

Jack was looking at the flickery television set on a
shelf above the bar when the woman sat down next to
him. Her gender was hard to overlook, but he wasn't
into specifics, having long since given up hope of being approached by a gorgeous young actress in search
of a passionate one-night sexathon. His sixtieth birth-
day had passed without such a phenomenon taking
place. Not much had happened since, for that matter.
He was older and grayer, although not especially
wiser. For years he'd come to the corner tavern to
have a beer, maybe two, and a little conversation. Depending.

"Can you believe that guy?" he said without turning
his head. "It's like he thinks this is gonna change our
minds about his guilt. The only people in this country
who believe he's innocent are the twelve jurors. Where
do they find wimps like those to serve on juries, any-

way? I'll bet not one of them's ever read a newspaper. Hell, I'll bet not one of them knows how to read."

"You're Jack Julian, aren't you?" she said.

Now he looked at her. She had drab hair, yellowish skin, and dark, puffy circles under her eyes as if she hadn't slept in weeks. Her stained sweatshirt and lack of makeup suggested she wasn't a hooker, but he wasn't sure. Hookers were about the only women who came on to him—and they were usually junkies.

"Yeah," he said. "Who are you?"

"Someone who made a point of reading your pieces in the newspaper. You were good."

"I suppose I was." Jack beckoned to the bartender. "Give the lady whatever she wants to drink."

"Nothing, thanks," she said. "I'd like to talk to you about Spider Durmond. You wrote as much as anybody about the case. You forgot to write about me."

"What should I have written?"

"Maybe I'll have a club soda." She took a tissue from her purse and wiped her forehead, even though it looked to be as dry as parchment. "Let's begin with the proposition that we both know he did it. This big, beautiful blond jock had a history of beating women, of roughing up photographers, of drinking too much and driving too fast and doing too many drugs. He bought off his one known rape victim. On the night of July fifteenth, he went to his estranged wife's rented beach house and stabbed her to death. His alibi was laughable—he was home, alone. Spider never went to bed alone." She took a shuddery breath. "You didn't seem to buy that in your articles about the case."

Jack glanced at the television, which was currently depicting some event in which everyone wore shorts and ran incessantly. "And a few minutes ago, while the cameramen jostled for room and the reporters knocked each other into the bushes, Spider staged a press conference and promised to pay five million dollars for evidence leading to the conviction of the real killer. I used to think those of us in the media had ethics—you know, a common moral ground. No more than a fraction of an acre, perhaps, but a little bit. I retired just before that bus veered, crashed through the rail, and nose-dived into the river."

He took a final swallow of beer. "Spider's a wonderfully photogenic guy, broad smile, dimples, not too bright, helluva great basketball player and paid accordingly. Endorsements for everything from athletic shoes to cat food. The money pumped up his brain, made him think he was invincible. Shit, maybe he thought he was invisible, too. He went to Suzanne's house, killed her, and then got all teary-eyed and claimed he was home with a cold. Jesus!"

"You think he did it," the woman said. "I know he did. I was there."

"Sure you were. Go peddle your story to a tabloid, baby. The trial's over, the jury's reached a screwball decision, and it's too late for you to make any money off this. You'll have a better chance with alien abductions in New Mexico or cattle mutilations in Iowa."

"The two of us can make five million dollars," she said, then slid off the stool. "Think about that while I visit the ladies' room."

Although Jack had been planning to leave, he sat. And thought. And got nowhere. She wasn't a hooker, and she didn't sound as if she was recently released from an institution guarded by burly men in white coats. Then again . . .

He didn't leave, though he wondered if he should have known better. "How'd you find me?" he asked the woman when she returned.

She took a sip of club soda. "You wrote a column about this place. I thought it might be your local hangout. I've been coming for the last few days, hoping to spot you."

"But you waited until tonight to speak to me."

"The jury came in this afternoon."

"And so they did," Jack said bitterly. "The trial lasted five months, and jury deliberations lasted two days. The evidence was so friggin' obvious—his blood on the scene, her hysterical phone calls to her friend, his car spotted a block from her house when he swore he was home. The woman walking her dog at midnight when she heard his garage door open." He waved to the bartender to refill his glass. "Why should I have written about you?"

"I'm one of Spider's ex-girlfriends."

"One of many. So what?"

The woman sighed. "Three years ago, I met Spider at a party. I was a model then, doing layouts for magazines like *Playboy* and *Vogue*. Spider came on to me, and I liked it. We looked really good together, like a pair of tawny lions. He promised to introduce me to movie producers. Most models see themselves as the next Audrey Hepburn."

Jack regretted his decision to linger. Pulling out his wallet, he said, "And then he dumped you and now you want revenge. It won't play in Peoria. It won't even play in Long Beach."

"It went further than that. He was escorting me to clubs, taking me with him on road trips, making sure I was seen on his arm when he deigned to bless night-clubs with his presence. He took me to the Oscar awards."

He tried to imagine her on the cover of a magazine, or even posing in a designer gown. As for a centerfold, no way. Her breasts hung like deflated balloons. Her lips were as sensual as earthworms. "I'm having some trouble with this," he admitted. "Spider made a point of being seen with good-looking women. Maybe you would have liked to—"

"My name is Abbie Cassius."

Jack's wallet fell onto the bar as he rocked back to stare at her. He knew the name quite well. He'd seen photographs of her. And there was a resemblance beneath her unhealthy, gaunt demeanor. The cheekbones were unattractively defined, but the nose was still straight, the green eyes wide-set and unblinking as they searched his.

"Abbie Cassius?" he said numbly. "I'm sorry for not recognizing you."

"But you recognize the name," she said, smiling. "I was a number with the so-called Spiderman. Now I'm ready to bring him down, at least financially. You game?"

Jack shrugged. "Were he a PT boat and I a torpedo. I know he did it, Abbie. All but twelve human beings on this planet know he did it. He not only got away with it, but he's trying to win back supporters with this five-million-dollar offer for the conviction of a nonexistent person. Pretty damn safe, isn't it?"

"You and I can screw him. It'll take the both of us, but it can be done. Why don't we find a more private place to talk?"

He looked at her for a long moment, not sure how to assess her. She was ill, obviously; whether or not she was paranoid or schizophrenic or whatever would have to be determined. He'd covered the investigation and snooped where he could, but had never found definitive proof that Spider Durmond had murdered his wife. If this washed-out woman could make the case, so be it. Screwing Spider did not appeal, except in the literal sense. And that appealed very much.

"Okay," he said at last, "why don't we move to a booth? If you have information, I'll listen. You want something to eat?"

"All I want is to teach Spider a lesson he won't forget," she said, heading for a corner booth. She waited until Jack had positioned himself across from her, then continued. "I don't know what you remember about me. I dated Spider for several months, and there were rumors that we might get married. What never came out was that I have a son, now ten, his biological father out of the picture. Ben's different; the clinical term is 'autistic,' and what it means is that he can't relate in a normal fashion. He tries to love me as best he can, but there are episodes when all I can do is remind myself of that. At the time Spider was around, Ben was spending weekdays at a residential facility and weekends at home with me."

"This created a problem?" said Jack, hating himself for lapsing into his old habits.

Abbie gave him a wry look. "Pull out a notebook if it'll make you more comfortable, or take notes on a napkin. Yes, Spider was pissed. He wanted Ben to idolize him like every other kid in America did. Ben was more concerned with astronauts and the space program; he couldn't have told you which day of the week it was, but he always kept track of the current shuttles and wanted to talk about Mir and the space telescopes. It made Spider crazy."

"How crazy?"

"Spider brought Ben a basketball for Christmas. When Ben reacted indifferently, Spider slapped him around. I became hysterical, and the whole thing erupted to the point that a neighbor called the police. I was ready to accuse Spider of everything from assault to child abuse when he made it clear that if I so much as pointed a finger at him, something bad would happen to

Ben. Spider said that he had plenty of friends who enjoyed hurting little boys." Abbie teared up, looked away. "So when the cops came, I told them that everything was okay. Spider swore that he'd give me enough money to get Ben the very best treatment—if I kept quiet."

"But he didn't," Jack murmured.

"Ben lost hearing in his right ear, and he lost a lot more than that. Spider has never given us a nickel. I tried to talk to him, to remind him of his promise, but he hung up when I called and pushed me aside when I came up to him in public. Eventually he got a restraining order that barred me from attempting to make any contact or setting foot on his property. When I violated it, I was sent to the state mental hospital for evaluation. Thirty days in a snake pit. I don't recommend it."

"I know the story. You didn't have any way to make him pay you off. Why didn't you just let it go?"

"You remember how I used to look? Curves in all the right places, firm muscles, golden hair?" She paused until he reluctantly nodded. "And you didn't recognize me when I sat down. It seems I have something called plasmocerciasis, caused by a microscopic worm found in the lakes and rivers in Brazil. It's exceedingly rare in this country. At first I thought I had the flu, but when it got worse, I started going to doctors. A specialist at Walter Reed finally made the diagnosis, but the prognosis is grim. Antibiotics are ineffective. Odds are I'll be dead in a year, maybe less."

"How'd you get infected?"

"A fashion magazine wanted an exotic background for a layout. The money was good. One of the teachers at Ben's school took care of him for the ten days I was there."

Jack considered offering sympathy, then decided she wouldn't be receptive. "Okay, let's go back to

something you said earlier. You were at Suzanne's
house when Spider killed her? That's hard to swallow,
Abbie."

"I know," she said. "After I was released from the
hospital and threatened with jail time if I violated the
restraining order again, I stayed away from Spider.
Then I learned how sick I was. I can't even hold down
an office job, and I don't have enough money to make
sure Ben will be taken care of after I'm dead. I went on
welfare, which gave me lots of free time to stalk Spider,
but this time from a prudent distance. I watched his
house. I followed his car. I couldn't afford tickets to his
basketball games, but I was always parked nearby
when he left the arena. When he and Suzanne were
married, I was in the crowd on the sidewalk across
from the church. I sat outside restaurants while they ate
lobster and drank champagne. I called his house from
pay phones, but hung up if anyone answered."

"Planning to accomplish what?"

"I don't know. I guess I hoped he would somehow
sense my presence and worry that I might blow him
away when he turned his back. I wanted him to feel just
a fraction of the anxiety I feel about the future." She
took a deep breath and exhaled slowly. "But let's talk
about the day Suzanne was killed. I was there that afternoon, parked down the street, when Spider drove to her
house and stayed for about half an hour. When he came
out onto the porch, I could see he was turning on the
charm, smiling, nodding at her, probably making prom-
ises to take her to Paris and the Riviera when the basketball season was over. He's a very slick performer."

"He admitted he went to her house that day," Jack
said. "According to his story, that's when he scratched
his arm on the screen door and dripped blood on the
carpet. How do I know you didn't read it in the newspaper?"

"I can describe her house."

"The address was published, as well as photographs of the house and street. Newscasters did broadcasts from the sidewalk out front. There was footage of the jury as they were escorted inside. Ninety percent of the people in this tavern can describe the house, Abbie. You'll have to do better than that to convince me that you were there."

"Which is what I'm going to do," she said. "Spider testified that on the night of her death, he went out to dinner, then went home. If anyone had asked me, I could have backed up that much of his testimony, since I was following him. He parked in the driveway. After a few minutes, all the downstairs lights went off and shortly thereafter the light in his bedroom came on. I was about to leave when I heard a car door slam. Seconds later he drove out the gate, his headlights dark. I followed him, naturally, and realized pretty quickly where he was headed."

Jack felt a chill, as if the air conditioner had been turned up. "Suzanne's?"

"Forty-five minutes later he turned onto her road. I parked behind a grocery store and walked the half mile to the house. His car wasn't there, but the lights were on and the front door was open. I was standing in the shadows, wondering if I ought to go home and say a prayer for her, when headlights came on further down the road. I jumped behind some shrubs as Spider drove by."

"You're sure you recognized the car?"

She laughed contemptuously. "Yes, I'm sure; my hobby was such that I could have spotted his car in a blizzard. I figured he'd tried to insinuate himself back into her good graces and she'd thrown him out. The open door bothered me, though, so I waited. An hour later, the door was still open and the same lights still on. I finally decided to go into the yard to get a better look. I ended up in the living room. She was on her back on the floor with the knife in her chest. There was blood all over the place, but I made myself feel for a pulse. She was dead."

"And you didn't call nine-one-one."

"Obviously," she said. "I'd been warned that if I had any further contact with Spider, including following him, I'd face felony charges. I couldn't prove he'd been there. My word against his, and I'd spent thirty days in a mental institution for stalking him. Crazy woman versus insanely popular athlete. No, I didn't call nine-one-one or anyone else. Would you have?"

Jack regarded her soberly. "If what you're saying is true, you committed a felony by failing to report the crime."

"What's your point?"

"Okay, okay," he said, almost ashamed of himself. "Then what happened?"

"I took her wedding ring off her finger. Maybe it was an awful thing to do, but all I was thinking was the last thing she deserved was to be buried as the wife of a monster. I didn't try to sell it or anything. I've still got it, as well as my blood-stained shoes and trousers. I was in such shock that I stuffed them in the back of a closet. Now I'm glad I did, since they're proof that I was at the scene."

"Not proof that you killed her, though," Jack said. "The detectives determined early in the investigation that you weren't a suspect. You told them you were home, and since you hadn't bothered Spider for over a year or ever threatened Suzanne, they crossed you off the list."

Abbie shrugged. "Here's what is going to happen. When Spider was found innocent, you started thinking about other possibilities. Tomorrow, you'll come to my apartment and interview me. You leave with some troublesome ideas. You reread all the police reports and talk to your pals who were on the case, then return to interview me. I break down and admit that I went to Suzanne's house to convince her . to resist Spider's sweet-talk. I describe how she realized who I was and became verbally abusive, how I grabbed a knife from a drawer and stabbed her, then yanked out the knife and later threw it out the car window while driving up a canyon road. I'll tell this to the prosecuting attorney, and to the judge when the time comes. No excuses, no insanity plea. I expect to get twenty-five to life, but that's not a concern. Later, you hold your own press conference and say that because you feel sorry for me, half the money is going into a trust fund for Ben." She stared at him. "I've arranged for a lawyer to draw up the papers and administer the trust. You'll keep half of whatever's left after taxes. Not a bad day's work, is it?"

"What if your doctor tells the press that you have this terminal disease?"

Abbie looked at him as though he was particularly dim-witted. "For one thing, he's bound by doctor-patient confidentiality, and I'm not about to give him permission to ever mention I was a patient. For another, he took a sabbatical and is in Brazil working with tropical disease experts there. If I'm questioned about my health, I'll just say that my consuming guilt ruined my appetite and prevented me from sleeping. There won't be a trial. My lawyer will negotiate a sentence in exchange for my full cooperation. All you have to do is play your part."

Jack envisioned himself at the precinct, telling the detectives that he strongly suspected Abbie Cassius, scorned ex-girlfriend and known harasser, had not only killed Suzanne Durmond but also retained evidence of her complicity in the crime. No matter how skeptical they were, they'd feel obliged to talk to her.

To add the icing to the cake, Spider's expression when he learned of her confession would be worth more than five million dollars. If he admitted his own guilt, double jeopardy would protect him from a second criminal indictment, but expose him as an easy target for a civil suit by his victim's family. That could cost him ten times as much.

"Do you have absolute faith in me?" he asked. "What if I forget about the trust fund?"

"When you come to my apartment, you're going to sit down and write a letter disclosing your role in a conspiracy to commit fraud, obstruct justice, and engage in theft by deception. You used to be a good reporter, Jack. I know you'll be able to capture the essence of this conversation, as well as describe your subsequent intentions to lie to the detectives and prosecutors. This letter will be in your own handwriting, of course. You'll then hand it over to me, and get it back as soon as Ben's share has been deposited in the trust account."

Jack was becoming impressed with her attention to detail. "What if Spider claims he's broke and refuses to cough up the money?"

"At the press conference he said that he can raise it by selling his mansion and his ranch in Colorado. He's on record, and you can sue him if necessary. Poor old Spider will be broke, without any expectations of multimillion-dollar basketball contracts and lucrative product endorsements. No more glitzy parties, movie premieres, celebrity tennis tournaments, television talk shows, complimentary suites in Vegas. He won't end up in prison, but a crummy one-bedroom apartment might begin to feel a little bit like a cell."

"One last question," he said. "Why me?"

"Why not?" she murmured, then wrote an address on a napkin and shoved it across the table. "Come over tomorrow morning and we'll get the show on the road."

Within a matter of weeks, Abbie Cassius had been transferred to a federal penitentiary, her prediction of twenty-five to life uncannily accurate. Spider Durmond had called a press conference during which he claimed to be pleased by this triumph of truth and justice, but his eyes had blazed with enough fury to melt a camera lens. Jack had been badgered by the media as well. Public sentiment had rumbled against him until he'd announced plans to establish a trust fund for the innocent, emotionally disabled boy.

The furor abated for several months, then flickered briefly when Spider publicly presented a check to Jack on the steps of the courthouse. Battling nausea and feeling no sense of virtue, Jack had accepted it with a grimace. Only then had he made the four-hour drive to visit Abbie behind the foreboding gray walls. She'd adjusted to the routine, she said, and was allowed to call Ben once a week. When her calls stopped, she doubted he would notice.

The day after he finalized the trust, a messenger delivered a thin package. Inside was his handwritten letter; there was no indication anyone had tampered with the sealed envelope. He burned it, then gathered the ashes and flushed them down the toilet.

It was three months later, while sitting beside a pool in a luxurious hacienda in Baja California, sunburned after a day of deep-sea fishing and on his third margarita, that Jack wandered across the article buried within the back pages of the *Los Angeles Times*. Researchers at a hospital in Rio had found an antibiotic that could reverse, or at least impede, the debilitating symptoms of plasmocerciasis, a disease virtually unknown outside of certain regions of the Amazon rain forest.

He thought back to Abbie's confession at the sentencing hearing, when the judge had required her to describe the particulars of her crime before accepting her guilty plea. She'd either embellished her fantasy with the polished skill of a best-selling horror novelist, or the twelve jurors had been right. Hard to know. In either case, Abbie had gotten what she wanted, and justice had been served, albeit lukewarm and difficult to digest.

He decided to send a postcard to Abbie the next day. "Wish you were here," he'd write.

Why not?

SARAH SHANKMAN's ten highly acclaimed novels include seven in
her comedic-mystery series starring reporter Samantha Adams.
When the author isn't writing about beauty queens, voodoo prac-
titioners, Elvis impersonators, con women, and assorted southern
obsessions, she sometimes moonlights as a food critic and magazine editor. In "Love Thy Neighbor," she brings us a young
woman driven to frenzy by an unseen—but certainly not un-
heard—neighbor.

LOVE THY NEIGHBOR

by Sarah Shankman

I'm going to shoot him." Julie glared at the digital
clock on her bedside table. Six a.m. She hadn't gotten
to sleep until three: left the restaurant at one, a couple
of hours to unwind, study a script, fool around with
Patrick. Then, as usual, she'd had trouble nodding off.
And now . . .

"Hunh?" Patrick rolled toward her but didn't open
his eyes. He was only a millimeter into consciousness.

"That bastard!" If the hand Julie flung had been a
knife, it would have pierced the heart of the man in the
apartment upstairs. "He's killing me. *Tromp, tromp,
tromp* ever since the day he moved in."

It didn't take much to awaken Julie. Sleep—or the
lack of it—was her bête noire, her cross to bear. Her in-
somnia had begun when she was a child back in North
Carolina, no napper she, and now her sleep deficit was
nearly thirty years deep. Some nights she couldn't drift

off. Others, she awoke in the wee hours, and that was it. She had to learn to deal with stress, her present shrink said. The one before that had given up, opining that some people are simply hardwired to toss and turn. Julie had all the insomniac's paraphernalia: blackout shades, earplugs, a white-noise machine. She exercised regularly, took no caffeine after noon, ate lightly before bedtime. Her apartment building had, thank God, installed double-paned windows a couple of years earlier. Still, neighbors were the one thing over which she had no control.

Patrick flopped over, giving her his bare back, and began snoring immediately, tangled in the hot sheets of summer.

Julie gritted her teeth. Bad enough that Patrick was in her bed anyway. It wasn't as if she loved him. Most of the time she didn't even *like* Patrick, with whom she worked at Lippi's, where they, both actor-waiters, served up exorbitantly expensive pasta to those who had already hit the big time. But Patrick had good connections. He was up for a role with a hot young independent director. Besides, Julie's most recent doctor at the sleep clinic had said, "I want you to use your bed for nothing but sleep and sex." She was getting precious little of the former, so . . .

Now the upstairs neighbor began his morning march. How could anyone walk so much, simply getting dressed? He circled and recircled, doglike.

"Damn you!" Julie cried. "Sit!" Then she jumped up, grabbed her red-handled broom, and jabbed at the ceiling. Already there was a rash of scarlet pockmarks in the plaster.

The man above answered with an angry stomp, his hard-soled shoes resounding on his hardwood floors. Wall Street shoes, Julie called them, though she had no idea where he worked, what he did, even what his real name was. There were only initials on the building's directory. *JL*. Nothing on his mailbox but the apartment number. *John Lennon* was what her crazy super had told her when she asked. *John Lennon*.

What a sick joke. Everyone knew John Lennon was long dead, struck down by an assassin's bullets about two miles north and west of her building on the fringes of Murray Hill. Lennon had lived in grandeur at West Seventy-second Street and Central Park West, in the Dakota. He'd died out in front of that fabulous old building, the setting for the movie *Rosemary's Baby*. The Dakota was spooky and dark with Gothic arches and gargoyles, a nineteenth-century castle with thick, thick walls and floors through which no one could hear your screams.

Julie's building was nothing like that. Red brick, square, with no adornment, it had been cheaply constructed in the 1950s. A friend of Julie's once told her that she'd grown up in a housing project in Rhinebeck that was its twin. The building's main drawback, other than its proximity to the traffic of the Midtown Tunnel, was the fact that its plaster ceilings were separated from the hardwood floors of the next apartment by nothing more than two inches of air.

"Visualize yourself somewhere else," her shrink had suggested. She'd come up with a dandy: a magical chamber, floating out of time and space. The room was lined with cork and eiderdown, a pillowed and perfumed bower for the Princess and the Pea.

But, in reality, Julie had no magical chamber, no famously thick walls and floors, as she lay wide awake chewing on her curdled thoughts. For example, it occurred to her that despite the dissimilarities between her building and the Dakota, if someone were shot out front, the crime scenes would look the same on the eleven o'clock news. The crumpled figure on the sidewalk, the pool of blood, the yellow tape, the cops holding back the curious crowd.

John Lennon, indeed.

"I'm going to shoot him," Julie said to Lisa. The two friends were eating hot dogs from a pushcart. Water sheeting down a brick wall to one side of the vest-pocket park provided a modicum of relief from the sticky summer heat.

Lisa said, "Doesn't your air conditioner block out some of his noise?"

"Not nearly enough. He's up at dawn every morning. *Even* weekends. *Tromp, tromp, tromp.* And sometimes he gets home later than I do. *Tromp, tromp.*"

"You said you tried a note?"

"Three or four. They started out sweet and rapidly progressed to ballistic."

"He has *no* carpeting?"

Julie shrugged. "Some. But nowhere near what he ought to. What is it the city requires, seventy percent?" Julie herself had lots of thick carpets. Even so, she never ever wore her shoes in her apartment. She was a *considerate* neighbor.

"You complained to the landlord?"

"Of course."

"And?"

"He'd love it if I moved."

"Oh, right. You have that great rent."

"How else could I afford to live in the city? I don't see my star rising anytime soon."

"No callbacks?"

"Callbacks? I'm lucky if I ever get through an audition without blowing the lines. I'm telling you, Lisa, the man is ruining my life. I can barely remember my own name. And check out these circles under my eyes. I look like a hag."

"You do not." Then Lisa, afraid that Julie would see the lie in her eyes, changed the subject. "How's Patrick? Have you two kissed and made up?"

"Are you kidding? We're civil to one another at work, but it's definitely over."

"Have you tried talking things out?"

"What's there to say to someone who thinks you're crazy? He says I'm obsessed with the man upstairs. That if I weren't such a wacko, good sex would make me sleep like a baby. I said, 'Yeah, *good* sex might. . . .' "

"You didn't!"

"Of course I did. What am I supposed to do, protect his delicate feelings?" Julie was getting a migraine. She pushed her damp bangs back from her forehead. "He certainly doesn't care about mine. Patrick's a beast, not even worth shooting."

Just then, around the corner on the Avenue of the Americas, a car backfired.

Lisa jumped.

Julie smiled.

"I'm going to shoot him."

"Julie, darling, I wish you wouldn't talk like that."

Julie stared out her dirty windows at the Thursday afternoon traffic. All the rich rats were heading for the Midtown Tunnel to the Long Island Expressway, then on to the Hamptons for the long weekend. "Ma, I'm almost thirty. I'm not a child."

"I know, dear. I'm sorry. It's just that I worry about you in that city."

Julie sighed.

"Wouldn't you like to come home for a week or so?

I'd love to see you. We could go swimming every day. It's been a while."

"It's even hotter there than here." Summertime in North Carolina was always brutal. But at least there were no sidewalks lined with rotting garbage, no subway platforms reeking of hot piss.

"We could go up to the lake. Or to the beach, if you want." Julie's mom wasn't giving up easily. She wanted to get her daughter home, fatten her up a bit. The last time she'd seen Julie, she'd been drawn and peaked.

"I have to work."

"All right, dear. But let's put our heads together about this hideous neighbor of yours. Have you offered to buy him house slippers? Wouldn't that help?"

Have you tried earplugs? Have you considered acoustical tile? How about splitting the cost with him, at least in his bedroom, of wall-to-wall? How many suggestions had Julie heard from well-meaning friends? Suggestions that drove her wild. *Considered giving up coffee? Tried meditation? Acupuncture? What about melatonin? Chamomile tea? Getting out of bed when you can't sleep?* As if she were a fool. As if she hadn't tried everything on God's green earth to solve her sleep problems. "I left slippers outside his door, Ma. Ages ago. He won't wear them."

"Well, dear, maybe they weren't his size."

Julie had to bite her lip to keep from screaming. "Bigfoot's *shoe size?* Huge. That's what I bought. Huge! Hell, Ma, I've never even seen him!"

Not that Julie hadn't tried to confront her neighbor. Many's the dawn Julie had grabbed her robe and raced up the stairs hoping to catch him. But she'd never been successful. She could feel him skulking behind his peephole. He knew what she looked like, while he remained Mr. Mystery Man.

Once or twice, she'd lost it and pounded on his door. "I know you're in there, you son of a bitch!"

Another time, she'd crept up and crouched against his door so he couldn't see her through the peephole. She'd waited for a long time, but still he didn't show. He could smell her out there, she was sure of it. A Wall Street wolf, he had a predator's keenly developed sense of danger.

"Or how about the mountains, dear?" Mom was still on the line, still pitching. "Remember how much you used to love the mountains when Daddy was alive?"

Oh, yes. They'd had lots of sweet times back then. Hot dogs on the grill. Toasted marshmallows. Ghost stories round the campfire. Her father, a loving, patient man, had spent many an hour teaching her how to cast into fish-rich streams. And how to shoot a rifle. Julie had never been afraid of guns. She'd loved the smell of the oiled blue steel, the *snick* of the cartridges' slide. Julie was a natural, a good shot. She'd punched many a tin can right out of the blue sky. She wasn't bad with a handgun either.

"I could fly down, take the train back," Julie heard herself saying, that reptilian part of her brain knowing, before she was conscious of it, why.

"I'm going to shoot him," Julie said to her friend Cassandra, the two of them waiting to pick up orders at Lippi's service window.

"I thought your little trip chilled you out."

"I wish. Bigfoot never takes a vacation. He's right there, every morning, six on the dot." Julie picked up her two dishes, one scallop, one sea bass. Who could stomach anything heavier? HEAT WAVE GRIPS NORTH-

EAST FOR SEVENTH WEEK! It had actually been cooler in North Carolina.

"I've got a friend back home who can put a curse on your neighbor. Want me to call?"

"No, thanks. A couple of slugs ought to do the trick."

Cassandra's eyebrows took a hike halfway up her forehead. "Whoa, girl. You feeling all right?"

"No, Cassandra. Actually, I feel like shit."

Sleep deprivation will do that. A night or two causes that feeling like a hangover or the flu, headachy, a kind of all-over malaise with which most people are familiar. Weeks, months, years can wreak much more serious havoc. Julie constantly wobbled on the edge of tears. Some days, she couldn't speak at all. Her chest thrummed with exhaustion, and a deep breath was impossible. Her dulled brain ached constantly and felt as if it were bouncing off craggy places inside her skull. Perhaps, she thought, her intracranial fluid had evaporated. She could feel her bones too, within her skin.

She said, "It's bad, Cassandra. Really bad. I really do think I'm going to have to kill him if he doesn't stop walking on my head."

But Cassandra was no longer paying attention to Julie. "Wouldn't mind having *him* walking wherever he wanted to."

Julie turned to see a tall lanky man she'd noticed in the restaurant a couple of times before. He had the kind of looks that grabbed you, even in Lippi's, where movie stars were thick on the ground—a thatch of dark hair shot with silver, a wide sexy mouth, dangerous brown eyes.

"He's probably an ax murderer," Julie said. "Those gorgeous ones usually are."

"Whatever. He's still got to eat. And he's in your station. Now you go, girl. Sell him some expensive wine. Earn yourself a big tip."

The handsome man had a heartbreaking smile. "Good evening yourself," he replied to her greeting. Then he and his dinner companion, an older man, proceeded to order a lovely meal: quail eggs with caviar, a frisée salad, lobster ravioli, a hundred-dollar bottle of champagne. They were fun to serve, savvy diners without pretension. They both flirted with her, mildly.

It was the older man, on his way to the men's room at the end of the night, who stopped Julie and pressed a card into her hand. Too bad, he was much too old and not the one she would have chosen. "I'm sorry," she was about to say, "but my boyfriend. . . . "

"Please call my son." He smiled. "He's too shy to ask you himself. I swear he's a great guy, though probably I'm prejudiced."

Julie stared at the business card for a long time. *Jonathan Lemmon.* He was with one of the big Wall Street brokerage houses. *Jon Lemmon.*

"I'm going to shoot him," Julie whispered to herself the next morning at six A.M.

She lay in bed staring up at the ceiling. She thought that she could *see* the footprints there.

It was just a coincidence, right? *John Lennon. Jon Lemmon.* It didn't mean a thing.

Her upstairs neighbor was not the man whose card was tucked in her purse.

(Was he?)

She jumped up, found the card, and dialed the office number printed there, Jon Lemmon's private extension. He wouldn't be in, of course. It was way too early.

(And perhaps he was still upstairs.)

(And perhaps she was losing her mind.)

"Hi, this is Jonathan Lemmon. Sorry I'm not in to

take your call, but leave your name and number and I'll get back to you soon."

It was the voice of the man she'd met the night before. Julie had never heard the voice of the man upstairs, not even the baffled tones of an answering machine. Only his footfall.

Julie hung up without leaving a message.

Then she fell back on her bed, clenching and unclenching her fists. Tears ran from the corners of her eyes and onto her pillow. She was going crazy. She had stepped way over the line. She no longer knew what was real and what was imaginary. Her sleeplessness was killing her.

"I'm going to shoot him."

The actress up on the stage delivering that line was young and thin like Julie, but blond, whereas the sleek curtain of hair Julie pulled back to gaze at Jon's profile in the theater was inky dark.

Jon caught her look and aimed his wonderful smile at her. She felt the electricity down her thighs. She'd been tingling with excitement since he'd answered the message she'd left at his office the second time she'd called. He'd seemed so pleased. Dinner and the theater? He just happened to have house seats for the biggest hit on Broadway. Cassandra, what an angel, had agreed to work her shift for her.

Julie found Jon easy to talk with. So sweet. Funny. With lovely manners.

"Feel like a nightcap?" he said as the actors took their final bows. "How about the bar at the Rainbow Room?"

Oh, yes, indeed. For she was Cinderella at the ball, dreading not the pumpkin but Jon's turning into Bigfoot, fearful of hearing his step overhead moments after arriving home. It was an insane notion, she knew that, but she couldn't help herself. She wanted to stay here forever, at the top of Rockefeller Center, gazing out across the dazzle that was Manhattan, the center of the universe, her adopted home. She had a cosmopolitan, a drink first created at this very bar, then another. She didn't want to go, didn't want to know. But she couldn't drink all night.

"Ready?" John was smiling at her.

She slipped from the barstool, and his hand grazed the small her back. Oh, God, how long had it been since she'd felt like this? Had she ever, really? Exactly this way?

Jon saw her home. The very most a woman expected in this city was that a date would put her in a cab and hand the driver a twenty.

But maybe Jon wasn't just seeing her home. Maybe he was going home too. Maybe all he had to do was take the elevator one floor up.

Yet he didn't release the taxi. "I'll just be a minute," he said to the cabbie. He kissed her hand at her lobby door. "I'll call you tomorrow," he promised, then watched until she was safely inside.

She couldn't very well wait to see if he paid off the cab and sent it on its way. She blew a kiss to him as the elevator doors closed.

But once in her apartment, she waited. And waited. And waited. She counted to one hundred, but there wasn't a peep from above. She strained and strained, but all she heard was the ringing of her own ears, then a fire engine outside.

Finally Julie undressed, climbed into bed, and slipped between her smooth cool sheets. She stretched langorously, happier than she'd ever known she could be, and nodded off.

It was after two A.M. when Julie awoke to the familiar echo of hard-soled shoes. "I'm going to shoot you," she whispered into her pillow, then plummeted effortlessly back into the void.

"I'm going to shoot him."

"Who?" Jon said lazily, drugged by their lovemaking.

"The bastard who lives upstairs. Wait and see. He'll wake us up at six." She paused. "You are staying over, aren't you?"

"Unless you kick me out."

"No way."

"Good. Tell you what. If he wakes us, I'll go upstairs and blow his brains out. But right now . . ." He reached for Julie's warm flesh, held her tight.

"You would never torment your neighbor like that?" She couldn't help herself. She had to ask.

"Never. I'm only interested in tormenting you." He nuzzled that little indentation at the top of her breastbone, then tickled her ribs.

She fell happily into his heat, a delicious contrast to the icy air from the AC. Jon Lemmon was so wonderful. He was the best thing that had ever happened to her.

"What are you giggling about, you sexy wench?"

"I was just thinking. When I first heard your name, I thought you said *John Lennon.*"

"I get that sometimes." His tongue was lazy and oh so sweet as it traced a route south. "But somebody shot John Lennon dead a long time ago."

"I know. In 1980. Shot him stone dead."

"I'm going to shoot him."

"Correct me if I'm wrong, Julie, but I thought you

said your neighbor had laid off. Or, we agreed, perhaps it's that you don't hear him as much anymore since Jon's come into your life. Since you're happier, more relaxed."

Julie stared across the room into her shrink's kindly face. He was such a nice man. He truly did care about her, she'd always felt that. He wanted to help her. But what was he going to say when she told him that the apartment upstairs was silent only on the mornings that Jon was in her bed? He was going to think she was *really* crazy. He might even want her to check into a hospital for observation.

"Let's go to your place," she'd said to Jon more than once. He'd told her he lived in a loft in TriBeCa, on North Moore. The night before, she'd really pushed.

Jon said, "Sure, hon. We will. But, like I told you, I'm in the middle of renovations. It's such a mess. I don't want you to see it like this."

"But I'd love to. The before and after, you know?"

"Okay. But wait until there's a floor in the kitchen. A couple more weeks."

"I'm going to shoot him," Julie moaned into her pillow. "When he gets back, I'm going to shoot him."

Jon had been gone for a week, on business to Hong Kong, he said.

He'd called her a couple of times. He was awfully sweet on the phone. But after each call, she'd been more miserable than before. She couldn't shut off the questions in her head. How did she know where he was calling from? He could be anywhere. Though for sure he wasn't upstairs. There hadn't been a single sound from there since the moment Jon had left for wherever

he was. Was Jon really John? Julie couldn't stop weeping. She hadn't slept a wink.

She'd figured out how to prove it once and for all. Julie
had a plan. She knew exactly what to do. All she had to
do was wait.

Jon's plane had arrived at JFK two hours earlier.
One hour to claim his bags, go through customs. Another for the ride in from the airport. And now, right on
schedule, came the first footfall.

"No!" Julie screamed in anguish. "No, please God!"
Her heart was broken, her worst fears realized.

For a moment, she forgot her plan. Instead, she
grabbed for her broom and pounded and pounded as if,
with the force of her pain, her fury at the unfairness of it
all, she could change the reality of the man upstairs. She
pounded so hard, the handle broke through the plaster
ceiling, and dust and debris drifted down around her.

But the sound didn't stop. Instead, the footsteps
grew louder and faster. The man, Jon, oh Jon, stepped
and stomped and kicked. He tangoed. Do-si-doed.
Riverdanced. She pounded again and again, and he
clogged. His Wall Street shoes smacked the hardwood
in a fusillade of blows. Then, finally, he bellowed. His
voice was muffled, but she could understand the words.
"You bitch!" he cried. "You crazy bitch!"

His words snapped Julie back to her plan. It was
now or never, do or die. Julie snatched up the phone
and dialed Jon's number, the number he'd given her for
his loft in TriBeCa. "Please, God," she prayed, but
there it was, the incontrovertible evidence. The phone
rang once in her ear, as it rang upstairs, and then it
stopped. Julie doubled over at the anguish in her gut.

"Hello? Hello?"

"Jon?" she gasped.

"Julie? Sweetie? Are you all right?"

"Where are you?"

He laughed. "You called *me*. I'm home. I got in only a few minutes ago. I had my hand on the phone to call you, darling. Are you okay? You sound terrible."

"I heard your footsteps. I heard you answer the phone. I know it's you up there."

There was a long silence on the other end of the line. Then Jon said, "Julie, sweetie, dear heart. We've got to do something about this."

"I know what to do. I know exactly what to do."

"I'm going to kill him," Julie said to herself with each step as she climbed to the floor above. To Jon, to her tormentor, her sweetheart, the love of her life. Waves of grief washed over her. Her brain pounded, *Why?* That was all she could think. Julie couldn't get past the first word of the question. *Why?* She was so tired. The torture had gone on so long. Far too long. So many years.

She unlocked the door at the top of the stairs.

She stepped into the hallway and made her way slowly to the door of the apartment directly above hers. She pounded once, twice.

The door flew wide.

The man standing there in the doorway, the man with fury inscribed across his face, was no one Julie had ever seen before.

"You're crazy, you know that?" he shouted, then he pushed out past her, slamming and double-locking his door.

He headed down the stairs. Julie followed. She was right on his tail.

"You've *made* me crazy!" she screamed. "You wake me up every single morning. This is all your fault."

"Ha! That's a good one."

Down, down, they went, the man in his Wall Street shoes, clattering on the stairs, Julie silent and swift in her bare feet.

They whirled through the bottom door, through the lobby, past the fake palm trees, the low benches, and out onto the sidewalk.

"I have to talk with you!" she shouted. "You have to stop this!"

But the man didn't slow. So she grabbed the back of his suit jacket and whirled him around. They froze, an odd couple, one fully dressed, one in her night-clothes, out in front of their building, just outside the lobby door.

"Outta my face!" the man who was not Jon Lemmon shouted. "Get a life, why don't you?"

People, smelling of shampoo and aftershave, slowed in their rush toward the subway station, staring at what looked to be an al fresco marital dispute.

"I *have* a life," Julie cried. "Had." The sadness in Jon's last words to her echoed in her heart. Then from a pocket of her pj's she pulled the sleek Glock 19 revolver she'd brought back from North Carolina on the train. No metal detectors on the choo-choo. "But you've ruined it. Destroyed it. And now I'm going to have to shoot you."

But Julie was hesitant, derailed by the toll her sleeplessness had taken. By confusion. By tears.

Then John Linden, Julie's upstairs neighbor and a junior-high math teacher whose summer-school students daily terrified the bejeezus out of him, pulled a .38 from the shoulder holster he wore, illegally, beneath his jacket. "Not if I shoot you first," he said.

And then he did.

PETE HAUTMAN *has written seven novels featuring dead-on por-*
trayals of con men, gamblers, hustlers and good-enough guys
with crazy ideas. He has been nominated for an Edgar Award,
and his novels have been selected as New York Times *notable*
books. As Peter Murray, he has written numerous nonfiction chil-
dren's books. In "Showdown at the Terminal Oasis," a group of
bar regulars are still working out a thirty-year-long grudge.

SHOWDOWN AT THE
TERMINAL OASIS

by Pete Hautman

I'm topping off the Stoly bottle with the cheap stuff which is just as good when Mike Cullen comes downstairs mad as a wet tomcat, banging the door against the wall. For revenge the door clips him on the shoulder. Mikey takes a cut at it, misses, curses, swings again. The door dances back and Mikey just brushes it with the hairy back of his fist but it is enough. That door settles right down.

Twenty, thirty years ago Mad Mike Cullen mighta put his fist right through the thing or since it is one hell of a thick slab of oak busted his hand on it. But Mikey went and got old the way a lot of guys do and he knows better now. He looks almost comical. Head sucked down between his shoulders, liver-spotted fists waving back and forth in front of his scrunched-up face. Most people seeing him like that would laugh, an old man just clowning around, but I can tell Mikey is genuinely ticked.

Something musta happened upstairs at the card game. Mikey probably got a good hand snapped off, or maybe he'd been losing right along like usual. Either way, I know what he needs now. I pour a shot of Beam, set it on the bar.

Back in the fifties before my time Mad Mike Cullen boxed featherweight, 120 pounds, lots of heart but getting his brains scrambled by a succession of older, smarter veterans. A few years later he got older and smarter himself but by then he was carrying an extra ten pounds, boxing lightweight class, and he didn't have his legs no more. Nineteen sixty thereabouts a kid named Gonzo Gonzalez did him the favor of permanently detaching his right retina with a short left hook. Mikey retired from boxing with a record something like 15 wins and 150 losses. In short, as a boxer, Mad Mike Cullen was a bum.

The door has shut itself now. Cullen is swiveling his head back and forth scanning the room for other sources of danger. Not a hell of a lot for him to worry about. Monday nights are always slow except for the card game upstairs, which has been going on since Friday. This particular Monday the bar is practically comatose. My big customer is Mrs. Lipke playing with her empty Miller bottles in the front booth, arranging them in drunken patterns on the table, occasionally discovering the one bottle still half full and taking a sip. She never lets me clear the empties. She likes to count them over and over, adding up her pleasure every way she knows. Mrs. Lipke use to be a CPA. Everybody use to be something. I use to be a professional golfer only I never won a dime and then I went and got married. Everybody makes mistakes. I still let Mrs. Lipke do my taxes every year. She does a fine job according to my cousin Jerry who I always have look over her work just to be on the safe side. Jerry works for a bank and is one of the few people I know never use to be something else. He was born a bean counter.

My only other customer this night is Lanny Wiseman the bookie. He use to run a cigar shop down on Third Avenue twenty, thirty years back but he'd been making book even then come to think of it. Lanny is sitting at the table next to the pinball machine punching numbers in his electric notebook, making cluck-clucking sounds with his tongue and shaking his head. Every few minutes he picks up his glass of Harveys and sort of licks the rim. Lanny can make a glass of sherry last a week. Nobody else in this town drinks Harveys Bristol Cream or if they do then they do not frequent the Terminal Oasis. That's my place. Smokey's Terminal Oasis. It is called that because there use to be a Greyhound bus terminal next door and because Smokey is my name. I am like a big bear they say.

Most ways Lanny Wiseman is an old-fashioned guy. After seventy-odd years he's got the right. But he loves his electric notebook. Half a century scribbling bets on scraps of paper and matchbooks and backs of coasters got Lanny's hands too twisted and tender to hang on to those pencil stubs. We are all falling apart—even me and I am young enough to be Lanny's kid god forbid. I figure Lanny for one of the point men, fighting back with his electric notebook, his slip-on shoes that don't need tying, his plastic pill box with a different compartment for each day of the week and a lifetime of street smarts. For instance he always has on his person an umbrella because in this town you never know when it is going to rain or when you might have to give somebody a poke in the ribs. Ever since I can remember Lanny has had his umbrella and hat and his seersucker suit. His shirt collars are an inch too big around now and his Panama hat bends out the tips of his radardish ears but you can tell he takes the time to look good. Even just walking the two blocks from his apartment to my joint for his glass of sherry he always manages to get his phony diamond links fastened through his French cuffs, a trick for any guy and one that must take Lanny's arthritic fingers the better part of a morning. You got to respect that kind of effort.

Mike Cullen naturally is acquainted with Lanny, both gentlemen being regulars and both of them from the neighborhood, however they do not care for each other. I know this without ever having heard it said straight out by either of them. You see two guys in the same place over and over again for twenty, thirty years and they never look at each other or talk, you get a clue. I never knew what it was happened between them. Probably neither of them remembers. Sometimes a guy says something you don't like, or doesn't do what he says, or laughs at the wrong time. You decide he's a jerk and the years go by and you forget what happened but you never forget he's a jerk, and most of the time he will think the same of you. Not that I give it much thought. I just pour the drinks.

I watch Cullen, now that he's got that door settled down, relax and straighten up to his full five-foot-five-inch height, then fix his eyes on the shot of bourbon I poured him. He crosses the room, hikes himself up onto the stool, puts his battered hands on either side of the shot glass, rolls it back and forth between his palms, the glass clicking his silver and turquoise rings. This means that he is thinking a thought. Pretty soon he will want to share it. Sometimes it takes him a while which is fine with me. Mike Cullen's thoughts are not what you would call worth waiting for. He tosses off half his whiskey, sets it back on the bar and keeps his thought to himself.

I deliver Miller number seven to Mrs. Lipke and collect one dollar twenty from the sticky pile of change on her table. She likes for me to take an extra dime for myself but after the fourth or fifth beer she doesn't notice so I don't bother. By the time I get back to the bar Cullen has finished his whiskey. I pour him another shot.

Again he rolls the glass, listening to it click against his rings.

"You know whatsa matter with that goddamn game?" he says at last.

"What?" I ask. I take his comment personally since the game to which he is referring is the one goes on upstairs of my bar three, four nights a week and which is known as Smokey's game. It's a friendly game, been going on years now. I say who plays, who doesn't. No one ever gets shot or stabbed or robbed or beat up. Mostly they play seven stud. High card brings it in for five, ten-twenty limit, table stakes. Now and then we raise it up. Some guys get stung pretty bad, but I never heard of anybody cashing in an IRA or pawning their wife's jewelry. Not that these guys have wives with jewelry or IRAs, but that's another subject. My game is an okay game. Nothing the matter with it.

Cullen shakes his head like he's trying to get blood out his eyes. "Damn rabbits," he says. He sips his whiskey. "Swear to god, Smoke, I got drawed out on five times runnin'. Had me a set of aces, two in the pocket and one up top. Three friggin' aces."

I am starting to get the picture. There is not a lot of honor and very little fun in playing against rabbits but to keep a regular game going you got to have them. Rabbits are to poker what Mad Mike Cullen had been to boxing. Born to lose. Only now and then the system breaks down and a rabbit gets on a run and goes hopping off with a wallet full of lettuce and we should all be happy because it means he will be back to play again, but to a guy like Mikey such behavior is an offense against nature.

"Those guys'll kill you," I say.

"You ain't kiddin'. Son-of-a-bitch got no business being in that pot. My pot. Son-of-a-bitch backs into a belly-buster his last card. He shoulda got out. Any sane person woulda folded, Smoke. I swear t' god—who can sit there and keep playing after something like that? I hadda come downstairs, take a break."

I shake my head in sympathy. "Those guys'll just kill you. Who was it?"

"Some drunk stockbroker, you can believe that."

The stockbroker had stumbled in a couple hours ago in his suit and tie, looking for action. He knew Swede, one of my regulars, so I sent him on upstairs. Too bad for Cullen.

"Worst card player I ever seen, up there playing with my money. Flashing his hand right and left, betting out of turn, wanting to see the next card every time he folds which, come to think, was maybe three times all night. Big fat jackass rabbit. He sure burned my ass."

"Bad beat, eh?" Lanny Wiseman sets his glass of sherry on the bar and props his skinny ass on the next stool over.

Cullen lets his head sink a couple inches down into his shoulders and raises the shot of whiskey to his lips.

Lanny says, "I been in this business sixty-four years now, taken my share of bad beats—cards, horses, prop bets, you name it. Bets I never shoulda lost. Only thing you can do is pay it and forget it. Only thing you can do." Lanny's got one tone of voice, a sort of creaky whine that sums up his personality about as good as anything. He hates to pay off a bet the way most of us hate to pay our taxes but because he has got to stay in business he always pays, carping all the way. Winning money from Lanny Wiseman is almost worse than losing it which was why instead of being rich he is still taking two-dollar bets out of my bar. No one with serious money to wager would go out of their way to look him up. Plenty of other bookies will pay off without making you feel like a jerk for winning.

"One time a guy bets me ten bucks he can bite his right eye," Lanny says, then waits for us to ask him to continue.

Cullen sort of growls. Lanny's voice makes people do that. Besides, we've all heard the old joke too many times from guys who tell it better than Lanny.

Lanny takes Cullen's growl as permission to go on. "I hear this, I can't get my money out fast enough. I figure the guy is drunk or crazy so why shouldn't I take a piece of his action? Then the guy pops out a glass eye and bites it!" He pauses here for effect, smiling and looking from me to Cullen then back again.

"So then the guy says," Lanny continues, "he takes my ten bucks and he says, 'I'll go you double or nothing I can bite my left eye. So now I figure he's this nice guy and this is how he's gonna give me my money back and besides, I know the guy don't have two glass eyes. So we bet and the guy takes out his false teeth and bites his own left eye. I tell ya. Sucker bets and bad beats. They don't never go away. Years later you're eating your goddamn chicken soup and you remember getting beat some way never shoulda happened and next thing y'know you're blowing noodles out your nose. I remember this one time musta been twenny, tirdy years ago, my cousin-in-law Mitchell who married my first cousin Marsha, who shoulda known better even back then, the guy still thinks he's Mitch the Greek or something, lays a bad beat on me still makes my ass burn.

"I never liked Mitch, y'know, a little putz trying to make like a mover-shaker goes and marries Marsha so I got to be nice to him. Take his little nothing bets, y'know, maybe show him the ropes. I don't mind that so much except the kid don't have no class. Kid wins a two-dollar bet on a cockfight he's Mr. Mouth, tells the whole world how he's beating poor old Lanny up down and sideways. Kid loses a bet he cries a river. No respect.

"So I figure when I got a chance to take a few bills off him on a sucker bet I was due it, y'know? I mean, all the noise I took from him I took for my cousin Marsha's sake, but I figure a chance to teach him a lesson was not to be passed up.

"See, Mitch had this buddy, some kind of neighborhood threat, and Mitch wants me to set him up, y'know? Introduce the kid to the right people, set him up as the next Henry Armstrong, on account of he knew how well-connected I was."

I nod to show him I am listening, not because I think he was ever well-connected. Well-connected guys do not frequent my establishment.

Cullen is not looking at Lanny, but I can tell he is listening.

Lanny continues some more. "Now this kid was a kid who never even seen the inside of a ring. A Jewish kid, f'chrissake, I know his mother. How many Jewish boxers you know? Mitch, he'd seen his buddy throw a few punches, something, take on a couple guys in a schoolyard, something, I don't know, and decided he was gonna be the kid's manager and make a fortune. Something. I say, 'Mitch, I never seen this guy fight. How am I suppose to introduce him, use up a favor, I never seen the kid so much as work a bag?'

"Mitch says, 'So let him go a few rounds with one a the guys you know. One a the pros works out down at Casey's. Show what he can do.'

"'Fugedaboudit,' I tell him. 'Kid gets his teeth knocked in I'm the one'll get blamed for it. You think I want his mama all over me next time I go to synagogue?' I mean, not that I ever went, but I make my point with young Mitchell who then says to me, 'He ain't gonna get his teeth knocked in. I'm willing to put money on it. A hunnert bucks says my guy wins.'"

Lanny looks at me and at Cullen and raises his wispy eyebrows up high.

"Now you guys know, like just about anybody would know, that you can take the fastest toughest kid ever threw a punch, and you can put him in a ring with the most beat-up, no-talent pro boxer and if that kid has never fought in the ring before and if that pro isn't dead drunk or asleep, the kid don't got a chance. It's a fact of life. The pro is going to win ten times outta ten. I figure this is my opportunity to teach Mitch and his buddy a valuable lesson, so I set it up with this guy I know who knows his way around the ring. Not a top guy, y'know, but a guy knows how to duck. I even pay him twenny bucks for his time. And then I take Mitch's hunnert-dollar bet and, because I am feeling generous, I give him two to one. Why not? I'm sure as hell not gonna lose.

"The next Saturday morning we meet up at Casey's. Mitch's guy is not as big or as hairy as I had imagined, and he has these nice white teeth. I tell my guy to try not to break 'em if he don't have to. We get them both gloved up and up into the ring and twenny, tirdy seconds later it is over and I am out two dimes." Lanny is looking at Cullen. "Now that is your bad beat, my friend."

"The kid won?" I ask.

"Tirdy seconds. My guy takes one on the chin, a little bip wouldn't stun my mother, and my guy goes down like he been sapped."

"The kid got lucky?"

Lanny doesn't reply. He is looking at Cullen in a way that makes me feel distinctly uncomfortable. I am getting the idea that I know the reason why these two do not care for one another.

"You want another Harveys?" I ask Lanny.

He shakes his head. He never wants another Harveys.

"A course, I got even with Mitchell in the long run, y'know. Won my two hunnert back and more. But I could never get straight in my mind why my guy went down. I know it wasn't the little tap on the chin he took, which he must've seen coming a mile off on account of Mitch's buddy was not all that fast and in fact the next time the kid climbed into the ring he got a couple of those nice straight teeth folded in by a guy half his size and nearly as green. Which has got to make you wonder how my guy went down that way, don't it?"

Cullen tosses down the rest of his shot. "Lanny," he says, "you still mad at that doctor gave you your first whack on the ass?"

"Son-of-a-bitch didn't need to hit me that hard," Lanny says, his rheumy eyes still stuck on Cullen.

Cullen stares back for ten, fifteen seconds, his knuckles wrapped white around the empty shot glass. I am wondering if I still got it in me to jump over the bar if things get uglier when Cullen yanks a roll out of his back pocket, peels off a twenty, slaps it on the bar in front of Lanny.

Lanny Wiseman looks at the curled bill. "What's that for?"

"What d'you think?"

Lanny pushes the money back toward Cullen, but not all the way.

"I just want to know what I ever do to you that you'd toss a fight against me like that? Only one reason I can think is Mitchell paid you to do the dive."

"There you go," Cullen growls.

"He paid you?"

Cullen shrugs.

"And you took it? After I pay you twenny outta my own pocket?"

"You paid me twenty to fight the kid and not knock

out his teeth, remember?" Eyes on his shot glass. "You
didn't tell me I had to win."

Lanny looks at me, then back at Cullen. His twisted
fingers creep across the bar and devour the twenty.
With a practiced motion that has so far escaped his
arthritis, he gives the bill a deft, one-handed fold and
makes it disappear. Touching the brim of his Panama
hat, he says, "I got to go see young Mitchell, see about
getting my two hunnert back. Statue of limitations
don't count with fixes."

Cullen and I watch him totter out the front door,
electric notebook clutched in one hand, umbrella in the
other.

I pour Cullen another shot. "On me," I say.

Cullen glares at me. "What for?"

"You're a good guy, Mikey."

"Not really," he says.

"You gave him his twenty bucks back and told him
what he wanted to hear, didn't you?"

"Yeah, I done that." He tosses off the shot. "I'm
gonna head back upstairs, look at a few more hands. See
about puttin' a beat on that stockbroker. I think I got my
perspective back now." He starts for the door, then turns
back. "Smoke, I didn't lay down for that kid."

"No?"

"No, and Lanny's cousin never paid me nothin'
neither."

"But then . . . why give Lanny the twenty?"

Cullen shrugs. "You think I want that cheap son-of-
a-bitch thinking I couldn'ta won that fight if I wanted
to? Thirty years now I been burning my ass remembering him watching me get knocked down by that skinny
little kid. I swear t' god, Smoke, the kid had the fastest
hands I ever seen. I was out cold before I even threw a
punch. Lanny thinks *he* was surprised, he oughta been
the one got hit." He shakes his head. "You talk about

your bad beats, man . . . anyways, I wish I could be there to watch Lanny try to get his two hundred back from Mitchell. That'd be worth another twenty bucks, minimum."

I watch him leave, then I deliver Miller number eight to Mrs. Lipke who is listing about fifteen degrees to starboard. This will be her last beer tonight. Back in her heyday, decades five and six, she could drain an even dozen, but not these days. Another hour, closing time, I'll ease her up and walk her the one and one-half blocks to her apartment and help her with her key and leave her propped up and smiling all loose on her cat-shredded sofa. After that I'll maybe swing back to the bar, head upstairs, sit in for a few hands. I'm curious to see how Mikey is doing now he has his bad beat behind him.

FUN WITH FORENSICS

by Eileen Dreyer

The first reaction most people had upon meeting Wanda Mummerson was openmouthed stupefaction. The second was disbelief. By the time the impulse to act finally resurfaced, it was often too late to stop Wanda from accomplishing whatever it was she was trying to get away with.

No one was more aware of this phenomenon than the secretary for the fledgling forensic science organization to which Wanda sought membership. The secretary, a thin, small, vole-like woman who specialized in forensic statistics, could most likely have fended Wanda off quite successfully if Wanda had approached her for membership through normal channels: the mail, the phone, the Internet. Any of the various means of communication that would have protected the secretary from the full brunt of Wanda's presence.

But Wanda, who was nothing if not resourceful,

presented her case to the secretary while that good woman served as registrar at the yearly forensic conference, where the secretary had neither the time, attention, nor stamina to withstand the assault. So before they knew it, the new Forensic Sciences Association, which was struggling to claim its place in the pantheon of professional organizations devoted to the burgeoning field, found itself saddled with a member who was not only completely unqualified, but a full-fledged psycho to boot.

"She wants to learn about forensics," the still-trembling, badly perspiring secretary offered three hours later in the lobby bar of the Los Angeles Hilton Towers. "I have a suggestion or two."

The other six people tucked around the knee-high cocktail table shook their heads in uncomfortable commiseration.

"Amateur," one snorted into his margarita.

The secretary looked up. "You don't know," she whined.

The snorter, a nearly seven-foot-tall death investigator named Max who looked as if he wrestled bears on his off hours, simply raised an arm to reveal a near-perfect oval of old scars no more than a millimeter south of his elbow.

The forensic odontologist who sat next to him, always on the prowl for a good slide of bite marks to show at conference time, sighed in envy.

"The Medico/Legal Death Investigation conference last summer," Max explained as he shucked his shirt back down over the evidence. "I made the mistake of trying to scoop the last of the lime Jell-O from the lunch buffet."

"I thought she wanted to be in forensic psychiatry," one of the drinkers offered.

"That's this summer," Max said. "Last year it was

death investigation. The year before it was undercover narcotics. I figure if we can just wait her out, she'll move on to something really hot, like angel catching or earthquake forecasting."

Tina, the secretary, was still riveted by the bite marks. "Didn't you press charges?"

Max smiled. "She claimed post-traumatic stress."

"She was in Vietnam?"

"Barney's during markdown days. She says she still can't go anywhere near bras or those little plastic things that hold sleeves in place on hangers."

"How about deodorant?" somebody asked. "Any reason she's so afraid of that?"

"Fluoride," another offered. "Communist conspiracy."

"Nah, that's not deodorant," Laura, a compact brunette trauma nurse from Detroit, disagreed. "That's the toothpaste she doesn't use either. She doesn't use deodorant because it interferes with her aura."

"It's interfering with my appetite," the odontologist claimed. "She sat next to me this morning in the arson victim panel, and I almost didn't last through it. First time I've ever been sick at the sight of dead people."

"Try eating at the same table," Laura retorted, inhaling her neat scotch as it if were the only water on dry land. "I don't think Godzilla has worse table manners."

"And then to make matters worse," another of the drinkers offered with a shudder, "in the middle of smearing stewed prunes all over herself, Wanda decides it's time we all share her childbirthing experience."

"She's been breeding?" three people asked in appalled unison.

Laura shuddered again. "A little girl. Pretty thing, too. She showed us the picture. My feeling is we should grab the baby and burn the nest while we have a chance."

Max considered his drink as if it were making him queasy. "Anybody know what the . . . uh . . ."

"Male of the species is like?" Laura shook her head. "She says she won't talk about him. My personal feeling is that after mating, she killed him and ate him."

"Although she did say she likes big, strapping guys," Margaret, the forensic radiologist, told Max with a salacious grin.

Everybody but Max thought that was really amusing.

"If she courts like she applies for memberships," Tina offered with heartfelt sincerity, "I'd run so fast even Jesus couldn't catch me."

There was a moment of silence, especially among the men who considered themselves vulnerable to attack. Finally, though, Tina, who took her position very seriously, got back to business.

"Isn't there anything we can do?" she begged. "Do you know what she's going to do to our credibility if anybody sees her membership identification?"

"Laugh until they have a seizure?" the odontologist asked.

"Commit her for delusions of sanity?" Margaret offered.

"Discount the rest of us as not worth consideration," Max was forced to admit. "Tina's right. We need to do something."

For a few moments, there was just silence and the soft sound of slurping as everyone concentrated on the problem.

"I say we kill her," Tina offered.

Max shook his head. "Don't forget that little girl."

"We could hold closed session and vote her back out," Laura suggested.

"She'd sue. She's already sued three workplaces, Barney's, and the manufacturers of two different kinds of breast implants."

"Not to mention an ex-husband who failed to impregnate her after she went to all the trouble of having the damn things put in."

"But what about that little girl?" the odontologist asked.

"It wasn't the husband."

"It probably wasn't even human."

"How 'bout just ignoring her?" Laura asked, hand up for another scotch. "After all, she can call herself anything she wants, but if we don't acknowledge it, she just looks as nuts as she is."

"She has the ID card," Tina reminded her.

"Steal her purse."

"Burn down her house."

"Carjack her van."

Laura laughed. "How do you think she got pregnant?"

Max spoke up for every man at the conference. "I'd rather go soap-diving in the state pen."

"I'm not so much worried about what happens when we leave here," Laura said. "But what about during the conference? Do you realize the caliber of speakers we have coming in? In a single day she could alienate every quotable forensic expert in the Western Hemisphere."

"Not to mention the fact that the conference ends with grand rounds with Dr. Arnot. You know what it took to get him here."

Dr. Arnot was currently the world's most famous forensic pathologist for his brilliant work on and testimony in the recent Jackson Williams murder case. Dr. Arnot, it was said, was the only professional in the contiguous forty-eight states who could make Johnnie Cochran sweat. The forensic conference had been sold out for eight months on the strength of his presence. The possibility that Wanda could somehow ruin that singular coup was enough to send everyone into flat despair.

"There has to be a way," Laura assured him. "After all, we're scientists. We're organized, methodical, detail-oriented, leaders in our field." Glasses were raised all round in salute, and Laura smiled. "Surely we can outsmart one stinky psycho."

"I'm telling you," Tina said. "Kill her. Make it a forensic experiment to see if we can get away with it."

"And you're going to raise the kid, I guess?"

No one jumped in to volunteer for even that much contact with the woman. So rather than rehash old war stories or complain about budget cuts, bad administrators, worse press and appalling working conditions, the seven drinkers who clustered at the edge of the plum and silver lobby bar spent their next three drinks working up a plan to effectively sidetrack the bane of their existence. Shift schedules were drawn up, maps studied, psychological warfare discussed and body armor considered. By the time Bruce the bartender shut off the track lighting and locked away the alcohol that night, the group decided that, barring unnatural acts of God, they had matters well in hand.

Whether or not Wanda Mummerson could be called an act of God would be forever debated. But the point of the matter was that although Wanda was crazy, she wasn't dumb. In less than twelve hours, even with the concerted interference of every one of the original seven stalwarts and every other conference attendee with a hand to raise, she single-handedly managed to alienate every speaker who stepped up to a microphone.

"You don't have a friggin' clue what you're talking about, do you?" she demanded in a voice that ground like bad gears to the world-famous expert on child abuse who was outlining investigative techniques.

Max, whose job it had been to keep Wanda busy for

this sixty-minute period, was caught midsentence in his whispered discussion about Wanda's desire to seek out a movie star to father her next child.

"Kevin Costner," Wanda confided to him with a ghastly smile before she whipped back to the open-mouthed psychiatrist who had been caught flatfooted at the front of a suddenly silent room. "I've started a Web page for people wrongly accused of child abuse, and your name's going to be on it as an overzealous, uninformed danger to parents everywhere. You got an answer to that?"

The psychiatrist, a trim, sleek, professional woman in her forties, had never been surprised to silence in her life. But faced with the dumpy, short, polyester-clad brunette with skin the texture of wallpaper paste and eyes that glinted maroon in the conference room lights, she couldn't seem to manage more than a bemused shrug.

"I, um, wonder at the advisability of ignoring quite an accumulation of literature on the subject," she finally managed.

"Are you sure about Kevin Costner?" Max whispered desperately to Wanda, one hand tightly around a doughy arm. "I think he's had a vasectomy."

Wanda even forgot to whisper. "No, he'd love to have my babies. Babies I'm sure this stupid bitch would be happy to snatch right out of my arms, just because I disagree with her. Isn't that right, Doctor?"

"Shut up, Wanda," somebody snapped.

"You can't shut me up," she snapped right back. "I'm a member, and there isn't a damn thing you can do about it."

An hour later, she struck again. This time it was Laura's watch, and the lecture was on rape investigation.

"When I was raped, nobody believed me," Wanda all but howled, on her feet, spittle flying.

"That's because she said it was by aliens," somebody whispered in the back of the room.

"Are you feeling well?" Laura asked behind her, already sweating in the air-conditioning. "You know how easy it is to contract something in a hotel this size."

Wanda didn't even acknowledge her. "I sued the police, because, of course, it was a cop who raped me. Here in Los Angeles, and you really think they're going to do a fair investigation? Asshole said he loved me."

". . . and then he made me eat it," she continued at lunch later after managing to push her way to the table where the rape expert was trying to eat in peace. "There isn't any meat on this salad, is there? There's meat? I'm a vegetarian. I can't have meat. Hey, you! What the hell is this meat doing on my salad?"

"I'm sorry, ma'am," the waiter apologized, yanking the plate away as if afraid of getting contaminated. "You never asked for a vegetarian menu."

"What, do you think I'm nuts or something?"

Since the question was unanswerable if the waiter wanted to keep his job, he just scuttled away.

"People think they can screw with me and get away with it. Well, anybody who's faced off with me knows better. Wanda always wins."

After Wanda had called the FBI profiler a selfish bastard and the armed forces air disaster expert an idiot, the original team members met in emergency session back with Bruce the bartender, three more conference members, and the FBI profiler, who offered the professional opinion that the "chick was batshit." They had, by then, only twenty-four hours left before Dr. Arnot was to make his appearance.

"I'll adopt the kid," Tina pleaded. "We're forensic experts. If we can't kill her and get away with it, who can?"

"Everybody at the hotel hates her," the odontologist

pleaded. "Let's just stuff her in a linen closet until Arnot goes home."

"Hell, let's stuff her in the incinerator."

"We're going to the LA County coroner's office in the morning," Max said. "She's not on the list. Maybe we can think of something while we're away."

"Maybe she'll have such hot sex with Kevin Costner the bed'll catch on fire and we won't have to worry about it."

The only real resolution that evening produced was a vote to warn Kevin Costner and a hope that five hours without their problem would offer objective insight.

They should have known better. The doors of the tour bus had no more opened the next morning to display the side view of the Los Angeles County Medical Center when a too-familiar whine wafted over on the breeze.

". . . thought they could keep me off the bus, did they? They don't think this city has goddamn taxis?"

"Oh, God," Tina moaned, almost collapsing right there on the asphalt.

Debarking right behind her, Laura almost knocked her over a second time. Then Max bumped into Laura, who was busy praying that she was suffering from hallucinations.

No such luck. There was Wanda, hauling herself out of a taxi that didn't even wait for payment before skidding out past the bus. Her hair sweaty, her face a ghastly color unknown to humans, and some unknown food detritus clinging to the corner of her mouth, she squinted at them all in rage.

"I'll sue this chickenshit organization," she hissed, waving her purse at them so that a condom packet and three hotel salt shakers shot out like ammunition and hit Laura in the chest. "Just see if I don't. You were going to keep me away because you knew that Arnot was going to be here at the end of the tour."

Laura blinked like a head injury victim. "Arnot? Here?"

"Of course. Didn't you hear them yelling that as you were pulling away? Why the hell do you think I called the damn taxi when you left me behind on purpose? I told you before. You're not getting rid of me in this lifetime, you snotty bitch. Now let's go or we're going to miss talking to the great man." She turned, muttering under her breath. "I have a few things to say to *that* asshole. . . ."

As Wanda walked away, Max sidled up to where Laura was rubbing her chest and looking at the spent ammo on the ground. "Tina's right," he said. "We could kill her. After all, we're already at the coroner's office. Think of the paperwork we'd save."

"The little girl," Laura countered, seeing their credibility vanish as fast as OJ's alibi.

"One look at Wanda, and Arnot's not going to darken our doors for the big speech tonight. Let's kill her now while we have the chance."

"And the baby?"

"Baby?" somebody echoed as they walked by. "What baby?"

"She's got a baby," Tina said. "A little girl."

The woman, a thick African-American burn nurse with sensible shoes and fluorescent nail polish, snorted in derision. "Girl, you get a look at that little girl's picture?"

Laura watched Wanda's dingy, disheveled back as it waddled toward the front door, and sighed. "Yeah. She's a cute little thing, damn it."

The burn nurse let off a laugh like a car horn. "'Course she is. She's Drew Barrymore. That crazy bitch carryin' around a picture from *ET* sayin' it's her baby. Where you been?"

Just about the entire busload of people came to a stop on that one.

"You serious?" Laura demanded.

"Does she need a vat of Haldol and a snorkel? Of course I'm serious."

Laura nodded. "Okay, then, we can kill her."

"We can make it a science experiment," Max offered, still standing there like a crime witness. "Just like Tina wanted. Then we'll present it as a paper at next year's conference, with charts and graphs and four-color glossy photos."

"A treatise on how easy it is to get away with murder in the United States," Laura agreed.

"An apology to every person she's insulted this weekend."

But they all still stood there for a minute, knowing damn well they were sunk. It was already too late for any kind of intervention, no matter how outlandish. And to a person, they knew that they weren't going to be outlandish. It was too late and they were too altruistic. Wanda was about to meet Dr. Arnot, and there was nothing anybody could do.

Ten minutes later Wanda seemed to clinch it when their host for the tour introduced himself.

"Garcia, huh, your family got a lot of representation on the other side of the sheet down there, don't they?"

Assistant Coroner Garcia, not sure whether he'd been racially slurred or simply personally insulted, just blinked and went back to his presentation.

"Our policies are pretty rigid here," he said as he took his place at the head of the classroom where the tour first gathered. "I'm sure you can understand why."

Wanda snorted. "Barn door, you ask me. This factory has the quality control of a pig farm."

Obviously accustomed to dealing with hostile press,

Garcia didn't even falter in his delivery. The rest of the tour group shushed Wanda like an unruly patron at a movie. She didn't say anything more through Garcia's recitation of statistics and procedures, nor offer any particularly germane questions. Laura and Max, not in the least deceived by her passivity, positioned themselves near her as the class rose to file out of the room.

"We'll be wearing masks down on the working floor," Garcia said as he passed around boxes. "Touch nothing, and please don't talk to any of the staff. Again," he said with a flash of very white teeth in a smoothly tanned face, "office regulations."

"What about feeding them?" Wanda asked, dislodging the leftover breakfast by her mouth as she snapped on her surgical mask.

The rest of the tour swept past her like a river around a slimy rock. Garcia simply unlocked access doors to usher the tour into the heart of the building. His posture had become more rigid, however, his smile a little more forced.

An older edifice in which the working floors were basement levels, the county morgue looked tired and smelled stale. Typical big-city institutional with a good dollop of protection of privacy and safety tossed in, it looked like nothing more than an unredesigned government office.

Until the morgue level, that is. With an average daily census of over three hundred patients, nothing could camouflage the purpose of that floor. The smell of bad meat clung to skin and hair, and bug zappers at the bay doors stuttered continuously. Garcia, oblivious to the impact of the place, wore his surgical mask like an Armani accessory and kept up a smooth commentary on the monumental workload that, as anywhere, had to be carried by too few people on a too-small budget. The members of the tour slowed slightly, winced, opened mouths to breathe. They followed quietly and maintained respect for the staff and the victims housed there.

With one inevitable exception.

"You can see what kind of volume we get here," Garcia was saying. "In any given year, we have some five thousand Jane and John Does alone."

"And the only person we have to rely on for ID is that hunched-up geek with the bad teeth back there?" Wanda asked. "Makes you wonder just how much free time he gets in with each dead body, ya know?"

Laura made an instinctive move to get between Garcia and Wanda. Max laid a restraining arm on her.

"We're gonna get tossed out of here," she protested under her breath.

Max considered the torque on Garcia's jaw and gave a considered shake of his head. "Wait."

"We identify all but about fifty people a year," Garcia said, walking on down the hall. "Considering how big our transient population is, I think that's pretty impressive."

"If you're not one of the fifty, sure."

"We have three holding rooms," Mr. Garcia said, hitting a button that forced the stainless steel door to slide open. "Also a room for oversized victims that don't fit on our shelves."

"Pretty full house," Max offered.

"Even with our fast turnaround," Garcia said as everyone peeked into the cooled room tiered with plastic-wrapped bodies, "you'll see on the flow board that we have some three hundred fifty-seven people down here right now."

"Stacked like cordwood," Wanda inevitably whined. "No wonder I had to sue this office when my aunt committed suicide. Took us days to get her back. I guess I should be surprised you guys found her at all. Hell, she probably could have been stuck under one of those fat guys for years before anybody knew about it."

"That was you?" Garcia retorted, his amazing composure completely deserting him.

Wanda gloated. "You guys paid me over a million dollars for that little piece of laziness. I could have gotten more if I'd pressed."

"You could have—" Garcia stopped, his face mottled with the effort to keep his mouth shut.

Laura, to his left, couldn't decide whether to reach out to him or not. That particular lawsuit had been ugly. She'd heard about it even in Detroit. And, if she remembered correctly, the allegations weren't just about disorganization. Wanda seemed to like that "what are you guys doing with dead bodies?" theme a lot.

"Everybody makes the mistake of thinking that I'll just go away if they ignore me," Wanda was saying, fresh spittle dotting the corner of her mouth. "But I won't. Ever. And there isn't a damn thing anybody can do about it."

Laura made another move toward Wanda, ready to yank her ass back to Detroit if she had to. Max held her back.

Every other person was focused on Garcia, more than one face red and uncomfortable over the masks. Nobody saw the door start to close. Except Wanda. When it caught her foot in it.

"You son of a bitch!" she screeched.

Garcia acted immediately. Wanda's foot was cleared without so much as a scuff mark on her Dr. Scholl's tennis shoes.

"You're fine, Wanda," Max soothed.

"Shut up!" she screamed. "I'll tell you what's going to be fine! My damn pocketbook! First I'll sue this office again, and then this pissant forensic organization,

and then your precious Dr. Arnot! You don't think I remember your name, do you, Ernesto? Do you think Dr.
Arnot is going to let you stay through another suit, you
jerk?"

"No, you won't," Max said quietly.

Wanda glared. "See if I don't. I think I'll be the first
person to greet Dr. Arnot. Unless, of course, Mr. Garcia
here wants to talk me out of it."

Garcia stood there twitching like a landed carp.

Max stepped into the breach. "Why don't you guys
discuss it with Dr. Arnot after the tour, Wanda?"

Max withstood a veritable barrage of silent outrage
from his comembers. Wanda, though, got a feral look
in her eye and nodded. "Sure, what the hell? I'm just
dying to see another member of this staff on his knees.
Let's go."

And she stomped off. Left behind, Max seemed the
only person not stunned to silence.

"Probably should finish the tour," he said quietly, his
hand on Garcia's arm.

"Yes," Garcia managed, his handsome features
ashen. "Yes, of course."

"Inspector Garcia," Max said in his silkiest, sweetest
voice as they walked away from the oversized room toward radiology. "Do you do many forensic experi-
ments here?"

Garcia seemed to have trouble pulling his thoughts
together. "Yes, of course. Why?"

Max smiled. "I'd like to talk to you for a moment."

Oddly enough, when Dr. Arnot stopped by to see
the tour an hour later, nobody argued with or insulted
him. The entire tour smiled and nodded and thanked
him for his presence. His speech the next day was a hit
and was covered on CNN. And later, much later, the
hunched-over geek whose job it was to ID Jane and

John Does found himself in the oversize room with Assistant Coroner Garcia while they harvested thumbs for fingerprints from one of their residents.

"Hey," he said, noticing a pasty white hand beneath the four-hundred-pound man's thigh. "What's this?"

And Assistant Coroner Garcia, who was in a fine mood, simply shoved the limb back under enough adipose to hide a truck. "Oh, nothing," he said. "I'm just doing an experiment for some friends."

Lia Matera is the author of twelve novels in two series featuring San Francisco Bay area lawyers. Her books have been nominated for Edgar, Anthony, and Macavity Awards, and she is the winner of a Shamus Award for Best Private Eye Short Story. She is a recovering lawyer. In "If It Can't Be True," a brother and sister try one last time to stop believing the impossible.

IF IT CAN'T BE TRUE

by Lia Matera

She regained consciousness seconds before the helicopter crashed. Gauges and instruments hurtled from one side of the claustrophobically small space to the other. Someone in the front was shrieking a panicked tone poem. Paraphernalia—stethoscopes, medicine bottles, clamps—hit her with the force of pinballs in a machine gone mad. An oxygen mask over her nose and mouth offered little protection.

She surfed a wave of dread, realizing this had happened to her before. She prayed it was just a bad dream this time.

When next she opened her eyes, she was still inside the helicopter but it was no longer in motion. A sheet of crushed laminated glass, glaring like glitter on glue, dazzled her. She was on her side, tipped toward the cockpit, the gurney wedged and buckled. A woman—a flight nurse?—was trapped beneath the gurney, her uniform soaked with blood. The nurse looked dead, red and wet like supermarket meat.

She supposed her own survival was a testament to good packaging and the tensile strength of the gurney. The plastic mask cut into her face, still feeding her oxygen.

Despite the fact that the gurney had twisted, the wristbands held. She jerked at them. Last time this happened, she'd been seat-belted like a passenger, not strapped down like an animal.

She could hear wind whistling through gashes in the metal sides of the helicopter. The crumpled windshield ballooned toward her, spilling bits of safety glass from its sticky laminate.

She wrenched her hands through the restraints, scraping off skin. It felt like a grease burn, shocking and scalding, but a monstrous dose of adrenaline helped her ignore it. She pulled free.

She couldn't remember what had put her into the helicopter, which she assumed to be a medical transport. It wasn't the airplane crash, that was a long time ago. She'd been a child then, they'd taken her to a foreign hospital where none of the nurses spoke English.

But whatever had put her here now, all she cared about was getting out. The door through which her gurney had been loaded was blocked, smashed against rocky ground. She crawled toward the cockpit, hoping for an exit there. But the window openings were flattened to slits. Broken tree limbs poked through parts of the metal. A branch no thicker than her thumb had skewered the pilot's body. She could see a second nurse's arm and shoulder, jagged bones poking through the skin.

She forced her attention away from them. She had to escape this grave of bloody flesh. There was a gash in the side, now the top, of the copter, maybe big enough to squeeze through.

She began squirming toward it. Her mask pulled off, and she could smell mud and pines and fried wires. As she hoisted herself out, frayed metal raked her clothes. She was surprised to see she wore a jumpsuit. Institutional clothes? She had a vague memory of locked doors and a tiny, unornamented room.

When she made it to the ground, she lay there panting, surrounded by splintered firs and scattered shards. A few minutes later, in horror of what had happened, she crawled a little farther away. And then a little farther still.

Drops of water from condensation on pine needles fell like light rain. Limbs creaked and rustled in a cold wind. The helicopter settled and shifted with deep groans that sounded like dirges.

She listened, watching the swaying evergreen pattern of branches against a gray and white sky. She must have been injured even before the crash; she wouldn't have been in a medical helicopter if not. But she couldn't put her finger on how it had happened, or even what kind of injury.

She had the notion, as she paused there, that she'd chosen to let her memories go. Or worse, that she'd jumped away from them as if leaping from sweat-soaked sheets in the middle of a nightmare.

Memories were strange creatures, anyway, sliding deeper into dark crevices even as they lured you with bright hints and teasers. She'd been thinking a lot about memories. But, ironically, she couldn't remember why.

Well, someone was bound to come for her soon. Then she would learn what had happened to her, like it or not.

She closed her eyes. And a memory bloomed: Her brother, George, was saying, "Either we've both gone crazy or reality is stranger than we ever dreamed."

He was squatting beside a dead cow at the time. He was only fifteen years old, in work boots and a flannel shirt. She was eleven, standing behind him clutching his shoulder. The dead cow had been part of their father's herd.

In life, the cow had been as dumb and clumsy and easily prodded as others on the ranch. It had become remarkable only in death, resting in a shallow indentation in the hard ground. The flesh on the right side of its jawbone had been bloodlessly and completely sliced (or maybe lasered) away. Its right eye had been removed, leaving a perfectly clean white socket. Its anus had been reamed out. And where the udder should have been, there was only a hole as precisely oval as a puzzle piece. And there wasn't a drop of blood on the ground. Not a drop.

She and George would later learn there was no blood inside the cow either. And that the cow's ovaries had been neatly extracted with its colon and anus. No flies had buzzed around the carrion. And nothing, not even an indiscriminate rodent, had taken tooth to it.

Their parents had been away in town for the weekend. So George had phoned the neighbors, he'd taken pictures, he'd called the sheriff. And he and his sister had learned an interesting lesson at a young age. When faced with the incredible, people chose to settle for any explanation they could persuade themselves made sense.

Shown the cow, their neighbors suddenly accepted the notion of cults. Or they said it must be predators, even though they knew predators didn't make clean cuts or surgically remove ovaries. People refused to listen by turning off their heads as well as their ears. As one neighbor put it, "If it can't be true, it isn't."

Maybe she'd been lucky to learn life's most important lesson at the age of eleven, standing behind her brother, George. She learned that reality is no small and controllable thing, no mere doll house of familiar props. She was changed forever in one instant, diverted from the mainstream and splashed into another river altogether.

A voice said, "Aw, no—she's dead!"

She opened her eyes, never happier to prove someone wrong. She expected to find a man standing over her. She was trying to smile up at him as she opened her eyes.

But there was nothing above her but tree limbs against a gloomy sky darkening toward nightfall.

She lifted her head. She had crawled into the brush, and greenery partly blocked her view. But she could see the commotion near the helicopter. She could see men silhouetted against its white paint. One was doubled over as if retching. He was being helped, practically dragged, away.

One of the remaining men reached into his jacket and pulled out a walkie-talkie. He clomped off without looking over his shoulder, without noticing her there on the ground.

The men had seen the pilot, the woman in front with him, and the one in back. Did they assume there was only one nurse on board? The nurse beneath the gurney, her uniform was obscured by blood. Maybe they thought she was the patient. Maybe they weren't searching for survivors because they supposed everyone was accounted for. She was about to call out, to tell them she was here, still alive.

But she heard someone say, "You think she brought the helicopter down?"

Another man said, "You believe all that bullshit?" Then, "Look at the sky, look at those clouds. It was a lightning bolt, has to have been." But he didn't sound convinced.

"All I meant was, maybe she got free and attacked the pilot."

"We told them to sedate her and restrain the hell out of her." The other man sounded angry. "God damn it, if we lose anybody . . . They should have stalled long enough for us to drive her."

"But how could something like this happen?" the first man persisted. "She must have gotten loose and done something."

Her hail died on her lips. These men seemed to blame her for the helicopter crash. What would they do to her if she announced herself?

She couldn't remember what she'd be going back to, but she began to have a feeling it was something she didn't like. Maybe her jumpsuit was from some prison, maybe they'd been transporting her someplace worse. Maybe she was better off out here, wounded but free.

She lay still, her head raised, watching for them, try-ing to catch some telltale detail of conversation. But they were out of her range of sight now, and the wind brought only murmurs. Or perhaps they'd switched to a foreign language. She rested her head. The effort of keeping it up, of remaining watchful, had drained her of energy.

She closed her eyes and drifted away.

She jerked her head up again, achieving full wakeful-ness in an instant. Tree limbs swayed overhead, strob-ing the diminishing light.

She heard men's voices again but they were too dis-tant to make out the words.

She'd been having nightmares about an institution where no one spoke her language, where she was herded and regimented and never understood why—a ranch where she was just another dumb, nameless cow in the herd.

Hearing people run toward her, she rolled to her stomach and began to crawl for cover. She crawled farther from the wreckage, as far as she could on weak and pain-stiff limbs.

Acid boiled up her throat and seared her mouth but she didn't stop. She put as much distance as she could between herself and the helicopter.

She stopped when the men were close enough to hear her scrabbling. She sat behind a big tree, back against it, lacking the energy to crane her neck and see what these people were doing. She tried to quiet her breaths, calm her heartbeats, so she could hear them.

A man with a harsh accent said, "They're stringing him along, but he's getting touchy. We don't have much time. Let's see if we can find *something* to help them out over there, any kind of proof of what brought this baby down." The voice, gratingly defeatist, made her shudder. She'd heard it before somewhere, and the associations weren't pleasant. She heard boots scrunching on the duff. "You know what to do."

A few minutes later, she heard commotion and shouting. There was a huge roar as fire exploded upward with a sucking noise punctuated by booms. Had they started the fire on purpose? Turned up the flow of the oxygen canisters? Punched holes in the gas tanks? Doused the wreck with rocket fuel?

With her back to the helicopter, she could see the shadows of trees and branches dancing in hot light. She looked out from behind the tree. The fire was a huge plume of red and orange tumbling with black clouds of smoke. It sent off waves of heat and chokingly acrid smoke.

She got to her feet. If the fire spread, it would move

faster than she could run. She knew that about fires, maybe learned it from someone. From George?

She tried to console herself with memories of her brother. She could feel the warm flannel of his shirt as she gripped him, looking down at their dead cow. The feel of his shoulder had provided reassurance. She needed that now.

She walked haltingly, painfully, as quickly as she could under the circumstances. She wound down a wooded ravine, away from the flaming debris of the helicopter that had brought her this far. She tried to take comfort in her homey memory of her brother, though it was spoiled by its association with the cow.

A few times, she had watched her father shoot cows. They would look startled, eyes opening wide and heads jerking back. Then they'd drop onto their front knees, pause infinitesimally, and keel over.

People killed each other pretty much the same way, she guessed. A stranger might kill you without anger, *blam,* for some reason or purpose of his own you would never understand.

As if you were a cow. Cows wouldn't understand being slaughtered for their meat because they didn't eat meat themselves. And as for being drained of blood and having their viscera pillaged, they could have no clue. That was beyond the understanding of any earthling, human or bovine.

She heard voices again—men moving closer. Hearing them through an inadequate curtain of redwood shoots, she tried to move faster. The men were bound to spot her soon. They might grab her and kill her—she had no reason to trust them. She needed more time, time to remember who she'd become in the years after finding the cow.

She shook her head as if to shake loose memories, to jump past her image of the cow. Her present life, her best interests, seemed to fall away as she turned that event over and over in her mind.

The discovery of the cow had ruined everything. Her gruff and level-headed father, for all his Rotary and Kiwanis Club and Ranchers Association contacts, had been derided mercilessly for stating the obvious: that no predator, no cult, no disease could drain a cow completely and remove its organs with laser precision. And he'd been too stubborn to back down, to pretend it was covens or coyotes. Her mother had been so mortified by the snickering, the graffiti, and the sneers that she overdosed on tranquilizers—which further convinced the neighbors they were all crazy, the whole family. For months every outing had been punctuated with jibes, or worse, pity. Her father began to lash out at everyone, especially his children.

She stopped. For a millisecond, she'd almost had it. She'd almost gotten to the heart of this. Her father had done something, and because of it she'd ended up here.

She could see movement in the brush. She knew she'd have to hurry, that she didn't have time to think about it now.

But wherever George might be, she silently saluted him for being right. Reality was indeed stranger than they ever dreamed.

The man holding the bomb was interrupted by the ringing of his cell phone. He answered. "Is she here?"

"George?"

George ran a hand through his greasy hair. He must look pretty bad after sweating in this building for ten solid hours.

"George?" The man's voice was calm with authority. "George, there's been a slight delay bringing your sister."

George wanted to hit the switch. He'd let himself grow expectant, almost optimistic. There had been a few minutes when he'd almost believed this man, almost believed they'd take Jane out of the hospital and fly her here—without incident. He had tried for almost six hours to believe it, in fact. God knew, he wanted to believe. It was better than the alternative.

"George, listen to me," the man said urgently. "We're bringing her, we really are. There's just been a delay."

"Did you fly her already?"

"Almost here, really. But remember I told you weather conditions aren't good? Electrical storms, lightning—we don't want to take any chances. Just a short delay, that's all."

The explosives strapped to George's torso made his skin ooze with perspiration. The itching was almost beyond enduring. But if he unstrapped the pack, they'd shoot him for sure. He knew they must have him in their sights. He knew they'd kill him even though he hadn't hurt the hostages, just herded them around and had his say, that's all. The hostages were lying behind him now, trussed up and silent except for some whimpering. They smelled rank after all these hours and no bathroom breaks, that was for sure. But so did he.

For the thousandth time, he considered ending it, just blowing up this plain wood box of a building—this pen—of people. He didn't care about any of them. And he'd just about had his fill of berating them.

It hadn't occurred to him to bring Jane here, not at first. It was the negotiators who kept asking him what he wanted. He was ranting at the hostages when he got the idea. If they could fly Jane here, then he might be wrong, after all. The hostages might be right, they might deserve to live. If the negotiator could get Jane all the way up here from Los Angeles within, say, four or five hours, that would mean they'd flown her for sure. You couldn't drive it in that amount of time.

But the hours had ticked by. And now the man on the phone was stalling him. Lying to him to keep his finger off the detonator.

"You're driving her here, aren't you?"

"We wouldn't do that, George. We made you a promise," the negotiator said.

George pictured him as avuncular and gray-haired with a potbelly and broken veins in his cheeks. But that was only because he'd once had a foster father who looked like that. For all he knew, the negotiator was lean and tough and decked out in SWAT team black with a bulletproof vest, like in the movies. It was hard to picture something so Hollywood in a cow town like this.

"Because the whole point of me talking to you at all," George repeated, "is you proving to me I'm wrong. Because I'd rather be wrong, I want to be wrong. I've always wanted that."

"We understand," the man assured him again.

But they didn't understand about Jane. Just like the hostages squirming behind him didn't understand.

"I knew you wouldn't bring her," George said. "I knew you were just stalling."

"She'll be here anytime. You'll see your sister, George, I promise."

It had been a long time since George had seen Jane. She'd been in the hospital since she was twelve years old, since their mother killed herself and their father went on a rampage against them for finding the cow and ruining his life. George couldn't take it. He'd run away. Later, he'd been shipped off to foster families. But they wouldn't let Jane go with him; she was too tweaked after the beatings she took.

At first they hoped with the right treatment she

would get over it. They couldn't see it was that unknown thing, whatever killed the cow, that Jane really dreaded. Their father's thrashings might have damaged her brain, but mostly she was afraid of being sucked into the sky and having her organs cut bloodlessly out of her, that's what George thought.

But he hadn't seen her in years. He couldn't bear to look at her tied to a bed.

"You should have had plenty of time to fly her here by now—weather's not that bad. You're just stalling," he repeated.

"There are electrical storms over the mountains," the negotiator insisted. "I'm serious. You can feel the static in the air, can't you?"

But the air felt damp and heavy, not dry and charged.

George caught his breath. "That's what you're going to blame when she crashes. Isn't it?"

"There won't be a crash, George."

"Yes there will." He sat down, slumping with exhaustion. "There always is." He'd already told them what happened when they tried to fly Jane to a special home in Oregon. And what happened when they tried to fly her back to the first hospital. "Anything she flies in, it comes down. It has to do with the cow. Don't ask me how."

He knew it sounded crazy. God knew, he'd gotten used to sounding insane. And yet, proof was proof. Two airplanes had crashed with Jane aboard. The investigators settled on other reasons, of course. They found faulty wiring in the first plane and cited a collision with a flock of birds in the other. This time, apparently, they meant to blame some storm.

George had just thought—prayed—that maybe . . . maybe they would put Jane up in the sky this time, and she'd make it. That would mean the other times were just bad luck, just coincidence. That the cow—

Well, there was no getting around the cow. George

had seen it with his own eyes. Over the years, he'd researched it. There'd been thousands of similar cases from Mexico to Canada, always unexplained because there's no guessing how a cow can end up half embedded in the ground without a drop of blood around it or inside it, with its organs lasered out so perfectly the cells remained intact on either side of the incision.

In California, the Cattleman's Association was suing the government for information after dozens of members found their cows eerily mutilated. The association president discovered a steer with its three-foot horn embedded in hardpan all the way to its head.

But here, the ranchers still laughed at George. It hadn't happened again, it hadn't happened to any of them. And so they had that luxury.

"Don't you get it?" George spoke into the cell phone, his finger on the detonator. "Don't you get it about reality?"

"Look, everything's all right, George, really. Your sister's on her way."

"No. No, she isn't." He wanted to weep, thinking about Jane crashing again. And this time, it was his fault. He'd put her up in the sky to try to prove to himself that it couldn't be true. When he knew damn well it was.

"We understand about your worries," the man continued, "based on her bad luck before. But everything's going to turn out fine this time. We made sure your sister's comfortable and sedated. We're just waiting on the weather, just a slight delay, George. For your sister's sake, because we know she's paranoid about flying. You can understand that."

The negotiator's voice was as soothing as Mr. Rogers's. Maybe he could tell George had reached the end of his tether. Maybe he knew George was just about to hit the button.

"You're idiots, all of you," George fumed. "It's no

use sedating Jane. She's not paranoid. Every time she flies she gets knocked right out of the sky—what's delusional about that? She's got brain damage from our dad beating on her. She's got short-term memory deficit, she's basically stuck where she was at age twelve. And her language processing is all screwed up—she either can't understand or doesn't want to. That's why she's been in that hospital all these years. But she's not crazy."

Or if she was, she'd come by it honestly.

George felt his skin beneath the taped-on bomb itch as if it were on fire. He'd let himself be seduced by the idea of proving himself wrong. Of seeing Jane again. As if touching her, embracing her, could pull him back through all these hard years to the good times of child-hood. His longing was natural. But he blamed these smug officers for exploiting it.

"George, listen to me," the negotiator said urgently. "We can put your sister on the phone. We've got her, I swear. Just give me a few minutes, you can talk to her."

"She wouldn't understand me." Sometimes she seemed to catch a few phrases, but usually she looked bewildered and scared by what she took to be senseless chatter.

"Well, you can hear your sister, whatever she says or whatever sounds she makes. You can hear her voice. She can hear yours. You'll know she's on the way, George."

But he knew better than to believe the man. They were clearly desperate now, knowing George would soon find out that Jane had crashed. And once that came out, they knew it would be over. George would realize he'd sacrificed his sister's life just to try one last time to stop believing. How could he live with that? Even if he wanted to live.

Despair enveloped him. He lied: "If you let me talk to Jane, I'll wait a little longer."

But he heard booted feet on the old-fashioned veran-dah porch of the barnlike building. They could hear his intentions in his voice, he supposed. Oh, well.

George had the satisfaction of blowing them up along with the rest of the people cowering and weeping at the Cattle Ranchers Association Hall.

In the split second it took George to hit the button, he wondered what statement the press would derive from this. And whether the beings who killed that cow would understand what he was really saying.

The men who grabbed Jane spoke a language she didn't know. Just like the doctors and nurses at the hos-pital, just like the nurses in the helicopter.

That's when Jane realized she'd understood the men who first found the helicopter.

But how could that be? She hadn't understood any-one in a very long time. Since she was a child. Since her father went mad and clubbed her. She had awakened in a hospital bed with bandages over her shaved head, and no one had spoken more than random words or phrases of English to her since. Not ever again. Never till today. Maybe the helicopter crash had jarred something right. Maybe she would get her language back.

She felt the horrible tension of renewed hope. She tried to speak, to beg these men not to fly her back to the hospital, to drive her, for all their sakes.

But as always when she made sounds, the response was shaking heads and looks of incomprehension.

The frustration threatened to lift the top of her head off. She couldn't seem to breathe, as if she'd gone too deep underwater and suddenly realized she might not get back up in time.

This must have been how George felt, bolting from home so many years ago. He must have felt like a cork shooting from the bottle, helpless against the built-up pressure. Later, he blamed himself for leaving her alone with her father. She hadn't understood his words, but she had understood his heart. She had tried to tell him she forgave him for running away. What else could he do?

He had tried so hard to make the neighbors accept the reality of the exsanguinated cow, accept that it had happened, that they had all seen it, that whatever it meant, it meant it for all of them. But the neighbors had laughed at them, sneered at them, turned their backs. The neighbors seemed to know instinctively that people who didn't believe such things, their families stayed together. Their mothers didn't kill themselves, their brothers didn't flee, their fathers didn't go on rampages. No, the neighbors had been smart enough to refuse to believe the unbelievable.

She hoped George had made peace with it somehow. That he'd stopped thinking about it all the time, like she did. She just couldn't seem to hang on to newer memories.

Half walking, half dragged away by the men, Jane wished for the millionth time that she could stop believing what she'd seen. She wished she could choose to be normal, choose belatedly to close her eyes and close her mind and even close her heart if she had to. She would close anything, even the ability to understand. Even the ability to communicate.

She scanned the sky for a sign that she could still undo it all. But the sky looked as ordinary as ever.